Book one of the

Divinity series

Without Choice

Thank you for giving this book a chance. I promise you, you will not be disappointed. This book is full of twists, turns and cliches.

Enjoy...

By Author Elizabeth Andrews

First edition February 2021.

Published by Brandy Michel.

Article of ELIZABETH ANDREWS INCORPORATED.

ELIZABETH ANDREWS INCORPORATED IS OWNED BY BRANDY MICHEL

Book cover model, Kevin Michel

Book cover design by Paul Michel.

Photographer Matthew Adams

Chapter & Book names by Adam Michel & Kathy Diaz

Book edited by Elizabeth Reza reza.elizabeth4@gmail.com

Video editor- TIFFANY MICHEL

Contact info for the author and her team, Nicole Diaz, Brandy Michel

autherelizabethandrews@gmail.com

Chapter *One*

Going home

Aphrodite

I feel my fingers tremble, so I sip on my latte, breathing in the rich aroma.
Trying to calm my nerves. I take a look around me and frown, knitting my eyebrows together. The only thing I'm going to miss from London, Saint Aymes, my favorite coffee shop in England. I'm sitting outside on the patio with one leg crossed over the other, the slight breeze kissing my lips. The chair I'm sitting on is a little uneven, the little round table made for a perfect couple, is a little dented. I look up to the windows that are bordered in Wisteria and try to memorize the perfect lilac color. I look through the window and see my parents having a serious conversation as they wait for their order. They are discussing our flight plan back to Los Angeles. My stomach churns in anxiety. All I wanted all year was to be back there but now, I am dreading it. Ever since we moved to London for my father's studies, my life has been so quiet and lonely. I left my friends, my home, my school, and *him*. For the last few months, not one call, text, or email has been answered by him. After I heard what happened to his mother, I rushed to get a hold of him but no luck. At first, I figured he wanted space but then I realized he just didn't want anything to do with me. I grab my phone and sigh as I scroll through my messages with him, all unanswered. You'd think after so long, a girl would take a hint, but not me.

'HELLOO!'
'ARE YOU THERE?'
'I'm here for you.'
'Why are you ignoring me?'

As I look through the messages, I realize I'm typing;

'I'm going home…'

I sigh as there is no response, even though it was delivered. I don't know what I was expecting. I'm such an idiot. The sound of boxes hitting the table with a loud thump, startles me a little. "You're all set for the flight, I got you quite a few things." my mother chuckled. I rolled my eyes "I just wanted a muffin mom, not the whole menu." I look at her pretty hazel eyes and chestnut hair, she has completely different looks from mine. I Have my father's black hair and electric blue eyes. What I got from my mother is her heart-shaped face, round tip, slim nose and full lips. Our car pulls up and my dad rolls down the window, "Lets go ladies, we're gonna be late for our flight." My mother and I both sighed and got into the car.
On our way to the airport, I texted my friend Roxy, who I have known since middle school, to let her know what time I will be landing, at her request. Her reply makes me roll my eyes with a smile.

'Hell yes! Can't wait to see you!'

Remembering her craziness, I laugh a little and hide my phone.

AS MUSIC IS BLASTING through my ears during this very long flight, I open the window shutter and look out at the darkening sky, clouds scattered softly. I close my eyes tightly at the song that starts playing. '*Always been you*' by Shawn Mendez. As the chorus starts, I close my eyes and lean my head against the window.

Flashback

As we slow down our bikes on the boardwalk of Venice Beach, I look up at a tattoo parlor and an idea pops into my head. Tomorrow I'm leaving for London and honestly don't know when I'll come back or if I even will. What better way for my best friend to remember me than to get a matching tattoo together. It doesn't hurt to ask, even though this is a really bad idea and he will never go for it. I turn my head and look at him with a smirk on my face.
He gives me a flat look already knowing what I was going to ask and straight out says, "No." You can hear the finality in his voice and my shoulders slump.
"Oh come on!" I whine, "Why not?!" I knit my eyebrows together with a slight pout. I knew if I got it, my father would probably yell at me for an hour and then ground me for a month.
"No" He said again the same way.

"Give me three reasons why not." I demanded as we walked towards a bike rack nearby and parked our bikes. I look towards him waiting for his answer and he sighs, "One, my father would kill me. Two, it's stupid and three, no."
"Fine then," I uttered, "Can you at least take me to get my favorite ice cream? I'm gonna miss Darla's so much when I'm in London." I pouted a little to drag it out. I inwardly laugh as I try to guilt trip him, the way I have since we were kids. I look up to his tall Hight. He is easily six foot two, while I'm nearly five foot seven. I see His pale green eyes shine with guilt, and I bite down on my lower lip to keep from smiling. He runs a hand through his almost black hair and sighs. That's when I know I won. "Okay, babygirl," the nickname he calls me when he babies me, " Let's get a tattoo."

My eyes go wide in excitement and slight fear. This is actually happening, I realize I'm going to get in so much trouble. I squeaked and grabbed his hand and pulled him towards the store. He laughs nervously as we walk in the tattoo parlor.

As the memory fades from my mind, so does the smile. I look at the tattoo that we got in the exact same spot, at the top of our forearm. One simple word, the word he chose. A word he didn't live by, written in cursive letters. *Always. T*he stewardess stops at my chair and I take my ear bud out. "Ma'am, we are landing soon. If you could please fasten your seat belt?" I nod and she smiles walking away.

Chapter Two

Unexpected

As I step out of the car, I look up to our new house with a weird look. How the hell did he get a house and a car from England here in Beverly Hills? What is he, Superman? Don't get me wrong the house is beautiful, it was a light cream color with big windows with white shutters surrounding them. There were wide rounded steps at the front with a balcony overhead and big white columns holding it up. On top of the balcony were french doors leading to, what looks like a room. I look back to the car and knit my eyebrows together in confusion. It was a brand new black-on-black, top-of-the line Jeep truck and in the driveway was a dark grey Range Rover.
I look at my dad and he has a huge grin on his face, still holding luggage in his hands, "Dad? Where did this come from?" I ask confusingly.
Now he's the one that looks confused, "What, do you mean?" He asked.
"This house, these cars? how did you do all this from London?"
He looks at me confused again, "Didn't Don tell you?" he said while walking up the stairs to the big double doors and punches in a code on a digital lock. He walks in, my mother following him in with a sheepish look on her face.
I stay in place, shocked at the name that passes my fathers lips. What does he mean by that? I finally walk in and look around. There is a big foyer with twin staircases, twisting up towards a big balcony. In the back of the foyer, is a set of french doors, with linen curtains draped nicely. I walk towards the right and there is a beautiful living room with a fireplace. The couches are a cream color with dark wood framing them. The coffee tables are the same color.

I walk back to the foyer. Towards the left, there is a really big dining room and a threshold leading to the kitchen. I pass the dining room that has at least twelve chairs and walk into the kitchen. My parents are in there talking in hushed tones.
I look to them and ask, “How did you guys even get it decorated?” I am so confused right now.
My mom looks at me sadly and begins to speak but my father cuts her off. “ Honey, Adonis helped me with all this. He got the decorators, he got me and your mother cars. He even got people to get groceries in the house.”
So this whole time he has been in contact with my father, but hasn’t been able to answer one of my freaking text messages? That makes no sense to me. Did I do something wrong? I quickly run over our last few calls and texts in my mind and try to think if I overstepped in any way.
“Great. Do either of you know which one is my room?” I ask sharply.
“Choose whichever one you’d like, sweetheart,” my mother says with a sad smile. I sigh and quickly walk back to the car, grab my luggage, and walk back in and up the stairs.

I pass a few rooms but none of them catch my eye, until I get to a room that has my exact aesthetic. The bed frame is a white, four poster bed with lilac and white drapes over it and in each corner, the drapes falling to the floor. The dressers are white and rustic. The couch in front of the bed is a pale lilac color with cute decorative pillows, the coffee table in front of it had a large vase in the middle with fresh white and lilac peonies. *My favorite*. There were a few other decorations in silver, white, and lilac. The frames and tapestries on the walls were perfect. I walk straight to

the french doors and peek out the curtain. It's the balcony leading to the front of the house. I let the curtain fall back into place and turn to see the room again with a small smile. I already love this room. I walk around admiring everything, then walk to the door leading to the walk-in closet. The things I sent over from London are already in place and organized. How would they know I would choose this room? I walk out a little freaked out and walk towards the in-room bathroom. It had a really big shower and a really big bath tub, a two person sink, and a vanity with a velvet lilac chair.
As I sigh and walk out I hear my parents talking to someone and my stomach bottoms out. Is it him? OH GOD.. What will I say? What will I do? If it is him, he is probably here to make sure my parents found the house ok. He's obviously not here to see me. I walk out of *my* room and walk towards the balcony, looking over the foyer. I get this weird feeling in my stomach, I don't know if it's happiness or disappointment that it's not him. Standing there, talking with my parents is none other than the famous Roxy. Sensing my presence, she turns to look at me with a big smile. Her light brown eyes brightened with excitement. I looked her over, her hair was the same, really curly and dark brown. She was tall and lean. The only difference I notice is the makeup coating her flawless light brown skin.
I run down the stairs and pretty much leap into her arms, she squeezes me just as tight as I do her.

"I missed you so much Aphrodite!" Roxy exclaims and pulls back keeping me at arms length.
"Oh, I missed you too girly! Gotta say, I'm loving the makeup! You look really good!" I say honestly.

“You do too, that body though! You didn’t have those curves last time I saw you.” she says as she looks at me from head to toe and I do the same to her. I turned to see my parents weren’t there and guessed at some time they left the room. “So did you pick a room yet?” she asks.

“Yeah actually, but the room picked me. C’mon! ” I tilt my head towards the stairs, and we start towards them.

“This is a really great house, A.” Roxy said, as we walked up the stairs.

“I know right? Apparently, Adonis helped them set everything up.” The words sound bitter, even to me, as I let them slip from my lips.

As we walk into my room Roxy says, "I see why you say the room chose you, it literally screams Aphrodite.” She walks around my room admiring everything, sweeping her delicate fingers over the different materials and surfaces. “He designed you the room.” she said matter of factly.
I look at her, taken aback, everything finally clicking into place in my mind. I don’t understand why he would take the time to design my room, but can’t take the time to answer a freaking phone call. “That makes no sense.” I say quietly.
She looks at me with a flat look and then rolls her eyes. I don’t know what to think, my mind is boggled. “What- I- um-“ I keep trying to form a sentence but I don’t even know what to say to this. That’s when Roxy says, “You haven’t seen him yet.” she said with recognition clear in her voice.
“Why do you make it sound like a bad thing?” I ask.

"Have you spoken to him since you left? When was the last time you saw him? Over FaceTime or a picture?" Her serious questions kept coming and they were making me feel anxious.
My heart starts to race, my hands start sweating as a million different things cross through my mind in three seconds, "Why? Has something happened to him? Is he hurt?"
"No, no he's fine..." she looks away and bites down on her lip nervously.
"What's wrong then? tell me!" I exclaim.
"Aphrodite, he's not the same guy you know and remember, he's changed."
I look at her frowning, what could she mean by that.
"Roxy, what do you mean? What are you talking about?"
She sighs, "You need to see for yourself." I purse my lips with my eyebrows furrowed.

I spent the rest of the day with Roxy. We talked more, mostly mindless things, catching up and about colleges we applied for. We watched movies but all I could think of was what she meant about him.

I WOKE UP THE next morning, had breakfast with my family, and then they left for work. It's so great the hospital is giving them back their surgical positions. I quickly clean up the kitchen and head to my room to get ready. As I enter my room, I get a quick text from Roxy telling me she will pick me up soon and that she's bringing a friend. I take a shower, brush my teeth, then get dressed in my favorite jeans, black Vans, and a white tank top and throw a short, double-breasted jacket on top. I style my hair in slight waves

and put a little makeup on. I have to admit, I'm a little nervous to meet the friend Roxy mentioned.
As I grab my bag, I hear honking coming from outside. I never liked meeting new people. It was always hard for me to get along with people I barely met but Roxy said she's cool, so that means I need to try. I run down the stairs, walk outside, and lock the door with the code my dad gave me this morning, which is my *birthday*.
I turn around to see Roxy in the driver's seat of a red convertible with the top down. I'm guessing the girl sitting in the back seat, is Erica. I smile and take a seat in the passenger chair.
Erica jumps up and quickly hugs me and introduces herself, "Hi, I'm Erica. So nice to finally meet you!" I introduce myself too, with a smile and notice her looks. Pretty olive toned skin, hazel eyes, and brown hair with soft caramel highlights in a long bob.
"Let's get this show on the road girls!" Roxy exclaims as she turns out of the driveway and turns up the music. I couldn't help the smile that blooms on my face, the summer breeze perfect on my skin.
We end up going to The Grove, a little outdoor shopping mall. We shopped a little, had a quick lunch, and got our nails done. Erika and I clicked pretty fast, which I wasn't expecting, she is so cool, down to earth, and a little shy. I see us becoming quick friends.
Roxy pulls up in front of my house and I quickly step out and I watch them drive off with a wave goodbye. It's funny how time can pass so quickly when you're having fun. I didn't realize it was getting late till now, it was almost dark. I turn towards the house and see my father talking with a man. I can't see much of him because his back is facing me. From what I can see, his arms are full of tattoos and his shirt is two sizes

too small for his big muscular frame. I walk towards them, curious to know who this mysterious man is. “Dad? Who is this?”. My dad looks at me with wide eyes. The mysterious guy's head turns towards me and I run my eyes over his sharp features; strong jaw, long nose, high cheekbones. His almost black hair is shaved, almost to nothing on the sides and long on top. It was a perfectly styled undercut, slicked back with gel. His eyes, his eyes were a pale green that seemed very familiar. It was that green that was so clear it almost looked grey. The one that you had to get closer to realize the color.

It's him...

Chapter Three

What Have You Done To My Best Friend?

It can't be him. My Adonis is skinny. This Adonis is muscular. My Adonis' cream skin is flawless and perfect. This Adonis' skin looks like a map of art. What I know of my Adonis, *My best friend* is, he would never tattoo his skin purposely.
I mentally shake my head from my shocked state and notice how he is looking at every piece of me as if I am someone he has never seen before. Our eyes meet and his green eyed gaze is so intense I quickly look away.
"Oh is that Melissa calling me? I better go." My dad says and quickly turns on his heel and walks back inside. My eyes go wide at the realization that I'm left alone with this new Adonis. I'm gonna have to have a word with my father later.
"Sup," He says awkwardly, putting his hands in his pockets and rocking back on his heels.
I turn back to look him in the eyes as I say ignoring his lame greeting, "Why?" He opens his mouth to say something but I stop him with a hand gesture. "Don't give me any excuses...", I look down for a moment with a deep breath, "How could you?", I say disappointedly. I Look him over with distaste and say, as my eyes collide back to his,, "What have you done to my best friend?" His eyes blaze with rage at my words and he steps towards me, "What do you want me to say?!", he yells and I cower back unexpectedly, a little frightened at the anger in his voice. Who is this person? This definitely isn't the person I remember. His eyes go wide in shock and regret is clear on his face. He reaches out a hand towards me and I step away from it, "I didn't mean-" I cut him off again with a loud sigh. "Look, I'm sorry for what's happening with your mother. I am truly heartbroken and I know you're going through a lot, but I was supposed to be there for

you...but you didn't let me." I rub my hands over my arms in slight comfort.
"You shouldn't have left." He whispers, not wanting to frighten me again. I laugh humorlessly, "You shouldn't have let me leave." I say matching his voice. We both knew it was useless. Neither of us had a choice in my departure. He looks at me with an intense look in his eyes, as if that look was going to tell me everything he has been going through but the only thing I see is a broken man in the place of my Adonis.

He sighs and runs a nervous hand through his hair, "I wish I had that choice."

"You had the choice to answer my phone call and you decided against it."
He shakes his head in disagreement, "I had my reasons."

I throw my hands up in exasperation, "Care to enlighten me?"

"You're better off not knowing," He says seriously. I'm not going to let myself believe his lies. He had no real reason why not to answer except that he didn't want anything to do with me. He just can't say it to my face. I start towards the door and pass him but he grabs my arm to stop me. I look down to his hand on my arm and unknown knots form in the pit of my stomach. Tingles flash up my arm and heat rises to my face in what I think is anger. "Is this it then? Let me explain."
"You already decided I'm better off not knowing. So what are you gonna explain?" I say and pull my hand out of his grip and start walking again.
I hear him from behind me say, "So what? You're just gonna ignore me from now on?"

I turn to him with my hand on the door and say, "I guess pay back really is a bitch," I slam the door in his face.
"That's very childish of you!" He screams from the other side of the door.
Those words make me want to open the door and give him a piece of my mind, instead I turn towards the stairs and walk up to my room. I look out the balcony as he drives out in a new, black Porsche.

I take a seat on my couch with a loud sigh. Everything that just happened is running through my mind and for some reason, I feel a longing in my heart. I wish we were back to the way we used to be. Nostalgia is clawing at my heart. The way this should have happened is completely different from what just happened. He should have been waiting for me with open arms. He should have held me in his arms and whispered to me how much he missed me. We should have ran up to my room and watched movies all night, while stuffing our faces with popcorn. Then after staying up most of the night, we would have fallen asleep together in my bed. The way we always did; but sadly that's not what happened. Instead of all that, I am sitting here alone, missing something that will never happen again. I won't be wistful any longer, I refuse it. So I push all those thoughts away and walk towards my bathroom and take a long relaxing shower.

AS I AM LYING DOWN in bed, watching a movie, hours after my encounter with Adonis, my mother walks into my room, "Hey sweetie how are you?" She smiles sadly at me. I turn off my Tv, sitting up I tap the spot beside me, she comes over and takes a seat,

"I'm good. How was everything at the hospital? Have you seen Mary?" I asked and leaned against her. I had learned that Adonis' mother was staying at the hospital because my father would be taking some special test to see what he can do about her lung cancer. My father is one of the best Cardiothoracic Surgeons in America. Mary is one of the reasons my family moved back to Los Angeles.
"Yes and she can't wait to see you. She has been talking about you all day. She is so excited for your visit tomorrow." I smile at that.
"I'm excited too." I look up to my mom and smile. "You didn't tell me about your day? Was everything okay?" She frowns and starts telling me how she lost an emergency patient on the table today and wished she was able to save him. She hated the fact that she lost her first patient, back at the hospital. My mom loves being a General Surgeon, same as Mary but every time she lost a patient, I saw it take a piece from her soul. We started talking about the internship she wants me to take under her and I sigh and laugh at that. My dream is to be a General Surgeon but I don't want to be her intern next year. I'd always wanted to be Mary's intern. I really hope I get that chance during med school the way we always planned. My parents and Mary took their surgical residency together and have been friends ever since. Adonis' father, Johnathon Clark, was a very wealthy man with a very strict attitude, completely different from Mary. He was a CEO of some architecture business he inherited from his father. The same business Adonis had to take over when one day. My mother and I talked for a long time until I ended up falling asleep to her hand running through my hair.

Chapter Four

Pretending...

I dust myself off a little as I walk out of the elevator, a little nervous to see Mary. I don't know why, this woman practically raised me but for some reason, I have knots in my stomach. I walk towards the room my mother told me she was in and take a deep breath before knocking on her door. "Come in!" she yells from behind it. I smile at the sound of her voice and walk in. My smile didn't falter for one minute at the sight of Mary. I don't know how I was expecting to see her but this was not it. She was wearing blue jeans and a white t-shirt. She had her black hair, like her son's, in a beautiful twist on top of her head. Her pale green eyes were shining in happiness. she was sitting down on her bed, her legs crossed under her and light makeup coating her cream face. She jumps from her bed, pulling the IV cart with her. She walks to me and pulls me in her arms. "I missed you so much Aphrodite! My days have been so dull without you in them sweetheart!" I wrap my arms around her and breathe in her familiar smell of jasmine. "I missed you to Mary. so much," my voice cracks on the last sentence and she pulls away to look at me.

"Oh sweetie, don't start now or we will never stop." She pulls me towards her bed and sits me down on it, taking a seat beside me. "Tell me about you. Your flight? How was it? What have you been doing that was so important, you haven't come to see me?" She gives me a mock glare and I smile shyly.

"I'm so sorry Mary, my friend Roxy insisted on taking me out. I should have come straight here." I look at her sheepishly.

She laughs and shakes her head, "It's ok sweetie, I'm just messing with you."

We start talking and joking around, laughing the whole time. Until there was a knock on the door and the person that walks in makes the smile from my face fall immediately. Adonis walks in with a take out bag in his hand. His step falters as he notices me, but then continues walking in anyway. Mary looks up at her son and smiles "Lunch again Adonis? I thought I told you not to bother with that. I don't want you to worry about me, I'm fine." He grabs the rollaway tray and sets the food there, "And let you eat the hospital food you hate so much? I don't think so," he says, in his velvety thick voice. His mother just smiles. I watch as he sets up her food nicely. After he is done, he puts all the remaining things back in the bag and sets it aside on the nearby sink. All the while, not even glancing my way.

He sets the tray in front of his mother and tells her to eat. He's about to leave when, to my dismay, Mary says "Wait!" He turns back to look at his mother a little impatiently, "Why are you leaving? Is there something going on between you and Aphrodite? Am I missing something?" She gives me a confused look. I can't allow her to know me and her son no longer get along. It would crush her, probably even more than it's crushing me right now and she doesn't need the extra stress. My eyes widen and my voice goes up a few octaves as I lie through my teeth. "No, of course not!" Adonis looks at me with shock and confusion on his face, then gives me a 'what the hell look'. "Don't leave Adonis, stay with us a little. We were just catching up." He raises a thick arched eyebrow at me and walks towards a chair a few feet in front of us. He takes a seat with his legs wide open, leans his elbows on his thighs and brings his hands to hang between them. He gave me a challenging look, as if to say, 'lets see what you got Aphrodite' and my breath stills in my throat. I take a quick glance towards his bulging, muscled tattooed arms and just as quickly, look away as a slight blush creeps up my cheeks. I catch a smirk on his face and blush even darker, knowing I've been caught. I look towards Mary and she has a smirk as well, which makes the blush creep down my neck but luckily Mary decides to clear the awkward silence. “Tell us about London Aphrodite.”

I smile in relief and my shoulders relax a little. I look back to Adonis and he is looking at me in interest. I mentally roll my eyes. He should have known everything about my time in London. I look back to Mary and say, “My classes were really good, school is a lot different there than here, that's for sure. But I learned so much. My favorite thing was visiting the museums, they were so beautiful and inspiring. I would go whenever I could.” I smile, reminiscing about studying all the artifacts and art pieces.

“That's interesting, and is Big Ben and everything as beautiful as they say? And the food? Please tell me about the food.” I shake my head and chuckle at Mary's words.

“Well when it comes to food, I really didn't eat out much. There was this really nice cafe I would go to sometimes and eat lunch there. The best thing about the food in London was the freshness, everything definitely has a different taste. Also, you can find the best Delis there. You go to any of them and it's amazing. Their bread, cold cuts-” I stop as I notice the look on Adonis face. He looked so wistful. His smile looked relaxed and sincere. He notices my stare and he quickly looks away, putting a closed fist under his chin, causing him to lean forward a little. It made his forearm bulge out, also making his veins pop out. I swallowed my spit and he caught my quick glance and paused, raising an eyebrow in question.

I look back to Mary and continue, "Don't get me started on the cheeses, they were all so good and different. The tourist sights were nice, just as you would expect. I loved going at night and seeing everything lit up." I nodded while smiling. Wanting to take the attention off me, I asked Mary, "What about you Mary, I heard you took time off your surgical practice. What have you been doing in your spare time?" She smiles excitedly, "As you well know, I always wanted to write a book about my work but I never got the time for it. In the last two months, I have gotten to almost finish it. I actually wanted to talk to you about that. Maybe one of these days, you can come by and read it, maybe do some editing or whatever else it needs." She gives me a hopeful look and I nod.

I feel his eyes on me as I say, "Of course! I would be honored to help out my childhood role model!" I glanced at Adonis, who was looking at his mother. As soon as he was going to look my way, I turned my head back to Mary. She gives me a sad smile, "I'm sorry, I won't be able to have you intern under me anymore." I give her an exasperated look. "Don't say that! You will be fine soon and you will be back working in the hospital and just like we always planned, I will intern under you." I started breathing a little heavily with every word.

"sweetie"- I cut her off.

"You're saying it as if you're... you're not gonna get better, as if-" this time Adonis cuts me off.

"It's gonna be okay, one way or another" I look at him and sigh. I noticed my hands were trembling slightly and I wrapped my arms around myself. I look back to Mary and she has a sad smile on her face. Her eyes are slightly glassy. “Did the doctors tell you anything today ma?”

“Yes, Robert told me the cancer has grown a little, from what he can tell from his new scans. He was comparing them to the ones they took two months ago. He said he wants to operate in the next three or four weeks. but he also said that he is almost done with his tests and I can go home in two days.” Mary smiles but it doesn’t reach her eyes. I look to Adonis and he runs a hand over his face, his bottom lip coming down with his hand and I can’t help but swallow spit again. “Well it's a good thing Robert’s here, I know he will do whatever he has to, to make you better.” he praises my father. I know that in his heart, he believes his words but I hope they are true. “You’re right sweetheart. Now tell me, how have you been spending your summer? I feel like I haven’t been talking to you lately.” Mary quickly changes the conversation. Adonis realizes too but he sighs and plays along.

“Yeah, it's been good, been hanging out with my friends,” he looks towards me then quickly reverts his eyes. I look at him curiously but he avoids me. Friends? I mean, I knew Adonis had a few guy friends he hung out with and played sports with but there weren't any specific friends. “Oh really? that's good, son, I’m glad. How are those boys? They really are lovely.” she looks towards me as she says the last part. Adonis leans back in his chair, pushing his legs forward while sliding his palms over his black jeans. He starts saying something to his mother. I don’t pay much attention as his white T-shirt is kind of see through. The tattoos on his chest and stomach are visible through the shirt. I look at his face and notice he has a small scar in his left eyebrow, that gives it a part in the corner before it ends. That little detail, that new detail, that my Adonis didn't have, gives his face a more fierce look. Not to mention, the shadows around his eyes and the stubble on his jaw. I bring my eyes down to his chest, my breath catches as he takes a deep breath and his chest lifts upward showing off all the details in it. My fingers tingle at the thought of touching him but I quickly shake that thought away. My heart skips a beat as he smiles and chuckles at something his mom said. For that little moment, that simple chuckle, that smile, that joy in his eyes, that joy that came from his mothers happiness; for that moment, he looked like the person I remember. He laughed louder and then a few strands of his hair fell on his face. He lifts an arm and runs a hand through his hair, putting it back into place. That gesture he does, makes me visibly widen my eyes. His arms are huge, so strong-- my thoughts get cut off by my name coming from his lips.

"Aphrodite?" My name coming from his mouth after so long of not hearing it from him, made my heart stop. I look to him and pull my hair to the side, trying to conceal my blush but fail miserably. "Look a little flushed there, you okay?" he smirks. The little embarrassment I felt vanishes and morphs into anger and I give him a flat look. He chuckles to himself as he looks away. Suddenly, there's a knock on the door and a nurse walks in.

"Hello. I'm gonna need the room please. So sorry to interrupt." she said shyly. She was a young nurse, maybe in her early twenties.

"You're good," Adonis says, not even looking at her. He stands up and walks to his mother's side and kisses the top of her head, his knee touching my leg slightly. “See ya later ma.” and he walks to the door. As I watch him walking out the door, I notice the nurse is also looking at him with some sort of lustful gaze. I don’t blame her. He is really good looking. I quickly say goodbye and kiss Mary on the cheek and walk out. As I do, I see Adonis leaning on the wall beside the room, obviously waiting for me.

Chapter FIVE

W.T.F

“What do you want, Adonis?” I ask, while giving him a raised eyebrow and walking away. He kicks off the wall and walks beside me. “Your cheeks are still a little red.” He puts his hands in his pockets and he smirks at me. I give him a side view, looking at him from head to toe, with a serious look on my face and decide on staying silent. But as I look at him, I notice more. From up close and personal, everything looks more defined. I swallow my spit again, like I did earlier several times. I feel an unknown feeling in the pit of my stomach and between my legs. “There it is again,” he smiles and shakes his head with a big grin on his face, showing his perfect white teeth. While he squints his eyes playfully, ”What is going on in that pretty little head of yours?” I walk a little faster, “Leave me alone Adonis.” I roll my eyes. He matches my steps and gets in front of me, walking backwards. I pause momentarily and then continue walking. *God, I hope he falls.* He leans forward and wipes at the corner of my lip with his thumb, causing my eyebrows to raise. I stop and look at him with a ‘what the fuck look’. He halts, saying, ”Oh sorry, I was just wiping off the drool from earlier.”
I push him aside and walk towards the elevator button and press it. I cross my arms under my breast and turn towards him to say, ”What's your problem?!” His smile falls as he says, “I thought we were still pretending.” He mocks innocently and winks. My heart leaps as weird images flash through my head of him saying those things in different scenarios. I quickly blink trying to erase those images from my mind. I mentally slap myself. What the fuck am I thinking? I hear the elevator doors open, his eyes stay on mine. He gets a weird look on his face as he pretty much stocks towards me. I walk backwards, not breaking eye contact. My back hits the mirrored wall

and I press my palms flat to it, trying to get as far from Adonis as possible. The elevator doors close behind him, trapping me in. He leans forward, our bodies about an inch apart. “I need you to stay away from me,” he says with no humor in his eyes. I know for a fact, hurt flashes through mine, I never thought I would hear those words coming from his mouth but what I realize, this isn’t the same person I left behind. Not even close. I try to conceal the look in my eyes with a flat one. I feel his minty breath fanning my face as I say, “Don’t worry I will.”
He runs a hand over his hair and blows out a harsh breath in my face, then pulls away, leaning on the wall on the left side of the elevator. He leans over, presses the button to go down, then crosses his thick arms over his perfectly sculpted chest. I walk towards the right side trying to put more distance between me and his new body. I lean on the wall and run a hand through my wavy hair with an exasperated sigh. I bite down on my lip trying to keep from saying anything but the words spill out anyway. ”As if I’m not already used to it...not having you in my life.” The painful words come out in a whisper. Something flashes there in his eyes but he quickly conceals it with a smirk, “Good, that's just the way I want it.”
“Good.” I say and cross my arms over my chest, not breaking eye contact.
I see how he sucks on his teeth then raises an eyebrow at me, accepting the challenge. I also raise an eyebrow but he doesn’t keep eye contact. He gives me a slow once over. His eyes show interest. My breathing quickens every millisecond. As his eyes reach mine, he gives me a cocky look, making me realize, this was his plan. He wanted to rile me up. He wanted an effect on me. and that's exactly what he got. I look away flushed. Luckily, the elevator doors

open and I walk out, walking quickly. I have one stop and that's my mothers car. I can hear and feel his footsteps behind me, his presence angering me with every step. As we walk out and reach the parking lot, I decide I had enough. How long is this going to last? I turn hot on my heals towards him and yell, "What the fuck is your problem?!" His eyes go wide in slight shock and he says, "You! You shouldn't have come back!" His voice was rising with every word. He raises an eyebrow and yells, "You don't understand! You can't be around me."

"Oh my God!" I run my hands frustratedly through my hair, "Do you realize how fucking stupid you sound right now?!" I exclaim!

He grits his teeth, "I have my reasons, to not want you in my life."

"So you keep saying! But you're the one who has been around me! Or haven't you realized! Are you that fucking dumb?!" I see anger in his face at my insult. He puts a hand in his pocket and pulls out a pack of cigarettes. A fucking pack of cigarettes! His words come out a little more calm but still as angry, "I'm not fucking stupid. I just want you to understand. I want it to get through your thick skull, that you-", he puts the cigarette to his lips, lights it then continues speaking after he takes a drag of it; "Need to stay the fuck away from me." He exhales the smoke from his lips.

I throw my hands up in the air in exasperation. "And what? You smoke now?! What else have you changed? Do you go out and kill people too?! You're definitely not the person I remember." My voice lowers in the last sentence. He takes another long drag from his cigarette, holds it a while then slowly exhales it. He looks at me narrowing his eyes,, "That person died a long time ago." He pulls on his lower lip

with the hand that's holding the cigarette between his tattooed fingers. I stay silent as he slowly releases his bottom lip, saying, “You need to forget him.”
I shake my head in disappointment, “What have you become?” He laughs humorlessly, “I’m not good for you.” He takes another drag from his cigarette then flicks it away.

“Who are you to decide what's good for me?” I look at him, waiting for him to reply but he doesn’t say anything. ”How about a better question; do you hate me?” Unshed tears gather at my eyes as he again does not answer, just looks at me with a flat look. I take that as my answer. I knew the truth all along. I knew he hated me but I just had to know for sure. “Well guess what? The feeling is mutual.” He sighs loudly as I walk away, straight to my mothers car, get in, start the car and drive off as a tear escapes from my eye.

Chapter
Six

Who Invited You?

The last two days have been...well, let's just say, bad. Roxy called me all day today and I couldn't get myself to answer the phone. Until finally, I had enough and decided to call her back. First thing she asked was, what's wrong? That's when I finally let it all out and told her everything that happened with him. I can't even bear to think of his name without getting mad. The thing that has me shocked is, as I'm ranting about everything that happened, the line goes dead. She hung up on me. I shake my head and throw my phone on the bed and go for a very needed shower. As I walk out of the shower and wrap myself in my robe with my wet hair framing my face, I hear the doorbell ring. I wonder who it is. My parents are at the hospital and will be there all night, so it can't be them. I slowly walk down the stairs, praying it isn't Adonis because I really don't know how I would react if it is him. As I open the door, I let my shoulders slump in relief looking at the two girls at my doorstep. My eyebrows knit together as I notice what they are wearing. I mean, I know it's Friday night but the only plans I had were getting in my bed and watching movies. These girls are wearing full blown outfits so they definitely plan on doing more than getting in bed and watching movies with me. Erika is wearing a deep purple bodycon dress with black pumps. Roxy is wearing tight black jeans, a see-through, long-sleeved black shirt tucked in, with a black bra underneath. I look down at Roxy's feet and mentally laugh, of course she is full on dressed and wearing black Vans. "Are you gonna let us in or are you just gonna stand there checking us out all night? Because we have somewhere to be tonight." Roxy said with humor filled eyes.

"'We' sounds like a lot of people." I say, as I move to the side allowing them to walk in.

"C'mon Aphrodite. We're going out tonight." Roxy says, as she tugs on my hand, pulling me up the stairs. I protest the whole way up.

"I really don't want to go out, girls. Can't we just stay here and watch movies?" I give them a hopeful look.

"Not gonna happen. She pretty much dragged me out of my house." Erika smiles as Roxy walks into my closet.

I groan and sit on my couch. Now I understand why she hung up on me. Her plan was to get me to go out. Erika walks into my closet as well to help her look for an outfit. They both walk out with smiles on their faces. Roxy's holding some clothes in her hand and Erika has my red pumps. They hand them to me and Roxy pushes me towards the bathroom, "Put these on and hurry up. I don't want to get there when everyone's already drunk."
I give her a flat look and she shrugs with a smile on her face. I walk into my bathroom and quickly get dressed. I look down at the outfit, it's pretty cute. They picked out a midthigh length, white skirt, with a black ACDC shirt. I tie up the shirt just over my belly button. I quickly blow dry my hair, then add slight curls in it. As I start on my makeup, the girls walk into the bathroom. They grab a few things to add more to their already beautiful faces. I finish with a cat eye and mascara, slip on my heels and we're off.

AS WE WALK TOWARDS the beach, I can hear music coming from a distance. I take off my heels and hold them in one hand as we start walking on the sand. As we near a Large rock. I can see flames. I can hear music, laughter, and yelling from here. We walk a little more and as we pass the rock, I start to see the scene in front of me. The first thing that catches my eye is the huge flames in the middle of the large crowd. They weren't too far from the shore but far enough where no one could get wet. This spot was perfect, with the big rock-like cliff surrounding the area, shielding them from view. To one side, was a big podium with a big DJ station. A girl with crazy blonde hair and big headphones was scratching disks and adding music on her computer. A few feet to the right of the DJ, was a bar. They managed to get four tables and make a boxed bar. There were three boys inside mixing and serving drinks to people. There was flat plywood to one side as a makeshift dance floor, which was pretty large, and there were people dancing and grinding to the music. There were chairs and tables all around. I look to the girls and smile. I don't think I have ever seen anything like this in my life. Roxy looks at me and smiles back while saying, "And you wanted to miss out on this." Excitement clear on her face, I giggle matching her excitement and Erika beams at us. I smile wider as the song switches to one of my favorites, "Don't Call Me Up" by Mabel. We start walking towards the crowd and I wince as we pass through sweaty and sticky bodies. Roxy starts leading the way to where there are a few people gathered around some tables and chairs. I kinda recognize some people from school. As we get closer, I notice who is sitting at the center of the group and I stop midstep. Roxy and Erika kept walking but I was tangled in the crowd, slightly swaying as people bumped me constantly. Adonis was surrounded by people, he hasn't noticed me yet. Everyone around him looked at him with such idolatry, they hung on every word he said. I finally noticed there is someone on his lap. A beautiful girl with the body of a supermodel. She had perfect tanned skin, long cascading hair, and gorgeous curves. I looked at his hand that was caressing her thigh, then to his other hand that was wrapped around a red solo cup. From what I could see, he was wearing a black, long-sleeved buttoned down shirt that was half way open, his tattoos on his chest showing through, with the sleeves rolled up to his elbows, with black pants, and black shoes. As I looked back to his face, our eyes met and the anger in his eyes was clear as day. I raise my eyebrow in question. I notice there is flat wood around and step on it. I slip on my heels without breaking eye contact. My lips curled as I walked towards them. Roxy and Erika are sitting down on some chairs near Adonis. Roxy jumps up and walks to me and says in a loud voice, while grabbing my hand and raising it, "Okay guys, this is my girl Aphrodite! She's back and hotter than ever!" She looks at me with mischief and continues, "Oh and she's single!" I pull my hand from hers and glare at her as everyone starts to wolf whistle. I walk towards Erika while shaking my head in disbelief and look down in slight embarrassment. I sit down next to her and look towards Adonis. He is looking between me and Roxy, clearly pissed. I look around and catch the eye of some guy with black shaggy hair. His brown eyes, a contrast to his fair skin, were playful as he says, "Hey Aphrodite, it's been a minute." He tilts his head in a what's up gesture.

"Hudson." I say in recognition.

“The one and only.” He shrugs one shoulder with a smirk. I roll my eyes as memories of him being a jerk to me in middle school run through my head. I haven’t seen him since I heard his family went broke and they had to move away. Roxy sits down next to me and winks. I have no idea what is running through her head, but it isn’t good.
“Wait wait!” Some guy exclaims and we all turn to look at him. He had clear blue eyes and brown buzzed cut hair, his skin was a soft tan. From what I can see, he had a few tattoos here and there on his sleeveless arms. “I want to know what happened between Hudson and Aphrodite. Was it a one night stand or something?”, he looked between me and Hudson and I looked at him in disgust from his words. I hear a slight angry tsk from Adonis but ignore it completely.

“That's Cain” Roxy rolls her eyes with a grin, she obviously gets along with him.

“Yeah, that’s me. Cain, but not the one that killed his brother. Though, I wish I could kill my brother.”

I laugh and shake my head. I open my mouth to say something when I hear Adonis’ cruel words, making me shut my mouth completely. “Why did you bring her?” I look at him with a glare but his eyes are on Roxy. I look at her and she has an angry look on her face, then look back to him and say, ”Excuse me?” His eyes pierce daggers into mine, ”If I would have known you were gonna bring her, I would have made sure you weren’t invited.” His words are towards Roxy but his eyes stay glued to mine.
I feel Roxy shuffle a little, “Come on Adonis, don’t be like that she belongs here, she’s your-“ He whips his

head to her and shuts her up with his glare. The girl on his lap smirks and takes a sip of her drink, enjoying the drama. With mischief, she says with a slight latin accent, “Well if you're staying, you're gonna need a drink”, she leans down and with a perfectly manicured hand grabs a drink from the table in front of her. She extends her hand, “I’m Adriana by the way.” I reach out to grab it but the drink is pulled from her hand roughly.
Adonis again glares at me as he says through gritted teeth, “She doesn’t drink.” He pulls her off his lap and practically throws her on the floor but she quickly composes herself with a huff and dusts herself off. She takes a seat right next to Adonis and crosses her legs, her dress riding up a little.
“A lot can change in a year.” I lean down and grab a new cup from the table, bringing it to my lips, my eyes never leaving his, "You should know that.”

Chapter
Seven
I Really Need A Drink

I tip my head back in honest laughter, gripping my drink in my hand tighter to keep it from falling. Cain has been keeping me company most of the night. In my opinion, he can make the guards in front of Buckingham Palace at least smile. The scene around us is just as booming as when I got here. With my already flushed face from the alcohol I have been drinking, the heat of the bonfire was really starting to irritate my skin. Cain points to another person, it was a guy with shoulder length hair, skinny jeans, and a loose, black t-shirt. “Gosh, man! What am I even doing here? I could totally be at the skatepark, shredding and smoking pot right now!” Cain’s impression of a skater dude was as funny as the jock with girl problems. I roll my eyes and giggle a little. “Okay, I think that's enough with the cliches.” I shake my head with a smile.
“Oh come on Aphrodite, I’m on a roll!” he whines.
I look to Adonis, who has had a sour face since I got here. His eyes have been on me all night. His other friends, who Cain introduced me to, Liam and James, were apparently cousins but looked nothing alike, were talking to him but he was giving them straight, flat answers. I get an idea, “Fine then, one more but I choose.” I point to Adonis, trying to keep him from noticing, ”Him. But make it good.” I look back to Cain and he has a smirk on his face.
“That's easy! But the thing is, are you ready for it?” He lifts an eyebrow.
I look at him with determination, “Oh I’m ready.”
“First,” He grabs two miniature solo cups from the nearby table and passes me one. “We need to drink these.” I give him a weirded glance but tap my cup to his anyway before downing the brimming cup of tequila. I screw up my face at the burn in my throat then put the cup down and Cain follows. He looks

back at me and sucks on his teeth before starting. “Why the fuck is she here?” He looks back at me seriously, his voice lowering, then continues, “He’s been asking himself this since you got here, also... Why the fuck does she have to look so sexy. Why do her legs have to look so perfect in that skirt? And there where he is sitting, he is insane with jealousy, he wishes you were talking and laughing with him instead of me. But he won’t allow that to happen. His problem right now is, he wants his hands all over you and he wants nothing to do with you. So there where he is sitting, he is fighting with himself and he can’t think straight.”
My head starts spinning slightly. I don’t know if it's from his words or that double shot of tequila. I force a laugh and slightly push his shoulder, “Okay, now you're just making things up.”
“Believe it or not.” He shrugs, “It's the truth.”
A song that I really like starts playing, “You know what? I feel like dancing.” I decided to ignore everything, the crazy feeling in my stomach, the things he said and the spinning of my head. I leave Cain to where he is standing and walk to the girls. “Let's go dance, girls.” Erica and Roxy get up without a protest and I walk over to where Adonis and Adriana are sitting. I lean over him to grab her hand but as I do I look to his inner forearm and I feel my heart ache. I look at his face but his eyes are not on mine, he is looking at my body as it is slightly leaning over him. I roll my eyes, pervert. I grab Adriana’s hand, ”Come on, let go dance.” She shrugs and jumps to her feet. Adonis has an unreadable expression as I turn away and we walk to the dance floor. I could tell from the way the girls are dancing, they also feel like me, dizzy and a need to dance it off. I sway my hips to the music and laugh a little as I

run my hands over my sides then bring them through my hair. I really am enjoying the buzz that is running through my body. The glare I have been feeling on me all night intensifies. Without looking, I smirk and grab on to Adriana's arm, pulling her towards me, I give her a little twirl then pull her body close to mine and we start dancing in sync. I turn us so her back is to him and I can see him perfectly over her shoulder. He sips on his drink as he watches us with those intense smoldering eyes. His back leaning against his chair, his legs stretched out in front of him. I turn Adriana around so her back is flush against my chest, I put my hands on her hips and we sway together. I see her look towards Adonis and she grins and looks back at me, she knows exactly what I'm doing. She turns towards me and rubs her hands over my body seductively and I feel a little weird about her intensity but go with it anyway. With every beat, Adriana's movements intensify, I push her off me and yell over the music so the other girls can hear. "I need a drink." They nod and I walk towards the crowded bar.
I have been waiting by the side of the bar for someone to take my drink order but with no luck. After a few minutes, I decide to leave. I notice a guy slide over one of the tables and walk to me in a hurry, "Wait!" I look at him perplexed, "I'll take your order. What would you like?"
"Isn't that their job?" I point to the other guys in the makeshift booth.
He waves his hand in a nonchalant manner, "They won't mind. C'mon tell me."
I smile and roll my eyes but still give him my order, "Give me two shots of tequila and a cranberry with vodka, please."
He smiles an impressive smile, "Coming right up!" He starts moving around the other boys looking for all the

things he needs. After a few minutes, he puts my order in front of me and two lemon wedges over a napkin. "Here you go pretty lady. I'm Nick by the way."
I smile but don't answer as I grab one of the shot glasses and down it, then grab the other and do the same. I grab my cocktail and suck on the straw washing down the burn of the tequila, abandoning the lemons. He smirks while watching me, "I'm Aphrodite. how much?" I nod towards the drink in my hand.
"Don't worry about it, it's on me"
"For real?" He nods and I smile big, "Thanks so much!" He shrugs it off.
"I haven't seen you around. Do I know you?" He asks and leans a little towards me so we can hear each other better over the loud music.
"I don't think so, I just moved back from London." His eyes go wide a little and then starts to ask me more about myself. Apparently, we went to the same school but he is two years older than me and that's why we never saw each other. He is really cute with his curly brown hair and brown eyes, he is really tall too, maybe about six foot four. He has a slight bended nose and a sharp jaw, his skin was pale but had flushed cheeks. After another shot of tequila and another cocktail, he asked me for my phone number and without a second thought, I gave it to him. I squeal as the song "Don't Start Now", by Dua Lipa, starts playing and says, without thinking, "Do you wanna dance?!" He smiles and says, "Yeah!" He jumps over the table in front of us and grabs my hand leading me to the dance floor. I hold on to his hand for dear life as my head is spinning way too much. At this point, I can hardly feel my face. Getting past all the people, we start dancing to the beat. I laugh at his funny dance moves then get closer to him, to steady myself. I turn around putting my back to his front,

losing myself to the music. He puts his hands on my hips as he gets even closer to me, and that's when I get ripped away from him. I turn to see Adonis push him even further away, giving him a harsh look. Turning that glare to me, he demands, “We’re leaving.”

Chapter
Eight
Like Old Times

"What the hell is your problem! I'm not going anywhere with you!" My feet falter as I sway a little. Nick gets closer and gets in between us. "Bro, the lady said no."
Adonis steps up to him with no trace of fear in his eyes, he is a little shorter than Nick but he is way more intimidating. Out of nowhere, Hudson appears by my side and he pulls me a little behind him, shielding me from the boys. I hold onto him to steady myself. Nick backs down as Adonis says harshly, "Get out of my way Walker, before I kick your ass... again." Nick walks away shaking his head in anger and Adonis turns towards me.
"I'm not going!" Without a word, he walks up to me, giving a fleeting look to Hudson, causing him to move to the side. *Now he doesn't want to protect me... stupid boys*. Adonis lifts me up and throws me over his shoulder with a little grunt. My stomach churns at the sudden movement. "What are you doing?" He doesn't answer, just keeps walking. We are now out of the crowd and walking on the beach. The sound of the waves crashing on the shore now evident, due to the music fading. I ask again, "What are you doing, Adonis?"
"Shut up." He almost growls, making me close my lips shut. At this moment, I am very aware of the position I am in. My ass is perked up in the air, pretty much in his face. My legs and arms are dangling. His arms tighten around me to keep me from slipping off. My stomach churns a little and I wrap my arms around his midsection to steady myself. I gasp inaudibly, the feeling of muscle under my arms is inexplicable. Light starts shining as we get near the parking lot. As we get close to his car, he sets me down on my feet. I instantly miss the feeling of his warmth. My head spins even more but I try to ignore it as I point

towards him. I open my mouth to yell but instead I say, "I don't feel so good."
I put my hands on my stomach as Adonis says, "Don't." But it was too late. I was throwing up right in the middle of us, he quickly moved to my side and grabbed my hair in one fist, using his other hand to hold me steady.
When I finally stopped throwing up my guts, I looked at him, his hand still holding my hair up, "I hate you."
He snickers a little, "Point taken. C'mon lets get you home." I don't fight him this time, just wanting to get out of here. He pulls me towards his car and to the passenger side, he unlocks the car and helps me sit down.
I watch as he stands up to his full height and I visibly check him out, "Where did this come from?"
He looks at me confused, "What do you mean?"
I move my hand forward in an exasperated manner gesturing to his whole body, "This! Why are you so hot?" He smirks and rolls his eyes without a word. He closes my door and walks to the other side of the car getting in. I close my eyes and lean my head on the chair as he drives off. The window rolls down and I feel the strong wind on my face. I sloppily turn my head to look at him. He has one hand on the steering wheel and the other on the clutch. With the little light there was in the car, I can see his muscles flexing as he tightens his grip on the steering wheel. I can't help but admire him, he has that whole sexy bad boy look going for him. The slick back black hair, dressed in black and the fierce look in his eyes. My heart hurts a little as I think of all the things I have missed this whole time. He glances at me and the words spill from my mouth without even thinking. "Why didn't you call me?" the words come out mumbled.

So many emotions run through his eyes, but the one more evident is regret. “I wish I had.”
My eyelids shut involuntarily and I drift off into nothingness. Feeling movement, I open my eyes. Adonis is holding me bridal style, while walking up the steps to my house. I watch him punch in the code and he opens the door. “Can you put me down?” He looks at me and releases my legs, allowing me to set them down. He doesn’t let go of me, keeping a hand on my arm to keep me from falling. He shuts the door and locks it. “How do you know the code?” I ask sleepily. He shrugs, "Don’t worry about it.” He leads me up the steps and towards my room. Walking into my room, the room he designed for me, he sits me down on my couch and goes to my closet without speaking. I squint my eyes frowning at the thought of him taking care of me. *Why is he doing this?* He comes back into the room holding a large t-shirt, he grabs my hand and pulls me towards the bathroom. I can’t form any words, I know I should be telling him to get out, but I can’t make myself tell him to leave. Having him with me, having him this close. I know it won’t last long, I know tomorrow we will go back to hating each other. So I decide to stay silent and enjoy his closeness and pretend everything between us is like it used to be. We step into my bathroom and he opens the cabinet under my sink pulling out mouth wash and makeup wipes. He grabs me and sits me down on the counter, he pulls out one makeup wipe and slowly wipes my face. I look to his pale green eyes, his lower lip is between his teeth as he concentrates on what he is doing. The smell of vanilla and white cedar mixed with whiskey, was strong between us, making my head spin even more. He finishes and he sets the wipe on the counter. I try to get off the counter and he helps me get down. I turn to rinse my mouth out and then

dry my mouth on the hand towel on my sink. I pull my shirt off and grab the shirt Adonis picked out for me. I try to put it on but literally can't. He turns me towards him, grabs it from my hands and helps me put it on. Our eyes lock as my head goes through the shirt's hole and I quickly look away. As the shirt falls to me knees, I reach under and pull my skirt down almost falling over in the process but Adonis keeps that from happening with a hand on my shoulder as I take my skirt off. Walking back to my room, he leads me to my bed and pulls the covers down. He helps me in then pulls the blanket over me. He moves my hair from my face and I whisper, "I missed you." With his hand still on my face he says matching my tone of voice, "I'm not him anymore."

Chapter Nine

Wrong Side Of The Couch

With a throbbing head, I climb out of bed. On my nightstand, I notice a bottle of water and some painkillers. I look at them confused but shrug and grab them popping the pills into my mouth. As I put the drink to my lips to wash down the medicine, last night's events flash through my mind. That's for forgetting everything when you're drunk, because I remember everything. I set the drink down and as I am walking to the bathroom I notice something on my couch and I look at it with wide eyes. Walking to my couch, I cross my arms over my chest and look at sleeping Adonis with my head tilted to the side. *What the fuck is he doing here?* I take a seat on my coffee table directly in front of his sleeping form, my arms still crossed under my chest. He has an arm over his eyes, the blanket is resting on his shirtless chest. His face looks so relaxed and he looks like he doesn't even plan on waking up anytime soon, he always was a heavy sleeper. I look around trying to think of an idea, then my eyes land on a glass of water on the coffee table I was sitting on. I smirk and grab it in my hand. First, I take a little sip then bring it right over his head thinking about my next move. *Should I do this? Eh, why not?* I tip the cup and the water falls on his face. He instantly pushes up with a huge gasp, he looks around frantically, then his eyes land on mine.
"What the fuck?!" He exclaims in exasperation.
"Why are you here?" He wipes his face on the blanket and stands up from the chair. He grunts loudly and walks around the coffee table to the open space. I move around to the other side of the table so I am again sitting right in front of him. He is literally just in his boxers, all his muscles on display, no shirt, no pants. He has Tattoos everywhere, on his arms, chest, abs, sides and legs and in a way they all sort of connect but at the same time they are separate. I try

not to look at them too much so I look up into his eyes. "This is really the treatment I get after last night?" He runs a hand through his wet hair while glaring at me. I cross my hands over my chest again and say sternly, "Last night didn't happen. It shouldn't have happened." He shakes his head in disbelief, "Your right, it shouldn't have happened and it never will. That was the last time you act like a child." He reprimanded me as if I was his daughter and he was my father. I stand up and poke him in the chest as I say loudly, "Me? I didn't act like a child! You were the one who dragged me out of there."
He throws his hands up in the air in annoyance, "I had to, you where practically fucking that guy on the dance floor!" I push his chest but he doesn't even budge as I say, "It doesn't matter who I fuck!" His eyes widen at my words and I gesture between me and him, "This doesn't exist. I'm not your friend. I'm not your anything." He chuckles but gives me a venomous look, "Good, you understand now. I don't want you at my parties anymore, or around my friends and especially not around me. I don't need you embarrassing me." I gasp and get in his face, "Oh, now you think you're some big shot! You think that you're the man!" I lift my hands in front of my face, "Don't worry I don't want to be around you. I couldn't care less about you." He smirks and lifts his eyebrow, "That's not what you said last night." Those words shock and anger me, in a way I have never been angry before, he has no right to talk to me like that! *Who does he think he is?* I push him harder screaming in anger, his step falters a little and I start to hit his chest with the sides of my fists, "I hate you! I hate you! I hate you so much!"
I keep hitting him till he grabs my wrist and yells, "Stop it Aphrodite!" Angry tears fall down my face and

I pull my hands from his hold roughly and back away a little. He has hurt me for far too long. He was a very important part in my life, he was the most important part in my life. And he's right, what he said the other day. That, that Adonis doesn't exist anymore. I rather not have him in my life this way. I need to let him go. He shouldn't have come back into my life again. I was better off not knowing who he became. I have tried a million times to get over this thing between us and when I was finally starting to, he came back into my life like this. "I don't need you in my life anymore Adonis. I learned to live without you. It was hard," I admit and look down with tears still falling on my face. "But I had no choice." The last words come out in a whisper. He is breathing heavily as he looks at me, his eyes glazed over. He looks up to the ceiling and runs both his hands through his hair, "Neither did I." he looks back to me, "I'll stay out of your life from now on." He turns and walks towards where his neatly folded clothes are. He slips on his pants, then his shirt. As he buttons his shirt, he mutters, "I'm glad one of us was able to move on." I stay there shocked as he walks out of my room and closes the door.

I scream loudly as soon as the door is closed behind him. I grab the vase filled with my favorite flowers and throw it to the wall watching it shatter. The tears are falling down my face faster now. I pull on my hair with both my hands and scream again. I ran to my dresser and threw everything to the floor in one long sweep. I turn to my bed and pull the streams of the canopy, pulling them to the floor completely. With another scream followed by a loud sob, I pull my covers and sheets and try to rip them with my bare hands. I yell in earnest at not being able to rip them. All I wanna do at this moment is run after him and beg him to come back into my life. To beg him to forget about everything that is keeping him from being in my life. To beg him to hug me and tell me everything is going to be ok, like he used to. I run to the door, but as I grab the door handle, reality sets in and I throw myself to the floor. He doesn't want me in his life. He hasn't wanted me in his life for a very long time. He proved that more than once. I sob uncontrollably and clench my shirt in a fist trying to keep my chest from hurting. The person I thought was always going to be there for me, is no longer there. The silence in my life was like a dark hole and I didn't realize that hole was in my heart, a hole left by the person who said always, meaning we were always going to be together and never let each other down. The only sounds that were heard were my cries and sobs. I lay my head on the floor and try to control my breathing and stop my sobbing. I put my hands to my chest, feeling my fast heartbeat under my palms. As my breathing finally settles, I hear footsteps fading down the stairs. I shake my head, if only he can see me now, lying on the floor looking like an unwanted, crumpled piece of paper.

Chapter <u>Ten</u>

New Friend

The sound of laughter, people chatting, and cars driving by fill my ears as we are sitting down outdoors on the patio of Brio, having lunch. Roxy, Erika, and I decided on a girls day. These girls always find a way to put a huge grin on my face. It has been three days since my incident with Adonis and honestly, I feel a little broken but I am slowly putting myself back together. As long as I stay away from him and the drama that comes with him, I will be fine. I spent the last three days pampering myself at home and binge watching all kinds of TV shows After I put my room back together. Sunday night, the girls showed up at my doorstep with pizza and ice cream. The relationship with these girls was just so easy and carefree. There was no judgement or snarky remarks. There was no attitude or bad manners, it was just so fresh and relaxing. It was as if we were all a different piece of a puzzle but put us all together and we fit perfectly. I really am happy to have them in my life. With Erika, the way she makes you feel as if she has known you all your life, is so blissful. It makes you act the same way, as if we grew up together. I feel so calm and relaxed with them. There is no pressure or need to act a certain way in front of them, it's like you can be yourself and you don’t have to try hard.
I shake my head and smile at Roxy’s words, "I am done with guys. That's it, I’m gonna love myself, just like Hailee Steinfeld.” Her declaration is filled with fake promises and we all know that.
Erika gives her a flat look, "She also Sings, I didn’t know that ‘I was starving till I tasted you’ song. That girl is as confused as you are.” I giggle and Roxy frowns while Erika smirks. I nod while saying, laughter still in my voice, “True.”

I hear my phone ping and I grab it out of my purse. I look at the screen and furrow my eyebrows in confusion. It is a text from an unknown number.

'Hi pretty lady.'

Roxy notices my face and asks, "What is it?"

I look back at her and shrug while showing her and Erika the message. "I have no idea who it is."

"Just go with it. What's the worst that can happen?" Roxy's right, I mean, there's no harm in just texting back. It must be a wrong number or something. I write and rewrite different texts till I decide on something simple.

'Who is this?'

I watch anxiously as the three little dots appear, signaling that the person is texting back. I grab a piece of bread and take a bite while waiting. The bubbles appear and disappear a few times, gesturing the person is trying to decide what to say. I look around at the beautiful view around me. The different types of stores that people walk in and out of in the outdoor shopping mall. I always prefer an outdoor mall versus an indoor mall on days like these. Not too hot and not too cold and the perfect amount of wind that you feel lightly on your face. When the text finally comes in, I realize who it is immediately.

'Were you really that drunk Friday night? You don't even remember me? WOW! I'm hurt.'

I smile and text back.

'Hi Nick'

He instantly texts back.

'Oh so you weren't that drunk! You do remember!'

I giggle and reply.

'I guess I wasn't drunk enough! lol jk. What's up?'

He sends me an emoticon of a laughing face then his reply.

'tbh haven't stopped thinking about you all weekend.'

I blush and the girls give me a questioning look, I explain to them and they lean over to read over my shoulder. I shake them off and they reluctantly go back to their spots.
I grin while replying.

'Oh really…'

He sends back the emoticon of the monkey covering his eyes in embarrassment, then again adding a message after.

'I was wondering if you wanted to hang out…'

I look at the screen with wide eyes, my brain runs through different ways to let him down easily till I finally decide on my decline.

'Sorry, can't. I'm going to be busy all week.'

I feel horrible at his reply. The truth is, I've never really dated anyone and I feel like this isn't the right time to start.

'Wow, that's a nice way to reject someone.'

I sigh as I tell him the truth.

'Honestly, I am not ready for a relationship.'

I look at the phone, taken aback but with a small smile. I read and reread his reply over and over again.

'We can be friends… for now.'

I smile while typing and put something simple and short then add a smiley face emoticon.

'Sounds good to me.'

We text back and forward throughout the whole day. He is really funny and so sweet. I never really got a boys attention in this way, even though I am nineteen and out of high school. When I was in school here in Los Angeles, Adonis was too over protective and never let me date. Heck he hardly allowed me to speak to any other boy. He always said boys had a one track mind and I had no business getting involved with them. I always agreed with him. And while I was in England, I was always keeping my head down, focusing on my school work. I didn't go to parties or anything like that. I had a few study friends in the library, who were girls, but our relationship was just that, studying. At lunch, I would sit down alone and read. The truth is, who would want to sit next to a girl that was studying, no one. I wouldn't even sit next to one. All I wanted was for the time to pass so I can graduate and go off to college here in California. That was the only thing that helped the time pass. Being back home and actually hanging out with friends is relieving. I didn't notice how much I needed it. Sitting down in the movie theater, in between Roxy and Erica, with two things in my hands. A small bucket of popcorn and my phone, excitedly waiting for Nick to text me again. And as The movie begins, my phone vibrates and a huge grin forms on my face.

Chapter Eleven

You Truly Are A Dick!

I watched the ball hit the wall right over my head for the thousandth time. I felt my eye twitch in frustration. I was trapped in a room with the person I wanted nothing to do with. Adonis Clark. The room is suffocating on its own. There was a wall full of posters of women, cars, and bands. There were a few guitars on one side. A large sound system and a record player next to a shelf filled with CD's and records on another side.

There were only a few bar stools in the room but no other chairs. Adonis was sitting on the floor leaning his head on the wall across from me, the wall that had all the posters. His third cigarette in his mouth. Luckily there was an ashtray next to him and he isn't destroying Hudson's house. I am sitting on my ass, cross legged in front of a pretty much empty area. There is just a signed record that was in a frame on the dark grey wall. The only thing keeping me sane was the light music playing in the background from the large sound system. His pale green eyes haven't left me once. He had one leg stretched out in front of him and the other tucked to his chest. The small red ball in his hand keeps bouncing off the wall over my head and back to his hand then back to the wall in an ongoing cycle. I look at my phone and sigh. We have been in here for forty minutes and haven't spoken a word to each other. If you're wondering how this happened, let me explain. I'm going to have to go all the way to the beginning.

Two hours earlier...

My hair whips around my face as Roxy drives down the road. She and Erika in the front while I sit in the back seat of her red convertible. The sun sets beautifully right in front us, making the sky shoot colors of purple, orange, yellow and pink. “Where are we going?” I whine for the fifth time and Erika laughs. They haven’t told me where we are going. They told me we are gonna hang out somewhere but haven’t told me where. I am a little anxious to say the least. These girls are a little too spontaneous for my liking. Roxy turns her head and grins at me with perfect teeth. She looks back to watch the road ahead of her as she says, “You’ll find out soon enough. Calm down, will you?” I groan loud enough for her to hear and she laughs loudly. I lean my head on the chair and close my eyes, waiting to see where she is going with this. It's not like I had anything better to do, I have been home alone for three days and Nick has been wanting to come over but I keep declining him nicely. Talking to him has helped the time fly. We upgraded from texting to talking on the phone and last night we actually face timed. I forgot how cute he was, I mean I remember being attracted to him. He had me flustered the whole time we were talking. I really enjoy the way he is, he is just so charming and kind hearted. I open my eyes as I feel the car stop completely after feeling the car move back and forward as Roxy tries to park. We are parallel parked in between a fancy dark blue, old fashioned sports car and a black motorcycle. I look up to the house. It's a blue one story house in a domestic neighborhood with a porch and a gate all around the property. The lawn was perfectly cut and bright green. I open the door and climb out of the car. Erika and Roxy walk up in front of the gate and wait for me as I close the door behind me. I walk up next to them and slide my hands in the back pockets of my grey ripped jeans. Because I didn’t know where we were going, I decided on dressing casual, a black t-shirt, grey jeans with black pumps. The girls were wearing similar outfits.

I look to Roxy with a questioning look but she ignores me and opens the door to the small gate. I follow her on the narrow pathway towards the cute little house. I should be ripping her hair out for not telling me what we were doing here but when it comes to Roxy, I just go with all her craziness.
We step up the porch and get close to the door as Roxy lifts her hand to knock. The door swings open and the person I see makes my breath catch in shock and slight fear. Oh no. She brought me around his group of friends. Cain stands there with a huge grin on his face, in jeans and a white t-shirt. He looks us over, his eyebrow raises as he sees me, "Hey ladies, come in." He steps to the side and the girls step in but I stay rooted to the floor. My limbs are not able to move. Cain walks over to me and reaches out to wave a hand in front of my face, "Hello?" I push his hand away from me with a glare. He rolls his eyes, "Come in Aphrodite." He reaches to grab my arm but I pull away, causing him to drop his hand. "He doesn't want me here," I say my thoughts aloud. "I need to leave." I can't see him. It has been good the last few days. I was finally okay. Everything that happened with him last week was finally in the back of my head but now I am here in front of this house that I didn't even know whose house it was. I know it wasn't Adonis' because I have been there plenty of times. Cain sighs and shakes his head, "I won't let him bother you, don't worry. Come inside. Everything will be fine." I look up to him with worried eyes and he says, "He's a dick, but he won't cause a scene in Hudson's house. Now stop acting crazy and come in. Just ignore him." He's right. I am just going to go in there and pretend Adonis doesn't exist. I nod and walk towards the open door. Cain interlocks his arm with mine and we walk in. We walk straight into a

living room with all grey, black, and silver decorations, with a huge flatscreen TV on the far wall. As we keep walking, there is a long hallway that looks like it leads to rooms. We don't go through there. Instead, we turn through a threshold on the left before the hallway and walk into a kitchen. The countertops were a salt and pepper granite and the drawers were back. The appliances were silver. We don't stop there. Passing the kitchen, we went through a half dining room, half living room area that was also in the same colorway as everything but the chairs of this living room were grey instead of black. There is an open sliding door that Cain pulls me through leading to the backyard. Everyone was sitting down on a set of patio furniture. There were a few couches and single chairs with a large umbrella overhead. I don't think we will be needing it as it is almost dark. There is a large square coffee table in the middle with all kinds of liquor bottles on it. A bucket of ice, a few fruit juices and some solo cups. Everyone turns their head to look at me. I smile at them awkwardly, purposely not meeting Adonis' eyes. Other than Erika and Roxy, sitting there was Adonis, James, Liam, and Hudson. Cain pulls me towards a three person couch that only Liam was sitting on. I take a seat in the middle and Cain sits too. Finally our arms untwine.
All the boys greet me in their own way, except Adonis. Hudson offers me a drink but I decline so he ends up pouring me a cup of juice and passing it to me. I notice he has a lollipop in his plump lips that were red from the candy. I take it with a small smile and a quiet thanks. Everyone starts up on different conversations but I look down to my cup and lean into my chair. I feel Adonis' eyes on me but refuse to look up. I feel a shuffle beside me and turn to see Liam turn his body towards me. His kind blue eyes are a contrast to his

caramel brown skin. He has buzzed brown hair with a straight part on his left side shaved in. He was wearing a light blue tank top and black jeans. Up his strong arms where a few tattoos scattered here and there. He smiles at me and says in a low but steady voice so only I can hear, “Can I ask you a question?”

I squint my eyes playfully and smile, “You already are.”

He chuckles, “Ah your cheeky, I like it.”

I roll my eyes, “Sure ask me anything.” I answer his question.

“Have you really known Adonis all your life? He says since you were babies but doesn’t really say much.”

He looks at me with interest, obviously really wanting to know our past. I had nothing to hide about my life with Adonis. He was the one that wanted to pretend it didn’t exist. My smile falls as memories flash through my eyes but I answer him anyways, “Yeah, actually. He is a year older than me but our moms have been friends way before they had me and Adonis so we pretty much grew up together.” A memory of watching a video of him visit me at the hospital from the day I was born pops into my mind. His mother walks in holding him and she leans over my bassinet and says, “Oh look at the baby girl, isn’t she beautiful?” Then Adonis, as cute as he was, with his big eyes shining says, “Baby girl.” Everyone in the room started cooing over his words. Apparently, they were his first real words, other than mamma or dadda. He used to call me that all the time as we grew up. I guess it stuck after a while. “But you guys used to get

along, right? Or was it like now, where you guys ignore each other?" His question was harmless, simply curious to know why his friend and I have bad blood. I would have wanted to know too. Somehow, I felt a little twinge in my chest. I shake my head with a slight smile so he won't think I am offended at his questions. "He and I were inseparable, up until I left for London. We used to talk all the time but after a few weeks of my arrival, he just stopped calling and answering all together." I shrug with a sad smile. It has been a little over a year since that happened and I remember freaking out but my mother would say over and over that Mary said he was fine. A few months passed and we heard about Mary and I remember grabbing my phone, tears in my eyes, dialing his number but he didn't answer.
"Well that's a dick move. I would have killed him if I was you." He looks serious but I just chuckle a little.
"Liam, stop bothering the girl! Leave her alone!" I hear Cain say from beside me and I turn to look at him.
"I was just talking to her man," Liam says with an eye roll. "Yeah Liam, leave the girl alone. She doesn't need your bad vibes, she already has enough going on as it is with this dude." Liam's cousin James says, while pointing at Adonis at the end. I look up to Adonis and he is glaring at James. James was sitting on a single chair, the same as Adonis but their chairs were close to one another so Adonis lifted his hand and hit him on the back of his head. With a chuckle, James rubs his head and shrugs. I took that chance to look over Adonis. He was wearing a light grey hoodie that made his eyes look the exact same color, with faded black jeans, and black shoes. Liam huffs and leans back in the chair. James' blue eyes looked amused and I couldn't help but smirk a little. He had

tan skin and brown hair, that was short on the side and longer on top. James looked mature, and smart. “No but serious, what's going on between you two?” Roxy says Looking to Adonis. Her arms crossed over her chest as she had a confused look on her face. Adonis gives her a flat look, “That’s none of your fucking business.” You can see his eyes were livid with his words. Anger boils inside me and I jump to my feet, ”Don’t talk to her like that!” I yell, looking at him dead on now. His fist turns white as he looks straight into my eyes, also standing to his feet. “I can say whatever the fuck I want.”
I give him a sour look, “I’ve met some shit people in my life, but I haven’t met anyone as bad as you. You truly are a dick.” Everyone stands quickly at my words. Adonis glares at me with so much anger and hatred, I gulp visibly, my cheeks heating up but I stand my ground, ready for anything he shoots back. Luckily, Hudson decides on breaking up this conflict, “Whoa whoa, c’mon guys, let’s not fight. We are all here to have fun. Let’s go hang out in the game room.” Hudson nudges James and he agrees.

Chapter Twelve

Best Friends?

We walk into the garage that is built for every boy's dream room. There were all sorts of arcade games on one side, two big flatscreen TV's with a big leather couch in front of it, and different video game consoles on top of a short shelf, filled with video games on the opposite side. In the middle of the room was a large pool table. I smiled wide and looked at Hudson, who was waiting on my reaction, "Cool, right?" he asks and I nod in encouragement. The room smelled of febreze and tobacco but it wasn't unpleasant. Cain and Liam run to the video games like two little kids and start fighting over what game to play. Adonis goes and sits on a bar stool next to the pool stick rack and a bar table and grabs a pack of cigarettes out of his pocket. I watch as he takes one out, puts it to his lips and lights it. James leads Erika to the old fashioned arcade games and she giggles as he says something to her. Roxy walks over to the pool table, "You guys up for a game? Girls against guys?" Roxy looks to Hudson and he shrugs with a slight nod. Then Roxy looks towards me with a smile and a glint in her eye. "What do you say Aphrodite? You and I against Adonis and Hudson?" I shrug, "Yeah, sure. Whatever." She looks to Adonis with a questioning look and he shrugs one shoulder, sucking on that tobacco stick. He then removes it from his lips and slowly exhales through his nose then back in his nose. Hudson goes to a small Red Bull fridge and brings out a few Red Bulls, giving everyone a can. Then he grabs the triangle from under the table and sets up all the balls. I walk over nervously, hoping I still remember how to play. "You can break Hudson." Adonis states, while tapping his cigarette in an ashtray, on the bar table he was sitting at. Roxy put's her hand on her hip, "Why does he have to to break?"

Adonis gestures towards the pool table, “Fine. Ladies first.” His words come out sarcastically and I roll my eyes. Roxy walks over and chooses a pool stick. She looks at me and winks. She walks towards me with a wicked grin on her face and like always, mischievous eyes. She hands me the stick and says, “Go ahead Aphrodite, show them how it's done.” I look at her with wide eyes and shake my head, “No! I haven’t played in ages, I don’t even know if I remember how to play.” Hudson chuckles, “Come on sweetheart, it doesn’t hurt to try.” He tilts his head towards the triangle. I sigh and walk over to the starting of the table. Hudson lifts the triangle and all the balls are perfectly in place. I look over to Adonis and he has the cigarette in his mouth, no hands holding it. He exhales from the side of his lips. His eyes on mine, he tilts his head in a “go ahead” gesture towards the table, then grabs the white stick in between his index finger and middle finger, replacing the cigarette to sip on his drink. I look at the balls and lean over the table, aligning the stick to the white ball. I breathed in and then hit the ball the best I could. I stand back up and watch as two solid balls make it into two different holes. Roxy claps her hands and calls our type of ball. I look back to Adonis with no expression on my face and he has a slight smirk with a lifted notched eyebrow. As the game proceeds, Adonis ditches the cigarette and actually starts playing. Roxy only hits two or three times but then takes out her phone and pays no attention to the game. She just stands there texting away. I ask her a few times if she wants to take her turn but she tells me to go ahead. Half way through the game, I watch Hudson as he leans over the table aligning the stick to hit. He is really good looking, he was wearing simple all black clothing but the black t-shirt was rolled at the sleeves to his shoulders, showing off his defined muscles. He had tattoos only on one arm and the other only had some on his knuckles. He had a few rings on both hands that were bulky but they looked good on him. He had a lollipop in his mouth and was concentrating on how exactly to align the stick to hit the ball in the right pocket. His shaggy hair was in different directions. I noticed Adonis glaring at me from beside his friend, he noticed me admiring Hudson. I give him a questioning look and he mouths, 'stop it', angrily and I smirk while shrugging one shoulder. He's always hated whenever I was around boys and back then, I used to listen to him because he had that right, he was my best friend and knew what was best for me. Now, he is nothing to me. The only reason why we are in the same room is because we have mutual friends. So in my book, he didn't have a say in who I checked out. After Hudson missed his shot, it was my turn to hit. As I lean over the table, My eyes meet Adonis', who is looking me over, then I look at Hudson, who is purposely trying to avoid me. I've seen this before, all my life actually. Boys avoid me to keep away from Adonis' wrath. I catch Hudson's eye and make a show of checking him out, just to get under his friend's skin. I then look to my target and shoot, making it in, then another two perfect shots until missing one. I stand up and strut over to the table with my drink on it. I grab it and take a sip, looking towards the boys finally. They are both giving me perplexed looks. Roxy was long gone, she was sitting on the couch with the boys. Hudson shakes his head, "I thought you said you didn't remember how to play?" I smile, "Muscle memory?" I said questioningly. Adonis had a pool table in his house and we used to play all the time but it really had been years since I last played. "Sure, let's call it that. Who taught you how to play?" Hudson asked

with slight awe in his voice. I smile and tilt my head towards Adonis, “Your friend did, actually.” I bit down on my lip and put one hand in my front pocket. He looks to Adonis in confirmation and Adonis nods, “Yeah, I did but the last time we played was years ago. That was all her.” Hudson looks to me then back to Adonis, “You guys really were best friends.” He states and Adonis shrugs. Hudson looks back to me “No offense but I don’t see it.” I chuckle humorlessly, “Me either.” Not anymore at least. Adonis clenches his jaw but says nothing. “It's just-“ Hudson gets cut by Adonis. “Can we just continue the game? Leave it Hud.” Hudson nods and we continue the game.
I catch Roxy and Cain walking out of the room with weird looks on their faces but decide on letting them be. After a few minutes, my phone rings and I take it out of my pocket. I give the phone a confused look when I see the name of the person that is calling me. It was Roxy. I hear another ring that comes from a different phone. I look to see Adonis answer his phone and I answer mine too. ”What’s up? Is everything okay?”
“No. Please come here. Can you come help me please?” I hear Roxy’s voice over the phone sounding weird. “Yes, of course. Where are you?” I say as I also hear Adonis say, ”I’ll be right there.”
She explains to me where she is and I walk out of the garage, into the house. I feel someone behind me and I turn my head to see Adonis following me to the living room and through the kitchen. I give him a questioning look and he shrugs. I turn and continue walking towards the supposed music room Roxy needs help in. Getting to the hallway with all the doors, I went to the room Roxy told me she would be in and turned the doorknob. Walking in, I don’t see her anywhere and it was a pretty small room so there

was nowhere for her to get lost. Adonis steps in the room too and looks around confused. “Roxy?” I call out her name but then the door closes behind us in a loud slam. I ran to the door and tried to open it but it was locked from the outside. ”Roxy!” I scream, pounding on the door. I hear snickering from the other side of the door then, “I’m not letting you guys out till you guys fix your problems!” She sounds serious. She’s actually serious. “We have all night!” Cain's voice also comes from the other side of the door and I groan loudly. I turned around towards Adonis, who’s eyes were wide in shock. His eyes meet mine and in that moment we both realize we are stuck together.

Chapter Thirteen

Ambushed

And that is how we ended up here...

As the ball hits the wall above my head again, I groan loudly. “Can you please stop that?!” The words finally leave my mouth. I have been trying to keep an indifferent attitude this whole time but it has been harder than you’d think. He pauses for a second, thinking it over. He takes a drag from his cigarette, holds the smoke a while, then releases it. He looks at the ball, bounces it in his palm a little, then looks back to me. With a small curl on one side of his lips, he throws the ball back to the wall above my head and catches it swiftly as it bounces back to him. He lifts his hand to throw it again and I wait silently. When the ball hits just above my head, I lift my hand up quickly and snatch it. I looked at the ball. I had two choices; one, throw it at Adonis but that will only cause him to throw it to the wall again. Or two, throw it into the trash can that was on the other side of the room so it won’t bother me again. Yeah, I think I’m going with that latter. I look up to Adonis glaring at me. His cigarette in his mouth, slightly tilted between his lips. I stand up and walk to the little trash bin. As I throw the ball in, I hear, “What the hell?” I shrug and walk towards him. I sat down right next to him, pulling my legs under me. He looks at me and stays silent. I look at the cigarette he has in his mouth curiously, I have never smoked in my life. The little things I know about cigarettes were all bad, except that it was supposed to calm your nerves. Right now, at this moment, I am the most nervous I have ever been. I feel my whole body trembling in anxiety. I reach over and pull it out of his lips, with my index and middle finger. He makes an angry tsk with his mouth but then closes it shut as he watches me put it to my lips. I take a drag of it, then pull my hand back. I feel the smoke tingle my throat and immediately choke on it. He chuckles and

grabs the white stick back from me putting it back to his lips and taking a drag. “What did you think was going to happen?”, he says, smoke coming out of his mouth with his words. I shrug, “I don’t know. I heard it's supposed to calm you down and right now, I need something that will do just that.”
He shakes his head, ”Cigarettes are just a quick fix. With time, smoking makes the nerves get worse. Addiction to cigarettes is what makes your hands shake and your eyes twitch until you finally have that temporary fix. What you're feeling now is nothing. It will pass.” I frown with a slight shrug, ”I just wanted to try it.” He sighs and smashes the almost done cigarette in the ashtray. I look at him confused as he grabs the pack that was on the floor and pulls out another one. He closes the lid and throws it back on the ground. He puts the filter to his lips and lights it with his silver zippo lighter. “This is how you do it-“ He hands me the cigarette and I take it from his hand, “Put it to your lips.” I do as he says, “Take a drag, but not too much, just a slight drag, just enough to inhale it.” I do just that and then he quickly says, “Relax, there's no rush,” I relax my shoulder and slowly inhale. ”Don’t hold it too long because you aren’t used to it. Release it slowly out of your mouth.” I do as he says and smile as the smoke comes out of my mouth without a cough. I pass back the cigarette to him but he shakes his head, “Go ahead it's yours.” I frown but take another drag, enjoying the feeling in my head. I lean on the wall and ask him, “How's your mom, is she feeling okay?” He also leans his back on the wall, crossing his arms over his chest and positioning his legs back to their original stance, one leg bent up and the other stretched out in front of him. “Yes, I spent the whole day with her yesterday.” The words come out flat and bored. “That's good. I planned on going

over soon, maybe tomorrow if she isn't busy." I pass him the cigarette and gesture to him that I don't want it anymore. He takes it and smashes it into the ashtray, while saying, "She's not busy and she would love your company. She told me you have been going over her book, that's good."
"Yeah, I really love it too. It doesn't need much work, actually."
He nods then looks at me questioningly, "Didn't I tell you to stay away from me and my friends?" He tilts his head to the side, faking innocence. I glared at him, "Trust me, If I would have known I was coming here, I definitely wouldn't have come."

He runs a hand over his hair, keeping his other hand in the crook of his elbow, then interlocks his arms again. "Screw Cain and his friendship with Roxy. Those two are like two high school girls on crack." He shakes his head. Anger boils inside me and I move away from him a little and say, "My plan was to ignore you all day but then I got stuck in a room with you." He laughs humorlessly, "I don't want to be here anymore than you do." I cross my arms under my chest, his eyes flick to my slightly, showing cleavage then back up to my face. It was so quick, I think I imagined it. I turn my body completely so I am facing his side, his head is facing me while biting his lip in thought. I look him over as I did countless times in the last few weeks, my mind finally understanding that this new look really suits him. The way he was before was just what his parents wanted him to be, when this is who he really is. I like the new look, I finally admit to myself. I like it a lot. After a few minutes of both of us silent in thought, I say, "I knew you better than you knew yourself. Now as I look at you, I feel like I'm looking at a total stranger." He stays silent, his chest

rising and falling faster. “I guess it is true.” He knits his eyebrows together and asks, “What is?” I give him a sad smile, “That friends come and go. I never really thought that you would though. I guess I took you for granted.” He uncrosses his arms and stretches his other leg in front of him. I watch as he grabs the hem of his hoodie and lifts it up, his t-shirt lifting a little with it. Showing a little of his sculpted abs, he grabs the hem of his shirt and pulls it down, throwing the hoodie to the side. He pulled the collar of his black t-shirt, his cheeks were slightly pink, obviously his body was starting to heat up. He looks back at me with those intense, almost grey eyes. “Do you think it was easy for me? You think it was rainbows and sunshine? You think it was easy for me to let you go? I did what I thought was right at the time.” I look at him confused and bewildered, “What do you mean? Why did this have to happen? You make me so confused.“ One minute, he tells me he doesn’t want anything to do with me. Then he says he had no choice. The confusion is making my mind boggle. “I’ll tell you one day but now is not the time.” I shrug and pull my lips in my mouth with a slight nod, that was the only thing I can do. I had no choice, he wasn’t giving me anything anyway.
“I just feel so stupid all the time..” I look down for a second, pulling my hair to one side. “I’m always missing someone who doesn’t want to be missed. I spend some nights falling asleep with dried tears on my face and most nights, I don’t sleep at all.” I don’t think he even notices as he reaches over and puts his hand on my knee in comfort. He opens his mouth a few times to say something but then closes it. With his other hand, he rubs his chest a little. He drops both his hands and finally speaks, “I’m sorry for all your hurting. I wish I could take all that pain away. I was

hurting too, you may not believe that but it's true." He pauses, thinking something over. Then he leans to one side and pulls his phone out of his tight jeans. He tilts the phone towards me as he opens the message thread with me. He scrolls through all the one sided messages I sent. A lot of unanswered goodnight's and I miss you's. I frown sadly as pain erupts in my chest, tears gather in my eyes but I try my best to keep them from falling. "I couldn't fall asleep without reading your messages. It was the hardest thing, to keep from texting you back." I take the phone from his hand and scroll through as he says," It has been eleven days since the last time you texted me. Ten days since the last time I really slept, not counting the night I slept over at your house and nine days since you realized who I am now." I look through the messages and go to the most recent one and he is right. It has been eleven days since I sent him the text saying, 'I'm going home.' Puzzled, I ask, "I don't get it." He smiles sadly, "No matter what, you would text me as soon as you woke up, then before you went to sleep. Somehow, that would help me sleep. From then until now. So much has changed between us. When you used to message me, you were texting your best friend." He smiles, a little wistfully and says, "I used to sleep better the times you would tell me about your day. I knew you were happy, I knew you were okay." I take a deep breath, "Yeah sure, I was happy." The words come out dripping in sarcasm. At least he slept, I always stayed up looking at my phone, waiting for a reply or a call to come in but it never did.

I pass him his phone and he turns it off, putting it on the floor. Looking back at me, he says, "You won't understand it now but it was all for you." A tear finally escapes and falls down my face and he quickly reaches up to wipe it away. “So what now?” I whisper, not trusting my voice to talk normally. “We just go back to ignoring each other again? We go back to hating each other?” I don’t think I can, after everything he just admitted to me. There is so much more he is hiding, but for now, I think I rather wait. I don’t want to push him away. He rubs a hand over his face and with a loud sigh, says, “I don’t know baby girl.” My breath catches in my throat and my eyes widen. I haven’t heard him call me that in what felt like years. His eyes open a little in recognition at the words that slipped through his lips by accident. He clears his throat awkwardly but then continues what he was going to say, “From what I can see, it's hard for us to be apart and not only because our friends always want to hang out together. I think we should try to be mutual, you know, when our friends hang out and stuff like that.” He’s saying he doesn’t want to go back to the way we used to be, just be in the same room together with the same people without fighting. “So you want to be acquaintances.” I clench my jaw and he grimaces, noticing how bad it sounded. He opens his mouth to say something but I say something first, “It’s fine, whatever. I guess it's better than fighting all the time or ignoring each other.” I quickly stand up and grab my phone, dialing Roxy”s number. She answers with a “Hello,” she drags out the ‘o’ and I roll my eyes. Adonis stands, watching me as I say, “Can you open the door please?” I was almost begging at this point. She chuckles. “One hour? That's all it took to fix your friendship.” I open my mouth to say something but my phone gets pulled away by Adonis, “Roxanne Jones! If you don’t open that door right now-“ His next words come out confused, “What? really? Okay bye.” He looks at me and smiles awkwardly, “Apparently they all left to go eat somewhere.” My eyes widen in shock and I whip my head towards the door, “So we’re stuck in here?” He walks over to the door and turns the knob, the door opening without a problem. My face instantly heats up in embarrassment. He chuckles and says, “Come on Aphrodite, I’ll drive you home.”

Chapter Fourteen

Mutual Friends?!

The whole drive to my house, I spent gritting my teeth together. We had light music playing in the background to break the awkward silence. No words were shared. Is this how it's going to be? I won't be able to handle it, seeing him and us just being...What? Friends of friends, mutual friends? I step out of the car, my blood boiling. I take a deep breath and turn towards him, holding tightly onto the door. "I can't fucking do this!" I can't help but to cuss at him. I am too damn angry. I walk towards my front door and hear him get out of his car and follow me. "What do you mean?" I spin around to glare at him and he gives me a puzzled look. "I just can't Adonis. I can't be your mutual friend. If that-" I gesture towards the car, "Is what it means to be mutual, then I don't want it." He sighs loudly and runs a hand over his hair, nervously. "You don't understand." The only thing I don't understand is how he can be okay with the fact that we aren't friends anymore. "I can't pretend like you do. I can't pretend we didn't used to be best friends. I can't! It hurts too damn much!" I yell, getting closer to him with every sentence. "I don't know how you do it." I turn towards my door to walk in but he grabs my arm, turning me back towards him. "You're right. It's not easy. I don't think you want to be in my life again. My life isn't what it used to be." He keeps saying that, always in different ways but it's always the same. I changed. I'm not him anymore. He keeps making similar remarks and frankly, I don't care who he became. I just need him in my life. I take a deep breath and pull my

arm away from him. “I don’t care what you do, or what you did. I wanna be in your life. I need to be. Please, let's at least try. Let's try to make this work. Whenever you're ready, you can tell me what you're going through. You know I wont judge you.” I look at him hopeful. I know this is wrong. I know I shouldn't be begging him, I should be making him pay for the last year. I should make him pay for everything he put me through. But I can’t let him go. He is right here in front of me. Everyday while I was away, that's all I wanted, just a chance to be next to him and talk to him again. He bites the inside of his cheek. I can practically see the wheels turning in his head as he looks from one eye to the other trying to decide which eye to look at. We were so close to each other, I could smell his strong cologne from here. It was making my head spin. He nods, “Okay.” I look at him, taken aback, “Okay, what?” He smiles and bites down on the corner of his lower, his eyes shining in happiness. “Okay let's try.” He reaches his hand out towards me, “Hi I’m Adonis Clark, nice to meet you.”
I stay still, confused at what he's doing, I gulp and look at his outstretched hand. I look back up at his pale green eyes, searching them for answers. A smile stretched slowly across my face, turning into a grin. He really is giving us a chance. I grab his hand and shake it sternly, “Hi, I’m Aphrodite Watson. Just so you know, I’m a little crazy.”
He chuckles lightly and leans in towards me, his breath fanning on my cheek as he puts his lips next to my ear. My breath stills in my throat as he

whispers, “Don’t we all need a little crazy in our lives?” He leans back and a smirk is plastered on his face. I roll my eyes at him, hiding my flusteredness. “Goodnight Don.” I turn and walk to my door, pushing in the code. I hear him say, “Night, baby girl.” I whip my head back towards him to see his retreating back. He looks at me as he gets into his car with a huge grin on his face, with a finger wave, he backs out of the driveway. I turn back to the door, pushing it open. I walk in and close the door quickly. With wide eyes and a big smile, I lean against the door. I cover my mouth and scream into it. I think I just got my best friend back. I run up the stairs to my bedroom. After getting ready for bed, I climb in and grab my phone off the nightstand. While biting my lip I open the message app and pull up my texts with Adonis.

‘Sweet dreams :)’

I send him the message, maybe tonight he will finally sleep and hopefully I will too. I set my phone on the bed, not expecting a reply. I jump slightly as my phone pings with a new message. I look at his reply, my heart skipping a beat every time I re-read it

‘Dream of me ;)’

I bite down on my lip while smiling. His reply was so arrogant but also perfect. I felt my heart fill with joy. I set my phone aside to get comfortable and easily fall asleep with a smile on my face.

Chapter Fifteen

Wicked Grin

As I pull a shirt over my head, I hear my phone ringing from my room. I walk out of my closet and grab my phone from my already made bed. I see the caller ID and a weird feeling sets in my stomach at the person calling. I guess I kind of hoped it was Adonis instead of Nick Walker. I answer and greet him easily. “Hey, how are you?” He asked. I walked over to the couch at the foot of my bed and took a seat. “I’m good and you?” I really was good, I woke up feeling really refreshed and well rested. How can one simple conversation change everything? My conversation last night with Adonis changed my mood completely, I feel as light as a feather. “I actually called to ask you if you wanted to go out with me today,” I open my mouth to decline as I have countless times with him but he quickly continues. “Before you decline, listen. I got us tickets to the LA fair and I know how much you would love to go. There will be funnel cakes and cotton candy. Oh and don’t forget the rides, I know you would love the rides, you look like a daredevil.” I giggle, “I really do love rides and cotton candy.” I sigh loudly as I finally decide to agree to go out with him. Nothing can happen, I have been talking to Nick for a few days now and he seems like a genuine guy.
“Okay”
“It's okay, I under- Wait what? You’ll go out with me?!” He practically yells. I shake my head chuckling. He tells me he will pick me up at seven thirty and that he can’t wait. After a few minutes we hang up and I walk down stairs and text Roxy about my date. Today, both my parents are home and I plan on spending the whole day with them.

MY MOM WAS SO excited when I told her about my date tonight, she was jumping up and down. She ran upstairs pulling me with her and helped me pick out

an outfit. My father didn't really like it but he said it was okay. He gave me a few rules but nothing too bad. As I set up the table for an early dinner, the doorbell rings and I look towards the door confused. I grab my phone to look at the time. Is he an hour early? Good thing I'm already dressed for our date. I set down the things I had in my hand and walked towards the front door and opened it with a smile. As quickly as the smile came, it faded. I swallow visibly on the stern look on Adonis' face. "Hey." The words come out a little bitterly but he was trying to mask it with indifference. "Hi. What are you doing here?" I move to the side to allow him to walk in and he does easily. "I.. Uh.. Came over to help your father set up a few things he had trouble with." I closed the front door and looked back at him. My father always used to call Adonis for help with all kinds of things like building stuff or whatever. He and my father had a great relationship, truly like father and son. "Yeah, cool. Dads in the kitchen helping my mom with dinner." I point towards the kitchen. He gives me a curious look tilting his head to the side. "Are you going anywhere?" My heart hammers in my chest in slight fear of his reaction to my date. He never liked it when I hung out with other boys. Before I can say anything my mom screams out my name. I take the quick save and walk to the kitchen. I feel a little self conscious as we walk in, feeling his eyes on me from behind as I lead him in.
As my mother is stirring something on the stove, her back turned towards me, she starts, "Aphro-" She stops short as she turns and notices Adonis right next to me. She smiles big, her eyes shining at the sight of him. "Adonis! Sweetheart! What are you doing here?" She turns off the stove and walks towards us passing the big island in the middle of the kitchen, she grabs

him in a big hug and he immediately hugs her back. “So good to see you sweetie.”
He chuckles and pulls away, “So good to see you too Melissa. It's been too long.” My mother noticeably checks him out, “Well. I have to say, you look really good. I love the new look.” He chuckles blushing a little, “Thanks.”
My father walks up to us cleaning his hands on a dish towel, “Honey, leave the boy alone. Hi son, how are you?”
I just stand there watching them act as if we never left. Adonis rubs the back of his head, obviously a little uncomfortable, “I just came over to help you with the thing you were telling me about the other day.” My father smiles, “Thanks Don. Please stay for dinner, we’ll get to that later.” He smiled and looked at me as if he was seeking approval. I gave him a small smile back. He looks back to my parents, “Sure, thanks.”

LAUGHTER IS ALL I hear around me as we sit down at the dining table and for some reason, I am the main attraction. My face is crimson as my father continues to say embarrassing things about me. Adonis looks at me with a gleam in his eyes, the look matching the big smile on his face. That look alone puts one on mine. His next words make my smile fall. “Remember the time she was dancing at a pool party, I think it was her birthday. Out of nowhere, she fell into the pool and the dress she changed into didn’t let her swim. She was drowning and freaking out. I had to jump in to get her out. After I saved her life-” he gives me a pointed look, ”she started hitting me as if it was my fault.”

My mother chuckles as she says, “She always blamed you whenever something bad would happen to her.”
I huff and cross my arms angrily, “Because, It always was his fault. That time I fell, I knew he was hoping I would.”
I feel his hand on my thigh over my blue jeans and he rubs a little, “C’mon, don’t get mad, we’re just messing around.” The words come out in a slight baby voice and he pouts a little. My mind gets clouded by the feeling of his hand on my thigh, they’re laughter is white noise as the only thing I can hear is my heart pounding in my ears. He removes his hand as my mother says, “Tell us Aphrodite, about this boy you're going out with tonight.” Everyone's expression changes completely, I gulp my eyes going wide. My mother notices the look on my face and her eyes quickly match mine. She looks to Adonis, understanding that he didn't know, she gives me an apologetic look but I look away. Adonis gives me an unfazed look but by the little crinkle in his eyes I can tell that wasn’t the case. “You have a date tonight. With who? Do I know him?”
I can feel my palms sweating and I quickly rub them over my jeans. I chew on my cheek a little, “Uh, I don’t know if you know him. His name is Nick Walker.” Anger flashes through his face but it quickly vanishes with a mock look of recognition, “Oh yeah, I know Walker.” I look to my parents for help, with no luck at all. They both had smirks on their faces. They know that Adonis is not going to react well to this. They love it. I frown at them but they pay no attention to me. I quickly stand up from the table, “Is everyone done already?” I pick up my plate and Adonis’ and walk to take them to the kitchen. I set it down on the counter and cover my face to try and calm myself down. I hear

footsteps, I look up to see my mother with a huge grin on her face. I scowl at her, “What?” She sets down the stuff she brought from the table and chuckles covering her mouth. I give her a flat look and she rolls her eyes at me, “Come on sweetie. You don’t see it?” I give her a questioning look, “He still reacts the same way about you and boys.” She shakes her head and walks back towards the dining room. I follow her and without making eye contact, I lean down and grab a few things on the table but quickly set them back down when I hear the doorbell ring. My eyes fly straight to Adonis, he quickly raises to his feet. I look to my father and he is shaking his head while chuckling under his breath. “Let me get that.” Adonis says, faking innocence. I move quickly to block his path and put my hands on his strong chest, “Oh no you’re not.” Adonis gives me a wicked grin, “I’m just gonna have a little chat with him, that's all.” I huff in annoyance and turn my head towards my dad for help, “Yes Adonis, go ahead. Aphrodite let him greet the boy. Adonis knows him. Go ahead son.” I gasp loudly, surprised by my father. Adonis moves me to the side and walks swiftly to the door in long strides. I follow right on his heels but as he opens the door he shoves me away and closes the door in my face. I go to try and open it but he is holding on to it to keep me from doing just that.
My phone rings with my text tone and I pull it out of my back pocket to see that Roxy sent me a message.

ADONIS KNOWS!!
He is pissed! He is on his way there!!

I huff, he knew this whole time and pretended not to know. I shake my head as I reply.

He's here. He's talking to Nick right now. Call you later!

She instantly replies.

I'm so sorry, I messed up.

I ignore the message and lean my ear to the door to hear what he is saying. There are only a few words I can make out. His words all come out threateningly though, that is clear. "*You know I'll hurt you. Don't touch her. You know who I am. Nothing stays in the dark*." The other words are more quiet and I can't make them out but you can hear the menace. I can't make out what Nick says but I do make out a deep chuckle that is definitely not from Adonis.

I lift my hand to knock on the door to interrupt them but the door swings open. I only get a quick glance of Nick standing on the front porch with his hands in his front pockets when the door is being closed on his face and Adonis is pulling me towards the living room to the right of the foyer. I give him a perplexed look and he matches it with a stern one. "Listen to me. I don't like this guy. I won't stop you on going out on this date. If anything, if anything at all, call me. Doesn't matter the time, I will go pick you up, without a question. Do you understand?" I gulp visibility and nod but that's not what he wants, "Use your words Aphrodite. I need to know you understand." I give him a flat look, I should be pushing him and cursing him out. He doesn't get to act this way after everything. But we agreed on trying again so I just said, "Yeah sure, I'll call you. Can you chill? I'll be fine." I wave him off and move past him to leave but he grabs my arm and I turn towards him again. "I'm serious, please call me if anything." His words come out softer and almost pleadingly. Searching his face, I nod and whisper, “Okay.” He lets go of me reluctantly and I walk to the door.

Chapter sixteen

Bittersweet Cotton Candy

We walked through the crowds, carnival music, chatter, and kids yelling all around us. All the rides are lit up in different colors, with a big smile on my face I pull a piece from my pink cotton candy and put it into my mouth. It's been a little awkward with Nick but he has been sweet. I look up to his tall height and watch as he stuffs his mouth with funnel cake. The times I went to the fair with Adonis, he would get all my favorite foods. We would stuff our faces, walk it off, then get on all the rides. I can't help but giggle at Nick, his face has powdered sugar all over it. He rolls his eyes jokingly and cleans his mouth with a napkin. We walked towards the game section after finishing our snacks, he said, "So tell me, is this your first date?" I feel my cheeks heat up in embarrassment. "Yeah, kind of." He turns towards me with an arched eyebrow. I can't help thinking of Adonis when he does it with his notched eyebrow.
He chuckles but it sounds half-hearted. I knit my eyebrows together. Somehow hearing Adonis' laugh in my ears. Adonis either chuckles humorlessly or full-heartedly. As I hear Nick laugh, it feels wrong and forced. I push the thought away and give him a small smile. We are standing in the middle of the crowds of people walking on either side of us. "You need to explain." He looks at me perplexed. "What do you mean?" I ask, tilting my head to the side.
He licks his lips and my eyes drift to them quickly. I love the slight gloss on his pink lips that were curved upwards. I looked into his eyes. My heart fluttered a little at the look in them. "How is it that a girl like you, has never been asked out on a date?" This time he tilts his head to the side looking at me questioningly. I have to admit, even with his towering height he looks cute. "What do you mean a girl like me?" I fake hurt and he shakes his head smiling.

"Beautiful, kind, and smart. Just by looking at you I would guess guys have always been all over you. I know I would have been." He looks honest with his words.
Trying to hide the blush in my cheeks, I giggle and push on his shoulder. "No, boys have never really looked my way actually." He squinted his eyes a little and anger flashed through them but he easily concealed it with indifference. "Because of Adonis, right?" I looked away a little. He continues as the words sound a little bitter, "Has he always been like that?" I shrug one shoulder and look up to him, "Yeah, pretty much." I look at the carnaval games and point to them. "Come on Nick, win me a bear!" He grins and says, "Alright, you're on." He grabs onto my hand and leads me towards the games. I was so glad for the change in conversation, I didn't realize his hand was wrapped around mine. It felt nice, there weren't any sparks or butterflies in my stomach. It was just that, nice. He leads me to a basketball game and I give him a flat look with an eye roll. "I guess I should have known. The tall guy likes basketball." We waited in a small line for our turn since there was only one person per game. He chuckled a little, "I actually played for some time in high school." I frown in confusion, "Why did you stop?" He shrugs, "I was okay at it. It's just that, it wasn't my thing." I picture him playing, basketball uniform and all. He would look so hot, sweat dripping on him. I visibly check him out jokingly while biting down on my lower lip, "I would have really liked watching you play and I would have really liked seeing you in the uniform." A slight blush creeps up his face and he nudges me with his elbow using the arm that was holding my hand, "Stop!" I smirk at him and admit, "What? You really are good looking and

you know it." His blush gets deeper and I chuckle under my breath.
He pulls me towards him and wraps his free hand around me, my breath catches in my throat. I look up at him and try to conceal my shock with a smile. He leans down, my heart is pounding loudly but out of fear. I don't want him to kiss me, this is too fast. How do I get out of this? What if I kick him in the balls? As I am plotting my way out the guy at the booth says, "Step right up!" I look at him and smile. I was so glad for the interruption. I pull away and Nick walks up towards the booth. I put my finally-free hands in my back pockets. I get closer to him and slightly rock on my heels. He grabs the ball from the booth and looks back at me with a smirk. I bite down on my lower lip, hiding my smile, "Let's see what you got, Walker." He winks at me and looks back towards the basketball hoop that was far away. He positions himself then jumps as he shoots the ball. He smiles cockily as it sinks perfectly into the hoop. After a few more shots, he wins a big stuffed elephant for me. It wasn't gigantic, it was maybe two feet tall. It was perfect. I hugged it to my chest as we walked back to the car. After the basketball game, we got on a few rides until we decided to call it a night.

"THAT'S WILD! YOU had a crazy day, Aphrodite." Roxy's voice comes through the group facetime call with Erika. I sigh loudly and roll onto my back on my bed, my chest was already getting sore from laying on it for the past hour. "Yeah, I know, my mind still can't fathom everything that went on tonight." The girls both laugh and Erika shakes her head. "Girl, all I see is two boys that are fighting over you." I roll my eyes.

“Whatever, I don’t even know how I’m gonna sleep tonight.” I put my forearm over my eyes and take a deep breath then slowly release it. “We’ll be over tomorrow to pick you up and we can hang out. Maybe go see a movie or something.” Roxy’s idea sounds good. “Oh yeah, I really wanna see that new Dylan O’Brien movie,” I uncover my face to see Erika fanning her face dramatically. I giggle a little at her actions, “Alrighty then, see you all tomorrow.” I go to hang up when Roxy quickly stops me, “A!?” I give her a head tilt telling her to continue, “Can I invite Cain and the boys?” I shrug, too tired to answer then click the end button. I throw my phone to the side lazilly and cover my eyes again. A ping on my phone makes me groan loudly. I reached for it to see what the girls texted and my heart skipped a beat.

Are you home?

Adonis texted me. He actually sent *me* a text. I looked over the text a few times before replying.

Yes. I got home like an hour ago. Thanks for asking.

I anxiously watch the bubbles signaling that he is gonna text back.

Did you have fun?

Heat rises to my cheeks a little at the mention of my date with Nick. I don’t know why but I guess I am a little embarrassed to talk to him about it.

Yes. :)

The bubbles appeared and disappeared a few times before he finally replied.

Did he treat you right?

My heart feels a little weird at his words. I guess he's always tried to protect me from boys. For one reason, so they won't treat me wrong. He always took care of me. I smile sadly as I write.

Yes, he was very nice.

The emotions I feel are all over the place and I don't know how to place them. He replies with something simple.

I'm glad you had fun, goodnight.

I'm happy he's back in my life again. My smile grows as I text back two messages in a row. I know my second message will make him laugh.

Gn.
Dream of me.

I wait impatiently as the bubbles appear. I look at his reply a few times, not able to think of a proper reply. So I decide to leave it at that.

I always do.

Chapter Seventeen

Looks Better On You

Looking at myself in the bathroom mirror at the cinema, I nervously run my fingers through my hair. I fidget with my clothes. I look at myself over again. I'm wearing a comfy black bodycon dress that has a split going up my right thigh. Paired with black tennies and a jean jacket. I chew on my bottom lip, there is no reason for me to be nervous, it's just Adonis and his friends but I have to admit, the thought of seeing him again makes the nerves in my stomach erupt. I pull my jacket off my right shoulder so it's resting off of it in a cute, chic way. I huff and decide on just getting out of the bathroom and stop stressing over my outfit. I walk over to where the girls are waiting by the entrance on the outside of the movie theater. They were in a full-blown conversation about Dylan O'brien. I roll my eyes and lean on the glass wall near the door. I look towards the parking lot and my heart skips a beat as I see *his* Porsche parking backwards in the nearest parking space. I see the other boy's vehicles too but I pay no attention as I watch Adonis climb out of the car. He shuts the car door and starts walking towards us. He pulls out a box from his back pocket and takes out a cigarette, putting it to his lips and lighting it. My eyes roam over his outfit and I subconsciously lick my lips. He's wearing a black long sleeve t-shirt, the sleeves pushed up his forearms. The black skinny jeans he's wearing are ripped at his knees completely. I look back up to see him flip his black baseball cap backwards on his head. As he nears us, he holds his cigarette in his thumb and forefinger while he says, "Hey girls." The girls greet him and I just smile at him unable to form words, they are stuck in my throat. He looks so good tonight. My heart is hammering in my chest and I'm sure everyone can hear it. He walks closer towards me and leans on the wall next to me, putting a foot on the glass wall. I look down at his Balenciagas and notice his cap is the same brand. He noticed my gaze and with a smirk takes it off his head and sets it on mine the right way. I shake my head, "What are you doing?" I chuckle and smile at him. He shrugs and exhales smoke from his lips while saying, "It looks better on you." He runs the hand holding the cigarette through his hair flattening it back. I turn to see myself in the reflection of the glass, thanks to it being dark outside. I smile and shrug, it does look cute with my outfit. I turn back to him to see his eyes are on me with a notched arched eyebrow. I feel my face heat as his eyes roam upwards from my shoes and slowly reach up to my eyes. I gulp at the intense look in his eyes. He has never looked at me this way. I hate to admit this to myself but, I really like it.

We are interrupted from our locked eyes as a loud clap is heard from in front of us. I quickly turn my head to see Cain rubbing his hands together. I roll my eyes with a smile. "Who's going with me to the bar?" Hudson, with dark wafers over his eyes says with a flat look, "Already ahead of you, Cain." He pulled open the door and walked in, leading the way for us to follow. Cain and Hudson walk towards the bar after Cain gets the boy's drink orders. The rest of us walk towards the concession stand. There was no line at any of the registers so we walked straight to them. As I walked to a register alone, the girl behind it asked me, "What can I get you?" I feel a presence behind me and Adonis' strong scent surrounds me. I open my mouth to order when Adonis puts his hands on the counter on either side of me, leaning his front on my back he speaks before I even have a chance. "She will have Red Vines and a large Coke; and let me get a large popcorn, buncha crunch, and bottled water." I turned my head to look up at him but didn't anticipate how close his face would be to mine. He looks down at me and smiles, "Anything else?" He whispers and I feel my stomach flip. "No, that's it." I turn back to the register and go to grab money out of my pocket. As I hand the money over, the girl is already charging his card making me frown. I turn my face back up to him again with a frown. "Oh come on. I wanted to pay." He chuckles, "You have to be quicker next time." He shrugs and I shove him with my elbow. He grunts pretending I hurt him badly. I roll my eyes, "Big baby." I say under my breath. "If you keep rolling your eyes like that baby girl, they'll get stuck that way." He says the words against my bare shoulder then pulls away completely. I miss his warmth immediately. I turn around to see him say something to Cain as he grabs a drink from him. Cain nods and walks over to Roxy as she's waiting for him to go into the theater. Adonis strides back to my side and I bring my gaze back to the register. The girl brings over the popcorn, he grabs it, and then she passes me the drinks and candy in a tray. "Come on Aphrodite, the movies gonna start soon." I follow him towards the theater with everyone else already ahead of us.

WE ARE NOW HALF way through the movie and I am sitting right next to Adonis. Roxy and Cain are sitting in the row under us whispering jokes about every scene. Those two really are like two high school girls on crack. Adonis was right. Erika and James were sitting directly above us. Hudson was all alone, sitting all the way up. From what I heard Cain say, he was apparently smoking weed up there. Liam was sitting in the row under Cain and Roxy. I lean over to grab popcorn from Adonis, my eyes still on the screen. I hear wet kissing sounds coming from above us. I slowly turn my head towards Adonis and he does the same. His eyes are as wide as mine. I give him a look of disgust and the corner of his lip curls in an amused smile. He shrugs and turns back to look at the screen and I put the popcorn in my mouth, slowly chewing on it. The noises behind me get louder and I lower in my chair and put my hand to my mouth trying to keep from laughing. I turn back to Adonis again and he's biting on his lip, also trying not to laugh. Our eyes widen at the same time as we hear a moan. His smile falls and he stands to his feet. Setting the popcorn down, he grabs my hand pulling me to my feet. I gave him a confused look but he answered by pulling me towards the exit. We jogged down the stairs and through the exit. As we get to the hallway out the theater, he turns towards me. "I'm not gonna take another minute of that." I nod in agreement, "Yeah, that was way too much on my innocence." He laughs full heartedly and I grin at him. "Come on Aphrodite, let's blow this popsicle stand." I knit my eyebrows together, "Where do you want to go?" He shrugs, "I don't know yet, let's see where the car takes us." I start to follow him as he walks back to the entrance. "I didn't know you had a Tesla?" He turns his head and laughs mockingly, "Funny."

Chapter <u>Eighteen</u>

Rooftop Memories

I looked up through the car windshield and gave Adonis a knowing smile. He turns into the parking garage of the Cedar Sinai Hospital. I chuckle and turn towards him as he parks the car. "This is the last place I thought you would want to go." He turns his head towards me and winks, "Well, like I said, the car was leading the way." He shrugs and turns off the ignition. I climbed out of the car, the valet already closed at this hour. I meet Adonis at the back of his car then he gestures towards the entrance of the hospital. He leads the way and we walk towards the entrance. As we walk in, I look towards the security at the entrance. He grins at Adonis. "Hey man! How's it going?" He's a man in his late twenties. Adonis tilts his head in a greeting way, "Hey Quill, Look I know it's late-" the man cuts Adonis short by waving his hand nonchalantly. "Thanks man. I owe you." Quill laughs, throwing his head back, "Don't worry about it, just get me in for free next time." The guy named Quill winks at him. Adonis stiffens a little and I give him a questioning look but he quickly smiles at Quill, "Yeah man, of course." Adonis grabs my hand and leads me towards the elevators. He leans over and presses the button to go up. As we wait for the elevator, I look up at him confused and take my hand out of his. "What was that about?" I ask him, confused. He gave me a questioning look and I looked behind me, giving him the idea of what happened with the security. He shrugs, "I don't know." The elevator chimes as the doors in front of us open. We step in and memories from the last time we were in here flood into my mind. I lean on the wall opposites of Adonis and by the smirk on his face, I know he was thinking the same as me. I give him a flat look. That day, he was teasing me because I was checking him out. Truth is, I really was. "When did you become so full of yourself?" He grins at me and lifts his arm, curling in his forearm, flexing his obvious strong muscled arm. He wasn't too big where it was nasty but he wasn't lean either. "I think it was when I got these." He puts his arm down and nods, "Yeah, I think that's when it happened." I lift my eyebrow while saying, "Yeah, well, that's what happens when you inject yourself with steroids." I shrug as if what I said was a fact. His eyes widen mockingly and he gasps loudly appalled by my accusation, "Me? I would never." He huffs then gives me a huge grin. "Yeah, sure whatever." I chuckle under my breath and the elevator doors open to the fifth floor, the highest floor you can go on with the elevator. It was also the surgical floor. Adonis looks at me with wicked eyes and grabs my hand, pulling me out of the elevator in a sprint. "What are you doing?" I whisper-yell. He turns his head towards me, "Come on Aphrodite, just run with me." I smile. This is what we always did as kids. We grew up running through these halls. We would constantly get in trouble. They would take us to the daycare here at the hospital but after we got older, we would sneak out. We would hide all over the hospital. As we run, we pass the nurse's station when suddenly, out of the room nearest to us, my mother walks out with a clipboard in her hands. With wide eyes, she yells, "What are you guys doing here?!" We pass right by her, still running and I scream, "I don't know! I'll explain later!" I look back and see her smile and shake her head. At the end of the hall, there was a door that led to the stairs. As we reach it, Adonis pulls it open and it hits the wall with a loud thud but we pay no attention as we continue to run. In the small space, all you can hear is our heavy breathing and loud footsteps.

He pulls me up the stairs and I laugh loudly at his actions. He joins in on my laughter and we start a new flight of stairs. There were several flights of stairs spiraling all the way up. “Adonis!” I whine loudly but he continues running, “I can’t run anymore!!” My lungs were burning already. I don’t know how he can do this so easily. I am definitely not fit for this. He looks back at me and out of nowhere, he bends down in front of me and I almost trip at the sudden halt in my step. In one swift movement, he grabs my other hand and pulls me on top of him. I yelp loudly at the sudden movement. He wraps my arms around his neck then brings both his hands under my legs, lifting me slightly higher. My grip around him tightens as he stands. “What are you doing?!” I yell with joy. I start laughing as he continues jogging up the stairs without a problem. “You said you couldn’t run anymore. I wanted to help. Plus, I had a feeling you wouldn’t be able to do it.” He keeps up his strides easily. We had two flights of stairs left to go and he seemed like he had no problem with it. “Wow! Hurtful!” I mock hurt and he chuckles under his breath. “We both know you're not in shape. Don’t pretend like you exercise.” He taps on my legs as he continues. We were now on the last staircase. “Well I guess you’re gonna have to help me get into shape then. You know, since you're obviously so fit.” I say half-honestly. I would really love to get into shape and I would really love to watch Adonis exercise too. He huffs out a laugh, “Obviously.” As we finally reach the door to our destination, a place we used to go to all the time as kids, he releases one arm to open the door and he steps out. The wind hits my sweaty skin immediately. He sets me down and I sway a little. I steady myself and grin as I look around at the beautiful night sky. We were on our rooftop, that's what we used to call it. I beam at him and he gives me a small smile. It's your typical building rooftop. There was an elevated section in the middle. There were no rails or ledges surrounding the edge; it's just a flat surface all around the building. On the hospital's building to the left, you can see the helicopter landing pad from here and all around, you can see the city lights. We both walk towards the middle of the edge without thinking. From this exact spot, you can see everything perfectly. We both take a seat, our legs dangling off the rooftop, my heart pounding in my chest at the tall height. I haven't been here in so long. I forgot how much I loved the adrenaline coursing through my veins while looking down. It was about 200 feet down. I look back up to Adonis to see him already looking at me. "How long has it been since we came up here?" He asked me, running his hands over his jeans. I squint my eyes together, trying to recall the exact last time. I bite down on my lip as the memory flashes through my mind. "Umm." I giggle, remembering the time exactly. "It was the time we both got in trouble for sneaking into the closed cafeteria." He laughs, tipping his head back, also remembering that time. "We lost the security guard that was chasing us and then we ran all the way up here." I pucker my lips remembering the guy who was built like a fridge running after us. He had no chance. "Was that the same night we stayed here all night?" I chuckle lightly and he nods. "Yes, we stayed up all night and planned out our whole future. Where we would go to school; what would we be; all kinds of things." He looks nostalgic and I know I must have the same look on my face as I look out to the city. "Yeah, we didn't even notice how long we were up here till the sun started rising. We both freaked out and got so scared. Our parents didn't even notice though." I look back at him with the same smile I had on all night.

"They never did Aphrodite, we practically raised ourselves. They were always so busy here at the hospital and my father was never home." The last words come out bitterly and I give him a questioning look. "Do you want to talk about it? It's cool if you don't." Lately, he doesn't like to share what goes on in his life and for now, I'll respect it. He puts his elbow on his thigh and rests his face on his palm. He turns his face towards me and says, "I haven't said it out loud yet. I haven't told anyone what my father has done." He takes a deep breath then continues, "He has been cheating on my mother for the last year." I gasp under my breath but he continues, "I should have known better. I shouldn't have walked in his office without knocking. I walked in to see him fucking some blonde chick on his desk. He begged me not to say anything. He even got me that car I have as a bribe. He said it would destroy my mother and I guess I believed him." I shake my head in disbelief, "I'm sorry to hear that. You're mother should know though. You shouldn't hide it from her." He grimaced, "I was going to tell her but then we found out about...you know and I didn't have the heart. Maybe she is better off not knowing." In that situation, he might be right. It would be really hard to tell her after getting really bad news. I put my hand on his thigh in resurance, "That was a good decision. It's better that way. He doesn't deserve her pain and tears anyways. She's too good for that. She's too good for him." He smiles and puts his hand over mine that was resting on his leg. "She really is too good. She's the best mom anyone could have." I nod in agreement, "Yes, yes she is. I don't know what I would have done without her in my life." Deciding to change the subject, I say, "Remember the time she bought us bikes so we can learn but apparently, she didn't know how to ride a bike either

and she was learning with us? My father was having a field day with all the jokes he was making about her." Adonis started laughing hysterically at the memory. We were so young then. I was only eight and Adonis was nine. It was so much fun. Now that I think back to it, Adonis' father was never with us, it was only my parents and Mary.
As our laughter dies down, we both sigh happily. I reach for the cap that is on my head and quickly set it on his, the right way. He rolls his eyes and flips it on backwards again. I tilt my head to the side, "It looks better on you."
He shakes his head, squinting his beautiful eyes, "I doubt that." I lean my head on his shoulder and bite down on my lower lip to keep myself from grinning like an idiot. My phone pings and I reach into my jacket to check who it is. I frown at the name that appeared on my screen, Nick Walker. I decide to ignore it and put my phone back into my pocket. I really don't want to text him while I'm having such a good time with Adonis. "So I see that's still going on." Adonis says sharply. I look up to him and frown. "Yeah we have been talking." The words come out timid and a blush creeps up my face. He notices my discomfort and he adds, "Just take care of yourself please. That guy really gets on my nerves." I look down and sit up straight, putting my hand on my leg instead. "He's nice to me." I can't help but defend him a little bit. I feel like I'm defending myself too. He puts his hand under my chin and lifts my face to look at him as he says, "Anyone else can be nice to you." I pull my face away and flip the switch on him, "Tell me about that girl. What was her name?" I pretend to think about it but I already know her name. "Oh yeah, Adriana." He gives me a flat look, "She means nothing to me." I scoff, "That's not what it looked like the other night."

He chews on the inside of his cheek with an annoyed look on his face he says, “She’s a little clingy.” I shove him slightly, “And you love the attention.” He grabs on to me dramatically, “You better not shove me again because if I fall you're falling with me.” He took that opportunity to change the conversation on me. I mentally roll my eyes at his attempt to lighten the mood. I chuckle, “You're still so dramatic.” He shrugs and lets go of me, “It's fun.” He raises his arm and looks down to his watch. “It’s late, we should go.” With my eyebrows knit together, I ask, “What time is it? Roxy’s gonna kill me for ditching her.” He stands to his feet and extends his hand out to me to help me stand up. I put my hand in his and he pulls slightly. When I’m standing right in front of him he says, “It's eleven-thirty. I guess time really flies by when you're hanging out with your best friend.” Butterflies erupted in my stomach at his last words, making me beam at him. “I guess so. Come on Don, take me home.”

Chapter Nineteen

Dream Of Me

Gasping loudly, I wake up from my crazed dream. I sit up in my bed and run my hands over my clammy face. I Feel my face heat up as the dream runs through my mind again. I grimace at the images that have never crossed my mind till today. I shut my eyes tight to try to erase them from my mind but all I see is Adonis kissing me and telling me how much he wants me. I shake my head and climb out of bed. I really need to forget about this dream. I grab my phone and walk towards my bathroom in need of a shower. I sent a quick text to Mary telling her I was going over soon and she replied with an excited emoticon. After getting ready and dressing in jean shorts with a button-up and halter top, I pull on some wedges, grab my purse and walk out of my room. I grab a granola bar and the keys to my mothers car from the kitchen and walk out. As I park into the Clarks driveway, I notice Adonis' car isn't there and I am glad. I don't know how I would react seeing him so soon after the dream I just had. I get out of the car and close the door behind me. As I walked up the porch, I looked up at the beautiful large house that was almost a mansion. I knock on the door and after a few minutes, the door is opened by a cute little old woman that I have known almost all my life. "Lily!" She smiles at me and pulls me into a hug. "Oh mija, how are you? It has been so long!" Lily was the housekeeper for the Clarks. She pretty much took care of Adonis and I for as long as I can remember. "I know, but I am here now." I pull back and walk into the beautiful home. My mother only gets help once a week to clean our house. She always said that we don't need a constant housekeeper because the house is never dirty. Lily frowns at me, "Adonis isn't here mija, he left a while ago." I hear footsteps and I look to see Mary walking towards us from the kitchen. "She's not here to see him Lily, she's here to see me." I smile at her and walk up to her to embrace her. "How are you sweetie?" she asks, after pulling away. "I'm good and you? How do you feel?" I look around the big foyer and up the grand staircase. This was a beautiful house and very modern. I look back to Mary as she says, "I am doing great. I won't have to go back to the hospital till next week." I smile and we walk towards her office. "Yeah I heard, that's why I came over. I finished editing the book, I sent it over this morning. I was thinking we can publish it today." We stepped into her office that was lined with white shelves, filled with books. Her desk was in the middle with a royal style chair behind it and a matching love seat in front of it. She squeals and sits behind her desk. She starts up her desk top computer and scrolls through her email, searching for the one I recently sent her. I take a seat on her white desk right in front of her and tilt my head towards the computer, watching as she flips through the chapters excitedly. I came over to help her self-publish her book on all the major websites. After a few hours of working on her book, we finally finish and we go into the kitchen and have lunch together. As I'm helping clean up the kitchen, Adonis walks into the kitchen and the plate I have in my hand slips out of my hands but I quickly catch it to keep it from breaking. I quickly look away from him and try to shake away the memory of his hands all over me from my dream. I put the dish where it goes when I hear him say. "Hey ladies, how's the book going?" I turn back to him and watch as he sits down on a bar stool at the large island that was in the middle of the modern kitchen. Mary squeals and claps her hands together, "So good son. Aphrodite helped me publish it and showed me how to advertise it. It took a few hours but we finished everything." He smiles at her and nods, “That's great ma, I’m happy for you. Thanks Aphrodite,” he turns towards me and my breath stills as images of his lips being between my legs flash through my eyes. I give him a tight smile, “Yeah, I’m happy to help.” He raises to his feet and tilts his head towards the exit, “Wanna go hang out?” He asked me and I looked towards Mary who nodded and shrugged. “Yeah, sure.” I set down the rag I was using to dry the dishes and follow him out of the kitchen and up the stairs.

We pass a few doors till we get to his room and he pushes the door open. He waits for me to walk in and I do. I look around the room and it looks exactly as I remember. A tall spine behind the large bed. Everything a dark cherry wood. The only difference is the sheets and curtains. Instead of the light blue and dark blue patterns it used to have, everything is in different shades of grey. The room was huge with a large closet and in-suite bathroom. There was also a large desk to one side of the room, surrounded by shelves with different things on them. Trophies, photos and books. I walked over to the shelves and picked up a photo of me and him when we were around 10. Adonis had his arm around me and I was hugging him from around the waist. We were at the beach that day, you can see the waves behind us in the picture. I smile and look back at him, he was taking a seat on his bed. I set the photo back down and awkwardly walk towards the middle of the room. *I want you so bad Aphrodite,* the words were whispered into my ear in my dream and it made goosebumps appear on my skin just thinking about it now. He gives me a confused look, “What's wrong?” “Uh nothing.” Comes my obvious lie.

"It's not nothing, what is it?" He stands up, grabs my hand and pulls me on the bed to sit down next to him. "Tell me."
I laugh awkwardly, "I...uh...had a real bad dream last night." I admit, because this boy can see right through me, he always had and he always will. He looks at me confused for a second then a smirk appears on his face with a lifted eyebrow and I groan loudly, tilting my head back in embarrassment. "Did you have a *bad* dream about me?" He said the word bad in a suggestive way. I put my hands over my face trying to conceal my embarrassment while shaking my head no. He chuckles darkly, "Yes you did. Tell me, what did I do to you."
I look up at him from my hands and give him a flat look, "C'mon Adonis. Stop it." He pushes on my shoulder so that I am laying flat on my back and raises himself so he is hovering over me, my eyes widen in shock. "What are you doing?" He gives me a wicked look, "I want to know what happened in your dream." I shake my head, "Trust me, you don't want to know." He looks me in the eyes, "Trust me, I do." He brings the hand that doesn't hold him up, to run it over my stomach and down towards my hip. "Was I doing something like this?" I stiffen and he chuckles under his breath, "I'll take that as a yes." He looks down to his hand on my body. I can't move, I am paralyzed. I gulp as I feel heat in my stomach. I close my legs together at the weird sensation I feel between them. His eyes flash to mine, his eyes looking shocked and heated. He lifts himself off of me and takes a seat on the edge of the bed in one swift movement. I take a deep breath and lift myself up, putting my bare legs under me. "Sorry," I don't know why I was apologizing, it felt right though. He looks back at me, "Don't apologize, it was just a dream. It's

not your fault." He pats the bed next to him and I crawl over to take a seat next to him.
I fidget with my hands looking down at them after a few minutes I ask, "So what does this new Adonis do these days? Where were you?" I bring my gaze up to him, my head still slightly tilted towards my hands. He runs his hands up and down his legs nervously as he says, "Just running some errands for my father." I look down to his tattooed hands and stop his movements, grabbing one and bringing it close to my face to examine it. To the naked eye you wouldn't be able to notice, especially because of the tattoos on his knuckles but I can see that there is bruising and cut skin there. I can also see old scar marks. I look up to him with wide eyes, "What happened?" He pulls his hand away and crosses his arms, putting his hands under each opposite armpit. "It's nothing, Don't worry about it." I raised my eyebrows with a small frown, a little hurt with the way he just brushed me off. "Sorry, I'm asking way too many questions. I know we're not the same as we used to be." I look back to my hands a little embarrassed by my prying. He puts two fingers under my chin and lifts my face up to meet his gaze that was the color of sage.
"Hey. Don't do that. Remember, we are trying here." I nod a little, my gaze not leaving his. Images of him devouring my lips going through my mind make me pull away from him. Looking towards the wall, I say, "I should really get going." I don't know why these images keep flashing through my eyes. I need to forget about this as soon as possible. I stand up and he follows. "Yeah, okay."
"I'm gonna go say goodbye to your mom..." I give him a tight lip smile. He walks towards his door and leans on the frame with a smile on his face, "See you later." I pull my lips into my mouth and nod, unable to form

any words as his smile looks exactly as the one from my dream last night. As I walked down the hall, I whispered to myself, “What the hell is wrong with me?”

Chapter Twenty

You Have No Idea

I smile at the waitress as she sets down glasses of water in front of Nick and I. He convinced me on going on a date with him again. I was so nervous on how Adonis would react about it so I told the girls to keep it to themselves. I don't know why I'm hiding it from him. It just feels wrong having him know about my date with Nick. It has been five days since the last time I saw Adonis but we have been texting back and forth throughout the last few days. It really did feel like we were friends again. "What would you like to order?" The waitress asked as she pulled out a notepad and pen. We were at a modern bar and grill. They sat us in a large booth in the back that was really comfortable. The tables were a dark cherrywood giving the restaurant a cozy feel to it. After Nick ordered, she asked me the same question and I answered, "Um. Can I get the house salad please?" I give her a slight smile. I don't usually order a salad but I didn't want to embarrass myself. This is our second date and I want to make a good impression. Nick puts his knuckles under his chin while asking, "Tell me about yourself beautiful. What school do you want to go to?" I smile and mimic his actions putting my hand under my chin. "Well, I don't want to be far from home so I'm thinking UCLA. I have been accepted into a few other schools too but they don't interest me." He lifts his eyebrow with a smile. "Wow that's impressive." I shrug, and he shakes his head. "Would you hate me if I said I hate school and I am so glad I didn't go to college?" I frown," Of course not, don't be silly. A lot of successful people didn't go to college." I smirk as I say. "Hopefully you're one of them." He widens his eyes in mock offence and huffs, " I'm already a successful person, thank you very much." We both

laugh. I stop mid laugh as I notice the door of the restaurant open over Nick's shoulder.
The person that walks in is the last person I wanted to see tonight. As Nick goes to turn his head to see what caught my eye, I quickly decide on interrupting him. The last thing I want is for those two to start fighting. “Tell me more about yourself Nick.” My voice comes out a little high pitched. Nick smiles, “Um, what do you want to know?” I shrug and he starts saying something about a car he is working on but I completely block him out as I can’t see Adonis anymore but I do see all his friends; James, Liam, Cain, and Hudson are all next to the door. I hear my name coming from Nick and I quickly bring my attention back to him. “Yeah?” I ask but then see a silhouette to my left and freeze completely as I feel him slide into my booth. I hear him say something but all I hear is the blood pumping through my veins. I can’t bring myself to turn towards him just yet because if I do, it will all be true. His strong smell was suffocating me. I know for a fact that only I can smell his cologne because it only affects me. It drives me crazy, I think about his scent constantly. His body gets pushed in closer to me as Cain sits right next to him. James and Liam scoot in next to Nick. Hudson grabs a spare chair from a table nearby, flips it around and sits on it with his legs straddling the back of it. I look at everyone except Adonis, even though his body is pressed completely to mine.
“What are you guys doing here?” Nick asked with a hard expression. “Like I said, there were no other tables and we’re here to eat.” Adonis says, his words coming out as sharp as a knife. I finally snap myself out of my shock and turn my face towards him, “There are so many other tables Don, do you really have to sit here?” I gesture towards the restaurant. It was

pretty packed because it's friday night but I'm sure there is a table for them. I look him over and gulp as I noticed the tight grey button down he is wearing. The shirt was stretched tight on his arms, showing off his thick toned arms. Just a couple of buttons were opened at the collar revealing a silver chain around his tattooed neck, with a silver boxing glove hanging from it. He looks towards me while raising an eyebrow. "I thought this was a one time thing." He gestures between me and Nick with one finger while wearing a smirk. The waitress appears and leans over the table to the side of Hudson and sets down our plates in front of us. Adonis looks at me, lowering his eyebrows together. The waitress asked the boys if they wanted to order anything and most of them order food. As the waitress is about to leave, Hudson, who like Adonis, didn't order food says, "Give me a whiskey neat." I look him over and notice his eyes are bloodshot red. He catches my gaze and tilts his head down. In one swift movement, the shades that were holding his shaggy hair back were now covering his dark shadowed eyes. As soon as the waitress is out of sight, Adonis says, "Salad Aphrodite?" I cover my eyes in embarrassment. He knows I would have never ordered a salad voluntarily. "You really are trying to impress this dick." I widened my eyes and looked quickly at Nick to see anger flash through his eyes, "What did you just say?" I look back at Adonis to see him giving a menacing look to Nick. This is where the saying comes, "if looks could kill", Nick would definitely be dead already. The first thought that pops into my head is to calm him down, I put my hand on his thigh and squeeze lightly. Adonis stiffens and takes a deep breath. I look at the other boy's face and they look like they are at the movie theater. Cain looks like he's about to ask for popcorn, he had a

huge grin on his face. Hudson is the only one who looked indifferent but part of me thinks he's drunk or high. Adonis leans back into the chair, showing me that he is more relaxed so I take my hand off his leg. "Look Walker, I know why you're doing this. I know you want to get under my skin. I have to admit it to you," he nods and looks at him with a glint in his eye that was mischievous, "It's good but people don't just go around trying to piss me off, they're all too scared at what I'd do to them...and Nick, you should definitely be scared." I give Adonis a questioning look but he pays no attention as his glare is on Nick. I don't know what it is but there is definitely something weird going on here. Whatever happened between Nick and Adonis, must have been bad for them to act this way around each other. Nick chuckles darkly and I lean back with slight fear. I haven't seen this side of Nick and I really don't like it. Out of nowhere, I feel Adonis' hand on my bare thigh, his large hand enveloping my whole thigh. I'm wearing a pink dress that reached up to my mid-thigh. He soothingly rubbed the outside of my thigh with his calloused thumb, making me realize he noticed my discomfort. "It's not what you think Adonis, I'm just here to hang out with Aphrodite. There's no other motive." He lifts up his palms in surrender.
Adonis nods, "That's good then. Just watch your back." I gasp inaudibly when I feel Adonis' hand move upward on my leg. My heart starts hammering in my chest and I shake my leg signaling for him to stop or take it off. He tilts his head towards me with a smirk and he winks. Adonis looks to Liam, "What did you order?" With that, his hand gets way too close to my underwear and my heart skips a beat. I instantly grab his hand and squeeze as tight as I can without making any facial expression. He pulls away wincing,

his hand hits the table with a loud thud. “You okay there Adonis?” I tilt my head to the side mocking concern. He squinted his eyes and smiled at me, “Yeah, I'm good, baby girl.” I widen my eyes and look at Nick to see anger and confusion flash through his face. Adonis said that on purpose, he did it to urke Nick. This is where his possessiveness starts showing. The way it always did with everything. He never liked to share, even as kids. He would only share with me. “Why do you care so much anyway?” Nick asked and sat up a little more straight. Adonis grits his teeth in anger, his strong jaw being more prominent. I again put my hand on his thigh to calm him down because he looks like he’s about to blow a fuse. “That Walker, is none of your business. You are here on this date with her by my grace.” I click my tongue in annoyance, who does he think he is! I go to move my hand off his thigh but he grabs my hand with his and puts it between his thighs locking it in place. Before I can say anything Adonis continues. “This girl right here, is with you as long as I will allow it. So consider yourself blessed.” I scoff loudly and Cain cackles. The other boys were silent. I turn towards him, “Adonis Clark. I think it's time for you to go.” He nods, “Your right. Let's go.” Cain moves, allowing Adonis to move out of the booth. He grabs my hand pulling me with him. I stand out of the booth and whisper so I won't make a scene, “I’m not going anywhere with you. I’m on a date.” He glares at me, “The date is over now. We’re leaving.” I turned back towards Nick. Liam and James were still sitting, preventing Nick from standing. I look back at Adonis, helplessness clear on my face. “Adonis, please.” I whine but so slowly, only he can hear. He leans over and whispers in my ear, “If we don’t leave right now, I’m going to kill him. It's your choice.” I glare at him

but he just shrugs arrogantly. I turn back towards the table and give Nick an apologetic smile, “I’m sorry Nick, I promise I’ll make it up to you.” He gives me a tight lip smile, “Yeah, okay, call me later.”
Adonis grabs my hand, pulling me towards the entrance of the restaurant. As soon as we walk out of the restaurant, I pull my hand roughly out of his. I cross my arms over my chest but he keeps walking and I follow him to his car. We get in and I immediately start yelling, “What the fuck was that about?!” He pulls out of the parking lot, completely ignoring my outburst. “I can’t believe what you just did Adonis. I always knew you were possessive and selfish! But this! Oh this was a new low, even for you.” He stopped the car suddenly and we were in the middle of a big street. Luckily there weren't that many cars around. He clenches and unclenches his jaw, his knuckles turning white on the steering wheel. His muscled arms flexing under his tight grey, long sleeved button down shirt. He turns his face towards me, “You know I don’t like that piece of shit but you still insist on seeing him. You knew I didn’t like it. That's why you didn’t tell me about your date tonight.” I throw my head back in exasperation, groaning loudly. I look back to him angrily, “The reason why I didn’t tell you is because it was always such a problem for you when I was around other boys. My own father doesn’t even act like this.” I throw my hands up in the air then let them slap over my bare legs. He looks down to my legs and then looks into my eyes, his were livid. “What the fuck are you even wearing? It’s like your begging him to fuck you!” I gasp loudly, slapping his shoulder, “Don’t talk to me like that! You're not my father!” Adonis scoffs, “Your father doesn’t know the half of what Nick Walker is because if he knew, you wouldn’t have gotten out of

the house and especially not dressed like that." I smirk at him menacingly, "You seemed to like it." He chuckles darkly as I say, "It really bothers you that I dressed up for him." I take a deep breath, feeling bold with my statement. He looks me over as he says, "You have no idea."

Chapter Twenty-One

Tell Me About London

I have been tossing and turning all night. I haven't been able to have a minute of sleep. Adonis dropped me off home without a word. I didn't text him and he didn't bother to either. I sat up on my bed and leaned over to turn on my lamp on my nightstand. I lean on the headboard and groan loudly. I grab my phone to see the time, it said four thirty AM. I look through my phone, opening my social media apps but finding nothing interesting. I throw my phone on the bed with a loud sigh. I can't believe what Adonis did. My mind has been replaying the events of the night before over and over again. Anger ripples through me again, thinking over how he acted so stubbornly. I turn off my light and lay flat on my back again, this is going to be a long night. I hear my phone ping from somewhere on my bed and I quickly search for it. My heart hammering in my ears. Finally finding it, I reprimand myself, what's your problem? You're mad at him. He treated you like shit, but I find myself grabbing my phone and as the screen lights up, I see the name of the person who texted me. I knew who it was before I even grabbed it but seeing his name lit up on my screen still makes my heart skip a beat. I slide the screen open and I see Adonis' question.

'Are you sleeping?'

I give the phone a dull look as if he can see my face, then I reply with a question of my own.

'How could I? '

My phone starts ringing in my hand; Adonis' name on the caller ID. I know it's stupid because we have hung out already and we have been texting but the fact that he is calling me, feels like something so different. Maybe it's because I wished for it for so long over my time in London. I answer and put my phone to my ear without speaking. I can hear him breath from the other end. Both of us not saying anything for a while, till he decides to break the silence, "I'm sorry." I take a deep breath, what am I going to do with this? "Adon-" he stops me with his words. "I know I fucked up, I know I never learn, but I am trying baby girl. I really am." His words come out pleadingly. "Adonis, you can't keep doing this. You can't control what I do. I know you're not used to me being around other guys but it's gonna happen, I can't keep staying away from them." I hear him sigh softly, "I know that you must have had a love life in London. I have to admit, seeing you with him really got to me but I promise I will try harder. If you really want to date that guy, then I will try to support it the best I can." His words come out tightly but sincerely. "I didn't have one," I admit to not having a love life in London. I mean why would I pretend I did have one. "What do you mean?" Comes his reply. "I didn't have a love life in London. I didn't have anyone." I stay still, waiting for his reply but it doesn't come, all I hear is his heavy breathing. After a minute or two I ask, "Adonis?" He clears his throat, "Yeah, I'm still here." I lay down on my side and ask, "Are you okay?" I hear shuffling on the other end of the phone. "Yeah, just tired." My heart breaks a little. "What are you doing tomorrow?" He takes a deep breath and says, "Nothing important. Hey, tell me about London." I chuckle under my breath, "What do you want to know?" His reply makes my heart stop, "Everything."

"Um...Where do I begin? Well, you would have loved the classic cars people drive in. I know that's for sure." His chuckle makes butterflies swarm in my stomach. "There was this little secret flower garden that you would have hated but I used to love to go there. I would take a book and stay there till the sun went down. The day I found it, I was so happy. There were all sorts of different flowers and it smelled amazing." I smile as he says, "Why do you say I would have hated it?" Thinking of how many times I went to that garden I say, "Maybe the first time you saw it, you would have liked it but after going with me over and over again, you would have hated it without a doubt." He chuckles again, because he knows I'm right. "The libraries were a reader's dream, they were so amazing and beautiful and not as strict as the ones here. Um…" I tap on my nose to think. "London at night, is way more beautiful than in the day. The bridge when it's lit up, is breathtaking." I start talking about the ferris wheel at night and Big Ben, when out of nowhere I hear light snores coming through the phone. I smile and whisper, "Good night Adonis."

Chapter Twenty-Two
Black & White

A loud knock on my door wakes me up from my deep sleep. I jolt upwards with a groan. My parents walk into my room, both of them with huge smiles. “Hey sweetie, sorry for waking you.” My father leans on my door frame as he continues to say, “We’re going out on the yacht today. Get up get dressed, we’re leaving in an hour. Call whoever you want to come with us.” I cover my face and throw myself back on my bed harshly. “We’ll be down stairs, sweetie.” Comes my mothers voice.Then I hear my door being shut. With a loud sigh, I grab my phone immediately calling Roxy facetime. She answers groggily, also in bed. “Why are you calling me this early in the morning?” I give her a dull look, “It’s noon, Rox. Anyway, my parents wanna go out on their yacht and they said I can invite whoever I want.” She quickly jumps to her feet and I see her running. I guess it's to her closet. “I am so in! What should I wear?” I see her moving around rummaging for stuff. “Can umm...you invite Erika and the boys too?” She stops her actions and looks at me dead in the eyes, a smirk slowly growing on her face. Her eyes were puffy with sleep but she was still mischievous. “You want the boys there?” I nod and she yelps in a high pitched voice. “Hold on, let me add them.” Before I can protest, she starts adding Erika, then Cain. “Hey guys.” Comes my timid greeting. “Cain! Add all the other boys in, Aphrodite has something to ask you guys.” I groan in protest and she grins at me. Then I see her start searching again, material flying everywhere. I shake my head with a slight smile. All the boys click in and start asking what's going on, except Adonis. Roxy keeps telling them to wait till everyones is on. When Adonis finally answered, he was rubbing his tired eyes and my heart skipped a beat. “Hey everyone, what's going on?” His voice was thick with sleep and sounded rough and

groggy. I notice he brings his blanket closer to his face to cover his bare tattooed chest. “Aphrodite?” Comes Roxy’s voice, snapping me out of my short daze.
“Yeah, like I was telling Roxy earlier, my parents want to go out on their yacht today and said I can invite anyone I’d like. So if you guys want, you guys can all come here and we can go together.” Looking at everyone's faces who were all looking at me, I was getting a little self conscious so I sat up on my bed and threw my feet off. I blush as I continue, “Or, uh, we can just meet there.” I shrug. Adonis smiles, “Yeah, baby girl, we will meet at your house in thirty minutes.” Cain speaks before everyone in a whiney mocking voice, “Yeah, baby girl.” Adonis’ smile falls from his face, ”Stop it Cain.” Cain's eyes widened in mock fear, “Oh no, I’m so scared.” Everyone agrees and I tell them I'll send them the address. After I hung up, I got up to take a shower, shaving pretty much everything. After my shower, I blow dry my hair, styling it, and then add waterproof makeup. Walking into my closet, still in my robe, I open a drawer in my closet and pull out a black bikini set where the strings from the bra wrapped around my midsection and put it on, throwing my robe on the floor. I grabbed a long black sheer coverup cardigan that had slits on the sides and slipped it on. I pull on a tan floppy straw hat with a black rim adding matching wedges. I walk over to my jewelry, put on a simple gold chain with a small compass hanging from it. This necklace held so many memories. I add gold stud earrings and a few thin gold bracelets. I grab a beach bag and add an extra set of clothes. Putting it on my shoulder, I walk out of my room and down the stairs. Walking down the stairs, I see my parents putting things in the back of my father's truck. I walk outside and I see Roxy’s car

drive through the opened gate, parking on the far end. Behind her car, is a guy on a motorcycle. It's a good thing the driveway was big enough to fit a lot of cars because in comes a classic car and a Dodge Challenger right behind it. As the other two cars park, I see Cain taking off his helmet as he gets off. I take a look at his motorcycle, admiring the black and chrome bike in awe. The girls get out of Roxy's car and walk towards me. I really was awestruck by the motorcycle and was dying to get on it but decided on just looking away towards James and Liam who were getting out of the Challenger. The last to get out of the car was Hudson. His car was the classic one and It suited him perfectly. He had that old fashioned feel to him too.
I knit my eyebrows noticing everyone is here but Adonis. They are all near me and I smile at them.
Cain grins, "Looking good, A."
My father walks out holding a box of beer on his shoulder and Liam is quick to take it from him.
"Thanks son. If you guys want to help, there is more stuff on top of the kitchen counter."
"Yes of course sir," James said quickly. "Hey! Don't call me that. I'm Robert." James smiles, "Okay Robert, just tell us where to go." My Father grins at that, "Aphrodite, show them where the kitchen is while I grab some stuff from the garage." Cain perks up, "I'll help you in the garage." My dad nods and gestures for him to follow him. I walk into the house and they follow right behind me. Roxy right by my side. "Is Adonis coming?" I ask her in a whisper and she smiles with a shrug. I give her a quick glance over. She was wearing a hot pink bikini with light jean short, shorts, the hot pink strings popping out of the waistband. With a cute scarf surrounding her curly head, to finish it all up, she has on silver hoop earrings. "You look good." She shrugs one shoulder

as we enter the kitchen "I know." My mom is there adding a few things in a big beach bag. "Hey mom, these guys are here to help." My mom looks up and I point behind me towards Liam, James, and Hudson. My mom blushes, literally blushes and she smiles at them. "I know Mrs. W, they're all smoking hot." I hit Roxy on her shoulder and she laughed. "What can we help you with, Mrs. Watson?" Erika asked, walking towards my mother. "Um, boys, you can take these things here outside." My mother points towards boxes of drinks, chips, and other stuff. She looks at us, "You girls help me make some sandwiches." The boys grab some boxes and walk out of the kitchen. My mother whispers, "Wow, those boys really are something." She shakes her head and we all laugh. As the laughter dies down, we all go to help my mother but she stops me, "Honey, take this last bag outside, please." I nod and take the bag from the counter and walk it outside. As I walk out, Hudson quickly takes the bag from my hands and sets it down on the bed of the truck. I look towards the gate as a black Cadillac Escalade drives in. Through the large windshield, I see Adonis wearing dark aviators and to his right is his mother wearing big dark glasses and a big hat on her head. I watch as they park their huge car. Adonis parked with the passenger seat towards me and I see Mary climbing out, struggling a little but pulls through. She was wearing a beautiful dress with a long cardigan covering her arms. From what I noticed, she is trying to cover herself the best she can to keep her sensitive skin from getting sun. I smile big and walk up to the car towards her. I pulled her into a hug, "I didn't expect to see you." She pulls back, matching my smile, "I wasn't coming, your mother and Adonis couldn't shut up about it. They forced me to come."

I hear his thick, velvety voice coming from my right, "I knew she was dying to come. She was just pretending she didn't want to." I pull her into another quick hug, "Well, I'm glad you're here. Let's go inside. Mom's making sandwiches." She nods and walks towards the house. I go to follow her when his voice stops me, "Sorry I fell asleep on you this morning." I turn around and tilt my head to the side, looking him over. He was wearing white shorts and a white tank top that said *"just do it",* in bold black letters and a Nike swoosh underneath. The white was a nice contrast to all the dark ink on his skin. I wave my hand nonchalantly with a mocking smile, "You look good in white." I look him over again, then meet his covered eyes. His lips curl at the side as he says, "You look good in black." I feel someone beside me and turn my head to see Cain standing next me. "You look good in black." He says mockingly, like earlier. He really is asking for it from Adonis. Adonis glares at him, leaning over Cain, hitting him on the back of his head. "Stop it." Cain smiles and rubs the back of his head. "Fine, I'll leave you and your baby girl alone." Adonis hits him again and walks away towards my house. I give Cain a flat look, "You asked for it." Cain shrugs, "I know." After we all got settled, Mary went with my father and mother in their packed car that was filled with all the essentials and all of us got into the Escalade Adonis came in. I called shotgun as I got into the passenger seat. James was pissed to say the least. Adonis climbed into the driver's seat and everyone else got into the car arguing the whole time till they finally sat down. Adonis looks at me with an annoyed look, everyone getting to him, I smile at him shrugging. As we drive off, he passes me his phone with the music app opened, I beam at him, "Really?" He smiles, "You're the copilot, you choose the songs."

I grin and go through the music. "You better not put girly shit!" Cain screams from all the way in the back. "You better not put Taylor swift!" I hear James grunt. I rolled my eyes and clicked the song I wanted. "Finesse" by Bruno Mars, featuring Cardi B. Everyone starts freaking out at my choice of music. Adonis turns his head towards me and smiles. He has one arm on the steering wheel and the other tapping on the middle console. I start moving my shoulders to the beat and turn my body to see Roxy with her arms out dancing and singing the lyrics. Erika is also singing but just moving her head to the beat. I sit up on my knees and turn towards everyone. I start snapping my fingers. To my actions, the boys in the back join in too and start singing. Hudson was the only one who wasn't joining in but I paid no attention. He was looking out the window the whole way, in the third seat, his shades over his eyes and a backwards cap on his head. Cain, out of tune, was singing louder than all of us over the blaring music. He had me laughing loudly. I look at Adonis, who was bobbing his head now with a huge grin on his face, showing his perfect white teeth. As Bruno says, "*Out here drippin in finesse*." I lean over and pull on Adonis' shirt, letting it fall as I sing out the words. He turns towards me and sings. "*Fellas, grab your ladies if your lady fine.*" I shake my head as we all continue singing.

Chapter Twenty-Three

Greek Goddess

My father's Yacht is huge. We have been on it hundreds of times, it's the only thing my father didn't sell when we left for England. He loved it, he named it "Greek Goddess". Apparently, after me. It was a three story boat. The first story, being all the way under the boat, were a few bedrooms and a kitchen. The second, being the most important part of the boat, there was a pool with a slide in the back of the boat. In the middle was a den that had floor-to-ceiling glass windows. There was a huge bar, a poker table, and a living room. In the front of the boat, was a spiral staircase leading to the top floor, where the pilot house is. Up here is a big lounging area too. That is where we all were at the moment, except for Mary and my mother. They were downstairs in the den. My father was driving the boat, there was music blasting through the bluetooth radio and we were all hanging out, laughing and joking around. The boys loved my father. He gave them all beers and told them that if they got drunk, he would call the cops on them himself. They were all nervous at first, except Adonis. Adonis was super comfortable with my father but now they treated my father like one of the boys. From where I was sitting, in between Erika and Roxy, I had a really good view of Adonis standing next to my father and all the boys. As Roxy catches me staring at him, she takes her sunglasses off her face and passes them to me, "At least put these on so you won't be too damn obvious." I give her a confused look, pretending to not know what she means, "What are you talking about?" But I grab the sunglasses and put them on my face anyway. I take off my hat and set it on the coffee table in front of me. "You haven't taken your eyes off him, Aphrodite," I look at Erika and smile sheepishly at her words, while running my fingers through my hair. She looked so cute in her

zebra bikini and white shawl on her hips covering her up. I look back at him, he took off his shirt a while ago. His strong tattooed body was on full show. There almost wasn't a clear part of him. Even with all his tattoos, his washboard abs were very prominent. My fingers were tingling at the thought of touching him. Adonis was nudging Cain and laughing at something he said. I look to Roxy then to Erika, "I mean, look at him. It's hard not to look." They laugh and Roxy shakes her head, "You haven't even turned your head towards the other guys."
I frown at her, while pulling my dark hair to one side I say, "I have." The words come out high pitched, even I can't believe them myself. Erika puts her hands over my shaded eyes, "What is Liam wearing?" I scoff, but then struggle with the thought. So I just decide on guessing, "He's wearing black shorts and a green t-shirt. With sandals." That was the worst guess ever. "Wrong!" Erika takes her hand off of my face and shakes her head. I look up to find Liam in khaki shorts and a black tank top, while wearing boat shoes. I grimace and look to Roxy for help. "You got serious problems, girl." I look back to him to find him looking at me. He smiles and calls me over with a hand gesture. "I can't help it, girls. He just looks too different from what I remember." I justify while standing to my feet. I give Roxy back her sunglasses. "Sure, that's what it is." Roxy rolls her eyes and puts her shades back on. Ditching my hat, I walked over to Adonis, who was on the other side of the boat. He smiles as I stand in front of him, "Hey bad boy, what's up?" He raises his eyebrows at me, "Bad boy? Is that what you're calling me now?" I make a show of thinking it over, then nod, "Yeah, I think it suits you. What's up?" I ask again. "Your father said to call you over so you can drive the boat, he's going downstairs

to get something to eat." These words come out louder as he says them and my father turns towards me. "Yeah, here sweetie, take the wheel. I don't trust these boys with my baby and Adonis here said you're a better driver than him." My dad smiles while standing up from his Captain's chair. I shrug, "Yeah, sure whatever." He walks away and I take a seat on the chair. As I watch the map to where the destination is, holding on to the steering wheel with one hand, I pull the lever to make the boat go again. As I look up, I see James leaning next to Adonis to my left, "You look good, Captain Aphrodite. It goes with you." I chuckle, "Yeah? I like it. Captain Aphrodite." I test the words out, feeling them out then nod once, "Yeah, It's catchy."
"Look out everyone, Captain Aphrodite in the house! You all better watch out!" I hear Liam, who was standing right behind me and I laugh loudly.
"What is it I hear?" Roxy and Erika walk up. "You're the captain now?" I nod at Roxy's words and she leans down, opens the small cupboard and pulls out a sailors hat my dad keeps there. "You need the matching hat." She sets it on my head and I smile, shaking my head. I looked over at Adonis to see him already looking at me and he was slightly biting on his lower lip, hiding a smile. I give a questioning look but he shakes his head then looks at my necklace. I look down but can barely see it. Looking back at him, I smile and scoot over in my chair then pat the large space I left for him. He walks over and takes a seat next to me, putting his awkward arm on the back of the chair. I hear a loud tsking noise and turn my head to see Cain frowning, "Adonis! I was gonna sit next to Aphrodite! You stole my spot!" I throw my head back and laugh in earnest. Cain laughs too, "Fine, you can sit next to the Captain for now but we all know she

wants to sit next to me." I see Adonis shake his head from my peripheral vision as I look to where we're going. Apparently, we aren't too far, just a few minutes out. I look down and see Adonis had a beer in his hand so without asking, I grab it and as I do Adonis raises his notched eyebrow. I raised mine mimicking him as I put the bottle to my lips and tip it back. I pass it back to him as I look back to the water. As we finally arrive at our destination, I turn off the ignition and lower the anchor. We were at a little sand bar in the middle of the ocean. As everyone starts shuffling down the stairs, Adonis turns towards me, still sitting on the Captain's chair together. "Didn't think you still had that necklace." He reaches up and touches it with his index finger. He gave me this necklace for my fifteenth birthday. He told me that if I ever really needed him, wherever I was, he would go no matter what. I smile at him, my heart hammering in my chest, "Of course I still do. It's my favorite necklace, even though you weren't good on your word." I give him a fake stern look. "You didn't really need me, Aphrodite but I needed you and here you are. It worked the opposite way." My eyes crinkle at his words and I push him till he stands up. I stand up and he says, "C'mon let's go down there." I nod and walk down with him. He's right, I didn't really need him. Nothing tragic happened to me while I was in London. The only thing was that I was missing my best friend. He on the other hand, went through so much and like he said, I'm here now and I'll help him get through whatever he needs.

I quickly grab my phone from my bag that was in the den and Adonis helps me climb down to the sand bar where all our friends were. As we got down, I saw everyone doing different things. Erika and James were sitting to one side, letting their legs get wet by the water. Cain, Liam, and Hudson were playing with a football. With Roxy is where I wanted to be. I ran towards her. She was laying in the sand making sand angels. I lay down next to her putting my phone on my stomach and mimicking her actions. I giggle at the feeling of the sand moving between my arms and legs. The heat of the sun makes my skin feel warm in a good way. The sun was super bright but I squinted my eyes just a little. I turn my head towards Roxy and she's grinning up at the sky with her eyes closed. I close my eyes too and then suddenly feel my phone being lifted. The fingers that graze softly over my stomach as they grab my phone, make tingles run along my skin. I open my eyes to see Adonis blocking the view of the hot sun. The rays of the sun surrounded him, making it look like the light was coming from him. He holds my phone out and takes a picture of us and I smile. After he snaps the picture I jump up to my feet and grab the phone from him. I turn the camera around and look at him, "Selfie?" I plead and he shrugs. I look at my phone, seeing our reflection, he lifts his eyebrow with a smirk, while I smile wide. I take the picture, then suddenly feel him tickle me and I scream out a laugh. "Hey!" He gives me a wicked smile and I back away from him, he gets closer and does it again while laughing. "Stop it!" I yell and run away from him, I fall in the process of trying to get away from him. He ends up toppling over me because he was so close to me when I tripped. He hovers over me, holding himself up on his elbows. I turn my body so I am now laying on my back as he says worriedly, "Are you okay?" I giggle and nod but then lose my breath as he starts ticking me again. My phone starts ringing and he stops while I answer it without reading the caller ID. "Hello?" I have a huge grin on my face as I look up at Adonis. I reach up and

grab his sunglasses, taking them off and putting them on my face. I can see his beautiful pale green eyes now. They were shining in happiness. “Hello? Aphrodite?” Nick's voice comes through the phone and my eyes widen. Anger flashes for a short moment in Adonis’ eyes as he somehow knows who it is. “Hey, how are you?” I say out of breath. My breathing coming in harsh pants from the tickle attack.
“Yeah, good,” I hardly hear what he says after that as Adonis gets a mischievous look on his face and starts tickling me again. I try my best to keep from laughing but it is so hard. Nick’s voice comes harsh as he says, ”Aphrodite, What do you think?” I have no idea what he said so I just agree with him. “Yeah, sure.” I laugh loudly, thrashing in Adonis’ hold, “I gotta go, Nick. Bye.” I hang up the phone and throw it to the side. I turn my whole body around, attempting to climb out of his grasp but he grabs onto my hips, pulling me back down and I yelp. Right before Adonis starts tickling me again, Cain says loudly, “Alright guys, are we gonna get in the water or what? And Adonis, Aphrodite, can you guys stop with the flirting. I’m getting jealous.” Adonis gets off me and stands to his feet, I extend my hand and he grabs it pulling me to my feet, I bend over and grab my phone. Then as I turn to look at Adonis, he asks me, “So we’re flirting now?” I roll my eyes and shove him turning towards where Erika and Roxy are sitting. I stride up to them.
I take a seat on my ass and Roxy lifts an eyebrow at me and I give her a “shut it” look. All the boys get in the water except for Hudson, he stands there watching them playing with the ball while having what seemed like a lollipop in his mouth. “You coming in, Hud?” Liam yells and Hudson lifts up the hem of his shirt, peeling it off his toned body. “Yeah, I’ll be right in.” As he throws his shirt on the ground, Roxy

whistles, making Hudson turn towards her with a smile. "Remind me to put you on my to-do list, Hudson."
"Sure thing, Rox. You better not take it back." Roxy looks behind him, where Liam is looking at her with a weird expression on his face. "Of course not." She says, then Hudson gets in the water, catching the football on the way in.
I look around at the dark blue water and watch as the water ripples. Also, I am trying so hard not to look towards Adonis. "Just look." I whip my head towards Roxy, who is giving me a sarcastic look. "What?" I ask, perplexed. She raises an eyebrow, "Just look at him. You're wearing his shades. You won't get caught." My hand flies to the side of my face as I feel the leg of Adonis' sunglasses. "I don't know what you're talking about." I cross my arms over my chest and look away. "Stop acting dumb. You know you're attracted to him now. You always kinda were, to be honest, you just didn't know." I look at Roxy and my mouth falls open at her bold words. "Don't worry, he's attracted to you too." This time I whip my head to Erika as she makes this accusation. "You girls are talking nonsense again. I'm leaving you guys. I'm going in the water." I stand up, throw off my cardigan, slip off my wedges while throwing my phone and the sunglasses on top of my cardigan and I walk into the water, a little to the left of the boys.

Chapter Twenty-Four

You Wanna Play?

With every step I take into the water, it rises up my body. I feel a heated gaze on me but don't look up. As the water reaches my waist, I sink down. The water feels fresh on my hot skin. I feel my hair swaying in the water. I finally opened my eyes underwater and could see everything, it was just a little blurry. From where I am, I can see all the boys bodies underwater. Looking far ahead of me, I see how the sand goes down deeper into the water. I don't see any fish but I do see big rocks covered in moss and seaweed surrounding them. I swim a little and as I do, I catch a glimpse of white to the side of me. I turn my body to see Adonis' tattooed legs and some of his tattooed back. He turns around a few times as if searching for something. I smile as I know exactly what he is looking for. I watch the other boys and notice how they jump up in the water as they play ball. I got an idea and started swimming towards him. He isn't that far from me. His back is turned away from me. As I get closer, putting my feet on the sand, I lift myself up slowly, then with a grin, I wrap my arms around his neck and chest. In one swift movement, I pull him with me underwater. He comes down easily but what I wasn't expecting was for him to turn swiftly in my hold. Our eyes meet, green on blue, matching the colors of the ocean. He grabs onto my hips and pulls me down deeper into the shallow water pinning me down with his arms. I shrug at his attempt to keep me down and wrap my arms and legs around him accepting his challenge. Pulling my body closer to his, he raises us back up to the surface, we both take deep breaths of air as soon as we make it up.
I grin at him and his eyes crinkle with a menacing look. I feel him gripping my hips tighter and my eyes widen as he suddenly pulls me from him and in one quick movement, he throws me about three feet away

from him. My body makes a big splash and then I sink into the water. I quickly turn my body in the crisp water and submerge up. As I stand, I look towards Adonis and watch as he runs both his hands through his wet hair, smirking at me. I swim towards him but don't get too close. I look towards the boys and see that somehow, we are now pretty far from their game. I swim around Adonis and he follows my movement with his gorgeous eyes. "That wasn't very nice." he says, as I was in front of him. I continue swimming around him, "Payback." He throws his head back laughing. Looking back at me, he says, "Oh, Aphrodite, you don't want to start something you can't handle." As I was in front of him, I said, "I can handle a lot of things. Try me." His eyes meet mine and the color in them darkens. "Oh yeah?" He says, but his voice comes out choked. He clears his throat a little then he says, "Are you sure?" I give him a mischievous look as I say, "Do your worst." I watch as he glides his tongue over his teeth. His back is now facing me and he says, "I will."
I stand to my feet and walk towards his muscled back, "You think you can handle me?" I reach up and run my hand over the black feathered wings on his back. I hear him intake a breath as my fingers touch his warm skin. In the middle of his back, running along his spine, vertically, was a word or two in Greek letters. I trace over his spine and feel him shudder under my touch, I grin to myself. "I know I can." Comes his whispered reply. The wings took up both sides of his back beautifully, I reluctantly pulled away from them and walked around towards his front.
I shake my head tsking, then look him over till I reach his face. I see him visibly gulp and I walk closer to him. He grabs on to my hips to keep me from him. I give him a questioning look but then try to wiggle out

of his grip to get closer while putting my hands on his arms. "You don't want to get too close to me right now, baby girl." I look at him confused, then turn my head as I hear Roxy yell from the sand, "Can us girls play too? Or is it a just guy thing?"
I look back to Adonis still holding on to my hips and me still holding his large arms. He has an embarrassed look on his face and my eyes widened in recognition. "Hey boss! You in or you plan on making out over there?" We turn our heads to Hudson as he is looking at us with a grin. Adonis looks back to me, "You wanna play?" He asked me timidly. Both of us ignore Hudson's remark about making out. I smile and nod, "Yeah, sure, as long as I'm on your team."
"Alright, deal." He releases me and we swim closer to everyone else. Roxy and Erika are already in the water.
"Yeah, we're in." Adonis said, then Hudson looked at us while quickly doing a headcount. "One problem, Don. We have one too many, that makes us uneven." Hudson speaks while holding the ball. "That's not a problem." Out of nowhere, I feel Adonis' hands on my sides and I scream as he bends down pulling me over his shoulders. I quickly grab onto his head to steady myself. "Now we are even numbered." He says, while adjusting me so we were both comfortable. I looked at the girls who were both grinning at me. Adonis looks up at me, raising an eyebrow with a small smile, "You okay?" I give him a pat on his cheek, "Perfect." We played and joked around for quite some time. We also played chicken with the other girls on the boy's shoulders too. It was so much fun but then we all got hungry.

WE ARE ALL SITTING down in the den, eating sandwiches and chips. My parents and Mary are

telling us some pretty crazy surgical stories. “After you boys finish eating, I want to show you something.” My father said rubbing his hands together.
Adonis looks over at him, “Oh, they're gonna freak, Rob.” My father nods, “Oh yeah, they are.” I know exactly what they are talking about and my father must really like these boys to show them his jet skis. I take a bite of my sandwich then I hear Roxy murmur to me, “Oh, you're fucked.” I give her a look and slap her on the shoulder. “What’s your problem?” I exclaimed, silently. She was sitting right next to me as we shared an accent chair. She shrugs while saying, “Oh, nothing.” I look towards where Adonis was sitting, his shirt back on. He has his ankle over his knee and his hands resting in his lap as he sits, leaning back on a chair. He was listening in on a story my father was saying. He managed to look so sexy, rugged, and sophisticated at the same time. He truly was striking. I look back to Roxy and whisper, “You’re right, I am fucked.” Her mouth opens wide and she laughs silently while shaking her head. After we all finish eating, the boys walk out to the front of the boat. From where we sit, we can see everything. My father presses a button on a clicker and I know the small garage opened where he hides the two jet skis he owns. I see the boys react like they have never seen one in their lives. They help my father somehow put it in the water and the first to drive them is Adonis and Hudson. I sit on my knees to raise myself higher for a better view. Adonis looked happy to be on the jet ski. As he leans over to grab the handle bars, his biceps and shoulder blades flex. I know my eyes must be wide because Mary says, “He looks really good, doesn’t he?” I look back to her, heat spreading on my cheeks. I take a seat again looking to everyone else for help but they all look at me knowingly so I have no

choice but to answer truthfully, “Yeah. He really does.”

Chapter Twenty-Five

The Man In Charge

Somehow, we established a group text after that day on my father's boat and it was just nonstop all day. Cain kept whining about a special name we needed for our said "group" and we all kept shutting him down. He came up with the weirdest things. I don't even want to mention them. Right now, as I sit in my living room watching TV on the big flat screen, I watch as Roxy and Cain banter back and forward through our group messages. I reach into the bag of popcorn as a question comes in for me, it was Cain asking, ignoring Roxy:

'What you up to Ditee?'

He insisted on calling me Ditee. Instead of my full name, he used the last half. It was pronounced die-tee. He added the extra "e" because it looked off as just "Dite". I smiled as I answered.

'Nothing, watching a show.'

A reply quickly comes in by Liam.

'What show?'

I quickly reply with an embarrassed emoticon, then add an actual reply.

'Grey's Anatomy.'

Roxy replies instantly.

'Again, A?'

I have seen the whole series multiple times but I just can't help it. I love it so much.

'Yes. I have nothing better to do. Gonna be home alone for the next couple of days.'

I send a shrugging emoticon with my reply, then quickly comes a chain of messages from everyone stating that they're coming over and what snacks they're bringing and that I better shut off that shit show before they get here. Adonis' reply comes last.

'Be there in two.'

My eyes widen at that and I look down at my outfit. I was wearing a big shirt and a fluffy robe. I set down the bag of popcorn and sprint towards the stairs, taking two at a time. Running into my room and into my closet, I quickly put on some black yoga pants with a white crop top that said "*heartless*" on it in red letters. I slip on my black Vans and quickly run to my bathroom to look myself over. My hair was a mess so I quickly ran a brush through it. I grab my mouthwash from under my sink and quickly rinse my mouth out. I look at myself again. Thankfully, my eyes don't have dark circles underneath. I actually had a really good night's sleep. As I pinch my cheeks to add some color to my pale face, I hear the door chime signaling it was opened. I always forget Adonis knows the code to the lock on the door. I looked at myself in the mirror one last time, my bright blue eyes widened. I walk out of my room and towards the staircase. Looking down, I see Adonis walking in as if he owned the place. He was wearing a black leather jacket with a black and white striped shirt underneath and blue jeans. He looked up at me after shutting the door behind him, a grin spreaded on his face. "Hey, beautiful." I walk down the stairs, my stomach doing flips. "Hey

yourself." I say as I stand right in front of him." I was close by when I read the messages so I figured I'd just come right over." He explains why he got here so fast. I nod. "It's cool." I tilt my head towards the living room. "Wanna sit while we wait for everyone else?" "Yeah," He answered and we walked into my living room. As we sit down on the couch, I turn my body so I'm facing him, one leg under me and the other one with my foot on the floor. "So you decorated everything in the whole house?" I ask him, remembering my father told me Adonis helped him with everything. He turns towards me, mimicking how I'm sitting on the couch, so now the free seat in between us was occupied by our legs. "Umm. No, a decorator chose everything in the house. I just watched as they put everything together." I lean my side into the couch and nod at his words confused because my room is perfect. "Oh." Then he says, while rubbing the back of his neck, "I did tell them what I wanted for your room though." I bite down on the corner of my lip and his eyes fly straight there, then back to my eyes quickly as I responded with, "It's perfect." A loud knock comes on the door and as I am about to stand to get it, Adonis put his hand on my knee, "I got it." I turn my body towards the door so I can see who's there. I watch as Adonis opens the door and everyone starts walking in, all saying different things and talking. I smile and stand to my feet to meet them in the foyer. Cain and Roxy were holding bags in their hands and Hudson had a bottle of vodka in each hand. I look at James, who was holding jugs of juice. I smile as I see Liam holding a bag of solo cups and ice.
"You guys really thought of everything." I state. "Oh yeah, we did." Cain said, holding up the bags of snacks making his point. I look around and notice

Erika isn't there. "Where's Erika?" I looked to Roxy for an answer but James answered without thinking. "She couldn't make it because she's with her mom." We all turned towards him and his cheeks redden a little. "I fucking knew it." Cain said, shaking his head. I lead them towards the living room and they set everything down on the coffee table. "Really, Cain? We all knew it. They were sucking each other's faces at the movie theater the other day." Hudson says, then I remember he had a full view of all of us from where he sat that day. Cain gives us all an exasperated look as he sits down on the couch. "Why was I the clueless one?" I smile, shaking my head, as I walk out of the room to go to the kitchen to grab some stuff, I hear, "Uh, cause you're an idiot." Roxy insults Cain like always. As I'm searching for the essentials, I hear music coming from the living room. Walking back, I see they started the TV and were playing music videos. I put the ice in the bucket I brought and organized everything on the table. I set aside napkins and paper plates. I hear Roxy groan. I look back at her in confusion. "No one cares if everything looks nice! Sit your perfect ass down!" She pats the chair that was empty in between her and Cain and I take a seat with a huff. I may or may not have a slight case of Obsessive-Compulsive-Disorder. I can't help it, I like everything in a special way. I think I get it from my mother. That is also why she doesn't really like having help around the house. She prefers to do it herself. Cain flips his body around so he is laying his head on my lap uninvitedly, his legs dangling over the armrest. I stay still with my hands floating over his head awkwardly. He looks up at me, grinning. He grabs my hand and sets it on his chest. I would have run my free hand through his hair but it was cut so short, there was almost nothing so I would just be patting his

buzzed head. I just set my hand on the chair next to my leg. I hear an angry sound coming from Adonis and I lift my head to see him glaring daggers at Cain. Cain turns his head towards him and smirks. “Oh chill, Adonis. I’m just relaxing on your baby girl here.” I smile and lean my head back on the chair. Adonis looks at me, questioning if I’m okay with it and I shrug my shoulder. “Pass me the remote,” Hudson says to Liam, extending his hand so he can pass it over. Liam groans, “I don’t want to hear your shitty old fashioned rock.” Hudson, who was dangling his feet over the armrest of the chair he was sitting on, now sits up straight, “You think I want to hear your shit music?” Hudson looked pissed to say the least. “No one wants to get depressed and emotional like you.” Comes Liam’s angered reply. “I don’t give a shit what you want. Give me the remote.”
I look down from the scene to see Cain chuckling. I give him a perplexed look and he answers with, “These two always fight like an old, married couple.” “Shut the fuck up, Cain.” Hudson gritted through his teeth, glaring at him in the process. “What crawled up your ass today?” Cain asked with a glint in his eye. “Something huge, that's for sure.” Liam said, under his breath. Hudson raises to his feet and grabs something from the table throwing it at Liam. Luckily, Liam crouches down in time and it hits the chair behind him instead. Liam stands up, anger clear on his face. In between him and Hudson, was the coffee table but that didn’t stop Liam from jumping over it. Before he gets a chance to get to Hudson, James grabs him, holding his arms behind his back. “What's your problem?” James asked his cousin. Liam was huffing in anger, Hudson had a smirk on his face, enjoying the whole scenario. “He threw something at me!”

“That’s because you acted like an ass.” James said quietly. I always thought Liam was the quiet, calm one but from what I just witnessed, he is temperamental. “Ok everyone, that's enough!” Adonis stands and glares at the boys angrily. Hudson pulls his lips into his mouth to keep from saying anything further. Liam pulls out of James’ hold and walks back to his chair sitting straight and looking down at his hands in his lap. Cain looks away towards the ceiling. I looked at Roxy bewildered as all the boys pretty much fell in line at Adonis’ orders. As Adonis sits back down, James walks up to Liam saying, “Give me the remote, Liam.” Liam quickly passes his cousin the control and James passes it to Roxy, who looks at it as confused as I am. The boys all looked like they were reprimanded by their father. Roxy puts a music video on and after some time, Cain breaks the silence, “Can we order a pizza? I’m starving.” He looks at me and I shrug. “Sure, why not? I’ll order it.” I grab my phone from the table and dial the number. After I ordered the pizzas, we all just chatted and joked around till the pizza got there. I stood up to pay but all the boys beat me to the door I fought with them until Adonis won, stating he didn’t bring anything so it was only necessary he paid. I frown at them as we go into the dining room to eat. Everyone sits around the table to eat and I take a seat right next to Adonis as he sits at the head of the table, Roxy sitting to my left. After we finished eating, my phone pings and I grabbed it to see who texted me. It was a message from Nick. Sliding it open, I look at it with wide eyes.

‘Hey pretty lady, be there in 30 minutes for that date you promised.’

I lean over and show Roxy, "I didn't know you had a date tonight," She whispers. I shake my head, "Neither did I." I search my head for my last phone call with him. It was a few days ago when we were on the sandbar and I paid no attention to what he said while Adonis was tickling me. My eyes widen again. "I think It was when we were on the sandbar. I didn't even understand what he was saying." I whisper, "What do I do?" She looks to Adonis who had a questioning look as he was staring at us. Then she gets an evil glint in her eye. She turns her head to me. "I think you should go." I grimace, "But I really don't want to. Plus, everyone's here."
"I think you should go and tell him you don't want to see him anymore," She nods as she continues, "and that's that. Don't worry about us."
"What is it?" Adonis finally asked. I look to Roxy for help, not able to say it myself. She looks at Adonis with her evil smirk and I grimace, knowing it won't be good. I look back to Adonis as Roxy says, "Apparently, she has a date tonight she didn't even know about." Adonis raises an eyebrow while clenching his jaw, "What do you mean, she didn't know about it?" I explain to him about what happened at the sandbar. "Then cancel. Simple as that." I look down to my hands. "You want to go?" He asked with anger lacing his shock. I look up at him, "It's just, I'd feel so bad to cancel on him after I promised him I'd make it up to him." He stands to his feet, almost tipping back the chair he was sitting on. "Adonis, you said you would try to support this." I stand on my feet too and so does everyone else. He walks out of the dining room and into the foyer. I follow him out, hearing shuffling and whispers behind me. I touch his arm while saying his name. He pulls his arm away from me, "I didn't say I was going to sit around and

watch." I look at him with wide eyes. "Adonis, c'mon. Please don't do this." I look at him pleadingly. "I can't do it, Aphrodite. I can't stay here knowing you're going to leave out that door," he extends his arm towards the door, "with that piece of shit. I'm leaving." I'm at a loss for words. I was stuck and my throat felt dry. I didn't know what to do. He opens the door and walks out. The boys pass me, giving me an apologetic smile as they walk out behind him. I turn around, looking at Roxy in disbelief. I put my head in my hands and take a deep calming breath. "Don't worry Aphrodite, he'll come around. Go get ready and I'll clean up." She said while rubbing my arm soothingly.

Chapter Twenty-Six

A Complete Disaster

I walk up to the ticket booth at the movie theater with Nick, I smile at him as we wait in line to get our tickets. He reaches out, grabbing my hand and I look to our interlaced fingers, knitting my eyebrows. Where are the butterflies? Where are the tingles? I should be feeling them. I so desperately want to feel them because I shouldn't be feeling them for the person I do. After we grab our tickets, we walk towards the entrance but before he opens the door, we hear someone yell out his name. We both turn around to see a few guys looking at Nick with a grin on their faces. Nick releases my hand and walks up to them. He gives them each a slap to the hand then pulls them in for a half hug. "Hey guys, long time no see. What are you guys up to?" One the guys, the one with long shoulder length hair and pale says, "What's that Walker?" He cups his ear as if to hear him better. "Are you trying to get nosey again?" I don't understand what that guy was trying to say. I look at Nick questioningly but he ignores me completely as he says with a grin on his face, "Always, Greg. You know that." Greg shakes his head, smirking to himself, "Take your girl inside, I'll find you later."
"Alright, deal." Alright, this was getting weird really fast. We walk in, grab a few snacks, then go into our theater room. As we take a seat, he puts his arm around my chair, making me feel awkward. "So um, who were those guys? Were they your friends or something?" I ask curiously and he turns his head towards me. "Oh, just some guys I know from high school. We have been friends for a long time." He said, then looked back to the screen as the movie commercials started playing.
My mind drifted off to Adonis and how he reacted to my date with Nick after he agreed on being supportive of my decisions. Remembering the anger and hurt in

his eyes, my heart breaks a little. I really hope this doesn't bring us back to square one. He was so mad at me. I frown a little at my thoughts but can't help it. I'd rather break off this thing I have with Nick than lose Adonis for a guy that I hardly know. Thinking of Adonis pulling out of my grasp before he left, I realize I should have gone after him and I shouldn't be here. I shouldn't be here with this stranger's arm around me. I really need to talk to Nick and explain to him that this won't happen again. I don't feel right sitting here with him, knowing that my best friend is mad at me for being here. I feel like I am doing something incredibly wrong. I was always the type of person that followed the rules. I always tried to be kind. I didn't like to be in conflict situations so thinking about admitting to Nick that I didn't want to see him anymore, made me feel nervous and a little scared. The first thought I get after that is wanting to be in Adonis' arms and know that everything will be okay and he won't let anything happen to me. From the corner of my eye, I see Nick pull out his phone and he starts texting someone. I think it's kind of rude to be texting someone while you're on a date. After a while, he puts his phone away and turns his head towards me. "Hey, um. I'll be right back, okay?" I pull my lips into my mouth and nod awkwardly, "Okay." I shrug. He stands and walks down the stairs, not even turning back to look at me. He walks out of the exit and I lean back into my chair looking back to the movie that started a while ago. I haven't even paid attention to anything that happened. After about 20 minutes of waiting on Nick, I decide to get up and go search for him. As I walk the empty halls of the movie theater, suddenly, Nick walks out of the bathroom laughing and the guys from earlier walk out with him. He noticed me and looked at me with widened eyes. I noticed that his eyes were

dilated to an extreme amount. What was he doing in there?
I see as he pulls on his nose a little, then he asks me, "Hey, what are you doing here? Did the movie end already?" I look at him, taken aback, "Uh, the movie isn't done yet but after a while of waiting for you, I figured I'd come looking for you." He looks to the boys then back to me with a smirk. "You missed me, huh?" The boys laugh at his words. I give him a confused look. I really need to leave, I can't be here with him any longer. He is acting really weird. "Can you take me home?" His eyebrows lift in amusement, "Already?" The boys behind him cackle at the innuendo. I take a deep breath. "Please, Nick." He turns to the boys, "Alright guys, it's been fun. Gotta go. See you guys." The boys say their goodbyes as they go back into their movie theater. Nick and I walk out of the theater. As we do, Nick covers his eyes with his hand. The fluorescent lights affecting him. They were bright but they didn't really bother. I looked back to him as he adjusted a little. I notice his eyes were red rimmed and bloodshot, also with the dilation. I knew exactly what was wrong with him, everything clicking into place. He was high off his ass. Wow, I couldn't fucking believe it. He starts walking towards the parking lot and to his car. I follow him, contemplating what to do next. I can't get in the car with him in his state. God knows what will happen to us. As we get to his car, I cross my arms over my chest defensively. "Are you high, Nick?" He turns towards me and laughs exactly the same way he did when we were at that restaurant. I step back a little frightened by his behavior. "Get in the car, Aphrodite." "I'm not going with you like this." I say, sternly. "Get in the car." He grits his teeth. I uncross my arms as I say, "At least let me drive or something." He walks

closer to me and opens the passenger door, “Get in.” I gulp and shake my head no. He grabs my arms, his grip tightening to the point of pain and pushes me trying to get me into the seat. “Nick! You're hurting me! Get off of me! ” I thrash in his hold but he doesn’t release me. He sets me down on the chair and without thinking, fight or flight mechanism sets in. I push my knee up into his ball with all my force. He grunts in pain, he instantly releases me and falls to the floor, clutching himself. I jump to my feet and dash as fast as I can. As I’m running I grab my phone, quickly dialing Adonis’ number. I hear Nick grunting as he follows me. “Hello?” Comes a voice that belongs to one of Adonis’ friends. I hear noise in the back but pay no attention as I scream, “Help! he’s going to hurt me!”

“Where are you?” I realized it was Cain on the other line.

“I’m at the Edwards cinema, please Cain, I need you to come pick-“ sharp pain runs through my skull as I am being pulled aggressively by my hair to the floor. I scream loudly. When my head hits the cement, a yelp leaves my lips in pain. I look up with wide eyes to a menacing look on Nick's face as he straddles my stomach, his hand still in my hair. “Who was it, Aphrodite? Who did you call?” I don’t answer him as he grabs my phone from my hand. He looks at me with wide eyes, “What the fuck did you just do?! You crazy bitch!” He lifts his hand from my hair, forming it into a fist, colliding it with my jaw. I scream out in agony. He grabs my phone and smashes it to the ground. As he quickly stands up, I grab onto my aching jaw, groaning in pain. He gives me a glance and I turn my head as he walks away to his car. He gets in and drives away.

What the hell did I get myself into? I sit up, my head spinning a little and immediately taste blood in my mouth. I quickly spit it out and gag a little at the strong coppery taste. I put my hand to my face. From what I can feel, he busted my lip. I pull my hand back to see more blood on my fingers. I reached out to grab my phone and there was no way it was going to start, it was completely shattered. I click the button to the side in hopes of it starting but nothing. I hear a loud engine in the distance and quickly stand to my feet, hoping it wasn't Nick coming back to finish me off but then I catch a glimpse of Cain's motorcycle in the distance and I feel a weight being lifted off my chest. He speeds right in front of me parking his bike without shutting it off. He takes off his helmet quickly and runs toward me. "Oh my god! Are you okay? We're gonna kill that mother fucker." He leans forward and quickly brings me into his arms and I start to sob into his jacket. "Oh God, Cain. I should have listened to him. Adonis was right." He pulls back and examines my face with a frown. "Don't worry about him, Aphrodite. He won't be mad at you." He knew exactly what I was thinking. "Let's go, I need to take you to him now." He grabs my hand and pulls me onto his motorcycle and I straddle it. "Where is he?" I was confused, Adonis isn't here but Cain has to take me to him. That makes no sense at all. Cain frowns at me again while setting the helmet onto my head cautiously. "You'll see in a little bit." He climbs onto the bike right in front of me saying, "Hold on tight, Ditee." I do as he instructed and wrap my arms around his waist holding on super tight. He drives off and I lean my head on his back closing my eyes tight as tears fall from them silently.

\

Chapter
Twenty-Seven
I should Have Listened

Cain parks his bike inside of a rundown shopping center parking lot. I look around confused while climbing off of the motorcycle. I take off the helmet and pass it to Cain, who sets it down on his bike. My face felt sore and swollen but I tried to ignore it the best I could as I tried to understand where Cain brought me. I look at Cain questioningly but he shakes his head, grabbing my hand and pulling me towards a little alley in between two stores and I noticed a staircase going down along a wall and a dark railing going down it. Cain pulls me down and I follow him, “Where are we?” I ask but don’t get a response as we continue down the large staircase. I start hearing noises coming through the large steel double doors at the end of the stairs. It sounds like screaming and yelling. I halt immediately and Cain turns towards me, worry, clear on his face, “Don’t worry, Aphrodite. You’re safe now. Trust me.” I nod and he walks down the last steps to the door. He knocks loudly and the door gets opened by a man that was almost seven feet tall, he had a huge neck and his arms were covered in tattoos. He was wearing a black tank top that said “The Undergrounds”, in bold letters on his chest. I hear loud cheers coming through the door and my eyes widen. “Hey, Cain.” He tilts his head towards me. “Who’s the girl?” Cain smiles but the smile doesn’t reach his eyes. “This is Adonis’ girl. He asked me to bring her.” The man nods and moves to the side and allows us to walk in. Whatever thought I had, vanished from my mind as we entered a large room that looked more like a boxing arena. Hold on...scratch that...it *was* a boxing arena. There were hundreds of men and women but everyone was dressed so elegantly as if they were at a party or

something. In the middle of the arena was a boxing ring and two men were fighting.
Cain pulls me through the isles of the chairs. Hoots and howlers were getting louder as the fighters got deeper into their fight. As we get closer, I look towards the fighters and my heart stops in my chest. Adonis was in that ring. At this point, Cain is literally pulling me as I am unable to really understand what was going on. I couldn't even register the fact that I had to walk. My heart was pounding loudly as we kept getting closer. Adonis was shirtless with loose black shorts. His hands were wrapped in white tape. As I got even closer, I noticed they had some blood on them. I noticed how close we were getting. We ended up on the side of the boxing ring. James, Liam, and Hudson were there. They all look at me wide-eyed but I don't give them a second glance as I look towards my best friend fighting in a boxing ring. I never would have thought of him doing this. It never even crossed my mind. Then his necklace hanging from his chest the other day flashes through my head. He had a boxing glove hanging from his neck. Should I have realized then. From what I can see, Adonis was good, he threw an uppercut into the other guy's jaw angrily. His whole stance was angry. Every punch was thrown in anger. His eyes were livid. The other guy did not even get anything in. He moves to the side and now Adonis is facing us, he hasn't seen me yet as his focus was on his opponent. As he throws a punch to the man's head, his gaze falls towards us and his eyes land on mine. Our eyes lock and shock and anger flash through his eyes, most of all, concern. He searches my face and his eyes widened. I swallow spit and like the idiot I am, I wave at him. Suddenly, the other boxer punches Adonis right on the side of his face and I scream out as his head flies to the side.

Before anyone can react, Adonis quickly recovers, takes a quick look at me, then turns back to his opponent. In one instant he throws two punches to the man. One to his jaw and the other, an uppercut sending the man's body flying backwards to the floor. My mouth dropped and I was frozen in shock from what I just witnessed.
Adonis quickly turns around and runs to the ropes sliding under them. He reaches me and grabs my face in his wrapped hands. His chest was rising and falling as he breathed heavily. His pale eyes examined my face and for some reason, I was shaking in fear. Fear of what he was thinking and I was also still a little affected about what happened with Nick. He pulls me into his arms and my heart starts pounding even harder and tears well up in my eyes again. He pulls away and grabs my hand. There was way too much noise going on so he didn't even try to talk. He leads me through the large crowds as they all try to get to him. The boys push people away from us and make a path for us to walk forward. We go through a long hallway, then reach a locker room. As we enter, he quickly turns towards me, "What happened?" His words came out stern and I couldn't help it. Tears started falling from my face.
"I'm so...so sorry Adonis. I... I didn't know. I should have listened to you." The words come out choked as I feel a huge lump in my throat. He grabs onto my face again, "Don't tell me it was him that did this?" He looks towards the boys, his hands still holding my face. His body is still centimeters away. "What happened?"
"She called your phone while you were in the ring and I went after her. I found her that way." Cain said, rushing over his words nervously. Adonis looks back to me, his eyes softening a little, "Baby girl, listen to

me. I am not mad at you. This is not your fault but you need to explain to me what happened." I swallow and then stumble over my words as I say, "He got mad because I wouldn't get in the car with him." His eyes squint in confusion, "Why didn't you get in the car with him?" I look down as I say, "He was high. He met some friends there at the movies and he got lost for a while. When I went to find him, he was super high." I shake my head, disappointed in myself. I frown sadly as I continue telling him what happened, tears streaming down my bruised face. He wipes my tears away and pulls me into his arms, hugging me close to him. "Don't worry baby, you're okay now. Nothing is going to happen to you. Let's go home." Those words make me feel so safe. Every fear and doubts I had were gone. I knew Adonis was going to protect me no matter what.

He pulls away from me and wraps his arm around my shoulder. He looks at James sternly, "Find him." My heart stops in my chest, knowing exactly what he was planning on doing. I look up to his face as he says, "And leave him to me." I looked at the boys, they all looked angry and murderous. They were all ready to do what Adonis wanted. I look around at the locker room and am awestruck at everything that happened in the last few hours. We walk out of what looks like a back door out of this place, away from the crowds. Walking up the stairs, I wrap my arms around Adonis and put my face in his chest. We got to the shopping center that I now realize was full of cars at this late hour. Cain gives something to Adonis, and I look down to see his keys and phone. Cain smiles sadly at me and reaches behind his back, pulling out his phone he says, "just in case." I grabbed it and right before I can reply he walks away towards his bike. Adonis tugs me towards his car, and I go to pull away

from him but he doesn't let me. He moved his arm around my waist as he opened his car door and took a seat. With one arm still around my waist, I again go to move away and walk to the passenger side.
"Adonis?" I whisper his name in question as he keeps me from moving again.
He pulls me onto his lap, "Please, let me just hold you." My eyebrows raise and I nod, not being able to say anything. He lifts me up and I straddle him. I realized that he wanted to drive while holding me and I quickly looked at him perplexed, "No Don, this is dangerous." He reaches over and shuts the car door. Without a word, he looked up at me as I was sitting on my knees, which gave me height over him. He starts the engine, his eyes still locked on mine.
He puts one hand on my hip and pulls me down so that I am sitting on his lap while still straddling him. He brings the same hand and puts it on my head, leading it to his shoulder. Once my face nestled into his neck, he wrapped that same arm around me. I wrapped one arm under the one he had on the steering wheel and the other around his shoulders. Our bodies were flush against each other. There was so much I wanted to know, there was so much I needed to say but at this moment, no words were able to leave my lips. He drives off and I feel the rumble of the car as he speeds up. How can one person make you feel so safe? Earlier, I was the most scared I have ever been and the first thought I had was to call Adonis. Having him this close, being wrapped around him this way, felt strange but at the same time, felt really good. He quiets my fears with one touch and with one look, I know I am safe. I kiss his neck softly and whisper, "Thank you." He turns his head towards me and kisses my cheek, "Don't thank me." My heart flutters in my chest and I can still feel the ghost of his lips on

my cheek. I relax a little more in his hold and he wraps his arm tighter around me.
After a few minutes, I felt the car slowing down so I brought my face out of its little safe place and saw that he was driving into my driveway. He parks the car and opens the door for us to get out. He helps me climb off him, then he follows me out. He walks me to my door, holding onto my hand. He unlocks the door and pushes it open. My hand still in his, we walk up the stairs and into my room. Looking him over, I noticed how stiff his whole body was, I can tell he was on edge. He leads me into my restroom and without a word, he leads me to the chair at my vanity and I take a seat. I watch him slowly pace in front of me, still only wearing his boxing shorts and shoes. Wraps still on his hands. I think he realized he still had them on too because he starts unwrapping them, his muscles flexing constantly as he quickly unwraps his hands angrily. He throws the first one onto the floor, then continues with the next hand wrap. His chest was lifting heavily with every breath. His jaw was as hard as granite and his face was flushed. His whole body screamed distress. As I sat there watching him, my breathing quickens, knowing this wasn't going to end well. I never needed him like this before. Throwing the other tape on the floor, he turns towards me and stands right in front of me, looking my face over, still breathing heavily, "Where else did he hurt you?" I search his face for answers. There are so many different emotions there but most of all, I see worry. I shake my head, "Nowhere. It's just my face."
He crouches in front of me, looking me over. "Is your head okay?" Not waiting for my reply, he reaches up and puts his fingers into my hair, searching my scalp for a bump. My head hurts a little but I knew he wasn't going to find anything. "Does your head hurt?" His

eyes meet mine dead, waiting for my answer. I nod my head yes and with a frown he said, “I need words Aphrodite.” I sigh, “Adonis, I'm fine.” My eyes, not meeting his as I say those words softly, trying to sound like I am telling the truth. I didn't want to get him more upset. I needed to find a way to make him understand I am okay. He gives me a hard look and grabs my face into his hands. “You're not fine. This is not okay. This will never be okay.” I frown sadly at the thought of what I went through and a tear slips down my face uninvitedly. I wanted to be strong, I didn't want him to see me like this but it was so hard. He lets go of my face and his face falls into my lap. He sighs loudly and I bring my hand to his head. “I'm so sorry. I'm so so sorry.” His words came out a little muffled, his breathing was coming out in pants. “It isn't your fault.” I say softly, my hand still on his head. He looks up to me, his eyes going straight to my busted lip. “Let me clean you up.”
He stands up and searches in the drawers under my sink. He pulls out a first aid kit and sets it on the counter closest to me. He opens it and gets out what he wanted. He brings out antibiotic cream and a cotton swab. He applies the ointment to the swab and then crouches in front of me again. He brings the cotton to my lip and gently pats it on, looking at my lips with a frown his forehead is wrinkled in concern. I want to take that frown off his face and I want to flatten those lines. After he is done, he stands up and looks for something else inside the box. He pulls out a little packet of painkillers and opens it. He grabs the cup from my sink and fills it with water. He passes it to me and I take it from him saying, “Thank you.” He doesn't reply as he watches me take the pills. He grabs the cup from me, puts it on the counter, and

washes his hands. He extends his hand towards me and says, “Let's get you changed.”
I take a deep breath and grab his hand. He pulls me towards my closet and before I can even look for something, he opens a drawer and pulls out one of my big sleeping shirts. He passes it to me and looks at me expectedly. I give him a questioning look, “What?” I realize he expects me to change in front of him. “Change,” He says plainly. I blink a few times, grabbing the shirt from his hand, “I’m not changing in front of you.”
“Change,” The words come out sternly this time. For some reason, I obey his command and set my shirt on a nearby shelf. Giving him my back, I lift my shirt over my head. My hot pink push up bra is now showing. I slip off my shoes, then peel off my pants, revealing my black panties. As I grab the shirt from the shelf, he says, “Turn around.”
I click my tongue and slowly turn towards him. I look to the floor, feeling his eyes run over my body, checking for injuries. With my face flushed in embarrassment, I say, “See? I’m fine.” He walks out of the closet and I slip my shirt on over my head. I walk out of my closet to find him leaning on my bedroom door, waiting for me. Walking up to him, I say looking up into his eyes pleadingly, “Don’t leave me.” He sighs leaning over and kisses me on the forehead, his lips staying there for a long second before he says, “I have to. I’ll be back before you know it.” He steps away from me and turns to walk away leaving me there.

Chapter Twenty-Eight

Let's Go For A Drive

I pace in my room, Cain's phone in hand. I waited impatiently for Adonis to call me. My mind runs through different scenarios and all of them end with Adonis full of blood. I try to swallow the lump that is stuck in my throat, but I am without luck. Instead of it going away, it just gets bigger and bigger as time passes. I shut my eyes tight and the only thing I see is Adonis getting punched in the face and his head whipping to the side as blood spits out of his mouth in the process. That will be sown into my head forever, I can't unsee it. I'm trying to understand why he didn't tell me. Does he think I was going to judge him for doing illegal underground fighting? Does he think I was going to hate him for it? If those are his reasons, then he doesn't know me at all. I don't care if that's what he likes to do. I do care if they are hurting him repeatedly and he allows it. That is the only thing that bothers me. He can get seriously hurt or worse. He is playing a dangerous game with this fighting thing. I take a deep breath and finally take a seat on my couch. Tucking my knees to my chest, I look to the phone again, for the thousandth time. With a deep frown, I look at the time. It was one in the morning. He dropped me off at home around eleven-thirty. It's only been an hour and a half but it feels like a lifetime. He shouldn't have taken so long, he should have been back by now. What if he really hurt Nick? What if Adonis got arrested? I rest my head on my knee and the phone rings loudly, startling me a little. I quickly answer without a second thought. "Hello?" I say timidly, not knowing what to expect. "Hey, baby girl. I'm outside." Hearing Adonis' voice makes my heart stop. What is he doing outside? Why didn't he come inside? I stand to my feet and walk over to the balcony door. I pull back the curtain and peek through. There he was, he was leaning against the hood of his black Porsche. His legs crossed, one arm under his chest and the other holding his phone to his ear, looking up at me. “Come down here.” He whispers and I give him a questioning look that I think he can’t even see. “Why aren’t you coming inside?” I say, sounding vulnerable and confused. “I want to talk to you first.” Talk to me? About what? Did something happen? Why was I so paranoid tonight? The craziest things keep going through my mind. “Let's go for a drive.”

I look down to what I am wearing, a big shirt and underwear. I frowned while nodding but then I realized, he might not be able to see so I answered him. “Okay, let me get dressed real quick. I’ll be right down.” I end the call and walk into my closet, I pick out white Calvin Klein joggers and a matching cropped hoodie. I quickly put it on, then slide on my tennies. I don’t even want to look at myself in the mirror so I walk out of my room and down the stairs, my heart beating faster with every step I take closer to the door. I open the door and step out, not looking at him just yet. I shut the door and locked it. When I turned towards him, the first thing I saw was that he wasn’t hurt. My hands were shaking for some reason but I still looked him over. He was wearing a clean white t-shirt and black jeans. His hair was wet from what looked like a recent shower and it was slicked back. Our eyes met, anger flashes through his pastel eyes at the way my face looked. His fist ball tightly but he tries to mask it all with a smile that doesn’t reach his eyes. I don’t blame him. I would have been livid if his lips were broken and swollen too. I walk up to him and wrap my arms around his waist, he instantly

wraps his around me too. His large arms drowned me completely. I breath in and his intoxicating smell of white cedar and vanilla fills my senses. “Are you okay?” I ask as I pull back from him just a little, my arms still on him. His eyebrows knit together as he says, “I’m fine. How do you feel?” Right now, I was a little numb because I took Ibuprofen. “I’m good. Those painkillers really helped.” I shrug a little and he frowns. “Where are we going”?” I ask him and he pushes off of his car. He grabs my hand and pulls me towards the passenger door, he opens it and helps me sit. I watch him, my eyebrows rising as he crouches down and leans forward. He grabs onto the seat belt and pulls it across my chest. My breathing quickened as he extended his hand, leaning over me to buckle the seat belt. His face was so close to mine, just centimeters away, I could lean in and kiss his lips. I mentally groan at that thought. I want to slap myself, I can’t think that way about him. These thoughts can ruin everything between us.
“Safety first.” He whispers, his eyes meeting mine for a split second. Then he pulls away too quickly for my liking. He shuts my door and walks around to his. He gets in and quickly shuts his door. He starts the engine, getting ready to pull out of the driveway. I glare at him as I say, “Safety first.” He chuckles and continues to back his car out not even planning on putting his seatbelt. He drives off and I lean back into my chair, my nerves settling a little. He starts the radio, lowers the volume, then clicks shuffle. Music starts playing slowly through the speakers. I look out the window as we pass house after house at this late hour, no lights are on. The street was dark and quiet. He suddenly turns off his headlights and I quickly look up to see the stars in the sky. When there are so many lights on, you can barely see the stars but now,

as I look up and there is no light around us, other than the ones coming from inside of the car, I can see the sky full of beautiful shining stars. I turned towards him and watched as he ran his free hand over his hair, his strong arm flexing. I so badly wanted to run my fingers through his hair. I looked him over, his white shirt stretched tight over his strong shoulders and chest. The shirt loosened just a bit as it reached his stomach. I looked at his hand that was resting on the middle console, trying to see if he had any cuts or bruises. Not being able to see anything, I grabbed it. His hand was heavy. I hold his hand in one of mine and inspect it with the other. His warm hand was sending sparks up mine but I tried to ignore it even though my stomach was filled with butterflies.
I noticed how his knuckles were swollen and red. I look up to him worriedly and he glances down to me, then looks back to the road. What did he do to Nick? I decide to put that thought aside and ask him later. Instead, I ask him, "Do they hurt you?" He looks at me again as he says, "No, I'm used to it." I blink a few times, then ask, "You're used to it?"
He looks back to the road, taking a smooth turn. "That's what I wanted to talk to you about." I want to know everything but if he isn't ready to talk about it, then he shouldn't. "Adonis, it's okay. I understand, you don't have to." He sighs, "Yes I do. I need to tell you everything and after you know everything, that is when you can decide what you want. If you don't want to be in my life anymore, I understand I won't fight it." What is he talking about? It's just fighting. Why is he making it seem worse than what I saw? "It doesn't change anything Adonis. I'm not leaving you."
He gives me a sad smile, then looks back at the road as he starts speaking. "It all started a few weeks after you left for England. I was just so angry all the time,

picking fights at school for the stupidest reason but it wouldn't lead to violence...well…that was until I saw my father fucking that woman in his office. Then I began getting into a lot of fights. Then I fought out of school too. This man kept following me, his name is Carter. He works for a very powerful man named Benjamin. Carter followed me for weeks. When he finally approached me, I was downtown at the police department." I gasped at that but he continued, "I was being charged for assault and battery. I was gonna see six months of the inside of a jail cell if it wasn't for Carter. My father didn't want anything to do with me. He wanted to leave me in there." I sit up straight in my seat, finally letting go of his large hand, "Why didn't your father want to get you out?" Mr. Clark is an evil man but he would never do that to his son. Adonis takes a deep breath, "That is an even longer story. I noticed my father was doing something weird. I didn't find out what it was until recently. Back then, he knew I was close to finding out so he wanted me to stay locked up." I slump my shoulders with a deep sigh. He continues looking at the dark road as he keeps speaking, "So, Carter got me out. I was shocked to say the least, to see a man I didn't know, bail me out. Not only that, he deleted any record of my arrest. He told me he has been watching me and likes the way I fight. I was very confused at first but I went with it. He took me to The Undergrounds, that is where I met Benjamin for the first time. Benjamin told me I had potential, he told me he wanted me to train and fight for him. He taught me how to channel all my anger in my fighting. After a few weeks of training, I had my first fight. And I won. That same night, Benjamin told me who he really was and what he did. I thought he was just a man who organizes fights for rich people to watch. I never have been more wrong. Benjamin is the leader of the American Mafia." He looks at me with a worried look waiting for my reaction. I honestly didn't know how to react to this. I turned my face towards the windshield, a million things running through my mind but right now, I only want to know one thing. "Are you in the mafia?" He takes a deep breath while making a left turn, before answering my question. "I help them." I give him a questioning look, "What does that mean?" I saw him visibly gulp, he was nervous. I grab his hand again, this time interlacing my fingers with his. "Hey, look at me." He slows down the car in the middle of the empty road. He turns his head towards me, worried, clear on his face. I rub the back of his palm with my thumb as I say, "Whatever you tell me tonight, won't change anything." My voice is filled with a thousand promises but I mean everyone of them.

Our eyes lock as he searches mine helplessly. He nods, then with the hand that was holding the steering wheel, he grabs his bottom lip in between his thumb and forefinger. With a loud sigh, he put his hand back on the wheel and pressed on the accelerator, going faster by the second. He tightened his grip on my hand as he started, "They need me to hurt people for answers. I'm sort of the 'hired fist'. That's where me and the boys all work together. Other than that, I have to fight for Benjamin whenever he wants, against whoever he wants." I furrowed my eyebrows, looking at his side profile as I asked, "Are you being forced to do it?" Adonis chuckles and shakes his head, "There have been a lot of times that I was without choice but with this, Benjamin always made sure that I was okay with this. I enjoy what I do, it makes me feel..." He breathes out heavily, then continues, "It feels like I finally have control in my life. I can control what happens to that person. I can choose if he lives or dies, no one can take that away from me. There was only one time I couldn't control myself while I was fighting." I look at him curiously as he takes a quick glance at me. "Today, when I was hitting Nick, I couldn't see straight. That doesn't happen to me. I'm always in control...but all I can see is the way he hurt you. Just thinking about it now, I want to turn this car around and go back and continue where I left off." I squeeze his hand but he continues, "James had to scream at me to come back. He had to explain to me that you were waiting for me and I needed to leave." He gives me another quick glance, "I needed to get back to you, it killed me to leave you after what he did to you." My breathing was heavy and I was a little bewildered at everything he just told me. I was also so worried about what he did to Nick but there was nothing I could do about that now. I frowned, my eyebrows lowering. I know if I ask him if Nick is okay, he will get furious. I'll ask one of the boys another time. There was silence and I knew Adonis was trying to put his thoughts in order so he could continue what he was telling me.

I run my free hand through my hair and I whisper, "Tell me more." He bites down on his bottom lip, contemplating his next words. I looked around to see we were no longer around houses and were now on a quiet street, filled with stores and shopping centers. There weren't any cars on the street, I think it was because it was the middle of the week and also the late hour. "Benjamin doesn't have any children, he can't have any. So he wants me to be his heir. I don't want to be. I never really admit that I am even in his mafia. The thought of me being a mafia boss is too much for me." Okay, that is too much. My mind isn't putting the pieces together at his words. I don't understand out of everyone, why Adonis? "Why you?"

Adonis smiles a little as he speaks, "Benjamin always says that he sees himself in me. We constantly fight about it." He chuckles a little and shakes his head. He was really fond of this man, you can see the respect he held for him as he talked about him. He never talked about his father this way, not even before. "Ben trained me himself. He has never done that for anyone. I really appreciate everything he has done for me but I won't take that title from him. I don't even know half of what it means to be a mob boss. He doesn't get it through his thick skull though." So all this has been happening to him. Is that why he stopped talking to me? Is that why he ignored me and didn't want to see me when I came back? "Is all this the reason you stopped talking to me then?" He nods, frowning a little, "Yes, that is exactly why. I didn't want to pull you into this life but then I didn't give you the option, now I am. If you want, I can leave you home now and you never have to see me again. We can go back to being strangers." Even thinking that, has my heart hurting. I know everything he's doing is dangerous and illegal. Everything he said, won't keep me from being in his life. The only thing that will keep me out is him. If he doesn't want me in his life, that's fine. I'll get out. But as long as he wants me in his life, then I'll stay.
"The only thing, Adonis, that can keep me from being in your life is you. No one and nothing can keep me from you. Nothing you do will come between us. I want to be in your life. I don't think I can stand to be away from you anymore. You're my best friend. We have been through everything together and I'll go through so much more with you, without question." I take a big gulp at the end of my speech and he looks towards me with shock and happiness on his face. I lean forward and give him a quick kiss on his cheek.

He chuckles and I quickly sit back down. He turns his face to look at me and says, “I’m glad you didn’t get crazy-scared and say you were going to run as far away from me as possible. I wasn’t expecting you to be so calm about it.” I snicker a little as I say, “It's not really hard to believe, Adonis. I mean, look at you. You look like a criminal, I wasn’t even that surprised when Cain took me down to that place. I probably wouldn’t have been surprised if you told me you sold drugs on the street corner.” I shrug nonchalantly and he fake gasps. “I would never stoop so low as to sell drugs on the street corner. We have people who do that.” I chuckled at that, shaking my head, and rolling my eyes. He was probably half serious too. With a small smile, I say, “Let's go home, bad boy.” He groans at the nickname but then gives me a grin. He makes a quick u-turn and then drives back towards where we came from. He smiles a beautiful smile, looking out to the road. His whole body was so much more relaxed now, from when he barely picked me up. His arm that held the steering wheel, wasn't clutching it in a death grip anymore. His jaw isn’t as hard as a rock like it was just moments ago. The fingers interlaced in mine were more relaxed. I look to our hands. My hands were engulfed in his completely but at the same time, our hands fit perfectly together. Butterflies started stirring up in my stomach again and I tried to forget about them but it was really hard.

Chapter Twenty-Nine

What Did I Do?

We walked into my room and I turned around to him smiling shyly. “Are you staying over with me?” He nods, giving me a small smile, “If you want me to.” I nod and he shrugs, “Okay.” I walk towards my bed, I pull down my sheets, and climb into it, sitting against the headboard and pull the blanket over me. I look at him as he stands there contemplating what to do. I pat the side next to me and say, “C’mon like old times.” He smirks at me and pulls up the hem of his shirt, my eyes bulging out of their sockets. His body looked alot more defined tonight. Maybe it was because he fought so much tonight or something. He looked so incredible, I wanted to run my hands down his chest. I wanted to feel every muscle under my fingers. He chuckles under his breath, shaking his head as he walks towards the opposite side of the bed. I watch his tattooed body climb onto the bed. I’d be a total liar if I said I didn’t like the idea of him being in my bed without a shirt. After he gets on the left side of the bed, I lay down on my side, facing him and he does the same, over the blanket, facing me. I know I was giving him a weird look because he says, “What?”
I decide on being honest, “I really like your tattoos.” I purse my lips and shrug. “Oh yeah?” He asked, a little amused. “Yeah, they really suit you.” I go to bite down on my bottom lip without thinking and I wince at the slight pain in my busted lip. He gives a remorseful look, “I’m so sorry that happened to you, Aphrodite.” I shake my head, “I’m okay. It’s not your fault.” He shuts his eyes for a second, then opens them as he

says, “Yes it is. I knew exactly what kind of guy he was and I still allowed you to go out with him. I should have never let that happen.” I put my hand on his cheek that was just about a foot away from me, “Stop, don’t do that. If we dwell on what-ifs, we won’t get anywhere. It happened, there’s nothing we can do now.” I look into his eyes to see he understands that I am okay and I don’t blame him. He nods, my hand still on his cheek, “You’re right. I just wish I can take all that pain away from you.” He leans forward and brings his hand to my lips. His eyes flashing to mine for a second before looking back to my lips and sweeping his thumb over them slowly. They part on their own accord. I look at his soft, plump lips as they part too and his breathing stills.
I look up to his light colored eyes and they meet mine, my breathing quickening with every millisecond passing. Suddenly, he leaned forward and all thoughts drowned into nothingness as his lips touched mine gently. His lips barely pecked my hurt bottom lip. Before I can react to the feel of his soft lips on mine, he pulls away. His eyes widened in shock at what he just did. He lifts himself on his elbow, “I’m so sor-“ I don’t know what got into me. Maybe it was everything that happened tonight. Maybe it was the fact that his smell of cedarwood and vanilla was floating all around me. Or maybe it was because the ghost of his lips pressed to mine was still there and I needed to feel it again. Before he finished whatever he was gonna say, I pressed my lips to his. I have never kissed anyone in my life but kissing Adonis was so natural to me. He sucks in a breath as I lightly suck on his bottom lip. It took him some time but he finally kissed me back. He brings his free hand to my cheek and continues to kiss me. Our lips didn’t move as if Adonis was waiting to see how far I wanted to take

this. All I know is that I didn't plan on stopping anytime soon. I kissed him again, this time with two long pecks in a row that made my stomach flip. I reach up to the back of his head and pull him closer. I tilt my head to the other side. This time, Adonis takes the lead and he kisses me deeper, his breathing and mine getting heavier. He releases my face and puts his hand on my hip, pulling me so I was flushed against him. Our lips started moving faster, the pressure in my lips stinging a little but I ignored it. I wanted more, I wanted to feel him all over. His lips on mine felt so exhilarating but his hand on my hip made me want to have them everywhere. I felt him being gentle and cautious but I wasn't having it. I push on his shoulder as we continue to move our lips against each other, making him lay back. I hike my leg over his, slowly straddling him, my body aligned with his. My chest pressed to his, he brought his hand that was on my hip, up my back and under my hoodie, then back down to the small of my back, making me shutter in anticipation. My heart was hammering in my chest and from the feel of him, I knew his was too. He grabs my hips with both hands and his grip tightens deliciously. My hips move mindlessly on his lap creating a friction I so desperately needed. I felt *him* under me and he breathed in heavily with a slight purr. At that moment, reality started settling in and the consequences of what this kiss will lead. The thought of him realizing that he doesn't want this, scares me. It scares me because our friendship will get ruined instantly and I don't want to lose him because of one simple act of impulse. Thinking this, I am still not able to pull away. The feeling of him was too good to stop. As his lips meet my bottom lip, he sucks on it making me wince. Before I can pull away, he sits up bringing me with him as our lips separate.

With wide eyes, he searches my face and as they settle on my injured lips, he brings his hand up and touches them lightly. “Are you okay? Did I hurt you?” He asked worriedly. I nodded slightly, “I’m okay.” I look to the side, not meeting his eyes, “I’m sorry, I don’t know what came over me.” With a frown, I lift up my hand and push a piece of my hair behind my ear. He reaches up to caress my cheek and I look back to him as he says, “It's okay, baby girl. Don’t worry about it. We should get some rest.” I agree and slowly climb off of him and lay on my side, bringing the blanket over myself again, looking away from him. My cheeks were burning hot, my heart was still fluttering in my chest. On top of all that, my whole body was shaking. “Goodnight,” I whisper, not trusting my voice to speak normally. I didn’t feel him move a muscle so he was still sitting against the headboard, I wasn’t expecting a reply from him because I know he was as shocked as I was. I bring my fingertips to my lips and close my eyes, a small smile covering my face. I sigh softly, then suddenly, hear his husky voice say, “Goodnight.” The words were thicker than normal, his breathing slowly calming with every second. As time passes, all I can think about is his body right next to mine. The feeling of his lips pressed to mine was still there and I wanted to feel them again. I feel him shuffling in the bed and know he finally laid down, still over the blanket. For some reason, I really appreciate that because if he was here under the blanket with me, I don’t know where that would lead.

I REACHED OUT A hand in search of the warmth from last night but didn't find anything. I keep searching more frantically with my eyes still closed. Memories from last night start flooding into my mind all at once. *Adonis leaving my house angrily. My date* *with Nick. Nick punching me in the face. Getting on the back of a motorcycle.* My breathing started getting heavier as the memories kept coming. *Adonis getting hit so hard blood spattered out of his mouth, Adonis running towards me and grabbing my face in his large hands. Adonis taking me home wrapped in his arms. Driving down the road without lights and Adonis admitting everything to me. A kiss being shared by two best friends right here in my bed.* My eyes pop open completely at the last memory. Oh no…what did I do? Fuck. I jump out of my bed, looking around my room in search of any signs of Adonis. When I finally looked at where he fell asleep last night, I realized with a heavy heart, he left me…I take a deep breath as I think. *This is all my fault.* I run my hands through my hair and take a seat on my bed, putting my face into my hands. After everything we talked about. After admitting to each other that we didn't want to be apart anymore, I go and fuck everything up with a simple kiss. I know he felt awkward and decided to leave so he wouldn't have to face me. I pull my face into my hands sadly, feeling tears well up in my eyes. What have I done to my best friend? Then, I remember how he kissed me first. That first kiss he stole from my lips. I lift my face from my hands and touch my swollen lips with two of my fingers, a tear slipping down my cheek. I hear a noise coming from my bathroom and I quickly wipe my face and blink a few times. As I do, the bathroom door opens and Adonis walks out in just his jeans, towel drying his hair with one hand. My eyebrows knit together and the words slip out of my mouth without thinking, "You're here?" He looks towards me questioningly, "Of course. Where else would I be?" I watch as he walks to the couch, blinking a few times. He grabs his shirt from the chair and I watch his muscles flex as he puts the shirt on. A lot of sinful thoughts run through my head. The one that keeps playing is, running my hands over his body, tracing his tattoos. He turns his back facing me as he puts his shirt on, after I got a perfect view of the beautiful black wings on his toned back. As he turns towards me, he smiles and leans his head to the side, examining my face with his eyes. I smile back, the smile not reaching my eyes. “Do you have plans for today?” I ask timidly. He nods, “Yes. I’m going to be busy all day.” I look to the side as I answer him, “Oh, that's good.” Then he continues, “I’m going to be hanging out with my best friend all day.” I look back to him and he shrugs.

Chapter Thirty

Pure Lies

Walking into the mall with Adonis by my side was a little peculiar, to be honest. Especially after last night. We have both been pretending nothing happened, even though the elephant was definitely in the room and it was suffocating me. I think we both silently agreed that we were going to move past it. He waited patiently for me to shower and get ready at home. He also made sure I ate toast with my pain meds, which was so sweet of him. Then, the car ride over was short and thankfully he filled the silence with music. I really need to swallow this awkwardness because if I don't, it will just get worse. As we pass Nike, I ask him, "Hey, I never asked; Is there a date for the surgery yet?" He looks towards me and shakes his head, "Not officially, no. Your father wants to do it sometime next week though." I frown a little, "How is she feeling? I haven't called her." I feel so disappointed in myself, I should call her daily to check up on her. "She's actually holding up pretty well, I was expecting her to be weak or something but she's good." I smile as we keep walking past a few stores. "That's good, I'm glad. She is a fighter." He shakes his head, agreeing with me. He then pulls me towards a department store. We walk in on the beauty level. "Do you need anything?" He asked me, looking around all the different makeup booths. I think it over a little. Do I need anything? Other than him kissing me again, no, I don't need anything. I shake my head, "No, not really." Passing the makeup department, we get to the accessories and I grab the first thing my hand touches, a pair of sunglasses. I put them on and look towards Adonis. He grins at me and grabs a nearby scarf, wrapping it around my neck. I quickly grab a big hat, setting it on my head as well. I walk towards a mirror and pose, trying to look posh. As I look myself over, I giggle a little, then look at Adonis

through the mirror, trying to put a straight face on. I attempt at a Russian accent and say, "Do I look like one of those rich mafia wives that go to your fights?" He chuckles, shaking his head, "Yeah, you do. And with that accent, you will fit right in." I look at his eyes, smiling a little, "Perfect. When's your next fight? So I can get ready, you know?" He raises his eyebrow, his lips forming a line, "That's not gonna happen." I quickly take the sunglasses off and set them on the table next to me. I turn towards him and put both my hands on my hips. He was closer than I was expecting but I pretended it didn't affect me. I give him a mock shocked look, "What?! You won't let *me*, your best friend, that you have known all your life, might I add, go see you fight?" I shake my head a little, adding to the drama, "That stings."
He smiles, his eyes crinkling a little. He knows I'm only half joking. "Yes. That place is too dangerous for you. You know I can't let anything happen to you." My shoulders slumped and I frown a bit, "What's the worst that could happen? I'll just be sitting down, watching you fight another man. I promise I won't get in your way." I walk past him and throw the scarf on the closest display table, leaving the hat on, and keep walking as Adonis is following me. I walk to the section with all the bags, grabbing one and putting it on my shoulder. I looked down at it, It was a brown alligator skin and it was hideous. I grimace and set it back down. I keep walking, passing the purses all together when I hear from behind me, "You could get seriously hurt." I give him a quick glance over my shoulder, then continue walking. "I don't think I'll be able to handle you getting hurt again, baby girl." I blink and spin around towards him. I look up to find his body almost flushed against me. His face was so close to mine, I can literally just get on my tiptoes a

little and press my lips to his. I take a step back, mentally shaking my head. I roll my eyes, “I'll be fine. Besides, the boys will be there. They'll protect me.“ I make air quotes with my fingers as I say the last sentence. He looks behind me as he says, “We can have this conversation another time.” Pure lies. That's what he said, pure lies. That's why he didn't look at me as he said those words. I shrug, “Yeah. Whatever.” I am definitely not giving up on this conversation.
I turn around and continue walking through the huge department store that was three stories tall. I get on the escalator going up without even asking him but he easily follows me. I turned my back towards the direction the stairs were going. “So tell me; what do the guys do? If you fight, what's their job?” His eyes weren't on mine, they were looking behind me, worriedly. He was scared I was gonna fall on my ass. “They all have a different job. Everyone has a part.” Before he can say anything else, he wraps his arm around my waist and lifts me up a little. I yelp but he steps off as the escalator ends, setting me on the ground. I look up at him bewildered and look back at the escalator. I nod at him, “Thanks.” He chuckles and gestures for me to keep walking and I do just that. I turn and walk towards the women's clothing, Adonis again following me.
Walking through the racks of clothing, I say, “Tell me more about the boys...well, if you want. “ I turn my face back to him and he shrugs. I grabbed onto a shirt I liked and passed it to him so he could hold it. He takes a deep breath but grabs it and slings it on his arm. He starts talking and I don't turn back to him. I just keep giving him articles of clothing to hold, “James, he is the organizer. We give him the idea and he puts the whole plan in motion.” I nod as I grab a

dress and pass it to him. I spot the dressing room and walk towards it, grabbing a few more dresses in the process, holding them myself. There isn't anyone there so I walk into the fitting room, Adonis sitting on a chair near the three connected mirrors where you can look at yourself perfectly. I look to all the dressing rooms and find the closest one. I opened the barn-style door and set down the dresses I had in my arms. I walk out, then go back and grab all the clothes Adonis was holding. "Are you at least gonna give me a little show?" I searched his face as his words had me a little shocked. The thoughts that ran through my head were completely different then what he meant. He adjusted himself on the chair, bringing his ankle over his knee. He put his elbows on the arms rest beside him and looked at me expectedly. Holding the clothes in my arms now, I shrug, "Maybe." I walk back into the room, the door swinging, closed behind me. Setting the clothes down on the bench and the hat on my head too, I lift my shirt over my head. He clears his throat and continues our conversation from earlier as I undress and put on a new outfit. "Liam is the technology man of the group. He can get you in and out of any building, any house, anywhere really. He can also find anyone and find out everything about them." I walk out wearing a cute, little black shirt with thick straps showing a little of my tummy and a black and white plaid skirt that reaches mid-thigh. "That's useful." Adonis was looking at his phone as I finished my sentence. He looked up, blinking a few times, putting his phone on his lap. He doesn't say anything as I walk up to the mirrors and step onto the platform, checking myself out. His eyes followed my every move. "Yeah, it really is." From the mirror, I can see his eyes looking me over. I try not to look at him so he doesn't know, I know, he is checking me out. This outfit is actually really cute and would look great with a leather jacket. I turn around and step off of the platform, walking back into the dressing room. He starts speaking again as I try on a new outfit. “Hudson is really smart too but in a different way. He’s good at reading body language.” I walk out of the room in a little pink slip dress. He looks me over and I do a little twirl for him. As I turn back to him, I see a weird dark look in his eyes. I looked back to the platform but decided against going up there. I just turn on my heel and walk back into the room. “You were saying?” I edge him on. That look was too much on my weak heart. I needed to hear him talking and I needed to stop picturing him walking in here and taking this dress off of me because that's all the look was saying. He wanted to do just that. And the truth is, If he opened this door right now, I would let him do anything he wanted. “Yeah, umm...” I hear him shuffling a little but then he continues, “Hudson can always tell if people are lying. Most of the time, he knows exactly what people are thinking.” I put on a white, lace dress that had a deep cut at the neckline, the skirt of the dress reaching just above my knee. I walk out and smile at him, “So like a mind reader?” He chuckles as his eyes rake down my body, then says in a thicker voice, “Yeah, I guess.” This time, I step on the platform and twirl a little, really loving the dress. I smile as I look myself over, “What do you think?” I turn my head towards him and he smiles a crooked smile, “Gorgeous.” I look back at myself. The swelling on my lips weren’t as bad as yesterday but they were still wounded. My chin and part of my jaw was a little bruised. I was looking my face over with a frown and he noticed, “That doesn’t change anything princess, you look beautiful.” I turn around and smile at him sadly, with a small shrug.

I walk back into the room and quickly change into another outfit. "And what about Cain?" I ask, when I walk out. I step onto the platform again and inspect the dress I was wearing. It was a red dress that reached mid-thigh with tiny flowers on it. It was off the shoulders and crinkled a little under and over my breast, with thin strings in the middle that formed into a little bow. I again watch as he looks me over, this time looking at him as I wait for my answer. His eyes meet mine in the mirror and he says, "Cain is our beginning and the end. He distracts when needed and always cleans up when we're done. He knows exactly how not to leave any traces of anything." I turn around and look at him, "And you? Other than fighting, what do you do?" He leans back into his chair, "Lets just say...what I say goes, no one questions me." I lift an eyebrow and smirk at him, "So you're saying you give all the commands?" He nods, "Yes. And I am commanding you to hurry up." I lift my eyebrows, "Do you like being in charge?" I watch him visibly swallow spit at my words. I don't know what got into me. Maybe it was the way he kept looking at me. "Yes, I like being in control." I purse my lips at his words and look him up and down as he sits on the chair, adding his hand to his face, his thumb under his chin, and his middle finger at his eyebrow. He looked like he was really trying to concentrate on something.
"That's good to know." I walked back into the dressing room, my breathing just a little bit quicker than normal but I tried to conceal it. "Okay baby girl, you're killing me. Lets go. Just get everything." He says, his voice coming out with a groan. He's right, this isn't fair for him. I quickly undress and put my clothes back on, stepping out with none of the clothes. As I go to say let's go, he was already standing and walking into the dressing room behind me. I turn to see him grab the

pink silk dress and he walks out. Turning back, I see his retreating back, he raises the dress in the air and says, “I’m getting you this one.”

Chapter Thirty-One

Strike!

After he bought me the dress, we went to fix my shattered phone. I'm glad they were able to fix it. We worked up a bit of an appetite and decided to head to the food court. Sitting across from Adonis, I was eating teriyaki chicken with brown rice while he was eating pizza. He was telling me a funny story about Cain and I couldn't stop laughing. "Are you serious?" I giggle again. He grins at me, "Yes. He was drunk and for some reason, when Cain is drunk, he loves everybody." I shake my head, "If I was that woman, I would have killed him. I can't believe him. I knew he was a total ass, but that?!" He takes the last bite of his pizza and leans back in his chair. After swallowing, he says, "She didn't have the chance to react, her boyfriend punched him square in the face." My eyes widened a little, my smile was still there, "What did you guys do?" He shrugs a little, takes a sip from his drink, then as he sets it down on the table he says, "There wasn't much we could do. Cain was in the wrong. We just pulled him away and walked out of the club." I close the container of the almost finished food and push it away, with a slight shake of my head and a smile. He puts his elbows on the table and leans forward, "So, I had an idea for what we can do next." I move the food to the side and mimic his actions, putting my chin under my interlaced hands, our faces pretty close to each other. "Shoot," I say with a nod. He looks at my face, over-studying it, then he looks from one of my eyes to the other. When he finally chooses an eye to look at, he says, "I was thinking we go bowling. We can-" Before he could continue, I groan loudly. I really hate bowling, I always sucked at it. Well, we went a couple times as kids and I said I will never go again. He rolls his eyes at me, his pink lips pursing. It was a weird look for him and his bad boy persona but it was still cute. "Stop whining. You haven't played in years. I bet you'd like it now." I lean back in my chair with a huff and cross my arms over my chest. "There is a reason I haven't gone, Don. We can do anything else. Whatever you want." I see him bite the inside of his cheek in thought. He looks around the crowded food court. When his eyes finally settled on mine, he said, "C'mon, I'll show you how to play. Or do you think you're that bad that you can't learn?" I looked over his face, his eyes squinting in challenge. I stand up pushing the chair back. As I do, I grab the food tray, filling it with the trash. He raises an eyebrow in question but I ignore him. Still thinking over what he just said. Do I really want to do this? Do I want to embarrass myself? I throw the food away and set the tray down. I walked back to the table, he was pushing his chair in after standing. "Fine. Let's go bowling." He grins at me and I can't help but smile back.

The bowling alley was here in the mall so we didn't have to walk very far. Passing a men's store, I turn towards him, glaring at him. "I can't believe you wouldn't try on clothes like I did. I wanted a show too, you know." He stops a second, raising his eyebrow at me like he always does. I stop to give him a frown and then continue walking. "I can give you a show anytime you'd like, baby girl. You just have to ask." I hear him say cockily from behind me. I smirk to myself, "What are you waiting for?" It's so hard to concentrate on him as my imagination runs wild in ways it never has before. "You're a naughty girl, Aphrodite." His words come out a little teasingly and with a chuckle. I continue walking without words. There was nothing I could say after that without taking our flirting to another level. I bite a small corner of my lip, trying to avoid my injury. The memory of his lips on mine flashes in my head again. I have been trying to forget about it all day. It was hard to say the least. Especially having him around me. I wanted him, it was a dangerous thought but it was the only thought I had at the moment. His arm suddenly wraps around my shoulders and he says, “What's going on in that pretty little head of yours?” I don’t look at him as I say, “Things that shouldn’t.” I then made eye contact. His smile falls, I look past him to see the entrance to the bowling alley. Pulling away from him, I walk in. After a few seconds, he walks in too. I look over my shoulder to see him coming in, his eyes a little dazed. At this point, I think we are just torturing ourselves. We both know if we continue, things will go south. So we needed to stop. But the thing was...could we? I walk up to the register, ask for his size and mine, then he walks up to me. We grab our shoes and walk to our lane after paying. The bowling alley was what you would expect. Just add a full bar and an arcade area. After we set up our game with our names and everything, Adonis takes a seat on a chair with a loud sigh, “I need a cigarette.” I couldn’t agree more with his confession. I nod and sit opposite him, “Yeah me too. A drink wouldn’t hurt either. Maybe five.” His lips curve a little, his eyes shining in amusement.

I REALIZED I’M NOT the only one who can’t say no to Adonis. The bartender was drooling all over him when he got us drinks from the bar. From here, I can see her twirling her blonde hair as she talked to him. He was looking irritated. He put a fake smile on his face as she passed him our third round of drinks. We have already been through a game. I was playing so bad, I refused to let Adonis show me how to play. The thing is, if I allow him to show me, then he would have

to get closer to me. Having him close to me would lead me to doing things I said I can't do.
But at this point, I think I'm just gonna have to let him teach me because this was getting really embarrassing. I'll just have to keep my distance the best I can. Plus, I started feeling good with all these drinks, so I was getting more confident. He walks back, holding the drinks and passes me mine, "Are you done trying?" I take a sip of my fruity cocktail and pout at him slumping my shoulders, "Fine. Show me how it's done." Wearing a cocky smile, he says, "I knew you were going to cave sooner or later." I roll my eyes and stand up from my chair, "C'mon then." I set my drink down and walk over to the bowling ball queue. After setting his drink down, he walks up to me rubbing his hands together, "Alright, let's do this." I go to grab my ball but he grabs it first. "Come on then. Let me show you how it's done." I shake my head, "You're so full of yourself." I follow him towards the lane and watch him. He aligns his body, the ball in his right hand. He looks back at me, "Don't just watch, come here." He tilts his head towards the lane and I get closer. I'm right beside him but still keeping my distance. He takes a step back saying, "Get in front of me." I don't move, I just look at him with my top lip sucked into my mouth. He gives me a flat look, "I don't bite." I chuckle under my breath but step in front of him, my heart starts to race. "Well...at least not hard." I turn my face towards him and elbow him in his stomach, making him grunt out a laugh. "You suck," I look around and see people playing and laughing. There was music playing with music videos on the big screens on the far walls aligning all the lanes. He gets close to me, not exactly pressing his body to mine. "Okay," He passes me the ball, then puts his hand under mind, sending sparks straight to my stomach. I

put my fingers through the holes and waited for his instructions. “Open your legs, shoulders length wide.” He kicks my feet with one of his so I can do just that. He further explains to me about how to aim the ball. But the truth is, it all sounded like gibberish to me. Especially with my heart hammering in my chest. My hands were shaking and I willed them to stop. “Got it?” His velvety voice whispers near my ear. Goosebumps automatically rise on my skin. I nod and he wraps his fingers around my hand, pulling my hand back. In a straight line, his breath fans down my neck. I held back a shiver with all my might...“Okay, so now halfway in the air, throw it.” He shows me exactly how to flick my hand. He makes sure I’m holding the ball right before stepping away, leaving me standing there, missing his body heat. I look back at him and he smiles, “You got this.” I look back to the pins. Okay, I got this. I need to do this. “I’m gonna do this.” I state and he laughs a little. I pull my hand back like he said and throw the ball like he showed me. I watch the ball, trying not to blink. I was surprised the ball didn’t go straight into the gutter. It hits the pins, not all of them, only like three to the left. I lift my arms up in the air and start screaming. I turn back to him and jump up and down in excitement. He was clapping his hands with a huge smile. “You see? I knew you could do it!” I run up to him and wrap my arms around him. He wraps his arms around my waist with a chuckle. I pull back with a smile, “Thanks Don, you were right.” He crosses his arms over his chest, “I always am,” He shrugs one shoulder. We started playing and I have to admit, I was holding my own. He was trying to teach me further on his turn but all I did was check him out, to be honest. His arms flexing, his chest rising. The white shirt he wore stretched tightly on his broad shoulders. I couldn’t breath, he was too good looking.

It was now his last turn and right before he went to grab his ball, a few loose strands of hair fell on his face. He reaches up and runs one hand through his hair, then the other, making me swallow my drool. He bends down and grabs the ball. I watch his toned back walk towards the lane from where I was sitting. His shoulder blades were moving and...okay, I really needed to stop, this was too much. I look down at my drink with a small smile. My mind was already buzzing with the alcohol in my system.

After his turn, I stand and go to grab my ball, then walk towards the lane. This needed to be good, it was the last turn. I align my body like he showed me. I turn back to him with a grin and shake my butt a little bit. He smiles amusingly and bites down on his lower lip trying to conceal it. I look back to the pins and pull my hand back. As I threw it forward, I cringed a little as I realized I threw it too hard. But my eyes widened as the bowling ball hit all the pins, making a loud sound as they fell. I turn back to him, my mouth hanging open in shock. He rises to his feet yelling, he runs towards me and lifts me up in the air, spinning me around. I start yelling too, in pure excitement.

He sets me down, “That was so awesome!” He grabs onto my face, his eyes as wide as mine and a smile that can blind you. “Did you see that?!” I exclaimed pointing behind me. His smile softens, “I did. It was awesome.” The words come out almost in a whisper. His hands were still cupping my face. As he finished his sentence, before I could even register what he was doing, his lips pressed to mine. I gasped into his mouth, shocked at the suddenness of his kiss. His soft lips felt heavenly on mine. As I close my eyes, enjoying the feeling and kissing him back, he pulls away. He quickly turns around and walks towards our chairs. I stand there blinking a little, trying to get my thoughts in order. What the hell just happened? He kissed me, obviously. But I thought we silently agreed we weren't going to do that again. We need to talk about this, we can't just drop it again. It isn't something we can just drop again. If we don't talk about this little thing between us, it will ruin everything. I slowly walk back to where he is standing. As he hears me approach, he clears his throat. With his back to me, he bends down to grab his shoes from the floor. I open my mouth to tell him that we should talk about this when he says, “Um...We should go.”

Chapter Thirty-Two

Our Terms

With a deep breath, I open the passenger door of Adonis' car. I slide in at the same time he does. I try my best not to look his way as we shut our doors in sync, making a loud noise that almost has me flinching. I feel my heart racing through my veins. I look straight out the windshield, my chest rising and falling with my deep breathing. I can hear his breathing coming out heavily too. From my peripheral vision, I see him running his hands over his thighs in thought. The sound of his hands gliding over material, is the only thing clouding the silence. As of right now, the tension between us is awkward and suffocating. This is exactly what I didn't want to happen. I didn't want my craving for him to interfere with what we have had all our lives. It was hard enough the last year of not being together. I don't want this to come between us, making us lose each other completely. In that instant, I decided to talk to him about it, and come to an agreement of trying to control our impulses. It was what we had to do in order to keep this friendship afloat. I turn my face towards him and say quietly, "Adonis?" Adonis, who looked like he was also in deep thought, turned his head, looking at me as if barely registering that I was here. As I wait for him to answer, he suddenly grabs my face into his large, tattooed hands and presses his warm lips to mine. *Oh fuck.* Every thought about talking through this with him, flew out the window. I kissed him back, matching his eagerness, I couldn't help it. His lips were kissing me passionately, both of us halting our breathing. His lips and mine, crashing against each other in need and want. My hands reach up and glide up his sculpted stomach, his lips still devouring mine. I continued up his chest, making him shutter under my touch, my hands stopping at his neck. I feel Adonis' tongue slide over my sore bottom lip softly, asking me

for something I never experienced. I gladly part my lips for him with a sharp intake of breath. His tongue enters my mouth and when it touches mine, I moan softly at the feeling. His hands leave my face as he explores my mouth at his own will and they grab onto my waist. He pulls me onto his lap without breaking our heavy kiss. As I am straddling him, thoughts of what could happen pop into my head again and I start to pull away, mumbling something I didn't even understand.
He signed against my lips, "We can talk later, baby." His lips crash on mine again, he becomes more forceful, making me putty in his arms. I wrap my arms around his neck, pulling my body closer to his. His long arms match my movements and they wrap around my waist, engulfing me completely. Even while on his lap, even having some height over him in this position, he still enveloped me. I loved that, I loved how he made me feel so protected and secure. I couldn't breathe anymore so I moved my face slightly away from his, breathing heavily. He wasn't planning on stopping though. His lips started kissing my cheek in big kisses, then peppered down to my neck. I was panting now, the feeling causing me to feel things I probably shouldn't. His tongue licked down to where my shoulder met my neck and my head moved to the side involuntarily, with a slight moan. I felt him smile against me, he kissed me there in big sloppy kisses. Not being able to handle his sweet torture, I grab his face and bring his lips back to mine. He kisses me back, hungrily, taking full lead. I feel a burning in the pit of my stomach, feeling him hardening under me. My panties are already dampening at the feeling. Needing friction, I start rocking on him slightly. He groans in the back of his throat and I smile this time. He grabs onto my waist,

stopping my movements. Unwillingly, he pulls away, his forehead pressing to mine. Both of us panting heavily, my eyes closed. “What are we doing, Aphrodite?” His lips brushed against mine with his question. I didn’t know the answer to what he asked, my mind was boggled. I shake my head, my forehead still pressed to his and my eyes still closed, “I don’t know.” He chuckled under his breath, “I want you.” The words come out serious and full of need. I look down to his lips and see him lick them, then bite down his lower one. All I want is to pull his lip between my teeth and do so many more things to him but these bad thoughts should stop because they will ruin everything. Looking up into his light green eyes, I say softly, “We can’t be together, Adonis. It will ruin our friendship.” I swallow, then continue, “It will ruin everything.” I pouted a little, his eyes went to my lips for a split second, then met my gaze again as I added, “What do we do?” His eyes ran over my face, then raked down my torso and led to his lap, as I was still straddling it. He visibly gulps, grabbing onto my thighs with both hands. He looks back at me, “I don’t know. I never wanted you this way. But the truth is, I never wanted anything this bad before.” His words alone had me panting again, he was still hard under me and I know I was still a little hot and bothered to say the least. His eyes were dark in lust, he meant every word he said.

I lick my lips and rock on his lap, feeling his tight jeans rub against me. He throws his head back with a loud groan. When he looks back at me I say, “Me neither.” He searches my face with his beautiful irises, in thought. You can practically see the wheels turning in his head as he thinks everything through. I wait for a few seconds, sitting on his lap patiently. “What if we don’t put a label on it?” I squint my eyes in confusion, resting my back on the steering wheel, putting a little distance between us, "What do you mean?" He looks down, raising his hand and sliding it up my arm that was now resting in my lap. He watched his slow movements, goosebumps rising on my skin with the light touch. "I mean, what if we do everything we want with each other without calling it a relationship." His eyes met mine from under his thick eyelashes, his face still tilted downward. I take a deep breath, "Explain." His hand continues up to my neck and into my hair. He pulls me abruptly meeting me halfway, his face in the crook of my neck, his lips near my ear. Feeling his hot breath on my skin as he says, "Like, I can do anything I want to you without the consequences." I pull a sharp shaky breath through my parted lips. He bites down softly on my ear with his teeth, then pulls back, grazing my ear. He leans back in his chair, releasing my hair. I lean back again, my hands still tremble a little, my heart racing in my chest. I looked closely at his heated gaze, he was serious. *He wanted me.* That thought had butterflies swarming in my stomach. How will this work? How can we just be physical? What does he mean by anything? So many questions run through my mind. But the one I ask makes my face heat up, "Anything?" He sucks on his teeth and gives me a quick glance over, "Anything." I look away shyly, allowing my hair to fall on my reddened face, "Umm…I have never done, *anything*." I say the last word bluntly so he understands what I mean. He pulls my hair behind my ear, then sets his hand on my other cheek and softly pulls my face to look at him. "Baby girl. If you don't want to, it's okay. I will understand." I shake my head, "I want to." I look at his face, then run a finger on his chest mindlessly. "It's just...I know that you have been

with lots of women who had lots of experience. Experience that I don't have."
He frowns, bringing his hands to my waist and squeezes as he says, "Hey, don't do that. Those other women were nothing. That doesn't change anything. I want you…so bad." He reaches up, running his fingers through my hair, "You're different, Aphrodite. You're my best friend." I look at him through my eyelashes, "It's not fair to you. You're so good at everything. I mean last night was my first kiss. I'm probably so bad at it too." His eyes fill with amusement, "Did I steal your first kiss, princess?" I cover my face with one hand in embarrassment and slap his arm with the other. He hisses and I look to see him rubbing his arm with a smirk on his face. "Stop it!" I exclaimed and then looked down at my hands, not able to look at his face. "You're so cute." I meet his eyes, giving him a flat look. He chuckles again and pulls me closer to him, our faces inches apart. "How did this happen?" I ask as I rest my hands on his thick arms. He brings his hands down and under my shirt, running his hands over my back. His warm hands felt amazing on my skin. "I don't even know, I just haven't been able to get my mind off you. At first, I tried to convince myself it was because I missed you. But then, I started having sinful thoughts about you that I just couldn't shake." I bring my face closer to his while rubbing my hands up his arms and down his chest. I know exactly what he means by that, I have been thinking a lot of sinful thoughts about him too. "Care to explain those sinful thoughts?" My lips graze his a little with my words that come out sensually. His arms still under my shirt, press down on me abruptly and bring my chest against his, making me inhale a sudden breath, "I can show you." His lips claim mine and I close my eyes at the feeling.

His lips were merciless on mine, not holding back like before. He took all the control of the kiss and I really appreciated it because I hardly knew what to do. His hands run down my back and he grabs my hips, his fingers digging into me. I moaned and he took that opportunity to taste me with his tongue. He made me forget everything I wanted to ask him with his lips. He made me want so much more. I released his lips and kissed down his hard jaw, hearing his heavy breathing in the air. I reached just under his jaw and licked a little bit, then bit down on his jaw teasingly. He didn't chuckle though, he breathed in deep and pulled me closer to him. I took that as a good thing and kissed lower down his throat, reaching his collar bone. I lick up his neck, feeling him shutter under me. Having him react to me was so shocking to me. I loved it, I wanted more. When I get to the crease between his neck and his shoulder, I lick and suck there softly. He tasted so good, the smell of him taking over all my senses. He grabs my face and brings my lips to his again, kissing me like he needed it. I wrap my arms around his neck, lifting myself higher on his lap, making him tilt his head up and mine down. He brings his hands to my ass and I pull away from him. I look down to him, squinting my eyes and smiling,
"Adonis?"
Our breathing was heavy but he smirked through it, "You said you weren't good at this. I gotta say baby, you know exactly what you're doing." I take a seat on his lap again, resting my hands on his chest, "Okay, what's your plan? Because this isn't gonna stop anytime soon."
"Well, for starters, we don't tell anyone. That will just add to the drama we don't need." He brings his hands up and wraps them around my wrist, lifting one hand, he kisses my palm, his eyes on mine. My eyes

widened a little and I lick my lips as he continues, "We keep this monogamous. I won't share you with anyone. If one day you find someone you want to be with, then we can break everything off and vise versa." I lift my hand and with two fingers, I go up his chest like legs walking up as he continues to talk, reaching up his neck. My other hand is still resting on his chest. He rests his hands on my thighs, rubbing small circles with his thumb. "When one of us decides we're done, then that's it. We forget about it and continue being friends." I bring the hand that was resting on his chest and run it through his hair softly. He closes his eyes, breathing in deeply. "Adonis, how will we even keep this from our friends?" He shakes his head and opens his eyes, "I have no idea but if Roxy knows, she will have a field day with it, that's for sure." I giggle and lean my head on the side of his, temple to temple. "The rush of sneaking around will be worth it." He whispers, leaning into my ear, making me shiver. "You're right about that." There is one thing I want to add. We can't fall in love with each other because that's where heartbreak comes in and that is when our whole lives will get turned upside down. I pull back again and look into his eyes, "We can't fall in love with each other. We have to just keep it physical." He nods, "I agree. I want something else from you if we do this." I give him a questioning look and he answers, "I want you to be honest with me." My eyebrows furrowed together, "What do you mean?" He runs his hands up my shirt, over my stomach, and to my waist. His calloused fingers scraping my soft skin. "You have to tell me what you want, what you like, and above all, what you don't want and what you don't like." I nod my head, blinking. "Are you sure you want this? Don't do this for me. You have to want this as much as I want it." I lick my lips and lift my hand to run it through my hair, pushing it to one side. I don't have to think this over. Of course I wanted to. I wanted him. "I want you, Adonis," the words come out softly but completely honest. I look into his eyes so he can understand that I wasn't backing down from this. Yes, I may be a little scared…okay, I am a lot scared but he is my best friend, he will never hurt me.

Chapter Thirty-Three

Murderous Blue Eyes

"No, Adonis. I'm not mad, " I say over the phone. I called him over but he said he couldn't make it, he was running errands for Benjamin. "I'll make it up to you tonight, I promise." I smile and continue cleaning my room, "How?" He groans out loudly, I can practically picture him throwing his head back in mercy. "I was thinking something along the lines of my lips all over your silky skin." My blood starts to race through my veins. "Adonis," His name comes out bashfully. I hear his breathing coming out from the phone, heavier, "Oh baby, the things I can do to you." I gulp at the thought of it, "Aren't you with all the boys right now?" He laughs, "Yes, but I'm alone at the moment." I walk to my couch and take a seat. I cross my legs together, trying to put pressure where I need it most. "Oh." I couldn't say much, my throat felt like it was closing up in my nerves. My stomach was doing all kinds of flips. "Hudson was saying something about maybe hanging out at his house tonight. What do you think?" I hear shuffling behind the phone, then I hear other voices. "Yeah, sure. That sounds like fun."

"Okay, Aphrodite. I gotta go. I'll call you later." His words come out more like he was paying attention to someone else. "Okay, bye." The line goes dead and I look around my room with a sigh. Thoughts of what he is probably doing runs through my head, making my heart start racing a little in fear. I hope he stays safe. I hear the door chime down stairs, signaling it was opened. I walk out my room and to the top of the stairs. I see my parents walking up the stairs tiredly. They are always so tired after their long shift, my heart hurts for them. They work so hard. "Hey sweetie," my mom said, not looking at me yet. My father's eyes are pretty much closed. "Hey guys, how are you feeling?" I ask nervously. I really hope they don't overreact when they see my face. Adonis and I thought of a story to tell them. They don't need to know what really happened. My mother's eyes finally reach mine and she gasps, Walking faster up the stairs, she reaches me. "What happened to you?" She lifts her hand to touch my face but I push it away softly, "I'm fine. I fell." My father, who finally is by my side, says, "How exactly did you fall?" I turn my head to him and sigh dramatically, "I was using my phone while walking down the stairs. I missed the last step and tripped, busting my lip like an idiot." I look back to my mother and she looks at my face with a frown. "Have you been treating it? This looks a couple days old." I look down at my feet, "Yes, I have. Adonis treated it the first day. It was like two days ago. I'm fine now. It doesn't even hurt." I shrug and move past them to walk down the stairs to go have some lunch.

AFTER A FEW HOURS, the group chat started blowing up. Everyone is talking about going to Hudson's house to hang out. The only ones not messaging are Adonis and I. I'm just watching everyone talk and argue. My phone starts ringing in my hand. The caller ID says Roxy. I pick up and without a word from me, Roxy starts, "I'll be there in twenty minutes to pick you up. You better look hot." I roll my eyes, even though she can't see me. "Alright, see you then." The line goes dead and I shake my head. I turn off the living room television with the remote control and stand up. I set the remote down and walk up the stairs, towards my room. I'm a little nervous. I have no idea what to wear. I don't even know how I am supposed to act now. I run my hand down my face as I get into my closet. After trying on several outfits, I decided on black short shorts, a white t-shirt that I tied a knot at the middle so it reached just over my belly button, with white chucks. I add some curls to my hair, then run my fingers through it just so it can be wavy. After putting on makeup, I walk back to my closet. I put on a belt with a thick Gucci buckle and some black studs in my ears. I lean over to shut the light when I see Adonis' hat on my shelf. Should I? I mean, it would look really cute with my outfit. With a shrug, I grab it and put it on my head. As soon as I walk down the stairs, my phone rings in my back pocket. I grab it and answer. "We're outside, girly." Erika's voice says through the phone. I smile, "Okay, I'll be right out." I hang up and go to my message thread with Adonis. I write and delete multiple messages, not knowing what to send him until I settle with just telling him I'm on my way to Hudson's house. He texted me back a winking emoticon after saying, *'can't wait to see you.'* I shake my head smiling while hiding my phone in my back pocket and walk out the house.

The sun was already down at this hour, so Roxy's roof was up. As I get into Roxy's car, she turns her body facing me as I sit in the back seat. Her eyes widened to saucers, "What the fuck happened to your face?!" She exclaimed. Erika turned towards me and gasped a little. I go into telling them what happened with Nick, skipping over the part where Cain took me to The Undergrounds. "Oh my god!" Erika covers her mouth, tears brimming in her eyes. Roxy hits something hard in anger, making me jolt a little, "I am gonna fucking kill him! Who the hell does he think he is?!" I reach out and touch her arm, "I'm fine. Adonis and the guys already did whatever they had to do." I look down and sigh. "That's good. I hope they fucked up his face. That piece of shit deserved it and so much more." She pulls out of the driveway and drives down the road, dialing Cain's number on the Bluetooth screen. Cain answers saying, “What's up, bitch?” Roxy sighs loudly, “I’m fucking livid bro! Who was gonna tell me that asshole hurt Aphrodite?” I hear Cain breath out, then I hear shuffling. I grab her shoulder, “Roxy, drop it. I’m fine. Everything is okay.” Cain speaks before Roxy can reply, “I was gonna tell you but I’ve been busy.” Roxy looks at me through the rearview mirror, “You had better made sure he was unrecognizable.” Cain chuckles, “Trust me bro, I thought he was dead after how Adonis left him. That man won't be able to recognize himself for a very long time.” My eyes widen at that and my heart starts racing. What the hell did he do? We get to Hudson’s house and as I walk up the sidewalk, I spot Adonis’ car across the street, my stomach fills with butterflies again. Knowing I’m going to see him after everything we agreed on, I try to conceal my feelings from showing on my face as we walk to the door. Roxy knocks on the door and after a little while, it gets swung open by Hudson. He smirks at us, “Come on in, pretty ladies.” Thoughts of Nick appear in my mind and I mentally shutter at the thought as we walk in. That's what he would call me, *pretty lady.* We followed Hudson to his back living room that was connected to his dining room. The couches where leather and the whole room was colors of black, grey, and silver. Adonis is nowhere to be seen. Liam, Cain, and Hudson were the only boys in the living room. There was a big hookah bottle on the coffee table with drinks and snacks set up. The room was filled with a thick layer of smoke that smelled of mint and pineapple and with that thought, I saw the pineapple wrapped in foil in the hookah bottle. I take a seat on the couch that was made for one. Erika sits on the love seat by herself, leaning her elbow on the arm

rest, and Roxy takes a seat in between Liam and Cain on the big couch. Roxy takes the hookah hose from Liam. As she puts it to her lips, he says, “It's laced with CBD.” She nods and leans back, taking a long drag of it, then passes it back to Liam. I cross my leg over the other and pull my hair to one side nervously. Hudson grabs a drink from the table and walks it over to me, “Relax.” I squint my eyes at him, pouting a little, then grab the drink. I look down to see a reddish-orange liquid inside. I take a sip and smile as he walks away with a shake of his head. There was music playing in the living room, I wasn’t sure where it was coming from. I look up to see Adonis stride into the room, looking as dominant as always. His strong shoulders straight, his step full of sexy swagger. James walks in behind him and takes a seat on the love seat next to Erika. Adonis grabs a chair from the dining room and pulls it near the big coffee table, taking a seat. His eyes meeting mine, they give me a quick once over, a smirk growing on his face. He was wearing a dark grey, short sleeved collared shirt that had a few buttons at the top that were all open. The black jeans on him were ripped at the knees, showing his tattoos there and he wore white tennis. I noticed that necklace he wore last time around his neck. I run my eyes on his strong, tattooed arms and notice how the sleeves tightened around his biceps. I gulp and look away towards the table in front of us. I was a little farther, not able to reach anything on it.
My heart was beating rapidly in my chest and I don’t even know why. When I looked back to Adonis, he was looking at me already. With one finger, he calls me over to him. I shake my head at his request. I bite down on my lip, trying to hide my smile. He gave me a flat look, “Come here.” I stand up from my chair and walk over to him, everyone in conversations around

us. Standing next to him, I tilt my head to the side, "Hi." He noticeably looks me over again, his eyes stopping at my bare midsection for a second before reaching my eyes. He wraps his arm around me and pulls me down on his lap, I inwardly gasp at his sudden movement. I adjust myself so my legs are in between his. Then, look up at him frowning. "Hi yourself." I ignore his greeting, "What are you doing?" I look around to his friends so he understands I meant why does he want me here with everyone around us. He shrugs his shoulders, "They don't care." He leans in so he can whisper in my ear, his minty breath that was laced with tobacco, fanning my cheek. "Plus, I want you right here where you belong." He lifts his eyebrows and I smack his chest angrily. "Stop being an ass." I hiss through my teeth. He smirks and tightens the arm that was around my waist. His eyebrows lower as he hums, "You're feisty today. Save that for later." I widened my eyes and tried to stand up to get away from him. "Hey. I'm just playing with you. Don't go." He tugs me back a little. I turn my face towards his, meeting his eyes. My breath stills at the closeness, one tilt of my head and I can kiss his perfect lips. My eyes look down to them really quick and then back to his eyes. That didn't go unnoticed by him though, because a full on smirk rises on his annoyingly beautiful face. I looked away to the hand that was on my waist. I reach over and trace the fierce lion that took up the whole space of the top of his hand before reaching his fingers. The lion had electric blue eyes that had a murderous stare. "He has your eyes." I look up at him, my brows knit together. "Really, they look like they want to kill someone." I widened my eyes for emphasis. He smirks, "I got that tattoo that day you told me so many things. You were so mad at me. You even said you hated me and you would never talk to me again so I told the artist to make his eyes angry and murderous. Even though the next day you texted me anyway." I blink a few times and look down to his hand again. I do notice the resemblance in color. My heart breaks a little at how I texted him that day so angrily and everything I told him. I even cursed him out. I even told him I wish I never knew him. He didn't mention that because I knew it hurt him. It hurt me to even think about it. He was going through so much and I didn't even know. "I'm sorry I said all those things. I regretted them all instantly." He puts a finger under my chin and slowly brings my face up to look at him. "Don't ever say you're sorry, not to me. Not to anyone." I nod his hand still under my face.

Chapter Thirty-Four

Teasing

Adonis holds out the hookah hose to me and I look at it like if it was something so foreign, “What is CBD? Will it get me high?” Amusement flashes through his eyes, his lips tilting to the side to keep from smiling. I don’t know how I felt about the hookah, to be honest. On top of that, the thick smoke was making my eyes water a little bit and I had no idea what was in there. But as Adonis holds the tip of it to my lips, our eyes meeting, I really wanted to do it. He looked so sexy looking at me this way, I wanted to do anything he wanted me to. With the right look and words, I think I can be at his full mercy. I tilt my head down and wrap my lips around the thin plastic tip. I hollow my cheeks as I suck hard, pulling in the harsh smoke. His eyes darken as he watches me sucking in the smoke. His lips parting, he blinks a few times, then his eyes meet mine. “CBD is extracted from marijuana. It's medicinal, it will just relax you.” I turned my head to look at Hudson as he finished his statement. Blowing out the smoke, I cough a little but not too bad. He was biting on a stick in his mouth as he continued, “But if you want something that will get you high, I can help with that.”

“Shut it, Hud.” I look back at Adonis to see him giving a flat look to his friend. I chuckle a little under my breath and Adonis’ eyes turn back to mine, his lips curing on one side. I took a sip of my drink, which was now my second one. “Have you ever gotten high?” I turn back at Hudson, shaking my head. “She’s a baby, Hudson.” Cain said jokingly, “She’s probably a virgin too.” I choke on my spit and everyone starts laughing around us. “Alright, come on you guys, leave our baby alone. She will get there.” I give Liam a flat look and he smirks at me. “Yeah, leave her alone. It’s okay for her to be a virgin, we need more of those around our group of sinners.” I turned to James, who wasn't smiling but had amusement in his eyes. I blink at him, appalled by everyone's teasing. "Aww, is our baby getting upset?" Before I can react to Cain, Adonis makes an angry noise in the back of his throat. "Whoever says 'baby' one more time, I'm gonna make sure you won't be able to talk ever again." Adonis' words come out menacingly, he looks to each and every one of the boy's faces, getting his point across. They all looked away, avoiding eye contact. He really was their boss, they couldn't undermine him for anything. My heart swelled in pride for some reason. It was something I never even thought of as a turn on. But let me tell you, it was so hot. He sets down the hose and reaches into his pants pocket. He pulls out his box of cigarettes and gets one out. The lighter strapped to the plastic around the box. He pulls it out, setting the cigarette to his lips. His eyes meet mine as he lights it. Putting everything he pulled out back, he takes a long drag, the cigarette resting on his lips. I swallow as he grabs it and puts his hand on his free thighs, the cigarette between his fingers.

I turn my face towards Roxy, our eyes meeting. She had a look of shock and a little amusement in her eyes. "I think I need to get a little high after that." I bite on my lip, trying my best to hide my smile at Roxy's way to lighten the mood. If only she knew the real reason they listened to Adonis. "I need another drink." This time I tip my head back laughing loudly at Erika's timid reply. Almost everyone joins in on my laughter. I looked at Adonis, who was looking at me with a glint in his eye. From there, everyone continued as if nothing happened, joking around and chatting. Adonis running his hands mindlessly on my arms and legs, I would watch him engage in a conversation. I would see every little reaction, his eyebrows lifting when he was shocked or intrigued. How the corners of his lips turned down when he didn't like what he was hearing. His pink lips moving as he adds something to the conversation. My favorite part was his smile when one of the boys said a joke. It brightened his whole face, making my heart stop. After some time, he looks at me with his notched eyebrow raised, "Take a picture baby girl." I purse my lips, containing my smile. I reach back, grabbing my phone from my back pocket, I pull up the camera app. I look up at him, smirking. I lean back, his arm around me tightening to keep me from falling. I adjust the phone so I can get a clear shot of him. He puts his thumb and forefinger under his chin and looks up to the side, in a mock thinking position. I giggle and take the picture. "There, it's perfect." I sit upright and show him the picture. He looks it over, nodding in approval, then he looks at me, "Yup, perfect." I meet his gaze, my cheeks heating up a little. His eyes were darkening as he looked into my eyes. The shadows around his eyes get more intense with his look. "Come with me." I nod and he pulls me up with him as he stands up. I took a look around to see that no one was noticing our departure. Adonis grabs onto my hand and pulls me out of the room and towards the front of the house, he turns his face towards me as we pass the kitchen, giving me a quick once over. As soon as we walk out the kitchen, he pivots around and pushes me slightly on the nearest wall. I gasp inwardly, my eyes widening. He pushes his muscular body on mine, grabbing my face in one hand and my hip in the other. His eyes were blazing into mine. As soon as his lips touch mine, I melt into a puddle. My eyelids closing slowly as I kiss him back, meeting his intensity. I reach up and wrap my arms around his neck, needing the hold to keep my knees from buckling as his lips

devoured mine. He brings his hands down, bending his knees a little till he reaches behind my legs, lifting me up. I gasp a little, wrapping my legs around his waist, he takes that opportunity to put his tongue inside my shocked mouth.
He starts walking with me wrapped around him. I pay no attention to where he was going, as his lips are still kissing me nonstop. His lips felt so good on mine, I couldn't get enough. I grab onto his bottom lip with my teeth and pull back, he groans out and my back hits another wall with a thump. We were now in a dark room. He pulls away and starts kissing down to my neck. He lifted me up a little in his hold and I noticed how he was positioning me against his tight jeans, making me feel the effect I had on him. I bite down on my lip and throw my head back hitting the wall behind me, a muffled moan leaving my lips. He licks up to my ear and shushes me softly. His hot breath made me shiver. He pulls his head away and switches to the other side of my neck, kissing me along my arch. I grab onto his hair on the top of his head, tugging on it in mercy. He shoves his hips into me, rubbing them against mine. The sensation was too much for me to handle, "Adonis." I moan out softly. He pulls back looking at my face, his eyes full of lust and need. His breathing coming out in pants. "So beautiful." He whispers before meeting his lips to mine again.
Needing the feeling he gave me earlier, I use my arms to help me move my hips into his. He brings one of his arms around, grabbing my hip with his hand and stopping me from grinding on his jeans, His lips still kissing me. I try to rub myself against him again, trying to ignore his strong hold. But instead, he just pulls me closer to him, keeping me from doing that.
He pulls away from me, one side of his lip curing up, "If you keep doing that, I won't stop." I blink at him

understanding what he meant. I tilt my head back on the wall and he leans his forehead on my collar, both of us trying to catch our heavy breathing.
He looks back up to me, my eyes already adjusting to the dark room. When I meet his passionate gaze, my heart flutters in my chest, an overwhelming feeling rising up to the pit of my stomach. He brought up the hand that was on my hip and slowly traced my stomach, "Where do you want me to touch you first?"
I swallow the lump in my throat and clear it a little. Searching his eyes, all I see is want. Suddenly, his hand presses over my jeans, right between my thighs. I suck in a sharp breath through my teeth. "How about here?" He starts rubbing a little and I bite down on my lip, holding in a groan. "Does that feel good?" He says, still holding my gaze. I nod slowly and he chuckles under his breath. That sound alone was so sexy coming from him. Feeling a little overwhelmed, I reach down and push his hand away. He slowly sets me down, my shoes hitting what felt like shaggy carpet. He pins me to the wall, cupping my face in both hands. Concern flooding his eyes, "I will never hurt you. I will take as much time as you want." I look up at him and his lips meet mine. My heart fills at the fact that he puts my worries before him but It's not that I don't want him to do things to me, I'm just a little nervous. But like I said before, this is my best friend and he won't hurt me. He just said it too, so what else do I need. I pull back and kiss his cheek, "I know, I trust you. I'm just a little nervous." He bites down on his lip, looking over my face in one quick sweep as if contemplating his next question. "Have you ever touched yourself?" My eyes open in shock and I push him away, "I'm not talking about this." I can see his huge grin from a foot away from me, his perfect white teeth pretty much glowing in the dark room. "So that's

a yes then?" I gasp loudly, "Adonis! Stop it!" I was super embarrassed by what he just asked me but I knew he could read the answer so easily. I could never hide anything from him. With a chuckle, he grabs onto my hand and tugs on it, he opens the door from the room we were in and we walk out into the long hallway. The sudden light made me blink a few times to readjust. I really needed to fix myself up before we went out to the living room where everyone was.

Chapter Thirty-Five

Natural Habitat

"So, where are we going?" I ask Adonis as soon as I step into his car. He called me this morning and just said to get ready, he would be picking me up soon. I looked him over and saw his attire, he was wearing a black compressed short sleeve shirt and grey loose shorts. With the shirt he was wearing, you can see the outline of all his defined muscles. He turns his head towards me after pulling out of the driveway, "We're going to work out." He sped down the street and I looked at him perplexed, "I don't know if you knew this, but uh…I don't work out." He chuckles, "Yeah, I know you don't but I do." There was music playing in the background, it was loud enough where you can hear it but also where you can talk freely. I lean back into my chair, actually kinda excited to watch him work out. "Since when do you work out exactly?" He turns down a street, then answers me, "Pretty much everyday, I normally work out around dawn." My eyes widened, "Why so early?" He reaches over putting his free hand on my leg that was covered in my yoga pants. He shrugs his shoulders and says, "It's just what I always do. I didn't go so early today so I could go with you." I put my hand on top of his and interlace our fingers while my hand was on top of his. I love how he wants to spend time with me, it puts a smile on my face. "You just love to show off. " I say teasingly and he turns his face towards mine grinning. He turns his hand over and grabs my hand in his, the right way, my stomach doing a flip at his movement. I look around as he parks after a few minutes in the back of the rundown shopping center where The Undergrounds was. I look at him questioningly, "What are we doing here?" He tilts his head towards the building, "This is where I work out." I nod and open my door to step out but he stops me pulling on my hand a little. I turn towards him and he presses his

lips to mine in a sweet kiss. He pulls away, releasing my hand too and we both step out of the car. As I meet him at his side of the car, he grabs my hand and leads me towards the entrance. He unlocks it with a key and opens the door. We walk and he closes the door behind us. We walk down the steep staircase, hand in hand, him still leading the way.
It's so crazy how he has a key to this place, Benjamin really does trust him. We step down and go through a hallway, we reach the locker rooms, there is only dim light in this room where you can see around the silver lockers. Also, to the far corner there were individual showers with curtains. We didn't stop there, we kept walking until we exited the locker room and entered another door right across the hall, this room was completely dark. We stopped at the door and he let go of my hand. I waited patiently, hearing him shuffling a few feet away. I hear a click and the lights go on. They were so bright, I immediately covered my eyes with my forearm. After a few seconds, I put my hand down and I blinked a little to adjust to the fluorescent light. The room was huge. The wall on the far right was all mirrored, there were rows of free weights right under it that looked like it went on for miles. There were different kinds of benches scattered near the weights. In the middle of the room was a boxing ring. On the back wall was a row of punching bags that looked to be in different sizes. On the far left side were all kinds of exercise machines and weight lifting machines. I start walking around, not looking at Adonis as he walks in the opposite direction of me to the mirrored walls. As I got near the exercise machines, I examined each one with awe and interest. So this is where he has been coming all this time? As I continue walking, I reach the punching bags and touch them with the tips of my fingers softly,

still walking. Every emotion he had was released in this room, in The Undergrounds gym. He has been through so much, I'm glad he found something to help him through it. I'm happy he found people to be on his side. Flashes of skinny, lanky Adonis working out here, runs through my imagination and I smile sadly. I turned around to look at the boxing ring and it looked sparkling clean. Now that I think about it, the room smelled of all sorts of cleaning products. I would have thought it would have smelled of sweat and body order. I walk up to it and pull on the ropes, watching as they swing back into place, I grin at that. "Having fun over there?" I turned towards Adonis who was setting down some dumbbells near an elevated bench. "This place is awesome." I say softly but loud enough for him to hear. I looked down to see the black foam floor had the name "The Undergrounds" in big white letters in front of each section in the gym. I finished my tour and stepped right in front of him, he was sitting down on the bench, his back in an angle. He grabbed the weights on either of him from the floor and lifted them. He put them on his chest and pushed out, I was far enough where the weights wouldn't hit me but close enough where I could see his features scrunch up as he breathed out with every push and pull of his arms.
I look over his torso and arms, examining every dip and bump. Feeling my mouth go dry, I lick my lips. Out of nowhere, he throws the big dumbbells on the floor and they fall with a thud. I look at them with wide eyes. I look at the number on them and swallow spit. I look back to his red face and watch as he stands from his chair, standing flush against me. I tilt my head up to meet his pale green irises. I take a deep breath in as he puts a hand to my cheek, I look down to it, barely noticing he had black workout gloves on. When

I looked back up, he was leaning into me, I closed my eyes, ready to feel his lips on mine. But instead, he leans in next to my ear and whispers, “Excuse me.” I open my eyes and realize I was indeed in his way. With heat rising to my face, I move to the side. He steps towards the free weights again, then I see how he reaches into his pocket and pulls out his phone, he clicks something on it, then extends it to me. “Put whatever you want to hear, it’s already connected to Bluetooth.” I grab his phone, skimming through his music. I end up choosing shuffle and the song, ‘For the night’ by Pop smoke, starts playing. I take a seat on a flat bench and watch as he bends to lift even heavier weights, then the one he was using earlier. I watch mesmerized as he works out on his arms, looking at himself in the mirror in front of him. I continue watching him as he rotates from one style of lifting to the next, my eyes following his every move. I watch the sweat falling down his forehead. The sweat coating his skin made me breathless. Every grunt he makes has my heart skipping a beat. I didn’t notice my lips were parted and my breathing was heightened till he turned towards me, his eyes dark and full of need. He stalks towards me from a few feet away. He puts his wrapped hands on my knees and spreads them, leaning forward so we are at eye level, “If you keep looking at me like that, I won’t be able to contain myself from taking you right here.” I gulp and try to put on a big girl act, “I don’t know what you're talking about.” I look to the side, not being able to meet his intense gaze.
“Oh yeah?” He leans forward, his breath fanning my collar bone, causing goosebumps all over my skin. His amazing smell took over all my senses completely. I close my eyes as his lips meet the arch of my neck softly. I grit my teeth together to keep from

making a sound, so I won't boost his ego. He pulls back, then moves to the opposite side, again kissing me in the same spot. But this kiss is deeper. Then his lips move higher up my neck, licking and kissing me, my breathing quickening more so. As soon as he gets to the area right under my ear, I whine softly. That noise was what he was waiting for. He wraps his arms around me and in one swift movement, he has me on my back on the bench, his bulky body over mine. His lips meet mine hungrily. I can't help it but to wrap my arms around him and pull him closer. As I kiss him back with whatever need that was building inside me for the past half an hour. I run my hands down his back and thoughts of feeling him shirtless over me has me moving to the hem of his shirt and pulling it upwards. Our lips are still colliding against each other. Feeling his hot skin under my fingertips as I pulled it up, he released my lips and pushed himself up, allowing me to pull off his shirt. I throw his shirt to the side and look him over as he straddles me on the bench. His knees on the floor, either side of me. His breathing was coming out in pants and his sweat coated skin was flushed. He gave me a quick look before leaning down and kissing me again. He took my bottom lip in his teeth and pulled down. He leaned down and kissed my chest. I tilt my head down to see him looking at me, watching for my reaction. He lowered with his hands to my sides and kissed me right above my stomach. As he lowers even more, he lifts my shirt up just enough to kiss over my belly button. I take in a sharp breath and bite down on my lower lip. My eyes follow his every move in anticipation. He lifts my shirt even higher and I hiss through my teeth as he kisses in between my chest over my bra. My nude bra was on full view to him, my nipples were hardened as they peaked through the padding. He pulled himself up a little, hovering over one of my breasts, he looked at them biting on his lip. My first thought was to cover myself up but the truth is, I wanted to see what he would do. He looks back to me, giving me a questioning look and I nod my head yes. Yes, because I want to give him everything. My whole body belonged to him to do as he pleased. He leaned down and kissed my bra just over my nipple. I lift my hands from the sides and push my fingers into his hair. Arching into him involuntarily with a soft moan, I tilt my head back with my eyes closed. That sensitivity wasn't anything. I feel his teeth graze my skin as he bites on the wire of my bra on the left side. He pulled it up and his breath fanning my nipple was enough to have me begging for more instead of pushing him away. With my eyes still closed and my back still arched into him, he suddenly sucks on my sensitive nipple. I couldn't contain the loud whine that leaves my lips. I tug on his hair and I hear a soft pur in the back of his throat. He slowly moves to the other side and does the same. This time I moaned out his name. I never felt anything like this and I didn't want him to stop. Ever. I felt myself clench in between my thighs and I knew I wanted more. The feeling of his lips on me was amazing. He stops and I feel him hover over me again, I look at him, my eyebrows furrowed. He looked like he was trying to focus. "What's wrong?" I ask, my words coming out in a whisper. "Someone's here." He puts a hand on the bench above my head and lifts himself up. He pulls me up to a sitting position and with a small smile, he adjusts my clothes back in place. He looks towards the door, then back to me. I look down my cheeks heating up a little, embarrassed of what we just did.

Chapter Thirty-Six

Benjamin

He stands to his full height running his hands through his tousled hair. I hear movement behind me, I stand to my feet and turn around. Walking towards us is a man I have never met before. I get behind Adonis in a way where I can still see the person but I feel more safe. The man gets closer with a pearly white smile on his face. He looked to be a lean man with shoulder length dirty blonde hair. He had a full on goatee and sharp eyes. From what I can tell, this man was in his mid fifties, he didn't look old, though from the lines around his hazel eyes, you can tell he has been through a lot. "Hey Adonis, didn't think I'd find you in here at this time." The man's voice is raspy but smooth. I look to Adonis' face and see his eyes lit up, "Hi, yeah. I came by to show Aphrodite the gym." The man's eyes meet mine and I blush a little, "Oh, so this is the famous girl I hear so much about." He walks closer and extends his hand towards me, "I'm Benjamin. It's a pleasure to finally meet you." I widened my eyes, I wouldn't have thought Adonis would mention me to this man. I extend my hand out and he grabs it, his smile widened as he shook our hands. "It's nice to meet you too, sir," My words come out timid. I want to slap myself in the face for being so shy all of a sudden. I bring my hand back to my side and the man steps back a little. "Please, call me Ben." I smile and nod. Benjamin's eyes go to Adonis, "Well, it's good you're here, I called the boys over so we can talk. I didn't bother calling you because I figured you'd be with your mom." Adonis shrugs it off as no big deal. "What did you want to talk about?" Adonis asked, his words getting serious, his eyebrows knitted together. Benjamin tilts his head towards me, "It's about work. Are you okay with your girl hearing all this?" Adonis looks down to me questioningly and I shrug. He looks back to Benjamin, "Yeah, it's fine."

Benjamin nods, “It's about the Russians. I need you guys to move in quickly. We can’t keep prolonging this. If we do, we will be sending a bad message to everyone else. They stole from us and we can’t let it pass.” He gives Adonis a stern look. Adonis nods and wraps an arm around me, as if to keep me from getting scared. But honestly, it was just interesting to me. “I understand, Ben. I was talking to James about that last night. We want to move in, in five days. We would have to be there for a few days to scope out everything.” We all turn towards the gym entrance as we hear people close by. In walks James, followed by Cain, Liam, and Hudson. “Adonis? What are you doing here?” James asked as they reached us. Cain looked us over with a huge smirk plastering on his face, “He brought Ditee to show off his glorious muscles.” I grin up at him making him smile back. “That explains why he is working out at noon and not the crack of dawn like he usually does.” Comes Liam’s unbothered statement. “How the fuck do you do that bro? I still can’t fathom it.” Hudson said, shaking his head in disbelief. Adonis ignores them all and looks back to Benjamin. Benjamin gives them all a look, “It's good you're all here. Adonis told me what you guys decided to do about the Russians. I agree completely. Just make sure you get all my shipment back. Also, make sure they all understand that they messed with the wrong person.” He looks at all their faces again, then says, “Keep me updated on that.” “You got it boss,” James said, not meeting the man's eyes.

Ben looks back at Adonis, “I set up another fight for tomorrow. I need you on full alert, Don. I have a lot of people who put big money on you.” Benjamin looks at me and smiles. I swallow, my heart hammering in my chest on nerves. “You should come.” My eyes widened and so did my smile at his words. “I would love to.” Adonis was quick to intervene and crush my hope completely. “That’s not gonna happen.” I look up to his face, my lips turning down. His lips were formed into a straight line. His eyes didn’t meet mine. I didn’t have to protest because Cain did it for me, “Oh come on, Don! Don’t be like that! Even the boss said she can come.” Adonis looks at him, anger coating his face, “She can’t come.” James gives him a look, as if saying you're being unreasonable, “All of us will be there to watch her. We won’t let anyone get near her.” Adonis blinks, his jaw clenched, containing his anger, “I said no.” His words were full of finality. I knew there was no fighting him at this point, he already made up his mind. And he was a stubborn man. I bite down on my lip and look down, not wanting to meet anyone’s eyes. “Adonis, you will only be in the ring for five minutes tops. Let the girl come. Let her watch you fight. When you're done, you can take her home.” Benjamin spoke reasonably but with authority. Everyone's eyes meet his, even mine. Adonis releases a heavy breath and looks at me, I meet his stare, a frown still on my face. He searches my eyes, then looks back to Benjamin, “I’ll think about it.” It really was up to him. He knew what was safe for me and what wasn’t and if he decided I wouldn’t go, then I wouldn’t and that would be fine. But if he says that I can go to his fight, then I would be extremely happy about that. Benjamin claps his hands together, “Alright, I’ll see you all tomorrow.” He looks to the boys, mostly eyeing Hudson, Cain, and Liam, “Can you guys please dress formally this time? I’m going to have a lot of important people over. You boys represent me.” Cain sighs dramatically, “Fine, I’ll take out my tux but don’t get mad when you see me in Jordan’s. I’m not gonna wear loafers.” Benjamin

shakes his head and walks away without another word.
Cain turns towards me, rubbing his hands together, “Are you ready?” I narrow my eyes at him stepping back from Adonis’ shirtless form, “For?”
“You’re gonna train.” He grins and I immediately frown. I shake my head, “I don’t work out. You guys go ahead I’ll just sit here and watch.” I point to the bench Adonis just had me laying on. I try to push away the thoughts of what would have happened if no one walked in. I turn my head towards James, who clicks his tongue, “Didn’t peg you for the lazy type.” My eyes widened at his words, “I’m not lazy, I just believe that I’m better off not sweating.” I look to the floor, “Maybe another time.”
“Look sweetie, if you're gonna hang out with us bad boys, you need to know how to defend yourself.” I give Hudson a sly smile. “Why do I need to defend myself if I have you boys to protect me?” I turned to Adonis, who was looking at me with a smirk. He knows how much I hate working out. “You know it would be good for you, Aphrodite.” His pale green eyes were shining in amusement. “Yeah, don’t knock it till you try it.” I give Liam a flat look and he smiles at me. I cross my hands over my chest with a huff, “Fine. What do you want me to do?” Hudson tilts his head towards the section where the machines are, “First, we gotta build up your stamina. Then, we will go from there.” Cain lifts up a finger, “Don’t forget to stretch.” I roll my eyes, “If I even feel out of breath, I am stopping.” They nodded at me and all of them looked like they were excited about this. I don’t understand why they are so happy to have me suffer. After fifteen minutes of telling me how to stretch, which I probably looked ridiculous, while they all looked like gods, we all got on the treadmills all in a line right next to each

other. I was in the middle, Adonis to my left, and Cain to my right. The boys were pretty fast and they didn't even look winded, I was barely even walking.
"So, there's a party tonight at Chad's house." I turned my head to Liam, who was right next to Adonis, "You guys in?" Adonis looks towards me, "What do you say, baby girl? Party?" I look at all the boy's faces, turning my head left to right, "Will Rox and Erika be there?" Cain answers quickly, "Like Roxy will ever miss a party. Of course they will." I nod, "Sure. Why not?" I shrug. Then, I think about a question I have been wanting to ask, "Do the girls know about all this? Am I the only one who was in the dark?" Adonis answers, "No, they don't know. We should keep it that way." Cain groans loudly and I turn towards him again, "I hate keeping all this from Roxy. Adonis and James keep busting my balls about it." I can't help but giggle a little. I then look back to Adonis, my body already tiring. "I mean, I don't see why you should keep it from them." I grin as I think about how Roxy would react, "I bet Roxy would join you guys in the mafia." The boys chuckle at that, Adonis shakes his head, "We'll see." After finishing our said "cardio", they have me lift some weights. Then, they told me they will start teaching me how to punch tomorrow. That did not put a smile on my face. I don't want to start kicking and punching at things. These hands are made for surgery, not hitting. After we discussed the party and what time we would meet, Adonis offered to drive me and I kindly accepted. Even though, all I really wanted was to be alone with him. I shouldn't be thinking like that, then I would just drown in him and that is not good for me.

Chapter Thirty-Seven

All Eyes On You

Climbing out of Adonis' car, I notice our friends waiting for us on the lawn of a huge two story house. There were people everywhere, the door was wide open and you can see the flashing lights from here. I wait for Adonis to reach my side, checking if my clothes are on right. I was wearing a lace body shirt that had black ribbon over my breast leading to the strap on each side. I was wearing a silk mini skirt with a slit on my left thigh, with black pointed leather heels and to top it all off, a black leather jacket with all sorts of zippers everywhere. My hair was in a high ponytail with a few loose strands here and there, my face was coated in bold makeup. As Adonis walks up to my side, we walk to where James, Liam, Cain, Hudson, Erika, and Roxy are talking. They turned towards us and Roxy narrowed her eyes at me. I walked over to her side and she raised a questioning eyebrow. "What?" I ask perplexed. She shakes her head, "Nothing. Nothing at all." I know she knows something changed between Adonis and I and soon, they would all probably find out. But until then, I will enjoy everyone being in the dark. We walk in, Adonis leading the way, we walk through a long hallway of people making out along the wall. The music was so loud, the walls had a slight shake to it. Smoke was everywhere and neon lights were flashing in different colors. We passed a living room that was crowded with people sitting down and smoking and inhaling all kinds of stuff. Drinks scattered here and there on the coffee table. Then we passed a large den where you can see people grinding on each other on the back wall. In the middle of the room was a small platform with a DJ who had huge headphones, directing the music. Adonis led us all the way to the kitchen, it was a really big kitchen. The island in the middle was filled with all kinds of liquor bottles. The granite counters

were filled with all the essentials. In the mix were the same guys from the last party, moving around the kitchen fixing drinks and passing it to people. I looked at Adonis, who leaned on a counter waiting for our turn to be served, I guess. “What's with these guys? Are they some sort of special bartenders?” He looks back to them, then at me, “Yeah actually. We always hire them to deal with the drinks and serve people. They make sure there isn’t any substance in the drinks and they stop people from drinking too much and only give drinks to the right people.” I blink at that. In here, the music wasn’t loud enough where you couldn’t hear, it was the perfect amount where you can talk.
“It's smart.” I turned my head to James, who was looking at the bartenders move around. “And they make a killing every party.” Hudson says, also looking at the bartenders. “That's really cool.” I looked back at Adonis and he was looking at me, searching my face with his icey eyes. He grabs my hand and pulls me so I stand right in front of him, turning me around he puts my back to his front and his arms around my midsection. I looked up to him and my eyebrows furrowed, “There’s too many eyes on you tonight, baby girl and I really don’t like it.” His voice comes out in a whisper, his breath fanning my neck, creating goose flesh all over my skin. I look back around towards the kitchen but don’t see anyone looking at me in this crowded room. He always had to be so possessive, I really hope he doesn’t get worse now that we’re…I don’t really know what we are. Hooking up? Friends with benefits? Best friends with benefits? I don’t know. I mentally shake my head. I look towards Erika and Roxy, they are both smirking at me. I look away trying to keep a straight face. One of the bartenders came up to the boys, “Hey guys! What are

you having?" The guy had short brown hair and matching eyes, he was tan and toned in a tank top with a logo on the front. Hudson and Cain order for all of us and the guy quickly gets to work. I feel one of Adonis' arms tighten around me and he whispers in my ear, "Did I mention how sexy you look?" I smile and shake my head, I hear him chuckle, the sound vibrating from his body to mine. "I don't think I'm going to be able to keep my hands to myself tonight." I turn my face up and our eyes meet, "Then don't." My words are serious and he knows it. All I know is that I want him to do whatever he wants to do to me. The bartender passed us all a drink, I looked down to see it was a blue liquid that was brimming the red cup. Adonis grabs his in one hand while keeping his other arm still around me. He easily takes a gulp, not even thinking it through. "What is this?" I ask, no one in particular. "It's an adios mother fucker." I blink up at Liam, who had a grin on his face. I put it to my lips and took a sip, it was really good. It tastes like sprite or something similar. It tastes really sweet too as if it didn't have any liquor in it at all. We all shuffle out of the kitchen and into the den where everyone was dancing. The music was booming in this room. To the left, were a few people sitting around some chairs but as they saw us, they all stood up, vacating the chairs immediately and walking away, not even looking towards the boys. I smirked for some reason. Is it wrong that I liked how the boys were treated? That I liked how everyone was intimidated by Adonis? Was it bad that I liked how he strutted into a room without a care in the world?
Everyone sits down on the couches and I take a seat on the coffee table directly in front of Adonis. He glared at me because he wanted me on his lap. I take a large gulp from my drink, looking Adonis over in the

process. He looked amazing tonight, so freaking hot. He was wearing a dark blue button down, with a few buttons opened, his arms bulging in the tight long sleeves. He paired it with dark dress pants and black shoes. I loved how he always dressed to impress. His hair was always styled to perfection, in a perfect undercut. He had tattoos everywhere but he managed to make it look sexy and sophisticated, not cheap and dirty. He looked like trouble and trouble never looked so damn fine. The drink was already giving my head a slight spin, it wasn't bad but I definitely felt it. His eyes look to the floor, then flash to mine, darkening as they sweep over me. With that look, I know what he wants. I smirk at him, raising my eyebrow. I turn my head away from him purposely, looking over to Roxy and Erika who were huddled together, saying something to each other. I stand up from the table and tower over Adonis, who looks up at me, his eyebrows lowering. I smile innocently and walk over to where the girls are. I park my ass on top of Roxy, leaning my head in between both of them. "What are you two talking about?"
"Are you done checking out Adonis?" Erika asked me, with a glint in her eye. I give her a flat look, then to make her laugh, look back to Adonis, giving him a quick once over. He was putting a cigarette to his lips and extending the box out to the boys, who each grabbed one. I look back to her, "Okay, now I'm done." They both laugh and I grin. "Erika was telling me how James finally asked her out." I turn my head quickly to Erika at Roxy's words. I look at her with lit eyes, "Really?!" She nods, beaming at me. "Well, finally one of you made a move." Erika blushes a little and her eyes move to the area where James is, "I know. I was just so shy. I was glad he finally did it, I thought I was gonna explode." I give her an amused

smile, then look to Roxy, “Now it's your turn to finally admit your feelings about Cain.” Roxy scoffs, “I have no fucking feelings for him and I never will.” She crosses her arms over her chest. I roll my eyes, “Sure whatever. One day you will tell me what happened with that.” She gives me a straight face, “That day won't be today.” I give her a look, which has her quickly look away from me avoiding eye contact. I mentally shrug it off and look around the room, I see everyone dancing and I decide on joining them. “Fine, whatever. Lets go dance.” They agree with me and I down my drink before walking to the dance floor with the girls following behind me. We stand only a few feet away from where the boys are seated. I turn my back to them and look towards the girls, dancing to the music. The liquor made my face a little numb, I secretly really liked the feeling. I start swaying my hips to the music, dancing and losing myself to it. The base of the music was vibrating into me and It was exhilarating. I couldn't hear my own thoughts and I was attracted to the song. As I'm dancing, Roxy leans in to my ear, “Don't look now but Adonis looks pissed. I give him two minutes tops before he is either pulling you off the dance floor or joining.” I pull back and give her a questioning look. I lean forward this time and ask, “Why is he mad?” This time she looks at me perplexed, “You really don't see it?” I look from her to Erika, “What!?”
Erika smirks at me, “You look freaking amazing, Aphrodite. Everyone's eyes are on you. Boys and girls.” I look over my shoulder to see for myself, even if Roxy told me not to. He was leaning into the chair, his legs wide open, the cigarette in between his fingers in the same hand that was holding his drink. His eyes were sharp and the shadows around them were darker than normal. His jaw was tense and his

lips were in a thin line. I turned my whole body towards him and continued dancing, his notched eyebrow raised and I smirked. I lift my hand and gesture for him to come over in a come-hither manner. He stands to his feet setting his drink down and mashing his cigarette in an ashtray on the table. He struts over to me, his eyes never leaving mine. He steps up to me and I instantly wrap my arms around his neck, "Dance with me bad boy." Without a word, he grabs me by the hips and flips me around, pulling me flush against me. I sway my hips and he follows me to the beat. He puts his face into my neck, whispering into my ear, "Didn't I tell you, I didn't like eyes on you?" A song that I really like starts playing, "Piece of You" by Shawn Mendes. I ignore what he said and lift an arm to put it around his neck, putting the other to one of his hands on my hip. I continue dancing into him and I feel his hot breath on my neck, making me shiver. I turn my body in his hold and wrap my arms around his neck again, his hands latching on my hips for dear life. He looks down into my eyes and I meet his gaze, trying to match his intensity. My heart was hammering in my chest and I wanted him closer. Somehow, he activates the naughty in me and I love it. The way he looks at me makes me feel like I'm the only thing he wants. I bring my hand down his neck slowly and reach the buttons of his shirt. I look at my hand as it follows the line of his buttons. As I reach the last one, my eyes flash to his and his lips part, his chest rising. I bite down on my lips and his eyes look at the gesture, his jaw clenching. How do I politely ask him to take me somewhere and do all sorts of bad things to me? He leans down putting his mouth against my ear, my eyes closing at the feeling of his lips. "I have a bad idea." Tilting my head up to his ear, I whisper, "I have a feeling I'm going to like it."

Chapter Thirty-Eight

You Drive Me Crazy

I bite down on my bottom lip as he pulls me up the stairs. He turns his head to look at me over his shoulder and my stomach erupts in butterflies. I don't know where he was taking me, the anticipation was killing me. As of right now, I couldn't care less what our friends thought. I couldn't even think about what I would do if they questioned me. Getting to the top of the stairs, he pulls me along a dark hallway filled with people. We get to a door and he turns the knob. We walked into a dark bathroom, the only light was from the large floor to ceiling window right behind the large bathtub that was connected to a shower. The moonlight was cascading over the double sink on the opposite side. To the left was a door that most likely led to the toilet. He closes the door and the music muffles behind it. He turns towards me and grabs my face in his large hands, "You drive me crazy." Before I can ask what he meant exactly, he smashes his lips to mine. I close my eyes and kiss him back, breathing in from my nose. I grab a fist full of his shirt, pulling him closer to me. He releases my face and grabs onto my side, lifting me up, our lips still attached. He set me down on the counter and opened my legs wide, getting in between them. He deepens the kiss and I easily join him. I bring my hands behind his head pulling him closer, making him crouch a little. I need to feel his body on mine, I need his warmth. His delicious smell of cedarwood was making my senses go wild, I wanted to taste all of him. I pull away to catch my breath and he continues to kiss me down to my neck, my chest rising and falling rapidly with my heavy breathing. I bring one hand up into his hair and as his lips meet the arch on my neck, I tug with a moan. He makes a sexy little sound and I wrap my legs around his waist, pulling myself impossibly closer

to him. He puts his hands on my bare thighs, exhaling deeply into my neck.
I was so glad I was only wearing a skirt because feeling him harden through the thin layer of lace panties I had on, was enough to make me tip my head back in need. My head hits the mirror behind me and he kisses along the ribbon on my breast, I look down and our eyes meet. I feel myself clench between my legs at the sexy look he gives me and a small noise leaves my lips, making him smile on my heated skin. Nothing is sexier than the fact that he wants me as much as I want him. He brings his hands up my thighs, slowly kissing along my collarbone now. He leaves one hand on my outer thigh and brings the other up to my waist and tightens his grip. With the hand that's on my outer thigh, he grabs the material of my skirt in his large hand and pulls up. My red lace panties now peaking through, I looked down to see what he was doing but his eyes were still on mine, assessing my reaction. He was slowly caressing my outer thigh now, kissing my skin softly and teasingly. I can't take it anymore so I pull on his hair and smash my lips to his in a hungry kiss, he kisses me back, his tongue exploring my mouth. I felt my underwear dampened and I needed friction so I squirmed around trying to feel him against me. I don't know why he always makes me so needy, I just need to feel him, at least for a little bit. He bites down on my lip, slowly pulling back, taking my lip with him. When he released my lip, it made a little noise colliding back to my teeth. He brings both his hands to my jacket and tugs it off, his eyes never leaving mine. He throws it to the side and it makes a noise as the zippers hit the sink. His eyes slowly rake over me from his towering height. His eyes darken as he takes in my blouse without the jacket. “This is the last time you wear this

shirt." I gulp and nod my head. "This shirt will only be for my eyes." I searched his face and licked my lips due to the fact that my mouth got parched on how sexy he sounded, his thick voice was filled with lust. He brings his fingers to my collarbone and slowly brings down his hand, watching his movements. I put my hands on either side of me, clutching at the counter top. His breathing was heavier with the lower he got down the lace fabric. He brings his fingers in between my breast and my breath hitched. With every second, my heart was beating faster and faster. As he reaches just below my belly button, my lips part and my breath comes out uncontrollably. Suddenly, his fingers touch in between my thighs and we both suck in a breath at the same time our eyes meet again. He visibly gulps and his fingers run up my slit through my underwear, his bottom lip was between his teeth. Releasing his lip, he whispers, "You're so wet for me, Aphrodite." My face heats up and I look away from him, slightly embarrassed. He grabs my face in his other hand and pulls it towards him, giving me a sweet kiss. His lips graze mine as he says, "It's so fucking hot." I release a breath as I feel him pull my panties to the side and run a finger over my wetness. He groans loudly and tips his head back. He pulls his hand away and I watch with wide eyes as he brings his finger to his lips. His tongue comes out and he slides his finger on it, his eyes colliding with mine and I clench at the gesture. "So fucking sweet princess." Clutching on the counter harder, I felt a knot in my throat and I couldn't even form words at this moment. I look to one of his irises, then to the next, not knowing what to expect. He brings his hand back in between my legs and slides his finger up and down. He puts his forehead to mine and I close my eyes at the feeling of his finger caressing me and I moan softly. Before I can even register what he is doing, he puts a finger to my entrance and my eyes widened as he slowly pushes it in. He looks at me through hooded eyes, his jaw clenched. I have never felt this before, I whine at the uncomfortable feeling and he waits for me to adjust to it. I was always a little scared to do this so I never even tried. “You are so tight, baby girl. I thought-” He shakes his head, not continuing what he was going to say. He leans forward and kisses my lips, slowly pulling his finger out just a little, then pushes it back in. I frown against his lips at the feeling, a small whimper escaping from my lips. He pulls his mouth from mine, “Do you want me to stop?” Concern covers his face from my reaction. I shake my head, “No. Please keep going.” He leans down, taking my lips back in his. With his thumb, he rubs on my sensitive nub. I moaned softly into his mouth as the feeling of pleasure was taking over the discomfort. He brings his other hand up to my breast and grabs it in his large hand, he runs his thumb over my nipple, then squeezes my breast. I bring my hands up to his large shoulders and moan as his finger slides out of me and he brings the wetness upwards and rubs up and down. This time when he enters me with his finger, I breath out in pleasure. He leans back a little, his pale green eyes looking at his finger entering my slit and disappearing between my folds. He closes his eyes in mercey then they flash to me in a heated gaze. He pulls on my legs till they’re wide opened for him. He puts his hand to my shoulder and pushes me back so my shoulders hit the mirror and my hands hit the counter helping me stay up. My breathing again was picking up as he slowly moved his finger inside me. He grabs one of my legs, still watching his hand, he sets my high heeled foot on the counter and I easily move it for him. With my leg now bent up on the counter he had a perfect view of what he wanted. His eyes flash to mine again for only a second before going back to his movement. I feel him take out his finger, then rubs me again this time in slight circles adding his other fingers for better friction, I close my eyes, “Adonis.” The words come out in full mercy and he groans at my reaction. I feel him continue rubbing me, his fingers speeding up and I can’t help the loud noise that escapes from my lips. It's a good thing we were at a party and whatever noise I made was drowned out to the people beyond this room by the music. When he enters me again, he does it with two fingers but my pleasure was so high, that I hardly noticed. He continued rubbing me with his thumb and pumping his fingers and I felt my stomach tighten and I knew I was getting close. He pulled out his fingers again and used the juices to rub me faster. I couldn’t contain the whining and moaning as I was getting incredibly closer. I squirm and he grabs onto my hip with his free hand to keep me from moving too much. “Adonis!” This time I yelled his name, His eyes met mine, “Come for me.” His encouragement is what I needed, with a buck of my hips, I moan loudly, coming. My eyes pinched shut in ecstasy. He grabs onto my neck and pulls my face to his, kissing me as I come all over his fingers. He slows down his pace helping me prolong my orgasm, his lips still kissing me. He pulls his fingers away and puts my panties back into place, then lowers my skirt. He pulls away from my lips, his body still close to mine. I open my eyes to see his running over my face. “You look so beautiful.” I put my hand to my chest trying to control my breathing and look down to his tightened jeans. I look up at his eyes and smile but he shakes his head, knowing what I wanted to do. “Tonight was just about you.”

Chapter Thirty-Nine

King Of The Jungle

Last night ended pretty well, we continued hanging out and we danced a little more. At the end of the night, Adonis dropped me off and I reluctantly walked inside the house. This morning, I had a crazy wake up call, to say the least. I woke up to all of Adonis' friends screaming my name to wake up. I covered my face and groaned, wanting them to leave me alone. When I peaked out, Adonis was just laughing at their antics. Cain even threw some clothes at me after rummaging through my closet and right when Liam was going to pull the covers off of me to get me out of bed, Adonis growled at him like some sort of animal. I finally threw them out of my room, promising I was going to get up and get ready. They took me to the gym and I sparred with each of them, Adonis taking the last turn. I really thought I was gonna hate it but instead, I was asking for more. At one point, I was bouncing on my heels and calling them forward to see who could take me, cockily. They were all laughing at me but they were proud of how quickly I was learning. After the gym, we got a quick bite to eat and now Adonis was dropping me off home. He was leaning on a column in front of my door and looking at me with a huge smile. "You did great today." I look down at the floor, my cheeks heating up from his compliment, "Thanks." I look up and he has a contemplating look on his face. I tilt my head to the side giving him a questioning one. A few seconds passed before he asked me, "Do you really want to go tonight?" I pull my lips into my mouth, thinking it over. I didn't want to go by force, I wanted to go because he wanted me there. "Only if you want me there." He takes a deep breath, "Fine." My eyebrows knit together in confusion, "What?" He stood up straight, "I'll be here at six to pick you up." My eyes glistened at his words, "Really?" He nods and I squeal, instantly wrapping my arms around him in a huge hug, “Thank you, thank you, thank you!” He wraps his arms around my waist hugging me back. Oh god! What am I going to wear? I pull back and he notices my worried look, “What is it?” I shake my head, “I have no idea what to wear.” I turn and walk through my already opened door, pulling my phone from my back pocket, dialing Roxy’s number. I need to call her to help me choose my outfit. I can’t do this without her. I put the phone to my ear and heard it ring, then I realized that I can’t just invite her without permission. I quickly turn on my heel and give him a sheepish smile, “Can I invite Roxy?” He looks me over, sucking on his teeth in thought, then takes a deep breath letting his shoulders slump, “Sure, why not.” I hear Roxy’s voice say, “Hey?” Then I quickly put her on mute and ran back to Adonis, “You're the best,” and gave him a quick kiss on the cheek. I pull back, unmute the phone and put it to my ear walking backwards, into my house, “Roxy, I need you.” Adonis chuckles and I wave at him then close the door. I hear shuffling and I can imagine Roxy sitting up on her bed thinking the worst possible situation, “What's wrong?” “There is this huge event tonight and we need to get dressed, all fancy. How long till you’re here?” I hear her take a deep calming breath. “Gosh, I thought I had to bury a body or something. Yeah, I’ll be there in ten, I’ll pick up Erika for back up. What is this event?” Erika? I think as I am walking up the stairs, I really hope Adonis…or James won’t mind her coming but I could use all the help I can get. I’ll just text Adonis to let him know. “I’ll explain later. Bring your best outfits! Bye!” I hung up the phone and ran into my room for a really long shower.

I LOOK UP AT an already done Roxy as she finishes the last piece of my curly up do. She was wearing a white, opened suit jacket with a lace strapless body shirt that had a corset style to it, tucked into white pants. Her hair was in a bun, parted through the middle, with light makeup. "So all this time Adonis has been underground fighting? And no one had the decency to tell me?" She brings up the situation again and I smile. I didn't exactly explain the mafia situation but she will most likely piece that together herself. I shrug and look to Erika for help, who was straightening her hair. She shakes her head and looks away, looking beautiful in her yellow satin dress with thin straps holding up the bodice. "Okay, girls." I look at both of them through the mirror and their eyes meet mine. "We need to stay next to the boys at all times. We can't wander off alone. There will be all sorts of criminals there and we don't know what can happen. We need to keep our heads down and keep to ourselves." They nod and Roxy sets down the hair tool as she is finally done with me. I stand up from my chair and turn to a full length mirror admiring Roxy's work. My hair was styled to perfection in a messy but elegant updo. My make up was bold but classy. The dress she chose was almost the same color of my eyes, Royal blue. It was a velvet, long sleeve dress that was completely backless. The neckline reached over my collarbones so I only wore long earrings. The split on the dress ran up my left leg in a rounded curve, paired with matching pointed heels. At that, I hear the door chime loudly, signaling someone walked in. I turn my head back to the girls who were also checking themselves out, making sure they didn't need anything. We walk out of my room and to the banister at the staircase. I look down to see all the boys there, dressed to perfection in tuxedos. They all turned their heads towards us and my eyes caught Adonis'. He was the only one without a suit jacket. He had a white tuxedo shirt with black suspenders and black pants, with a bow tie opened around his neck. I have never been so wildly attracted to someone, I can actually feel myself going insane for him. Roxy starts towards the stairs, stomping down them fuming in anger. Erika and I follow her slowly, worriedly. Cain walks to the edge of the last step, lifting his hands up in front of his face, palms up, "Rox. I have been dying to tell you," Roxy gets closer with every word he says, "You need to understand-" Cain doesn't continue as Roxy slaps him straight across the face, making me flinch. Cain puts a hand to his cheek and looks at her wide eyed. "I tell you everything. How could you keep this from me?!" As I get down the last steps past Roxy, I stand in between the boys, Erika joining me. I turned my face to glare at Liam and Hudson, who were holding in their laughter. As they noticed my glare, they actually laughed loudly. James glared at them now and they both suck in their lips at the same time to keep from laughing further. Roxy then points at me, "She knows for all of five minutes and she did not hesitate to tell me. God knows how long you have been hiding this!" Adonis stepped up from my side, the shirt stretched tight across his strong shoulders making my heart beat faster at the powerful atmosphere around him. "Roxy." Her eyes turn towards him and she blinks a little, her cheeks tinting red, also feeling his domineer. "He really has been wanting to tell you. It was I, who didn't allow him. I didn't want Aphrodite knowing about any of this." Her eyes flash to Cain, then back to Adonis, she nods and walks down the last step, walking to my side. Everyone stays silent and I look at Adonis' back, blinking at the fact that he has so much authority without even trying. James clears his throat and opens the front door, "We should get going, we have reservations." Reservations? What does he mean by that? I watch as everyone steps out and then I turn towards Adonis, who was already looking me over, his hands inside of his front pockets. I smile at him and he returns the gesture, "You look stunning." He starts towards me and I put my hand on my hip leaning my weight on that leg, making it pop out a little. I give him a noticeable once over, "And you look dashing." I smirk at him and he steps right in front of me, putting one hand on my bare back, pulling me against him. I look up at him as he looks down, our eyes meeting, green on blue colliding like the ocean. He runs his calloused hand up the curve of my spine. I try my best to keep from stuttering in desire, "Does this thing have a zipper? Or will I just be pulling it off?" I bite down on the corner of my bottom lip and bring my hands up to his chest, "Who said you were allowed to take it off?" He lifts his notched eyebrow at me with a smirk, "By the end of the night, you will be begging me to take it off." I narrow my eyes at him, "Is that a challenge?" With a shrug of his shoulder, he steps away and walks past me out the door. I watch the move of his shoulder blades as he walks out, like a lion in his kingdom. The boys took us to a very nice dinner at a fancy restaurant. Roxy sat at the opposite end of Cain, still angry at him. Everyone was trying their best to ignore them. Adonis got me an apple martini that made me bubbly. We all fought over the bill at the end but for some reason Adonis always ended up paying the whole thing. Throughout the whole dinner, Adonis' hand was on me, caressing me and creating a whole field of butterflies in the pit of my stomach. He just couldn't stop touching me.

We were now stepping out of the large SUV we came in. The girls looked at me in confusion as we were at the back of the rundown shopping center. As the boys start walking, I tilt my head to follow them and they do. We walk through the now opened door and we enter the dimly lit entrance, the girls cautiously follow me down the stairs.

Chapter
Forty
Get In And Get Out

Watching Adonis as he is sitting down on a wooden chair, the spine to his bare chest, his legs straddling it, James wraps one of his hands and Liam wraps the other. He was now in black loose shorts, his clothes long forgotten in the locker room. We were in the gym and Adonis was looking up at Benjamin as he told him what he needed to know about his opponent. The man Adonis is going to be fighting weighs more than him and is taller but Benjamin said that, that will make him slower. Benjamin also told him the fighter's usual routine. Adonis just stood there, his jaw clenched listening intently to his boss. I look between Roxy and Erika, who looked like they were still trying to wrap their heads around what's going on. As both the boys finished wrapping his hands at the same time, Benjamin said, "When you win tonight, you will officially be undefeated in all of California. These people are coming all the way from San Francisco and Lucas is also undefeated. You need to strip him of that title." Benjamin looks at Adonis, waiting for a reply but doesn't get one so he says, "Do you understand?" Adonis nods his head and Benjamin shakes his head with a loud sigh, he walks away and out of the gym. I walk up to Adonis and crouch down so we are eye level, his eyes meet mine and his jaw relaxed. "Are you sure you want to do this?" He stands from the chair and pulls it to the side as I stand to my full height. I look at him intently, trying to read his face but he gives me nothing as he looks at me with hard eyes. "I have been doing this, Aphrodite. I think I can handle this one fight." My eyebrows furrow and I frown, "I have won against men who were bigger than him." I looked over him, the skull that took up all the space on his abs looked like it was ready to pounce on his next victim. And the tribal lines that moved from his arms to his chest, looked darker with

the oils that were coating his skin. The fans came to see him for his tattoos and body so they had to make him look more defined.
I watch as he walks up to the boys, my ears ringing, the words not being registered in my head. All I'm hearing is white noise as flashes of Adonis getting punched in the face run through my memory. I stand there just watching as James was telling him something and Adonis nods. But as the boys talk to him, I only see their lips move. My heart was beating incredibly fast as fear creeped up my chest. At the sound of my name, I snap myself out of it and turn towards Roxy, "Ready?" I look back to see the boys looking at me, already halfway towards the exit. I nod, following them out the room, Adonis leading the way. As we entered the long hallway that opened up like a tunnel, I heard people screaming. As we get to the edge of the tunnel, music starts playing. Adonis turns his face back to me and his eyes meet mine. He looks at Cain and tilts his face towards me, pretty much telling him "don't leave her side". Cain nods and comes to stand next to me. We walked out of the tunnel and the crowds parted by men in black suits who looked like bodybuilders, allowing us to walk through. As we get closer to the boxing ring, I speed up my step in my high heels, trying to catch up to Adonis. As I do, I grab onto his arm, he turns his face towards me, his eyes moving from mine to my lips, then back to my eyes again. I couldn't help the worry that was showing on my face. I wanted to be strong but it was really hard. "Be careful." He smirks, cockily saying, "Always, baby." I smile and shake my head. He turned back around and Hudson was up on the platform holding the ropes open for him. Adonis steps up on the two steps leading to the platform, then bends under the top rope while putting a leg over the

bottom rope. He gets into the ring and stands to his full height. The yelling starts getting louder than the music and I look out to the crowd to see people jumping up and down at his presence.
A man in a black tuxedo with greying hair, steps up to Adonis and screams into a microphone "Adonis! The fallen Angel!!" My eyes widened at his nickname and they immediately went to the black feathered wings on his back and it made sense. So that's what it must say on his back, it had to. The other fighter steps into the ring and they say his name also. He had blonde hair in a man bun and bright blue eyes. He was huge, Adonis is tall, maybe about six foot two inches but this man was at least six foot five inches tall. "These two fighters are both undefeated. One from Southern California and the other from Northern California. Tonight's winner will take home the full California title!" People start cheering and when it dies down, the announcer speaks again, "Now boys, shake hands." Adonis stays still his stans, full of power, making Lucas walk towards him stretching out his hand. Adonis looks at it, then grabs it, shaking it and everyone starts screaming again. As we stand there in one corner of the ring, a woman in a red dress walks in front of us holding a cardboard sign in her hands. Her hair was cascading down her back in dark layers. Her dress was long but with a wide split up each leg and the cleavage reached to the top of her stomach, giving a glimpse of her perfect chest. I recognize her immediately as the announcer lets her in as he gets out. It was Adriana, the girl that was sitting on Adonis' lap the day we went to the bonfire. She smiles at the man, her tan face coated in makeup, making her look even more beautiful. As the fighters stand there waiting for the match to begin, she walks around the ring, her back straight and her

stride as perfect as a supermodel's. She holds up the sign over her face and as she gets close to Adonis, she turns her face towards him and throws him a wink. He didn't even pay attention as his eyes were on Lucas. I noticed my breathing was quickening and my face was heated and I knew I was full of jealousy. I turn towards the girls to try to rid myself of thoughts of his hands on her body. Roxy and Erika were looking at her with distaste, might I add. They met my eyes and Roxy grimaced with a crinkle of her nose. While Erika gave me a sad smile. Cain was right by my side but his eyes were on Adonis and Lucas, so were the other boy's. A loud noise was heard, signaling the fight had begun. I turn towards the ring and see how Adriana was stepping off on the complete other side of it. I notice a man in a red shirt in the ring with a whistle hanging from his neck. Adonis and Lucas start walking around in circles, both their fist up to their faces, both of them assessing each other. I look at Cain and ask, "I didn't think there were rules in underground fighting. Why is there a referee?" He turns towards me, his eyes going from Adonis to me slowly, "This is just like regular MMA boxing. We have most of the same rules. We just bet way more and are ruled by crime lords." He shrugs, "The crime lords don't want their best fighters to die or get seriously injured."
I look out to the crowds and my eyes sweep over all the classy dressed men and women and wonder what they do and who they are. I ask, my face still towards the crowds, "How much money exactly?"
"Millions," My head flashes to Hudson, who wasn't even looking at me with his statement. "Damn." I hear Roxy say from beside me. I look at the ring again, just in time to see Adonis block a hit to the face. I swallow a lump in my throat and put my hands to my hips to

make sure I'm perfectly steady. Again, Adonis blocked another hit by ducking and stepping to the other side, making Lucas follow his movement. The crowd cheers at every block. Adonis keeps doing the same thing, he doesn't allow his opponent to hit him and moves to the side, making him follow him so he is again in front of Adonis. "What is he doing?" I ask and Liam giggles. James answers me, "Lucas is a big guy, he will get tired fast." Hudson snickers, "And Adonis has no plan on staying in there for long." I furrow my eyebrows, about to ask what he meant when Liam says, "His plan is for a quick knockout so he can take you home." I look at him taken aback but totally understanding that Adonis would definitely do something like that. I look back to the ring and as Lucas almost hits Adonis. Adonis ducks and throws a right and left jab to his ribs, then stands to his right. Lucas' shoulders slump and his mouth opens in pain, his eyes wide. The dark room filled with silence in shock at how Adonis so easily broke the man's ribs. Adonis then lifts his fist, pulls back, and hits him at the top of his cheek with all his force. Lucas' face flies to the side, his jaw dislocating completely and he falls to the floor. I put my hand to my mouth with my eyes completely opened, my heart wanted to come out of my chest, and my stomach was in knots. The arena was still as they waited to see if Lucas got up, Adonis stood up straight and looked down to his unconscious rival. The referee checks Lucas and lifts his hands signaling knockout. The room erupted in cheers and hawlers, the crowd going wild as they realized he wasn't going to get up anytime soon. The announcer quickly steps into the ring, grabs Adonis' hand and puts his microphone to his mouth. "And our winner is Adonis, The fallen Angel!" Adonis gets out of the man's hold and steps towards us, his eyes not

meeting mine. He steps out of the ring and down the stairs. He reaches us, gives Cain a look and passes us completely, still not looking my way. I blink a little and Cain puts his hand on my shoulder, leading me to follow everyone else.
As we walk through the crowds, he continues walking ahead of all of us. *He probably doesn't want the criminals to see me with him*, is what passes through my mind. But as we are walking into the tunnel, I try to catch up to him but his step quickens and he walks into the locker room. As I get close to the room, I hear James say, "We should wait in the gym for Adonis to get ready." I look at him, my eyebrows knitted together in confusion. As everyone walks into the gym to wait, I stand there undecided on what to do. I look from door to door contemplating. I needed to know what was his problem, why did he close himself off that way. It was burning me on the inside. I suck on my teeth and walk into the locker room, hearing water run, I turn towards the showers. Adonis was in the middle one, his body covered by the curtain. I stomp over and without a thought, wrap my hand around the grey plastic and pull it back against the middle pole above. He looks at me, the water spraying over his head, steam surrounding him. I don't say anything as I stare at his face, trying to avoid his perfect body. I watch as he rubs soap into his hair, his eyes pinched closed, I keep my eyes up as he brings his hands down, cleaning his body too. The shower was large enough where the water wasn't ricocheting to me. I was bemused by his behavior. As he finishes, he turns off the water and walks towards me, dripping in water. I step to the side and he steps out, grabbing a towel that was hanging on the wall in between the showers. I quickly look him over before he wraps the towel around himself, putting my hand on my hip and

my lips pursed. He walks towards the lockers and with a sigh, I follow him. He gets to the one with his name on it and I flinch as he punches it harshly. I pull in a sharp breath and watch as he puts his forehead to the locker, breathing heavily. I took a few steps closer to him, standing to his left. "Adonis?" His name comes out in a whisper,
He turns his head towards me, his forehead still on the locker, "I never wanted you to see me this way." The words come out thick.
"What do you mean?" I ask softly. He turns towards me, completely looking me in the eyes, "When I said I am not the same person anymore, I meant it. I didn't want you to know this side of me. I kept you away for so long and that was one of the reasons." He looks down at his hands, turning them over, then looks back to me. The water was still dripping down his muscular body. "I'm sorry, I shouldn't have brought you here. It was a mistake. Just where you're standing right now, it's a risk. A risk I shouldn't be taking." I walked up to him and put my hand to his cheek, he leaned into my touch, closing his eyes, "Being here meant everything to me." His eyes open and it feels as if they are staring into my soul. He steps away from me and lifts his hand to his hair, clutching it in a fist. "You just don't understand. I'm dangerous for you. This is dangerous. You can't even comprehend what can happen to you." I look at him, analyzing his features, his eyes blazing in regret and anger. His lips in a thin line, his jaw clenched. I looked down to see his hand in fist as he tried to control his anger. "This didn't change anything. I told you, nothing will." I take a step towards him, reaching my hand towards him but he quickly says, "Please don't." My movement stops completely and I lower my hand to my side. "Adonis, please. Don't do this. Don't shut me out again." I look

at him pleadingly as I continue, "I won't handle it this time." He frowns sadly and takes the steps remaining between and stands right in front of me, I lift my head up to meet his eyes and see the conflict in them. He takes a deep breath, obviously losing some battle in his mind, "Trust me Aphrodite, I'm not able to do that again." He leans his forehead against mine and I close my eyes, enjoying the closeness.

Chapter Forty-One

Always...

Fluttering my eyes open with a deep breath, I turn my face to the side and my eyes land on a very much sleeping Adonis. He looked so peaceful. His usually tense jaw was relaxed, his long eyelashes resting over his cheeks. I looked at his lips and they were parted. I wanted to press my lips to his swollen ones but I didn't want to wake him. I closed my eyes, still feeling the pressure of his hand on my head as his fingers were through my hair, directing me just how he wanted. He slept over after, not wanting to leave me home alone. Last night, after Adonis got dressed, we walked into the gym and there waiting for him was Benjamin, he congratulated him happily. Then, Adriana walked in, she also came to congratulate him. She wrapped her arms around him but he literally shook her off. I wanted to rip her hair out for even touching him, I don't know why it bothered me so much. Adonis noticed my sour mood but didn't say anything until we were alone in my bedroom. Just knowing she has done stuff with him that I still haven't, made me seeth in anger. I wanted to ask what she was doing there but I couldn't make myself say her name. He teased me about my sour mood before he showed me how he only wanted me. He made me feel so sexy and confident, I don't even know how he does it. I open my eyes and look back to him. He was flat on his back and I was on my side, admiring him. My heart started beating faster and I felt heat pull in between my legs as memories from last night's activities started flashing through my head. His lips between my thighs. His hands gripping mine as he kept me from touching him. The way his eyes looked as I got to my knees telling him I wanted him. I grin and bite down on my bottom lip as crazy ideas run through my head. I lean forward and kiss his bare chest, feeling his warmth under my lips. I leave a trail

of kisses leading towards his arm. I feel movement and then hear his thick, hoarse voice say, “What are you doing?”
I looked up to his face and his eyes were still closed, “Minding my own business.” My lips graze his skin as I speak. Getting on my hands and knees to straddle him, I continue going down towards his abs. I kiss him softly as every piece of me aches for him. I wanted him to feel my need just by my lips. “Honestly, if you keep going any lower, I won’t be able to stop.” His words come out humoredly, but little did he know I wasn’t joking. I looked up at him, his eyes open but still tired as he watched my lips on him, “That's the point.” I feel him grab onto me and he flips us in one swift movement so he was now on top of me. His eyes met mine and they were shining in amusement. How could someone look so good in the morning, I probably looked like a mess. I was only wearing his button up from last night. My hair was super crazy and tangled. His face gets closer and he grazes his nose along mine, “Someone’s in the mood.”
“Are you planning to ruin it? Because I was thinking about going further this time.” The words come out in a murmur. He sighs loudly and peels himself off of me, throwing himself back on the bed beside me.
“Aphrodite,” He groans out my name. I get on my side again and prop myself on my elbow. I reach my hand and glide it down his chest. I look up to his face, under my eyelashes, puckering out my bottom lip, “What is it?” My hand reaches to the waistband of his boxers and he quickly grabs it in his large one, bringing it to his chest. “Before we take this any further, we need to take precautions. Are you on birth control?” I shake my head no. I never needed it, it didn’t even cross my mind till now. He was right, we have to take care of ourselves. “What do you think if

we go to the clinic and start you on it?" "Yes, I agree." He opens his mouth to say something when my phone rings. He gestures for me to get it and I turn to my nightstand and grab it, sliding it open as I see my mother's name and picture on my screen. "Hello," I say as I put it on speaker. "Hey sweetie, how are you?" My mothers voice comes through the phone. I suddenly feel Adonis hands run up my leg and under my shirt. I turn my face and give him a warning look and he gives me a smirk. Turning back to the phone, I say, "Yeah, I'm good, mom. What's up?" Adonis' hand creeps higher up my shirt and my breath hitches. "Oh, nothing Aphrodite, just wanted to check up on you." At my mother's words, Adonis' hand latches on my breast, I hike up my leg and kick him in the shin. He groans loudly in pain and I snicker. "Is someone there?" My mother asked, worriedly. I take a deep breath, rolling onto my stomach, Adonis pulling his hand out, "It's just Adonis."
I hear a sigh of relief come from her, "Oh, that's good. Hi Adonis!" She said loudly. Adonis chuckled and got right by my side, matching my position, "Hi Melissa." "It's a good thing you're there too. We are having dinner at your house and we want both of you there." I furrow my eyebrows at Adonis, "Dinner?" I ask my mother. "Yes. This is the only time we all have free time before Mary's surgery." I look to Adonis and watch as his eyes harden, "We'll be there."

"WHAT?" I ASKED, PERPLEXED at his statement. "I get a tattoo after every fight." We were in the car on our way to a tattoo parlor. So that's why he had so many tattoos. "So like, how many fights is that exactly?" He chuckled and I looked down to his hand on my leg that was covered in jeans. "The truth, I lost

count." I blink up at him and then look out the window as we arrive at a little store that was painted black and had a big sign overhead saying the store's name. He parks in front of the store and we climb out. I wait for him to reach me and he grabs my hand, pulling me to the glass door. He opens it and a chime is heard overhead. We stepped into the tattoo shop, the floor was black and white checkered. There were pictures of tattoos and people with them all over the walls. In the middle of the room was a large black receptionist desk. A man walked through a door that was ajar behind the desk. He had platinum long hair and black eyes. He was covered in Tattoos that also showed through his white shirt. "Won another fight?" The guy asked with a smirk. Adonis grins, "Why else would I be here, Marcus?" I smile and shake my head at his comment. "I had an appointment set up but I'll change it for later. Look through the book while I go shoot the lady a text." Adonis nods and Marcus walks back through the door. I wait for Adonis to walk towards the desk to look through the binder but he doesn't so I give him a questioning look. "Do you already know what you're getting?" He nods and pulls his lips into his mouth. "What is it?" He pulls his phone out of his pocket awkwardly and opens the screen, pulling up a picture. He tilts the phone towards me and I knit my eyebrows together. It was the number sixty-nine in roman numerals. I look up at him raising an eyebrow. He lifts a shoulder nonchalantly, "I didn't want to forget about last night." I swallow spit and feel my face heat up.
We both turn our heads to Marcus walking into the room again. "Alright boss, what are you having?" Adonis steps up to the desk and shows the man his phone. I watch as he runs his hand vertically on his upper left side, telling the man how and where he

wanted it. It would be right under his left arm pit. After about an hour, Adonis stands in front of a large mirror, completely shirtless with dark jeans hanging low on his hips. He was admiring the tattoo that was about seven inches long and three inches wide. His arm raised over his head, he looked at me through the mirror, "What do you think baby girl?" I smiled at him and my eyes crinkled a little in amusement, "I love it." Marcus comes up to him and puts a clear wrap on top of his newly inked skin. We walk outside of the room and enter the front of the store. Adonis pays the man and turns toward me. He reaches out to me, asking for the shirt I was clenching in my hand, I pass it to him and he pulls on his black sleeveless jersey. He leans his head towards the exit and I follow him out. Getting into the car, he starts the radio, asking me, "Hungry?" I was actually starving by now so I nod enthusiastically, "Yes." He nods at my words and starts the car. He rolls down the windows and I lean back as he speeds off. The breeze hitting my face made me smile wide. We park on a busy street and I step out of the car quickly running to the sidewalk, Adonis following me. Looking up, I see the name of the restaurant, *Mulberry Street Pizza*. Outside of the store, were a few tables with red and wite checkered tablecloths and black chairs. The front of the store was glass so you could see them cooking. "Take a seat and I'll bring us a few slices." I nod and walk towards the nearest table, pulling out a chair. I watch as Adonis pushes the door open, walking into the pizzeria. I looked around, surrounding the restaurant were all kinds of stores, nail salons, and offices. The bustle of cars and traffic was all I heard as I sat here smelling the aroma of Italian food. After a few minutes, Adonis walks out holding a pizza box in one hand and two soda cans in the other. He sets the stuff down and takes a seat. “It's been ages since I ate here.” I say as Adonis pulls open the pizza box. I look down to see the random slices of pizza; two pepperoni, two cheese, and two pepperoni and veggies. He looks at me, his eyebrows furrowed, “You’ve been back for weeks. I would have come straight here after my flight.” I just shrug and he shakes his head and takes a bite of the pizza he grabbed from the box. I got a glimpse of the tattoo on his forearm, the tattoo that I also had. I smiled and as he noticed my gaze, he stretched out his hand, still chewing on his food. He looks down at it, then back to me. After swallowing down his food, he says, “Let’s see yours.” I follow his actions and flip my hand around, stretching my arm out next to his. Both our forearms on full view, the tattoos were side by side. His arm was way larger than mine but the ink was the same size. The cursive letters that meant so much. *Always.* My arm looked completely different from his. While the middle of his forearm was clear, other than our matching tattoo, the rest of his arm was completely covered in black ink. While mine was completely plain. I look up at him after analyzing the art on our arms. But his eyes were already on me, a small smile on his lips. “I told you. We may have been apart for some time but that doesn’t have anything on the years to come. We’re *always,* baby.” I giggle under my breath and pull my hand back, “Let’s see about that.” I mumbled and grabbed a slice of pizza, putting the greasy goodness to my lips. He gives me a fake glare, as I chew on my pizza, setting it down. I roll my eyes saying, “Stop being dramatic. I’ll always be here to bother you, don’t worry.” He smiles, taking another bite with a mouth full of food, he asked, “Promise?” I nod once, “Yes. You're not getting rid of me anytime soon.” He looks down at the table, his lips turning up at the corners, "Good, that's just the way I want it." His eyes meet mine, humor coating his sage colored irises. I purse my lips at him, remembering him saying those same exact words in a complete opposite situation. He said those words to me when we were in the hospital elevator after I saw Mary for the first time back from London. Our worlds changed so much from that day and where we are now in our relationship. We went from "hating" each other to...I still don't know. He realized I understood and his smile widened.

Chapter Forty-Two

Uh Oh...

I stepped out of the back seat of my father's car and looked up to the Clark's house, it was a large two story home. I walk up to the front door with my parents following me. Adonis dropped me off at home earlier to get ready and he came home to help his mom. I ring the doorbell and wait, looking down at my outfit, making sure everything was in place. I was a little nervous because I was wearing Adonis' dress shirt from last night, which still smelled like him. I tucked the shirt in light faded blue jeans with a red belt and matching pumps. I set the shirt off my shoulder, my hair in a messy bun with loose curls framing my face. The make up I wore was simple on the eyes but I added red lipstick, just to feel confident. My heart fluttered when the door opened but instead of Adonis, it was his father, Johnathon Clark. He has a smile on his face that doesn't reach his dark eyes. "Hello everyone, come on in." His eyes crinkle and he steps to the side. We walk into a large foyer that has a grand staircase in the middle of the room. The ceiling was super high with a huge modern chandelier at the top. The floor was marble in a mixture of grey's that led up the stairs. Mr. Clark led us into a large den. There was a whole set of couches that were dark blue with white throw pillows and white accent chairs. In the middle was a large coffee table with a beautiful blue, silver, and white decoration on top. Behind the large couch was a dark desk with a floor to ceiling window behind it. I looked around, noticing neither Adonis or Mary were in here. My Father takes a seat and Mr. Clark tells him something about business while he pours him a drink from his liquor cart nearby. My mother and I look at each other and we both head to the kitchen without a word. I smile wide as I walk into the kitchen, Mary is moving about with Lily by her side. They were setting up all the food on plates. I

looked at my mother and her face was as bright as mine felt. "Alright, tell me what to do." My mother said, walking to Mary's side. Mary smiles at her, "We're almost done here but thank you." Mary looks to me, her smile turning into a grin, "Aphrodite, would you go get Adonis for me? He was getting ready."
Suddenly, I hear his voice and my heart stops, "I'm right here, ma." Mary looks over my shoulder with a slight surprise on her face, "I told you I wouldn't take long." Mary looks back to her food with a shake of her head, her smile returning on her beautiful face. She starts handing things to Lily to take to the dining room and Lily easily goes with a small smile. He gets to my side and I turn towards him, he gives me a quick once over, his notched eyebrow raising high, "Nice shirt." I mimic his actions, raising my own eyebrow, "Right? I borrowed it from someone," I give an indifferent shrug. He always looked so good in long sleeved button downs. Tonight, he was wearing a charcoal one and it suited him well. His muscles were bulging in the shirt as it stretched tight on his body. He chuckles, "More like you stole it from someone." I look up, pretending to think about it, then I look back to him after a second, "Maybe. You probably shouldn't have forgotten it…" We were mostly keeping to ourselves but I had a feeling we were being watched. I turn my face towards our mothers, who quickly look away, "Uh-oh." Adonis whispers near my ear. I look at him and bite down on my lip nervously. "We should get out of here before-"
"Adonis," Mary said, at the same time my mother said, "Aphrodite." Adonis widened his eyes mockingly, pretty much saying; "Oh shit, we're fucked". He turned his face towards them, my eyes stayed on him as I'm not able to look at our mothers. "Yes, mother?"

“Can you come here for a moment?” Mary said, her voice coming out with suspicion. My cheeks heat up from her tone. Adonis looks back to me for a second, then back towards Mary, “Do we have to?” My mother’s next words come out sternly, “Adonis, Aphrodite. Sit down.” He takes a deep breath and he starts walking towards the island bar stools and I follow him, taking a seat, leaving a chair in between us so they won't get any ideas. Even though they already know something is going on. I looked up and my eyes met my mothers, I was expecting to see anger or disappointment. All I saw was amusement. Why did I have to go and wear his shirt? I brought this upon ourselves, I’m such an idiot. “So when did this start?” Mary asked, with a finger raised and gesturing between me and Adonis. “What? Us being best friends?” He turns his face to look at me, putting his elbows on the counter in front of him, “How long has it been Aphrodite?” I look at him and click my tongue with a shrug, trying to sound nonchalant, “I don’t know, twenty years?”
“Cut the shit you two.” My mother says, slamming her hand on the counter top, I widened my eyes at the sudden words my mother used. I look at her bewildered.
“You two are dating.” Mary states and I again, look to Adonis. Adonis puts a hand on his face and tilts his head to look at me like a deer caught in headlights and he mouths. *What do we do?* Can he be anymore obvious? I put my head in my hands with a loud groan as my mother says, “You know, we can see you?”
“Yeah, we are,” Adonis said, exasperatedly and I flash my face towards him. What is he thinking?! Didn’t we agree on not telling anyone. He lifts his hand in the air dramatically and it slaps on the granite, “There I said it.” I face our mothers, my blood boiling and I decide

to flip the switch on him, “Yeah and you want to know how it happened?” I raised my eyebrows and nod once, I gave Adonis the same look, repeating myself before turning back to Mary and my mother. “Adonis was so miserable while I was dating that guy. He confessed to me on the night of my last date, his undying love…And that's how it started.” Mary leans her elbow on the counter, putting her face in her palm, sighing dreamily. My mother smiles and says, “Aww, I always knew he was in love with you. He would always get so jealous when you were with other boys.” I smirk at that and I glance at Adonis, who had his jaw clenched and his cheeks were a tinge of red. He gave them a fake grin, “Yup! That’s exactly how it happened.”
“Are you guys being careful?” I blink at Mary, my cheeks becoming impossibly hot. “Ma!” Adonis said in outrage. “We want grandbabies but not anytime soon.” It was my turn to give my mother a shocked look. “Come on, just tell us. It’s okay, we’re doctors, remember?” Mary said standing straight. I close my eyes for a second with a sigh. When I look up at the women who raised me, I say, “We haven’t done that…we planned on going to a clinic soon.” My mother shakes her head, “Why didn’t you guys tell us? I thought we taught you guys to tell us everything.”
“I guess we thought wrong, Mel. Our babies don’t trust us.” Mary frowned, “We have been waiting for this to happen for years. How could we miss it?” Adonis wakes up from his chair and walks around the island to his mother putting his hand on her shoulder, giving her a smile, “It’s only been a few days. We didn’t say anything because we didn’t know how you guys would react. I’m glad you two approve.” He looks to my mother for a second before turning back to his.

My heart was melting at the way he was treating his mom so kindly. He felt bad that he kept it from her.
“Of course, I’m so happy for you two,” Mary wraps her arms around her son, who hugs her back. He pulls away and steps back as Mary continues, “You take care of her, son. She's one of the good ones. I should know, I helped raise her.” She shrugs and turns to look at me with her lips turned up in a huge smile, her perfect teeth showing. Adonis’ eyes meet mine as he says, “I know.” Making me giddy on the inside for some reason. Being around Mr. Clark was just uncomfortable during a very awkward dinner. I always felt off about him but now that I know what he has done and the kind of man he really is, I just can’t stand being in the same room as him. My heart breaks for Mary. I wonder what Adonis must be feeling as he looks at his father and as he has to pretend that everything is okay. He really is a strong person, his father can never even reach his feet.
Adonis and I sit facing each other on two wooden armchairs in front of the desk in the den. Our parents were chatting on the couches, having a cup of wine.
Adonis looked me over and I tried to ignore him, I didn’t want to get hot and bothered in front of our parents. His gaze was intensifying with every minute, while mine was on our parents. I keep flicking him looks that said “stop”, every few minutes. As our parents continue to talk, I feel his eyes undressing me, “Can you stop?” I cross my legs, my elbows on the chair's arms. His face masked confusion, “Stop what?” He bites down on the corner of his lip, his eyes shining. He sat with his legs wide open, his arms dangling between them. I glared at him, “Stop those looks.” Our words are hardly heard over theirs.
“I can’t help it.” His eyes slid over my body shamelessly, “In my eyes, you're naked right now.”

My breath hitched in my throat and I took a quick glance to see if our parents heard but they were engrossed in their conversations. I looked back at him and the side of his mouth was turned up cockily, "The things I want to do to you will drive you crazy." I swallow the lump in my throat, my breathing picking up and I find myself whispering, "Tell me." His lips part and his eyes search mine but all he sees is the need to know what he has to say. He leans forward and I watch his arms flex through his tight sleeves as he grabs onto my chair and pulls it towards him, his eyes never leaving mine. My stomach does a flip and It clenches tight. I did not anticipate this.
I grip the chair and blink, my heart hammering in my chest. I can see the hunger in his eyes as he looked at me. "You don't know what you're asking." I lift my eyebrows in challenge, "Actually…I do." He licks his bottom lips and the gloss left there makes me even more breathless. He hums, "I want to to put your body in all kinds of positions. I want to watch your face as I take you to places you've never been before." I take a deep breath at his words, my body trembling, "That's it?" I put my high heeled foot to his chair in between his legs, the heel of my shoe barely grazing him. I pushed myself back and the legs of the chair scraped on the floor. Crossing my arms over my chest, I say, "I was expecting something better." Then, look away from him. Hearing his deep chuckle, he knows he affected me and I know that was only a taste of what he wanted to do but I loved to mess with his huge ego.

CHAPTER FORTY-THREE

Without Choice

I was shaking, I know I shouldn't be scared of needles because I wanted to be a surgeon one day. Putting a needle in someone and getting one in, is two different things. Adonis had amusement all over his face as he watched me from across the room. I couldn't even look at him as I was looking at the door, waiting for the nurse to come in to prick me. The doctor helped me decide on getting the birth control shot, it seemed like the best option. As soon as the door knob turned, my heart started beating faster in my chest. The nurse walks in holding a tray with all the essentials. She sets the tray down on the exam table beside me and smiles. "Are you ready, sweetie?" She asked and I looked at her like a deer caught in the headlights and I was about to be run over. "Is this going to hurt?" I ask worriedly. Before the nurse can respond, I hear a laughing come out of his mouth before he says, "Come here, baby girl." I give him a flat look but I decide on climbing off the table and walking towards him. He was sitting on a small armchair, he opened his arms and silently asked me to sit on his lap. I ignore his breathtaking smile and take a seat on him. He wrapped his arms around my waist and I felt myself relax in his embrace, feeling immediately safe. The lady gives us an adoring look as the corners of her lips turned all the way up. "Are you ready now, Miss Watson?" She asked and I nodded finally. "It's only gonna be a pinch." Adonis whispered in my ear and I mimicked him feigning annoyance. I felt the rumble of his chest as he chuckled and then pressed his lips to my bare shoulder as I was wearing a cami. The nurse walked over with the syringe and Adonis grabbed my hand in his interlacing fingers. "Don't flinch, sweetie. It will be over before you know it."

YESTERDAY WAS PRETTY uneventful after the clinic, Adonis dropped me off at home and went to go run some errands. I laid in bed and watched movies till my eyes couldn't take it anymore. Right now, we're at a fast food restaurant after training with the boys again. Cain was telling us a story about a raid he helped his father clean up once, when he was younger. It was kind of sad because his father was dead now and also because Cain was only ten when he would help him. He was really into the story though and I couldn't help imagining myself being there. Wiping everything down, getting rid of all evidence. Making sure there was no trace of anyone in Benjamin's mafia. It was crazy how Cain, at such a young age, had to clean up so much blood and gore. "You okay there, Aphrodite? You look like you're gonna faint." I blink up at Hudson who had an amused look on his face. "Yeah, you look like a ghost." Liam said, looking my face over. All the boys around me at the table were looking at me worriedly. Adonis wraps his arm around me, "What's wrong?" I shake my head, "I'm fine, I was just really focused on the story." He nodded and tightened his arm around me and I nestled into his side feeling the blood rush back into my face as everyone was still staring at me. Their eyes turned to James as his phone on the table started ringing. James eyes flick from the phone to Adonis, then he answers it, putting it to his ear. "Boss?" James answered in a way that said, tell me what you need me to do. James takes a deep breath, "Yes, we're all together." He looks towards me, then to Adonis again, "Aphrodite is with us." James closes his eyes in surrender, "Okay, that's fine. We'll go right away. Bye"

"What is it?" Adonis' back straightened ready for anything. "You're not gonna like it." James said, avoiding eye contact. My heart was starting to speed up and I didn't even know why. "Tell me." Adonis said, firmly. "We don't have much time. We need to go get some information from Steven Crawford before he leaves for his flight. Benjamin wants us *all* there." James' eyes widened at his last sentence for emphasis. Everyone around the table had their eyes on Adonis, waiting to see his reaction. "I need to take her home," Adonis takes his arm off of me and gets ready to stand up. "Adonis, he said to take her. We have no time." Adonis gives James a look, stating he was out of his mind. Adonis grabs my hand and I stand up, the boys follow my movements and we walk out of the restaurant. Adonis looked like he was lost in his thoughts. His eyes unfocused and his breathing was faster than normal. As we reach the parking lot, he lets go of my hand and paces in front of his SUV. "How the fuck does he figure I'm going to take *my girl* with me to get information from some criminal?" He says the words to no one in particular. He definitely was angry. My hands were shaking, I was a little scared. Not from Adonis, but from what was about to happen. "Fuck!" Adonis kicks the tire angrily and I try to keep myself from flinching. Liam opens the Escalade's trunk and pulls up a hidden compartment. As he does, you can see all sorts of weapons in there. He starts throwing the illegal items to the boys and they all check for bullets, then put their guns away. Adonis grabs his gun, cocks it, then after putting it in place, he puts it behind his back, his eyes meeting mine. Liam was about to pass me a gun when Adonis stopped him, putting his hand on it, "She doesn't know how to use it. Give her a knife." Liam nods, putting it back in its place and takes out a knife that was encased in a leather wrap, handing it to Adonis. Adonis looks at it, then his eyes meet James', "She'll

be fine. We won't let anything happen to her." James' words make my breath get caught in my throat as he consoles his friend. I had no words at the moment. Adonis puts the knife in my hand, keeping his hand there in mine. He looks into my eyes, his eyes telling me so many things that were running through his head; anger, worry, regret, fear, and so much more. "Listen to me. You will keep your head down. You will listen to all of us. And don't do anything stupid." He waits for my reaction and I nod. The boys climb into the car as Adonis continues, "You're going to see things that you have never seen in your life. Don't leave my sight." He leans down and takes my lips in his, not caring if the boys see, even if they were in the car. He kisses my lips as if with this kiss, he can tell me how much he wants to protect me, how much he cares about me. With this kiss, all the doubts fade away and I know everything will be okay. He pulls away and we climb into the car. James was driving and Hudson was in the passenger seat. I sit between Cain and Adonis. Liam was in the third row with a tablet in his hands doing god knows what.
The boys start talking strategies and who does what as Liam gives them the layout of the man's house and I just sit there pretty much paralyzed, not knowing what to do or say. My heart was pounding in my ears and my palms were sweating so I rub them along my jeans. What did I get myself into? I did not expect myself to get wrapped up in any of their missions or whatever. One thing is for sure, these boys know exactly what they're doing. None of them looked scared or worried about what they were doing. Adonis looked worried but about me, not the situation. His whole body was tense, even though he was joining the conversation of the plan. I grabbed his hand that was on his thigh and tangled our fingers, wanting him

to relax. He leaned forward and kissed my forehead, trying to show me that everything was going to be okay. As we get to a small, rundown neighborhood, we arrive at a house that is two stories, but small. "Go on, let me know when you guys have him in the garage." The boys get out of the car, close the doors quietly, and start for the back of the house. I pull back from Adonis and scoot down the chair and turn my body so I am facing him. He runs both his hands through his hair nervously. I was expecting this place to be swarming with bad people and for it to be incredibly hard to get in. This seemed easy. The boys go in, get the guy, and Adonis gets the answers. Why is he so nervous? "Hey?" He looks at me and I give him a small smile, "It's just one man. It's not that bad. We will be out of here soon." He chuckles humorlessly, "This is all too fucked up. You're not supposed to be here." I roll my eyes with a huge sigh. He will always have that need to protect me and keep me in the dark. Some things will never change. He looks at his phone as it beeps and he steps out of the car, leaving the door opened for me to follow him. We walked to the side of the garage and the door was already opened for us. The room was dark, the only light was the one coming out from under the garage door. Blinking my eyes to adjust to the dim room, I see a man taped to a chair in the middle of the garage. Hudson, Liam, Cain, and James surround him, watching as the man trashes. Adonis points to the garage door, glancing at me over his shoulder, giving me a silent order. I quicken my pace and lean against it. My whole body trembles in anxiety. The boys part, giving Adonis space to do what he has to do to interrogate this man. The man's eyes widened as he got a glimpse of Adonis. Adonis' back is to me and I can see how his whole body changes

intimidatingly. “Cain, get the lights. I want to see this man's eyes as he tells me how he stole from us and who he is working for.” Adonis pulls out his box of cigarettes and puts one to his lips as he takes it out of its container. He takes a drag of it, then says, “Don’t make this hard on me. I don’t have all day.” James pulls the tape from the man's mouth and it makes a loud noise as it peels off the skin. The man starts talking as soon as it's off, “It wasn’t me, Adonis. I didn’t do it.” The lights flicker on and I can see the man's face clearly now. His tan face was full of fear and his dark eyes contained regret. Adonis took a drag of his cigarette, his legs spread wide, “Okay Crawford, who are you working for? You definitely aren’t working for us anymore. You’re a traitor.” Cain chuckled, “You should have seen him, Adonis. He was packing his bags in such a hurry. He thought he was going to escape us.” Adonis laughs but it's such a dark sound. A normal person would have shuttered in fear, I on the other hand, shuttered for a different reason. “I’m going to ask you again. Who are you working for? Answer me or next time, I won’t be so kind.” Adonis said, menacingly. The man shook his head, “I only work for Benjamin. No one else. I didn’t do anything. It wasn’t me!” You can tell he was lying, there was no doubt about it. Adonis calmly took another drag from his cigarette, “Do you know what I hate more than a traitor, Crawford?” Adonis doesnt let the man answer as he gets closer to him, “It’s a liar.” Then, he suddenly presses his cigarette to the man's forehead, making him scream out in pain. My eyes widened as Adonis did that without even a second thought. The cigarette fell to the floor and was forgotten.
“Guy’s, please! I’m not lying! I’m being set up! You need to believe me.” I pressed myself to the wall, not

knowing what was going to happen next, my heart picking up speed. Adonis rubs a hand over his face, "Give me my wraps." His eyes don't leave Steven Crawford's as he speaks. Hudson pulls out white material from his pocket and passes it to Adonis. "Now, I told you not to make this hard on me but I guess you don't understand what that means." He grabs what Hudson passed him, only grabbing one bundle. He opens it from its socket, then wraps his right hand slowly, threateningly. The man watches with wide eyes, visibly gulping. Adonis' back was stiff, his shoulder blades moving as he wrapped his hand. I lick my dry lips as I watch him move so fluently. He looks back to the man, getting closer to him. I was trying to control my breathing, I didn't know what I was expecting to see here but this is mind boggling, Adonis was focused on what he was doing. His hand pulled back and he smashed it into the man's stomach, Crawford groaned in pain. "C'mon, you know this is going to only get worse. Tell the man what he wants to hear." Liam said, shaking his head in agitation. "Okay, listen-" Adonis pulls back and punches him again in the stomach, causing the man to hunch over in pain. Adonis stands to his full height, "Don't spit out lies, Crawford. I'm just going to have to hurt you." Steven looks at him, his face bright red in pain, "Adonis, I'm telling the truth. I didn't do anything. Maybe it was that new guy. It wasn't me." Adonis looks at James taking a deep breath in, "I didn't want to have to do this, Crawford." In one swift movement Adonis punched the man in the face. I flinch and pinch my eyes shut. As I open them, Adonis is stepping back. "Hudson. You give it ago man. I don't wanna kill him…yet."

I gulp at Adonis' words and watch as Hudson steps forward, towering over the man, he sighs loudly. "You know what I can do Steven. Just tell us the truth."
"Hudson, you know me. We have worked together. It wasn't me." Hudson's hand grabbed onto the man's face, "And you know me. I can see a liar from a mile away." The man groans in pain, signaling that Hudson was squeezing his face harshly. After a minute, he pushes Steven's face back with force, then he stands after crouching. "You did this Steven. You gave that someone our information and they stole from us. You are a first class traitor. And Benjamin doesn't like traitors." Hudson puts his hand to his shoulder and bends down to elbow the man, straight in the face. Making me look away instantly, my stomach was full of knots. I wouldn't be surprised if I threw up right here, right now. "Just say the fucking truth and the truth will set you free!" Cain said humorously, he was always trying to lighten the mood. "I am saying the truth! I don't know what else you want me to say!" The man spoke but he was full of pain, his mouth sputtering out blood. I see, with my mouth gaped open, Hudson uppercut him in the chin, Steven's face flying back again. "Can you just shut up! If you're not gonna say the truth, just shut the fuck up!" Hudson shakes his palm out as he probably felt pain in his knuckles, his word coming out in annoyance. "That's enough." Adonis' voice booms out as he steps forward, Hudson walking to stand next to Cain. "How much pain can you take, Crawford? Because we can go all night."
"Okay, yes! I told them where Benjamin kept everything." Steven breathes heavily, blood running down his mouth. "Who?" Adonis said, his words coming out angrily. "The Bratva. They threatened me and my family, Adonis, I had no choice-" Adonis

stepped forward and the man's eyes widened completely. “I'm not going to kill you. That would be too easy, I need to make a statement that whoever even *thinks* of going over our code of silence, they will get whatever you will.” The words are dark coming out of Adonis' lips and I find myself shaking in fear. “What-“ The man doesn't finish his sentence as Adonis starts hitting him repeatedly in the face. My hands lay flat on the wall as I try to shut my eyes completely so I won't be able to see this anymore. The problem is, I can't even make myself close my eyes. My irises stayed locked on Adonis' hands as they attached the man completely. The man had no chance of even defending himself, his hands were bound to the chair. Adonis gives one last punch, then stands to his full height again. Steven Crawford's face was red, purple, and swollen. Blood was seeping out everywhere. Adonis lifts his foot and kicks the half awake man in the stomach, making his chair fly back to the ground. “Take him to Benjamin.” James throws him the car keys and as Adonis catches them, he walks towards me. He grabs my arm and pulls me towards the exit. My breathing was coming out in pants as Adonis pretty much dragged me out the door.

Chapter Forty-four

Going To War

Feeling lips graze along the back of my neck, my eyes slowly open. Adonis' arms were wrapped around me and his legs were intertwined in mine. His breath was fanning over my skin and I smiled, scooting back into him. It felt so good to be in his arms. I loved feeling his warmth around me. His arms held me as if he never wanted to let me go, as if he can keep me like this forever. Yesterday, after what happened with the interrogation, Adonis brought me home. We showered, then got into my bed and haven't got out of it since. It's a good thing my parents were never home but even if they were, I don't think they would care. They loved Adonis and he used to always sleep over. I turned towards him and looked into his eyes that were full of sleep. He hasn't been up for long. "Good morning," I whispered and he smiled, nestling into my neck taking a deep breath. "Good morning, baby." "Why are you up? Let's go back to sleep." I run my hand through his hair. "I just got a message from the boys. They want to go out." His words are said on my skin and with every word, his lips move on me, making goosebumps raise all over my body. I groan loudly, "But I want to spend the day in bed. Right here in your arms." Adonis chuckles and I feel his body shake against mine. He pulls me tighter against him and I sigh into him. "It's either we meet them, or they come here and drag us out." I pull back to meet his eyes that remind me of sage, giving him an "oh shit" look, "You're right. I forgot how crazy our boys are." Adonis leans forward and kisses my nose in a quick kiss, "Our boys? I didn't know they were your friends too now." I grin at him, "Oh yeah, definitely. I guess they grew on me." I shrug, then put my face into his chest, breathing in his smell. I can't help but get lost in him, I know I said I wouldn't but it was so easy, even after what I witnessed last night. I just couldn't stay away from him.

ADONIS PARKED HIS CAR IN BETWEEN James' car and Cain's motorcycle. We were at this park that led into the woods. Apparently, we came paintballing. I don't know how this happened. I climbed out of the car and followed Adonis. We walked towards a little cabin-like area, where there were a few of them. We walked to the one in the middle and it was set up like a shop. Standing there, were all our friends, including Erika and Roxy. They all turned towards us and smiled. I waved as we got closer. "Hey!" I grinned, feeling happy to be in a normal environment. They all greet us happily and I am so glad to finally have something to get my mind off of yesterday. After a few minutes of all of us getting ready and geared up, a guy dressed in full camouflage tells us which path to take and how to play and all the rules. We started running, already divided into teams, on my team was Cain, Roxy and Liam. We took left as the other team took right. My heart was beating quickly in excitement. Cain gestured for us to get into a circle, "Okay, you guys. We have the upper hand here." Liam looks at Cain as if he had two heads, "How's that?" Cain blinks at him, "Because we have the opposing team captain's kryptonite right here." He gestures to me and I give him a flat look. "Adonis is competitive, he doesn't care if I'm on the opposite team as him." Roxy perks up, "No, Cain's right. Adonis is going to stay clear of you…He's not going to hurt his baby girl." Roxy picks up her hands and makes air quotes with her fingers as she says baby girl. I roll my eyes, "Guys, he's not going to back down because of me." They ignore me and go on making a plan around me,

taking down Adonis and I just go along with them. They're not going to listen to me anyways.
It's been about thirty minutes into the game and I haven't been hit by anyone, I have been ducking left and right. Adonis was nowhere in sight. I actually managed to shoot someone earlier but it didn't count because it was Cain. He wanted to kill me with his eyes. I was now alone. From a few yards away, I could see Liam and Hudson going head to head, ducking behind the obstacle course. I find myself going deeper into the woods, searching for someone to shoot at. Suddenly, a hand was over my mouth, I panicked for a second, until I recognized Adonis' presence. I feel pressure at my back and I know he has the mouth of the gun pressed to me, "Caught you." He whispered and I giggled into his hand. "Never let your guard down. Rule number one." I squint my eyes as an idea pops into my head. The hand that wasn't on the paintball gun, I ran it down his leg seductively and I felt him stiffen behind me. He moves his hand to my neck and tilts my head back so he can say something against my ear, "Don't even try. I know better than that." I felt myself clench in all the right places but I try to keep my body as relaxed as possible. I slump my shoulders with a sigh, "It was worth the try." He chuckles and I can't help the reaction it does to my stomach, any little thing he does always gives me, butterflies. He pulls away from me, "Give up so easily, baby girl? I thought you would have fought harder." I turned towards him with a shrug of my shoulder, then met his gaze for a second before smirking and looking down at the dog tags he had around his neck. I lean in and grab onto them examining them. I didn't want to look into his eyes because he would know I'm still up to something. One of his dog tags said his name and some other

information, the other one said, “keep your head up and no one will tear you down”. As I continue to fidget with his necklace, I say in a soft voice, “I love it when you call me that.” He hums, “Do you, now?” I nod and look up to his lips slowly leaning in. As soon as he starts to lean in to kiss me I say, “Never let your guard down!” And I quickly take a step back, with shock written all over his face, I shoot him in the chest. He looks down at his chest, then back to me, a smirk rising on his lips, “You shouldn’t have done that.” He throws his gun to the side and stalks towards me. My eyes widened and I turned to run away. I move through the trees, hearing our footsteps crunching over the leaves. He was close so I started running faster, my breathing picking up. I turned my head for a second and that was a big mistake, I missed a step and was about to fall. Right before I do, Adonis catches me, both of us ending up on the ground, his arms taking most of the impact. The gun slipped out of my hands during the fall. “I thought we agreed you wouldn’t fall for me?” I manage to turn my body around to face him after his words. I couldn’t help but smile at him. Our eyes met and his were full of amusement, “You just wanted to be on top of me.” He lifted himself slightly so I wouldn’t feel his full weight on me. I loved how his body aligned with mine in such a perfect way. He bites down on his lower lip, “You’re right.” Then he leans down, capturing my lips. I kiss him back, a sigh leaving my lips. He always knew how to make me forget about everything and everyone with just a touch of his lips. I bring my hands up and wrap my arms around his neck as he deepens the kiss. He grabs my waist in his free hand, his grip tightening as he devourers my mouth. His tongue worked its way to tasting me. When his tongue touched mine, I couldn't help but moan in at the feeling. Not paying attention to the noises around us, we missed footsteps closing in on us. “I fucking knew it!” I hear Roxy’s voice yell and Adonis quickly pulls his face away from mine. We both turned our faces towards her, she had a huge grin on her face with those mischievous eyes. I was so shocked, I didn't notice Adonis climbing off of me and pulling me up with him. Roxy’s eyes move from Adonis to me, “How long has this been going on?” Everyone starts slowly showing up, Erika being the only one to hear Roxy’s words, “What's been going on?” I look to Erika and give her a sheepish smile. Roxy turns as Cain gets closer, “Did you know about this?” Roxy points towards us, still looking at Cain. Cain furrows his eyebrows as he stands next to Roxy, ”What do you mean?” I get a little behind Adonis in embarrassment, not knowing what to say or do. My cheeks were so hot, I wanted to put my hands on them to cool them down but that was going to make things worse. I hear James’ voice from behind me, “What's all the fuss about?” At his voice, I grab onto Adonis’ arm for some reason, feeling way more embarrassed. Adonis looks down to me with a small smile. He was enjoying this, I wanted to slap him. This isn't funny, no one was supposed to know. James walks in front of us and stands next to Erika. “Did everyone just find out?” I snap my head to the side to see Hudson coming down a hill, his hands adjusting the bandana on his head. “C’mon, you guys, it has been so obvious.” “What do you mean?!” Cain yells, lifting his hands in the air exaggeratingly. “I just caught these two making out. They have been hiding it from us. They’re in a secret relationship.” Roxy puts both her hands on her hips, giving me a look. I loved her but she was annoying sometimes with her dramatics. Adonis finally decides on speaking, “We aren't in a relationship." Roxy gives him a questioning look as he continues, "We're just messing around, no labels." "So like, fuck buddies?" Adonis and I both turn our heads to see Liam leaning on a tree, his gun over his shoulder. "Something like that..." Comes my timid reply. I really hope they don't judge us for this. I really love all of them. I hope they don't distance themselves because of this or think differently about us. "And why were you guys keeping it from us?" Erika says, frowning in confusion. "It's just something we wanted to keep on the down low," Adonis says, his words coming out nonchalant with a shrug. "I have a question," Cain raises his hand as if he was in school. "When were you gonna tell *me* about this?" He looked us over with confusion written on his face but his eyes had amusement shining through. "Cain, leave them be. It's none of our business," James says throwing his arm over Erika's shoulders. "No, I wanna know." Cain takes a step forward but was stopped by a paintball shot to his leg. He growls in pain and looks to his right, Hudson was lowering his gun, smirking. "What the fuck was that for?!" Cain yells, glaring at Hudson. "Don't be an ass, Cain." Hudson says, giving him a pointed look. "He's the ass for not telling us." Cain says, as he points to Adonis and I can't help but giggle under my breath. "He is so dramatic." Liam says, rolling his eyes. Then, I feel a sharp pain in my arms and clutch it with a groan. I look up to glare at a smirking Roxy, who blows on the tip of her gun. "That's for keeping it from me." Roxy says and throws the gun on her shoulder. Adonis again, looks down to me, "Are you okay?" His eyebrows were knitted together. I shake my head yes and he looks back to Roxy, giving her a raised eyebrow. She shrugs him off with raised eyebrows. "So are we still playing or not?" I heard Liam say, looking at everyone questioningly. I look at everyone's faces, blinking at them, “So that's it?” Everyone looked back at me puzzled, “You guys are okay with this?” My words come out a little shocked. “Of course we are, Aphrodite! Why wouldn't we be?” Erika grins at me and I smile back. “I'm just pissed you hid it from me but other than that, I'm cool with it.” Roxy shrugs again, her lips turning down. “Let's see how long you guys last as friends with benefits. You two will be married by next year.” Cain shakes his head with his eyebrow raised. “Shut up, Cain. No one asked for your opinion.” Roxy nudges him and he glares at her. Out of nowhere, Cain lifts his gun and shoots all of us, one by one. We all groan in pain as he lifts his arms in the air. “I won, mother fuckers!” He groans loudly and clutches his private parts as someone shoots him there. Cain falls to his knees, “Fuck you, James!” I turn to find James with his gun aimed towards Cain, a huge grin on his face.

Chapter Forty-Five

Adrenaline Junkie

As I watch the sunset go down, I smile. Loving the colors in the sky, wishing I knew how to paint. If I did, I would have a canvas here and all the right colors but even if I was the most talented artist, I still wouldn't do it justice. And to add to the perfect view was Adonis sitting on Cain's motorcycle, talking to his friends a few feet away. After we were done playing in the woods, we went out to eat near the beach and now here we are at a parking lot, looking out at the sun rays hitting the dark water, enjoying the slight wind hitting my face, the smell of the ocean in the air. I was leaning on Roxy's car as the girls kept trying to take things out of me, I just shook my head and kept repeating the words, "Stop asking." Roxy was sitting in the driver's seat, the door open and her legs dangling out. Erika was leaning next to me on the side of the car. "Fine then, if you don't want to tell us how it happened, I don't even care." Roxy crosses her arms and looks away from me. I grin at her, "When you tell me what happened with Liam, I'll tell you what happened with Adonis." Roxy grimaces and I laugh under my breath, "You see? It's not that easy, right?" "He took my virginity," Roxy starts and I turn towards her. "Then, the next day, told the whole school how easy I was. I had such a huge crush on him and he fucked it up. After that, I had guys coming on to me all the time, thinking I was up for anything. Cain one day, punched a guy in the face for me and we became friends after that and no one bothered me again." I blink up at her, a knot forming in my throat, tears welling in my eyes. "When was this?" My words are choked and hoarse. "It happened about a month or two after you left. The bullying only lasted a couple of weeks till Cain stepped in. That's why I'm so close to him, he was there when I needed him the most. And I will never forget that." She looks up at me, the side of

her lip stretched out in a sad smile. “Wow. Rox, I’m sorry I wasn't here for you. I wish I was.” she shakes her head at my words. “It’s not your fault, A. You would have been there if you could have been. I didn't tell you because I didn't want you worrying about me all the way from London.” Her face brightens a little, “Okay, now your turn.” I groan and Erika giggles, “You asked for it.” I glare at her and she shrugs. I go on giving a short overview of what happened between me and Adonis. Erika gives me a sharp look, “I thought you were smarter than that Aphrodite.” I give her a perplexed look, “What?”
“Yeah, you and Adonis are fucking idiots.” Roxy shakes her head at me. “Why is that?” I frown at them, getting a little bothered by their statements. “You two are madly in love with each other.” Before I can reply to Erika, Adonis yells my name. I turn towards him and smile, he gestures with his hand to come over and I do, pushing aside any thought of the conversation we just had. “What’s up?” I ask him and he grins at me, running his hand on the bike. “Wanna go for a ride?” I widened my eyes, “Seriously?” Adonis nods, his eyebrows lifting up on top of his black sunglasses. I look up at Cain, “Is that okay?” He shrugs, “If the big guy is driving, that's fine. But if you're gonna drive it, that's a no.” Adonis stands from his chair glaring at Cain and I smile at him, “How do you know I’m not a professional?” Cain gives me a look, “I do not want to find out.”
“Now because of that, she's driving it on her own.” Adonis says harshly and Cain's shoulders slump, “Don’t worry, Cain. She knows how to ride. Her father taught her a long time ago.” Adonis says to make Cain feel better about me driving his bike. Cain takes a deep breath, “Good, I thought she was gonna hurt my Harley.” He really is so dramatic, he and Roxy

really are the same person, I mentally roll my eyes. "Thanks Cain, I promise not to hurt your baby." Adonis steps to the side and I climb on the bike and take a hold of the chrome and leather handle bars. The key already in the ignition. I look up to Adonis, beaming at him. Cain passes me the helmet but Adonis grabs it before I do and sets it on my head, pulling my crazy hair behind me. "You got this, baby girl?" He asked, knowing full well I did. I nod and hold onto the clutch, the boys moving to the side as I kick start the engine easily. Slowly releasing the clutch, I twist the handlebar and the bike moves forward.
I pull out of the parking lot and drive onto the small empty road. I loved the feeling of the engine beneath my legs. I loved the adrenaline pumping through my veins. I sped down the road, only hearing the sound of the loud motorcycle and the wind in my ears. To my left, was the ocean and parking lots and to my right, was mountains filled with beach houses. In front of me was nothing but road and I loved how the lines blurred into one as I sped up. I leaned forward a little, focusing ahead of me. As the street turns in towards the right, I follow it and enjoy the tilt to the side like the crazy person I am. As I get to a wider street, I decide on making a U-turn and going back because if I keep going, I won't want to return the vehicle back to Cain. Reveling in the last few minutes on the bike, I smile wide. When I finally get back to the parking lot, everyone waits for me, Adonis wearing a huge smile. I park the motorcycle back in its place and take the helmet off, my breathing coming out faster. I look up at Cain, passing him his helmet, "She was amazing. Such a smooth ride." Cain looks at me in disbelief, "I was not expecting little miss Watson to be such an adrenaline junkie." I shake my head, "There a lot of things you don't know about me, Cain. Stick around,

there's more to see." His smile shows his perfect teeth, then looks towards Adonis, "She's a keeper man." I blush a little and look down to my hands on the Harley. Adonis rolls his eyes at him, then looks at me, "What you think?" I stand up and throw my leg over the bike to climb off, "It was such a rush, I really enjoyed it." Adonis opens his mouth to say something when his phone rings, he grabs it out of his pocket and answers it. Putting it to his ear, "Hello?"
My eyebrows knit together, then Adonis replies to whatever the person says, "Yes, she's with me." He looks at me as the person talks again, then says, "Sure, we will be there soon." Adonis looks around, meeting the boy's eyes, "That was Benjamin. He invited us over. He wants the girls there too." My eyes expand, "Why does he want us there?" Adonis shrugs, "I have no idea." He puts his hand in his front pocket and pulls out his key, he throws it to Cain who catches it easily with a questioning look, "You take the Porsche, we're going on the bike." Cain gives Adonis a shocked look, then looks down to the keys, "I have always wanted to drive the Porsche" The words come out in a whisper and I shake my head, smiling at his antics.

WE DROVE THROUGH A LARGE GATE that had to be opened by a keypad. At the front of the mansion were two men dressed in full on swat style gear. A rifle slung across their chest by a strap. This place was so beautiful on the outside, driving around a water fountain that took up the front of the house, Adonis parks in front of the entrance. We climb off of the motorcycle and I look up to the estate. There were rounded steps leading to the large Victorian doors. From here, you can see the large windows, each one having a balcony. The house was humongous. There were all sorts of trees and flowers surrounding the grounds. The guards move to the side as we walk up the steps, allowing us to get to the entrance. Adonis twists the door knob and the door opens. I blink at the sight in front of me. I was awestruck, the foyer went on, for what looks like blocks, leading to twin grand staircases that curved up on each side, meeting at a wide banister. The floors were white marble, in the middle of the stairs was a black carpet leading all the way up. The matching carpet was in the center of the foyer with a big round table. On top of it was a beautiful arrangement in black and white. Hanging from the ceiling directly over the table was a crystal chandelier. We step into the manor and I look up to Adonis, still in awe. He smirks, “It’s amazing, isn’t it?” I nod and look up to see Benjamin descending from the stairs, holding to the black railing. His smile turns into a grin and I can’t help but admire him in his three piece suit he was wearing. “Aphrodite, Adonis,” He starts as he steps off of the last stair. “So glad to see you two.” He meets us at the door with long strides, his back straight. This man was very graceful. He grasps onto Adonis’ shoulder and shakes it. I smile at Adonis, who looked at the man in front of him as if he was out of his mind, his lips turning up. “Ben, how are you?” Benjamin releases Adonis and says, “I’m good, son.” Then turns towards me, “And you beautiful, how are you?” I blush crimson at his compliment, “I'm okay, thank you for asking.” I look down to the floor, slightly intimidated. “Come in. Come in,” He steps to the side and we step deeper into the foyer. “What a beautiful home you have, sir,” The words come out timidly and I can't help but mentally reprimand myself. “Thank you but it's going to be Adonis’ one day.” Adonis clicks his tongue loudly with a shake of his

head, “I thought we talked about this.” Ben smirks, “The offer is still on the table.” Then Benjamin looks at me, “Would you like a tour?” My lips turn up at the suggestion, “I would love to.” his eyes crinkle as genuine happiness appears on his face. He gestures to turn to the right and we step into a hall leading to a beautiful den with floor to ceiling windows aligning the left wall. The soft light from the dusk shining through the windows as it is almost dark. From these panoramic windows, you can see the backyard and how enthralling it was. The living room itself was gorgeous, in beautiful tones of white, grey, and black, with wooden decor and the wall behind the fireplace was grey brick. To the right of the room was a black grand piano. “I wanted to say, Aphrodite, I am very proud of you.“ My head flashes to Benjamin who was grabbing glasses from a liquor display nearby. I frown in confusion, “You are?” He chuckles and pours an amber liquid from a decanter into the crystal glasses. I look up at Adonis who just shrugs a shoulder. Benjamin walks towards us and passes us each a glass, I take it from him. My eyebrows furrowed. He grabs his cup and takes a sip before saying, “You are one brave girl.” His eyes meet Adonis’, “You better keep her by your side. You don't find women like her anymore.” Adonis looks down at me, one side of his lips turning up, “You’re right.”
“Why do you say that?” The confusion was still very much present inside me. “What happened yesterday. Not anyone can do what you did. You surprised me.” Adonis is the confused one now, “Benjamin, what are you talking about?” He takes one step forward towards his boss. I don’t understand what this man is saying. What did I do? I haven't done anything that I can think of. Benjamin takes a deep breath before saying, “Yesterday, she went with you to the

interrogation. I was expecting her to react way differently than how she did. Anybody else would have ran away and never turned back." Adonis breathes out heavily from his nose, recognition appearing on his face, then his eyes blaze in anger. "This was a test." Adonis states. "Yes, a test for her. After everything she saw, she is still standing next to you." My brain starts working on overload. He tested me? Does that mean the Steven Crawford thing was all a rouse to see if I would stick by Adonis? That was unsuitable of him. Adonis squares his shoulders, his nostrils flaring, "Why would you do that to me?" Benjamin rubs a hand over the stubble on his face, "We both know you need her in your life. I blame myself for the torment you went through this last year without her. Now she is protected by us because you need her by your side. Let's say…last night was her initiation and she passed it with flying colors." I blink a few times, looking from Benjamin to Adonis. The way they spoke was as if I wasn't even present.
Adonis' jaw was tight from how hard he had it clenched in anger. My heart was beating rapidly in my chest. What did this man want from me? I was no one. Just a friend of Adonis'. My palms were sweating so I clutched them to my thighs, gulping down the bile that was rising in my throat from nerves. "You know I don't want her involved in this." Benjamin's eyes meet Adonis' in a heated stare, "She already is." Adonis takes another step forward getting in Benjamin's face but at sudden noise, we all turn to see the rest of our friends walking down the hall. Adonis backs away and grabs my hand in his. I look up at him questioningly, but his eyes don't meet mine as they are on Benjamin. "What's up everyone?" Cain's cheerful voice filled the silent house and I turned to look at everyone stepping into the den, Roxy and Erika

looking as out of place as I felt. James walks over to Benjamin extending his hand out in greeting, “How's it going, Ben?” Ben grabs his hand, shaking it. James' eyebrows knit together, “Is something wrong?” I blurted out, “No at all.” I felt as if I needed to defuse the situation because Adonis looked calm on the outside, but I know he was blazing on the inside. Benjamin's eyes meet mine and he smiles fondly, making me quickly look away. Adonis turns his head and gives me a flat look and I bite down on my lip, looking away from him too. I run my hand through my hair. Benjamin ushers us all outside so we lounge in his beautiful outside furniture. A lady comes over with a tray of drinks and snacks. Everyone talks and jokes around, except Adonis. The whole time we were there, he didn't say a word. He had me sitting on his lap, his arm wrapped around me but his teeth were glued together. I tried to caress his arm to get him to relax but nothing was working. After some time, we all decided on leaving. As we stepped out, Adonis told me to wait for him for a little bit and closed the door. He obviously wasn't done with his conversation with his boss.

Chapter Forty-Six

Red Rose

I closed the passenger door of Roxy's car a little too harshly, it was the day after we were at Benjamin's house. I spent the whole day with Roxy, doing her stupid errand's. "Watch it!" Roxy smirks at me and I give her a flat look and walk away from the car to my house. I look around to notice both my mother's and father's cars are missing. They must be on another overnight shift. Adonis was out getting ready for his trip tomorrow. He is leaving for three days to Nevada and they need to plan out their whole mission. The thing is, he promised me he would be done hours ago and hasn't answered any of my calls or texts. I was a little agitated, to say the least. Looking down to my phone, checking for any missed calls, I open the front door. I close the door behind me, lock it, and walk up the stairs, pretty much stomping. I start an angry text towards Adonis, saying things I don't even mean. I open my door, looking at the screen of my phone. I'm about to hit send when I see him standing there in the middle of the room. My heart melts and my stomach does a flip. The room was illuminated by candles. I look around the room, slowly walking towards him, noticing he had a hand behind his back and the other in his front pocket. "What is this?" He meets me halfway, meeting in the middle of my room. Bringing his hand from behind his back, he pulls out a red rose, "Did you really think I wasn't going to see you before I left?" His smirk turns into a soft smile, his beautiful pastel green eyes narrow a little, happily. I take the last step towards him and put my hand on his chest needing his touch, taking the flower with the other. "Adonis." I look up into his eyes, biting down on the corner of my lip, trying to contain my smile. I tap his chest, even though my anger was long forgotten, I say, "You didn't answer me all day. I was so mad at you." I frown mockingly and he chuckles, leaning in to

kiss me softly. He pulls back, putting his forehead to mine and he whispers, "I'm sorry. Are you still mad at me?" His bottom lip pops out as he pouts a little and I smile at that, not able to keep it in any longer.
"No. Of course not." I nudge my nose to his and he wraps an arm around me, pulling me closer and pressing his lips to mine. I breath in, taking in his perfect scent of white cedar, vanilla, and something else more spicy. I bring my arms up and wrap them around his neck. The rose now behind him. We deepen the kiss and I can't help the flutter I feel in my chest. He grabs me with both his hands, lifting me up and I instantly wrap my legs around his waist, throwing the rose on the floor. He starts walking, my eyes are closed as I feel my back hit my bed, our lips still moving against each other. He lifts me a little more, moving me towards the center of the bed and he brings one hand up into my hair, pulling me closer to him. I moan into his mouth, loving the feeling of his body on mine, feeling the weight of him. His tongue massages mine and I am putty in his arms, loving the feeling. He kissed me so passionately. I wanted to be closer to him, I needed to be. I run my hands up and down his back and sides, needing to feel all of him as he kisses me hungrily. I wrap my legs tighter around him, pulling his hips closer to mine and he makes a little sound in the back of his throat as I rub against him. I throw my head back, breathing heavily, his lips trail down my neck, kissing me along the curve. He reaches just below my ear and I whine loudly as he sucks the skin there. His lips hover over my ear, "That's my new favorite sound," The words come out of his mouth raspy and full of lust. I breath in and manage to flip him in one swift movement. I put my hands on his chest, sitting up straight while flipping my hair to the side with a flick of my head. "Yeah? Do

you want to know what's mine?" His eyes meet mine and the fire inside them fills me with more confidence than I ever had. He unconsciously licks his lips as I slowly crawl down him. I bring my hands down to the hem of his jeans. My eyes leave him to look at the visible bulge in his jeans. When I look back up to his eyes, a smirk is on my lips and he bites on his bottom lip. I unbutton his jeans looking at him through my eyelashes and slowly pull the zipper down. He hisses between his teeth with that little action, my smirk gets wider. As I reach my hand in to take him out of his jeans, he grabs me and pulls me up towards him, kissing my lips tenderly. He flips us so he is once again, on top of me. His lips hover over mine, "You're making it hard for me to behave." He runs a hand up my thigh and my breathing stills at the contact. The smirk falls from my face and I look into his eyes so he knows I mean what I say, "I don't want you to." He bites down on my lips, then sucks it into his mouth. Pulling back, he says, "I do very bad things and I do them very well." His hand ran up between my thighs, his eyes never leaving mine. I lift my hips suggestively, "You haven't seen my bad side." He groans loudly at my words, grinding into me unconsciously. I look down between us and give him a questioning look, "Why are our clothes still on?" He breathes out heavily, "You're right." He pulls back, grabbing my shirt in both his hands and tugs, ripping it easily, making me gasp. He continues taking it off my arms, pulling it to the side, then grabs onto my pants, pulling them down in one quick movement, throwing them to the floor. I was left in a blue thong and a matching bralette. "Mmm, my favorite color. "His eyes met mine after scanning my body longingly, his head still tilted down so his eyes were looking at me through his thick lashes. My stomach was swarming in butterflies, their wings grazing along my lower abdomen. He sits up on his knees between my legs and pulls off his shirt. I put my hands on the bed and reached up to kiss his chest and down towards his abs. He grabs onto my face with one hand, the other, grabbing onto my side and he brings us back to laying down. His lips crashing on mine, I instantly wrap my arms around him, kissing him back. How do I tell him I want to finally go all the way tonight? How do I tell him I am ready for him to take me completely? We have done so many other things to each other but never more. “Adonis.” I whisper on his lips and he pulls away. His questioning look turns into an understanding one. “Are you sure that's what you want?” His chest was rising and falling rapidly from our kissing. “Who better than my best friend?” His eyes searched mine for reassurance and I put my hand to his cheek and slowly brought it down to his neck, pulling him back down to me. After a few minutes of kissing my lips, he releases them and starts kissing me down towards my chest. His lips knew exactly where to touch me to make my skin feel like it was on fire. He knew exactly how to make me pant and gasp loudly. In just a matter of days, he knew my body better than I ever did. He reaches my hip bone and my breath gets stuck in my throat as he sucks harshly, leaving a mark for sure. His hands grab onto my underwear and he pulls them down, making a clicking sound with his mouth as he gets a view of me. I feel myself clenched tightly at the heat in his gaze. He made me feel so wanton, I wasn't even partly ashamed that I was almost naked in front of him.

Flicking my underwear to the side, he bends down and licks up between my folds, causing a moan to escape my lips. He gets back up and after licking his swollen lips, he says, “I love how you taste on my tongue.” My mouth parts at his words, a breath coming out slowly. He gets off the bed and I watch as he takes off his jeans, his boxers going down with them. I reached back and unclasped my bra throwing it to the side. My eyes don’t leave his as he climbs back on the bed and over me. He takes a deep breath as he parts my legs and aligns himself with my entrance. “Tell me if you want me to stop.” His eyes are full of sincerity and concern. Fear crawled up my chest and I tightened my legs a little, “Baby girl, you need to relax.” I swallow the knot that formed in my throat and force myself to relax my body because if I don't, this will hurt more than it should. He kisses my lips softly, reassuringly. He pulls his lips from mine, his eyes gazing into mine as he slowly enters me, a sharp burning sensation has me hissing between my teeth. His lips turn down and he stops for a second, allowing me to adjust. After a second, he continues to enter me, the burning still present. Once he is completely inside me, he asks "Are you okay?” Not moving an inch, helping me get used to his size. I nod and he gives me a sad smile as he pulls back a little, entering again. I bite down on my lip and squeeze my eyes shut, trying to keep from yelping in pain. I feel his lips kiss my cheek and I relax a little, opening my eyes again, meeting his concerned ones. I kiss his lips so he knows that I am okay. He again pulls back and slowly thrusts into me, a breath release from his lips. I did feel a pinch of pain as he continued his steady pace but for some reason, being this connected to him filled me with this happiness. My heart was soaring and my lips moved against his ever so slightly. He leans up towards my ear and says in a husky voice, “You're so tight.” His teeth graze on my earlobe and I can’t help the soft moan leaving my lips.

My hands grab onto him as he continues rocking into me as I slowly ask him for more with every passing minute as the pain is residing and forming into pleasure. He makes a deep sound of mercy as I arch into him, my breast pressed against his hard chest. "You feel so good," He murmurs and I wrap my legs around him, pulling him closer, my eyes closed. His thrust becomes a bit longer and quicker and I moan every time he reaches a spot I never felt before. He grabs onto my face, saying, "Look at me." I opened my eyes and looked into his irises that were almost black from how dilated they were as he stared into my eyes. My lips were formed into an "O" as he rocked into me. His green eyes looked at me as if I was the only person in the world. He made me feel so special and wanted with just his intense look. The rush I start feeling in between my legs as he speeds up has me gasping his name. My release was getting close and I think he was too. He captures my lips in his, kissing me sloppily. It was oh, so sexy as he continued his pace. Our breathing was loud between our kisses. “Baby, please tell me you're close,” He whined against my lips and I moaned out a yes and he quickened his movement. The way he rocked against me, he rubbed me just where I needed him to so I could reach my peak and as I do, I threw my head back, his name being released from my lips multiple times, in a panted manner. He soon finished after me, slowing down his movements so we could come down from our high. He puts his forehead to my chest, collecting his breathing. He pecks my chest and I smile, bringing my hand up to his hair. My hammering heart slows down with my breathing. He pulls away from me and a gasp leaves my lips from the sensitive sensation. He lays down on his back beside me. I cuddle up to him and he wraps his arm around me, a sigh leaving our lips at the same time.

Chapter Forty-Seven

Miss You....

I tried to keep myself busy the whole day, Adonis texted me when he arrived in Nevada. I haven't wanted to bother him all day, I knew he was going to be busy but I feel so on edge not knowing if he is okay. Is this how it's always going to be? He's going to leave to go work and I'm gonna be left wondering about him, waiting for his call? To tell me he didn't die or worse. I lay down in my bed after a shower. It wasn't just any shower, I did a facial, put in a hair treatment, waxed my whole body, and I even fixed my nails. Everything I did was to keep myself distracted. I didn't want to bother the girls today, trying to pretend none of this bothered me. I close my eyes and all I see is him. Adonis. His eyes, his smile, him. Last night was so perfect, I wouldn't change a single detail. I can still feel his caress on my skin as I remember it. I can still feel his kiss as I press my finger to my lips. I sigh loudly, a smile creeping on my face as I remember how he left this morning, so reluctantly. After making sure I wasn't in pain, after giving me painkillers, he left. It was very early in the morning, the boys were waiting for him. But in his eyes, I knew he didn't want to leave me so I had to put my big girl pants on and tell him I was okay and he had to go. The smile on his face didn't reach his eyes but that's what made my heart melt. Any other boy would have left without a second thought but not my Adonis. His heart was too kind for that. I still felt a little sore, it wasn't too bad but if I am being honest, I kind of liked it. It was a reminder of him. He was so gentle and caring. Butterflies swarm in my stomach and a grin spreads across my face as my phone rings and I see the caller ID. I slide the facetime call to answer while adjusting my perfectly blow dried hair. Thank god I spent hours pampering myself today and I didn't look like a slob.

His handsome face appears on the screen and relief settles inside me. Glad he wasn't injured. He smiles, a heartbreaking smile, his pale eyes shining. He had a hand behind his head, laying in bed. The white sheets surrounding him were a contrast to the tattoos all over his skin. He wasn't wearing a shirt and the blanket was just barely covering his chest. His hair was a little wet, probably from a shower. “Hey, gorgeous.” His words come out thick and velvety, making my heart skip a beat. “Hi, baby.” I whisper, the happiness clear in my voice. I remember his face when I called him that this morning for the first time. He looked taken aback but he liked it. He always calls me baby, it felt right to call him that too. Last night, something changed, I know it did. But I’m just going to see how things go from here because if I admit it, or say it out loud, I am scared I might ruin a good thing. His teeth on full show as he smiles wide, making his face brighten, “I’m not going to *ever* get tired of that.”
“Did you get much *work* done today?” I lift my eyebrows as I say *work* for emphasis and he laughs a short laugh before saying, “Yes, we have everything figured out.” I nod, “That’s cool…are you alone? Do you have your own room?” I tilt my head to the side in curiosity. His eyebrow raises in a suggestive manner, “Why? Is there something you are planning on showing me? That…” He looks to his sides, then back at me, “Only I can see?” He gestures to himself and I mentally roll my eyes. I scoff, “You wish. I am not that kind of girl.” I raise my eyebrows and look away, shrugging one shoulder dramatically. He shakes his head, then licks his lips, humming, “I bet I can make you do whatever I want.” I give him a playful glare, “Don't even think about it, Mr. Clark.” The smirk falls from his face and his eyes darken. He puts his thumb to his lower lip and my heart starts speeding at his

lustful expression. What did I do? “I am alone and I’ll give anything to see what you're wearing underneath that shirt.” My face flames and I look away from his intense stare.
I close my eyes for a second and try to gather my nerves. I look back to him, “What if I said I had nothing underneath?” His lips part and a breath passes through them, “If only you knew...” He shakes his head and brings his hand up to his face, rubbing it down in desperation. He then brings it down to analyzing it. “I wish you understood how good your skin felt under my touch.” His eyes meet mine as his thumb runs over his finger tips, his hand still in view of the camera. “I want to feel your skin under my fingers. I want your skin to rise as I touch you.” As if he was really touching me, my skin blooms in goosebumps and a lump forms in my throat that just won't go down as I swallow spit. I bring my hand to my collar bone and delicately slide my fingertips over my skin, “Like this?” His eyes move over the screen, “Just like that. Jesus. I wish those were my hands on you right now.” This simple touch, alone, was affecting him so badly. I only wondered what else would drive him crazy. I bring the same hand up and bite down on the pad of my index finger, letting it linger on my bottom lip, “Did you miss me today?” My voice sounds foreign to me. I feel like a different person as I speak to Adonis in such a different way than I normally do. His chest rises as he takes a deep breath, his eyelids getting heavy in lust, “Can’t you tell?” He runs a hand through his tousled hair. “Tell me. Were you as distracted all day as I was? I couldn't get my mind off of you.” I shake my head slightly with a sigh, not taking my eyes away from him, “You don't even wanna know. My mind has been in a daze since you left.” He bites

down on the corner of his lip, a smile appearing, "Yeah? What have you been thinking about?" "Thinking? I can still feel you." He blinks at my words and my stomach flutters. "You're killing me here. I am gonna get my ass kicked by Ben if you keep saying these things." I give him a confused look and he rolls his eyes, "I'm going to ditch this mission and drive down to your house right now."

THE NEXT TWO NIGHTS pass by the same way. Hours of facetime and very heavy flirting. His words get more and more intense. His I miss you's turning into I wanna fuck you, in a matter of minutes. I couldn't help telling him my desires too. I spent most of the time wishing I could step through the phone and be next to him. Today, I couldn't take the smile off my face. Adonis was coming home tonight. I was getting ready, Roxy was coming to pick me up soon. The boys called us over to Hudson's house to celebrate that they weren't dead…Oh god, I just quoted Cain. I tried on multiple outfits and nothing worked, Roxy was on facetime as I showed her each outfit while she got ready. "You can't wear a bra with the shirt." She states as I am about to take off a shirt that she insisted I try on with my blue jeans. It was long sleeved and the back was bare with thin strings criss crossing down. "I am not wearing this shirt, Roxanne." She sighs loudly, giving me a death stare, "You are wearing that shirt. I'll be there in ten minutes. You better be done by then." I take a deep breath and just decide and stick with this outfit. After a few minutes, Roxy called me to tell me that she was outside. After walking down the stairs and closing my door behind me, I walk towards Roxy's car. As I step

in, Roxy tells me we have to pick up Erika on our way there. My stomach was in knots. I tried to calm my nerves down but nothing helped. I have no idea why I was so nervous to see him. I should be calm and cool. I shouldn't be feeling like I'm going to throw up. I am just going to see my best friend and his friends...my friends. It's so weird how I feel so close to the boys now. It's as if I knew them all my life. They were all so easy to get along with, even James who was more quiet. I was now in front of Hudson's house, my hands shaking. Adonis' car was here, which meant *he* was here already.
The door is swung open by a very cheerful Cain, "Hola, amigos!" Then he frowns, looking at Erika, "Did I say it right?" She gives him a flat look, "Just because I'm latin, doesn't mean I speak spanish." He gives her a confused look, "So you're not latin?" Erika shakes her head and walks through the door passing him, Roxy follows her slapping him across the head while hissing an insult. I take a deep breath and walk through the door. The boys were all in this front living room, lounging on the sofas. Adonis' back was to me on an armchair. His back was straight, his hair was perfectly styled...like always. He seemed to be in a conversation with Hudson. I walk towards him, my hands still shaking and bend down to say in his ear, "Hey, bad boy." I quickly walk away, walking around his chair to where Roxy was sitting but as I do, I feel his eyes on me, then his hand grabs mine, not letting me walk away. I turn my face towards him and his eyes meet mine, his face lowered towards the floor, his eyebrows raised, "Where do you think you're going?" I felt my stomach flip as he looked at me this way. I smirk with an arched eyebrow, "To sit down." I point towards the empty seat next to Roxy. He shakes his head with a tisk. He tugs on my hand and in a split

second, I was on his lap, "Your throne is right here." I look back at him with my lips turned up, "That was smooth." I look away from him and say, "Hey guys, how's it going?" I feel one of his arms wrap around my waist. They all greet me and then I lean back into Adonis, "How are you?"
"I'm good...better now." He squeezes me a little and I suck in my lips to keep from smiling. "How are you feeling?" I ran my hand over his thick forearm. For some reason, the feeling of his bulging veins under my fingertips made my stomach clench. "Better now," I repeat his words and I smile wide. "So, I have a surprise for you. Do you want it now or later?" His voice is loud enough for everyone to hear and I turn my head at a loud sound of a clap. Cain was rubbing his hands together. "Say now!" Cain looks at me pleadingly. I turn back to Adonis, "Now?" It comes out as a question.
He puts his hands on my hips and helps me stand before he gets to his feet. He puts his large hands to my eyes to cover them. I felt so nervous all of a sudden. He leads me forward, then I feel the gush of wind as the door is opened. We continue walking and I have to trust that I wasn't going to hit a wall. "Watch your step." He whispers in my ear and I feel his breath fanning over my skin. I take a step down and we continue along the walkway. I know everyone was behind us because they were not keeping quiet. You can hear all their remarks about how I am going to freak out or how I am going to cry. I just grin as we suddenly stop. "Keep your eyes closed till I tell you." I don't say anything and he says, "Got it?"
"Got it." I repeated. He removed his hands from my face. He adjusts me and I feel my stomach flutter. A thousand things run through my head. What could it be? I keep my eyes shut tight, not wanting to ruin the

surprise. My mouth was slightly parted and my breathing was heightened. I clutch my thighs with my sweaty hands waiting. “Are you ready?” Adonis asked, I nod, my grin still in place. “Open your eyes!” I open my eyes to see Adonis lifting a tarp and a beautiful cherry red motorcycle appears under it. My mouth and my eyes open wide in shock and I feel my eyes light up. “Is this for me?” I asked stupidly. Adonis walks up to me, smiling, “Yes, it's yours. I drove it down from Vegas today.” I look at him frowning, “Why?” He smiles and holds out the key, “You always wanted one so I got it for you.”
“Plus, we don't want to give you rides anymore!” Roxy yells from behind me and I give her a quick glance with a smile on my face. I take the key from Adonis and jump into his arms, wrapping my arms around his neck, “Thank you so much!” I pull away and look at the bike, “You shouldn't have.” He presses his lips to my cheek, “Well, I did. Your father knows too so don't worry about him.” I turned towards him, looking into his eyes, his were shining in happiness. “You're the best.” He slants his head towards the bike, his eyes never leaving mine, “Go for a test drive.”

Chapter
Forty-Eight
Waiting...

I watch as he takes a shaky breath, his back stiff. I wrap my hand around his and he turns his face towards mine. Adonis' eyes were weary and concerned. The annoying music in the elevator made my stomach feel more queasy than it already was. It's been two days since we were at Hudson's house. Today was Mary's surgery, my father was finally going to remove the cancer from Adonis' mother's chest. I put a hand to his cheek, "She is going to be fine." He nods, my hand still on his face. The elevator doors chime open and we step out, his hand clenching mine tightly. As we finally got to his mother's room, the door was wide open and the room was crowded with people. I smiled, everyone was bidding her good luck. Adonis releases my hand and leans on the door, just looking at her from afar and I lean on the wall opposite of him, watching his face, Mary out of view. His eyes were glazed over and you can see all his thoughts and fears in them. A sad smile appears on his face as his mother notices his presence, "Okay, everyone. Thank you all for coming but my kids are here to see me. I will see you all when I get out." You can hear the smile in her beautiful voice. As everyone walks out, my eyes are still on Adonis. He runs a shaky hand over his hair when a few strands fall on his face. As the last person walks out, Mary says, "Come in, you two."
I walk in, not waiting for Adonis as he seems frozen in place. She was sitting cross legged on the bed in a surgical robe. She smiles as I take a seat on the bed. I try to smile back but it feels like a grimace. My stomach was in knots and I felt like I was going to throw up right here. "How are you feeling?" Is what I ask and she tilts her head to the side. "Listen to me," she starts, ignoring my question, "I know I am going to be okay but just in case, I need you to know that I

love you so much. To me, you are my daughter, you always were. Being in your life was a pleasure. I need you to look after my boy." She smirks at me, "I know I won't ask him to take care of you. That's already wired inside him." I look down to my lap as a sad frown forms on my face, my lower lip jutting out. "He is a very strong man but he won't be for this. He won't want anyone but you by his side. So please don't leave him. I know you're going to be very good to him. And I know for a fact, you are going to be an amazing wife and an even better mother one day." A tear slips down my cheek and I finally look up to her face, her eyes the same color of her sons, were filled with unshed tears as she continues. "Don't let anything stop you from following your dreams. It's going to get hard, real hard but I need you to lift your head up, square your shoulders, and push forward, take one step at a time. And don't look back, you're not going that way." She takes a deep breath, "I love the woman you have become, so beautiful, so smart." She wraps her arms around me and I do the same, tears streaming down my face silently. "He loves you so much." She starts whispering, "Sometimes too much. Just have patience with him." I tighten my arms around her, my breathing coming out faster as the tears keep falling. She pulls away and I stand to my feet after kissing her cheek.

"I love you." My words come out in a croaky whisper.

"I know, sweetie." She smiles and then her gaze meets her son's. I walk to the wall in front of her bed and press my back to it, running my fingers over my tear stained face. Adonis starts walking towards his mom's bed with heavy footsteps. Mary lays down on the bed, stretching her feet out and moving to the side. She pats the empty side next to her, "Come here, baby." He climbs the bed, cautiously laying down beside her. She wraps an arm around him and he puts his head on her shoulder. As soon as he does that, his shoulders start shaking and sobs are released from his mouth. My heart breaks at the scene in front of me, tears of my own falling down my cheeks. Mary runs a hand over his head, whispering things into his ear and he just nods into her neck. I think back to where Mary said I was going to be a good mother and a good wife. Those thoughts never really crossed my mind. I never thought about it. I knew Adonis was going to get married and start a family one day but I never thought of my future past medical school. I know he will be a great father and he will make a special woman very happy one day. Pain ripples in my chest at that and I picture Adonis getting ready for work, a beautiful woman helping him with his tie, a toddler on her hip. The tears on my face go down quicker as it hurts me to picture him this way. Having a family, a life with someone else that wasn't me. I see him take a deep breath and slowly calms himself down as his mother talks to him, tears streaming down her face. No. I wanted that. I want what our parents want for us. I didn't want him to be with someone else. I wanted him to be with me. I want to be his wife and have his children one day. My breathing was coming out in pants, as realization settled in me. I loved him. And I wasn't going to let anyone take him away from me. I push all those thoughts aside and decide to dwell on them later. They are too much for my heart to handle right now. "Okay, you guys!" I turn my face to the door as my parents walk into the room, my father holding a chart in his hands. Adonis sits up, wiping his face and my mother continues, "Nothing is going to happen. She is going to be out of surgery and free of cancer."

“Do you two not have faith in me?” My father asks, faking hurt. Adonis gets off the bed and stands to his full height, his shoulders still a little slumped, “You’re right, Rob. Do your thing.” He turns to his mom and gives her a kiss on the top of her head, “I’ll see you in a few hours, okay?”
“Okay.” She smiles and nods her head once. Adonis turns to walk away and my father puts his hand on his shoulder. Adonis was a few inches taller than my father but you can see the respect he had for him. My father gives him a look that says, *don't worry.* Adonis nods and walks past him. Adonis glances at me and I say bye to everyone in the room and walk up behind him. I followed him down the hall, having to jog a little as his strides were too wide for me. He turns into the waiting room and I follow him in. His back hits the nearest wall and he slides down it, his hands meeting his face, his elbows on his knees. I sat down next to him, one leg stretched out the other tucked up to my chest. I reach a hand across my chest to put it on his forearm. Wrapping my hand around it, I rub my thumb along his skin soothingly. He felt so out of control, I wish there was a way I could promise him everything was going to be okay. I don't know what was going to happen but I hope it turns out okay. So we sit there in silence on that wall, switching positions every half hour or so. My mother came and brought us snacks and drinks but he didn't touch anything. Me? I ate almost everything. I may be a nervous eater. I don't know yet. The boys showed up for support, they stayed with us for a few hours before they had to leave. I know Adonis really appreciated it, even though he didn't say much to them.
I may have used this time of quiet to think over this new piece of information in my head. I realized something else. I was not only in love with Adonis, I

always was in love with Adonis. Well, for as long as I can think. I think back to the way I always felt about him. I needed him by my side and when he wasn't there, it was torture for me. I never really cared for other boys and whenever he looked at another girl, it would make me furious. I always tried to pretend I didn't care but that wasn't true. I don't even want to get started on the time I spent in London. It was like my heart was missing from my chest and I know I never want to be apart from him ever again. Maybe it was my insecurities talking but Adonis would never feel the same way as I did. As I sat there waiting for news on Mary, I decided on not telling him how I feel. I was too scared of the consequences. So instead, I am just going to continue whatever we have going on and hope that one day, he will fall in love with me too. My stomach falls as I remember saying that we can't fall in love with each other but I couldn't help it, my heart is his and only his...and always will be. It's now been several hours since Mary got into surgery and my mother and father walk into the room. Adonis had his arm around me and I was leaning on his chest but as we see my parents, we both stand up.
"How is she?" Adonis' words come out croaked, his eyes still swollen. He runs his hand over his hair nervously, his eyes locked on my fathers. My father gave him a small sad smile, he looked tired. He has been working nonstop for hours. "The surgery went perfectly. We managed to remove most of the cancer, luckily it didn't spread more than it should have." My father takes a deep breath and then my mother continues, "She will need to see an oncologist for a few months so we can get rid of the rest of the cancer." I smile, glad to hear everything is good, I look up to Adonis but his eyebrows are knit together. "What's wrong? What aren't you telling us?" He asked

worriedly. My father sighs, “All her vitals are perfectly fine but she hasn't been able to wake up from the anesthesia. It's normal to take a few hours-” Adonis doesn’t let my father finish as he starts walking out of the room. We quickly follow him as he walks towards his mother’s room. “Is she in her room already?” I ask and my mother is the one to answer as we continue walking, “Yes.” We walk in to see a pacing Adonis, His mother laying on the bed, her chest covered in bandages. She was still sleeping and she was connected to the machines beside the bed as they continuously checked her vitals. Adonis stopped his pacing and looked at my father with worry in his eyes, “How long do you think it will take for her to wake up?” My father takes a seat on the chair near the sink in the room, “It all depends on her, Don. Her body suffered a lot of trauma today. It could be hours.” Adonis looks at my mother who frowns sadly, he asks her, “Will she wake up?” She walks up to him and brings him into her arms, he just stays there, letting her hug him. I frown as my mother pulls away and says, “Of course, she will.” A few minutes later, my parents walk out saying they will be back to check on things soon. Hours pass and nurses and doctors walk in and out of the room, checking her vitals. They open one eye, put a flashlight in checking for brain movement, then check the next. They check her hands and feet for movement too, everything seems to be coming out perfectly fine.
Adonis kept asking questions, impatiently. At one point I brought him food but no matter how much I tried, he wouldn't eat. He paced every little while, then would sit down and just stare at her waiting for a reaction. Benjamin called a few times but Adonis would give me the phone to answer as he didn’t want to talk. It was awkward talking to his boss but all he

wanted to know was if Adonis was okay and he would also ask how Mary was. As visiting hours were coming to an end, we heard Mary start to groan softly and we both ran to the bed. I grab the remote to call the nurse. Mary tries to open her eyes and Adonis grabs her hand, “Hey ma, I’m here.” She groans again and her eyes open slowly as she turns her head towards her son. Her hand grabs his and he smiles at her, you can see the relief in his eyes, I know I felt the same way. A nurse walks in and my father comes into the room shortly. They fan over her, making sure everything is fine. We only get to stay with her for about an hour before we have to leave, she needs rest anyways. She was groggy the whole time but thankfully she pulled through. As we get to the elevator and I press the button with the arrow going down, the doors open to a very nervous looking Jonathon Clark. I looked at Adonis, his teeth were locked into place, his chest rising and falling, anger clear on his face. “Son,” Mr. Clark starts, stepping out of the elevator. I was shocked, I don't understand why he even bothered to show up now. He should have been here hours ago. “How did the surgery go? I was delayed at work.” Adonis doesn't answer his father, he lifts his fist and collides it with Jonathan's cheek. I gasp loudly and the man falls to the floor at the sudden impact. Adonis steps into the elevator and I stand there looking at his father, wide eyed. I look back at Adonis and he gives me a blank look, his fist clenched to his sides. I stepped into the elevator and the door closed right behind me.

Chapter Forty-Nine

Enjoy The Ride

"Adonis, slow down." I put my hand on his, that was on the gear shifter. His grip on the steering wheel was so tight, his knuckles were white. He doesn't slow down the car. Instead, he picks up speed as we drive down the road. His jaw was wired shut, his face was red in anger. I take my hand off of his and lean back in the chair. I took my eyes off him and looked out of the windshield and noticed we were headed towards The Undergrounds. When we finally arrive, he gets out of the car, slamming the door shut. I got out of the car and followed him as he stomped towards the back door of The Undergrounds. I didn't even question why we were here, I just went along with it. I felt nervous to see him this way but I said I wasn't going to leave his side no matter what. Even though he was furious, I was going to stay by his side. We passed the locker room and walked right into the gym. After starting the lights, putting music on, and grabbing his white wraps, he walks straight to the punching bags, taking his shirt off in the process and throwing it to the side. He wraps his hands quickly and I just stand there watching his aggressive movements. I gulp and cross my arms over my chest as he starts hitting the bag in front of him. He moved from side to side, ducking a few times, then kicked. He continued the routine over and over, his breathing coming out heavily, his face a mask of rage. An hour of his angry boxing, he walks over to the workout machines and I follow him, watching him in a trance as sweat beaded down his perfect inked skin. My heart started to race and I tried to keep myself calm as I analyzed his body. He was doing chin ups. His arms spread wide on a bar and legs crossed, hanging over the floor. I lean on a pole, crossing my legs as I felt myself pulsing with need. The way he worked his body with all his fury was making me feel some way. He was blind to everything around him, all he saw in this moment was red. I can only imagine what he is going through. His feet hit the floor with a loud thump and he runs a hand through his sweaty hair. His gaze meets mine, then they run over the length of me, making my heart skip a beat. He walks toward the butterfly machine, sets the weights to his preferred number, and takes a seat. My lips parted and my breathing was quickened. I wasn't able to keep my cool demeanor anymore. I felt like the room was turned up a few degrees higher than normal Even though I wasn't working out, my skin was coated with moisture. He was pulling the handles towards his face, his arms stretched out wide. With every pull, he let out a loud breath. His face was scrunching with the heavy weight he was lifting. My panties were definitely soaked. His corded muscles were flexing with every push and pull. I felt the lust wash over me as it was unbearable. He lets go of the handlebars and they slam back with a loud clunk. Before I know what I'm doing, I'm standing right in front of him, my eyelids heavy as I look into his darkening eyes. The air around us changed to a heavy atmosphere. He relaxed into the chair and rested his head back on the cushion. “Come here.” I take a deep breath at his words and straddle his lap, my dress rising up, my eyes not leaving his. I put my hands on his chest and led them down to his sculpted abs, he put his to my hips, our eyes locked. I sweep my hands up his sides and slowly reach his hair, “What do you need?” I felt him hardening underneath me and my insides clenched at the feeling of him. His grip tightened on my hips, “You…badly.” I pull his hair with both my hands and press my lips to his, matching his earlier aggression. He moved my hips so I grinded against him and I moaned into his mouth. He kissed me back so passionately, I couldn't breath. His tongue devoured my soul and I wanted to be closer to him. I lifted myself up and opened his jeans, his head tilting up, kissing my lips as I pulled him out of his tight jeans. He pulls back from me and I lean back a little as he brings his hands up. He starts to unwind his wraps but I put my hand over his, “Leave them.” He raised his notched eyebrow, a smirk appearing, “Yes, ma’am.” He grabs my waist and I reach down between us. I move my panties to the side and with the other hand align him with my entrance. He takes a deep breath and looks down at my movement. His eyes meet mine as I sink down on him, feeling him stretch me out. I threw my head back in ecstasy, his lips met my collar bone and he kissed me hungrily. I bring my hands up back into his hair and attach his lips with mine, slowly riding him. His lips leave mine as I moan loudly and they work their way down to the skin under my ear. “You like riding me, baby girl?” I’m not able to speak as my breathing was ragged, my body was bouncing on his. He brings his wrapped hand to my hair and tugs, “Tell me.” I gasp at the feeling of his hand in my hair. “Yes, Adonis.” His hold tightens in my hair, not enough to hurt but enough to make me release a breath, “I don't normally give control, Aphrodite.” His thick velvety voice has me panting louder. “So you better not get used to it.” My hands run down to his shoulders and I grasp them as I start moving faster. I sush him and say, “Enjoy the ride.” He chuckles darkly against my skin and I twist my hips a little, making him growl and pull me tighter against him, his hand on my back. After we finish, Adonis drives me home. He spent the night with me because he had no plan of going home to be near his father. He seemed to be better as we got to my house. I pulled him into the kitchen and made him eat something, which he does easily. After we ate, we went up for showers and got into bed, both of us falling asleep instantly. And let me tell you, having his arms around me as I fell asleep, was everything to me.

Chapter
Fifty
The Divinity

A couple days have passed since Mary's surgery. We were now walking into Benjamin's house. Benjamin invited us over for dinner to talk about something important. The nice lady, I haven't learned her name yet, she seemed to be a housekeeper, ushered us to a dining room. We step into the large room, all the boys and Benjamin sitting around the table. The table could fit about thirty or more people, the whole room was gorgeous. It had windows to one side that were draped in blue fabric that matched the tall chairs that surrounded the table. Adonis led me to a chair near the head of the table where Ben sat. I noticed there were a few people I didn't know, also sitting at the table. He pulls out my chair and takes a seat beside me. I wonder what I am doing here in a room filled with Benjamin's people. I still don't understand what the man wants from me. I give a tight smile at everyone and as my eyes meet Cain's, he throws me a wink, making me roll my eyes. Benjamin stands up and closes the button on his suit jacket, "Aphrodite, Adonis. Glad you two could make it." Adonis gives him a short nod and Ben continues, "I invited you all here today because we have important business coming up. We will all be flying to New York in a few days. We have a few things that need to be taken care of. I am going to need you all there." All of us? Why do I need to be there? Adonis looked towards his boss, "What is it that you need us to do?" Benjamin's eyes meet his, "We were invited by an allied mafia, they want you to fight against their best fighter. They heard about your title and want to see how good you are. Also, they need help with a few things. I agreed that we will be there for whatever they need." Adonis' jaw clenches because he had no choice in this matter.

WE WERE ON A LUXURIOUS PRIVATE jet. It was just our group of friends and Benjamin. Apparently, there was another plane behind us, filled with more members of the mafia. I asked Adonis why Ben wanted me here and he said his boss wanted me to meet his allies. Adonis has been staying over at my house, he went home only to grab his stuff. I was surprised my mother and father were so calm with the fact Adonis was sleeping over, even though they believed we were now together. They didn't even care that he slept in my room or didn't notice. It was weird how much they trusted Adonis. When he told them about New York, I was awestruck with how supportive they were about it. Adonis was so smooth too, saying how our group of friends wanted to take a short trip and check out colleges and the museums. I just stood there, my mouth gaped open, he was so believable, I almost fell for it too. Roxy and Erika came along, saying the same story to their parents. Roxy pretty much fought her way on this trip and Erika just came along for the fun. “How's your mother, Adonis?” Benjamin asked. His chair was on the left side of the plane but facing us. The man was a GQ model. He was wearing a three piece suit, his ankle over his other leg and a drink in his hand. “She is doing really well, thank you for asking. She’s home now.” I smile at his words. I am so glad Mary feels so much better. We have been visiting her everyday and staying with her for a few hours. She is finally home since yesterday and thankfully Lily is there to take care of her while we’re away. “That's good, I'm glad.” Ben replies, then takes a sip from his drink. “Your mom is a fighter bro. She fought cancer and won. That's great.” Liam grins from across the plane as he was playing a card game with Hudson, on a table in front of them. Adonis smiles and nods. “Has your mom

asked about me?" I look up to see Cain over our head. As he sat up on the chair behind us, "She is so hot, man." Adonis glares up at him and slaps him across the face. He grabs his cheek and juts out his bottom lip, "It was just a joke, Don." Cain slithers back down into his seat. Benjamin chuckles, "That's what you get, boy." And he shakes his head.
After a long flight, we were walking into our penthouse suite. First thing we see is a large den. It has a bar to one side, filled with all kinds of liquor. In the middle of the room was a pool table. To the right of it was a living area and you had to take a step down to get to it. The wall behind it was tinted glass, showcasing the beautiful streets of Manhattan. Before I can say anything, everyone is running up the spiral staircase leading to the second floor. Adonis was walking to the bar. I stride to the windows and put a hand to it, looking down at the crowded streets, a smile gracing my lips. It was dark outside so all the buildings were filled with lights. The air feels thicker here in New York, it hits you as soon as you step out of the airport. I always liked quiet and peaceful areas but I can't help but want to be down there in all the mayhem. I feel a hand wrap around my waist and I look down to see a cup being led to my lips. My lips touch the crystal glass and the liquid slips into my mouth. It was whiskey, the feeling of it burning my throat was actually nice. The bitter taste was laced with something sweet and it had my mouth salivating for more. I turn my head to Adonis and his eyes meet mine as he takes a sip from the cup himself. Before I can say something, his lips press to mine and the whiskey is back but so much better as now his impression was mixed in. I pull back and gaze up at him, the glow of the bright neon lights reflect on his skin, his pale eyes mirrored the view. My heart filled

and my stomach erupted in butterflies. *He is so perfect,* is what I think as my eyes run over his face. *I love him so much.* I just wish that, at this moment, I can tell him my thoughts but instead, I swallow and pull away. “Let's go find our room.”
He smirks, “Our room?” He raises his eyebrow looking as sexy as always. “Is that a problem? If you want, I can go up and share with Roxy.“ I start walking towards the stairs, “I’m sure she wouldn't mind.” I try to keep myself from smiling. He grabs my hand before I get any further. Giving me a once over, his eyebrows raised, his head tilted down and he said, “You're not sleeping beside anyone but me.” My stomach flips and I keep the nonchalance as I shrug, “If that's what you want. Someone has to appreciate my lingerie.”
His smirk falls from his face, his eyes darkening, he opens his mouth to say something when Roxy comes down the stairs. We both turn to her as she says, “There you are, I have been looking everywhere for you!”
“Whats up?” I lean my head to the side. “We’re going sightseeing. Go get ready.” Her eyes meet Adonis’, “You too.” She narrows her eyes at us, “Hurry up, there is so much I want to see.” She turns around before I can reply and runs back up the stairs, taking two steps at a time. Adonis leans over and whispers in my ear, “I definitely will be appreciating them.” I take in a sharp breath and he walks away towards a hallway at the end of the room.

ADONIS TAKES A SHOWER WHILE I style my hair, a wet towel wrapped around me. After he finishes, he dries his body and I watch with my mouth feeling like the Sahara desert. He puts on boxers and a pair of slacks before styling his hair with product and brushing his teeth. Music was playing throughout the whole penthouse, making everything feel fun and easy. We had the downstairs bedroom, which was huge. As soon as our luggage arrived, I started adjusting mine and Adonis' stuff in the closet to keep them from getting wrinkled. Adonis was as bad as me when it came to everything being clean and organized. So while I did the closet, he laid out all our toiletries without even a question. We worked so easily together. We were like two magnets. Wherever one went, the other one followed. After he is done getting ready, he walks to the closet and grabs his black dress shirt, bringing it out with the hanger. He presses a kiss to my cheek, making my heart skip a beat, "Take your time. I'll be waiting in the den." I nod as a lump forms in my throat and he walks away. As soon as I hear the door shut, I take a deep breath, put the curling iron down and put my hands on the counter, looking at myself in the mirror. My blue eyes were shining, my makeup coated, my skin was glowing. I looked so different. I don't know why my heart was beating out of my chest. Maybe it was because now that I knew how I felt about him, everything was different and seeing how easy it was to be around him, made my mind swirl in thoughts of what we could be or what we should be. I like the way we fit together. It was like two puzzle pieces and we were the ones that you didn't realize belonged together till the very end. I just hoped he realized we were meant to be more than this, whatever we had going on at the moment. I sigh deeply and finish up my hair. I walk to the closet and put on the hot pink slip dress Adonis bought me that one time we were at the mall. I laugh as I think about how much we have been through since then, as I put my heels on. I finish up and walk out of the room to find the den filled with half naked men. I blink and move my eyes around the room. James and Liam were playing at the pool table. Adonis and Hudson were at the bar, both with a cigarette in their mouths. I turn my head to see Erika walking down the stairs, her eyes widening. She was wearing a black lace bodycon dress, making her look bolder than usual. “I know.” I say as she stands next to me, I agree to the look she has on her face as she admires the guys. She shakes her head, releasing a whistle. “These boys are fine.” I sigh and give her a noticeable once over, “And so are you. I love this look on you.” She blushes and looks down herself, giving me a shrug. She looks back at me, “Forget me, you look like a supermodel.” I roll my eyes and look up the stairs as Roxy walks down them carefully, her eyebrows furrowed. She was wearing black jeans, a black bra and a tan blazer. The blazer was closed by one button and she looked super hot. As her tan shoes hit the floor, she says, "The divinity on you guys!” Her exclamation was heard over the music and everyone turned towards her. “You guys think of yourself as gods!” She puts her hands to her slim hips. No one says anything, then there is a door opened near the bar. Cain runs out holding his pants up as they are completely opened. He was also shirtless. Behind him was a bathroom, from what I can see. “That's it!” He trips in the process of yelling, then steadies himself on the bar counter. He lifted a finger in the air trying to catch his breath, everyone's eyes on him. “That's our group chat name!” a slight laugh leaves my lips and I cover my mouth. “What are you talking about, dumbass?” Roxy squints her eyes at him while shaking her head. “*The Divinity!”* His eyes open wide for emphasis, then he reaches down and fixes his pants. “I won't have any other name.” He grabs his phone from his pocket and types away. I hear my phone beep in my clutch and pull it out. I look at the notification on my screen and grin. It said the group chat name changed by Cain, *The Divinity.* My eyes meet Adonis and he mirrors my smile. I walk over to the couches and take a seat, the girls joining me. Hudson claps his hands together and rubs them, “Alright, boys. Before we go, let's all have a shotgun.” He turns around and opens the fridge on the counter, pulling out a few cans of beers. He grabs a knife and pokes the bottom of his can, then quickly puts it to his lips, popping the other side open and It makes a loud sound. He sucks the liquid down his throat, his Adam's apple moving quickly as he swallowed each gulp. Before I knew it, he threw the can to the floor, cussing out loudly. My eyes widened as Roxy's says, “Do you eat pussy like that?” And I choke on my spit. Hudson smirks at her with a wink.

Chapter <u>Fifty-One</u>

The Big Apple

We walked out of the hotel and headed towards Time Square on foot as we were only a block away. Before I know it, an arm is being wrapped around my shoulder and the smell of cedarwood and vanilla fills my lungs. I don't look up at Adonis, trying to seem composed but he pulls me into him, putting his lips to my ear, my hair bunching up, "That dress, baby girl, is going to be the death of me." I finally turn my head towards him, "You like it? My best friend bought it for me." He gave me a cheeky grin. We turn a corner, our feet finally hitting Time Square, Adonis' next words don't let me appreciate the scenery around me. "I regret not doing what I wanted that day." I swallow spit, "And what was that?" He chuckles and the noise sends electricity into my veins that start pumping loudly with my heart. "I wanted to throw your legs over my shoulders and feast on you in that dressing room." My stomach clenches and I look up and watch our friends walking ahead of us. "I don't think I would have protested." He pulls away from me, winking and walks towards the boys. I quicken my step and walk between Roxy and Erika. I watch Adonis' back as he steps in between the boys and strides so he is a little bit in front of them, leading the way. His black shirt was stretched tight across his shoulders, his strong muscles bulging through the sleeves. I finally look up and grin as I see all the big screens surrounding the buildings. I loved the weather around us, it wasn't windy but there was a slight breeze. It was a perfect summer night. I always wanted to see New York. It was better than what I imagined. "Where are we going?" I ask the girls. My eyes land on Adonis' back again and I watch as he pulls out his pack of cigarettes from his pocket. "We are going to get pizza from this place the boys know." Roxy answers, her face shining with excitement. "I never thought I would see this place." Comes Erika's gleeful voice and I wrap my arms around both of them. "You guys! We're in Time Square!" I exclaim and they laugh along with me. We get to a more crowded area and the boys get closer to us. Adonis glances at me over his shoulder and holds his hand out so I can grab it. I quicken my step and wrap my fingers around his. We walk a few blocks until we get to a little pizza parlor. We all over ate except for the boys. The boys ate so much, we had to pull them out of the store. After that, we walked back to the middle of time square to these red glowing stairs that were crowded with people. We took all sorts of photos. Liam kept going on about going to all the bars in Time Square so Cain had the great idea of going bar hopping, which was super fun. We were now on an elevator going up to a rooftop bar. It was our fourth bar so far and my head was starting to spin. My lips were numb and everything was funny to me. We were all crammed in the small space and Adonis' front was to my back. I looked around the room and noticed no one was paying attention to us. I step back into him and shift from one foot to the other, discreetly rubbing against him. He grabs my hip with one hand, his grip tightening. "Don't start." His husky voice says, into my shoulder and I giggle and repeat my movement, making Adonis press his fingers into my hip. The pressure wasn't enough to hurt but it definitely made my stomach flip. I face up as the elevator door opens wide to the night view. We step out to a beautiful garden themed rooftop. There were a few tables scattered around and the big bar to one side. Over the head of the bar was a tent of flowers, twinkling lights draping through. I felt like I was in a fairytale, it was so beautiful. Adonis grabs my hand, practically pulling me towards the bar. He sits me down on a stool and stands behind me, pressing his

front to my back again, while wrapping an arm around me. There were a few people behind the bar, moving around to serve customers. When one of the bartenders finally has time, he walks towards us, a smirk coating his lips as his eyes meet mine but I look away. “What can I get you?” The guy asked and Adonis ordered everyone's drinks. Our group was huddled around me as I had the only free chair. Suddenly, we all turn to a deep, Russian accented voice, saying, “Adonis, is that you?” It was a tall bulky, raven haired man, wearing a pinstripe suit. Adonis takes a deep breath smiling. He takes a few steps towards the man, the guys follow him. “Vladimir, how are you?” Adonis says, shaking hands with him. I turn to Roxy as she whispers, “That is one fine specimen.” I roll my eyes at her, a chuckle leaving my lips. Erika shakes her head with an eyebrow raised, “You find everyone good looking.” Roxy gives her a sharp look, “It's not my fault. I blame these hot ass mafia guys.” Before I can reply, the bartenders bring over our order. “Anything else I can get you?” He tilts his head to the side, shamelessly checking me out. He was really cute, in a boy next door kind of way. He had blonde, shaggy hair and brown eyes. My face heats up, “No, thanks.”
“Are you sure?” He says, Roxy elbows me and I look up to glare at her. The bartender nods and walks away, not before shooting me a wink. “What's your problem?” I hiss at her and she grins. “Come on, it was just harmless flirting.” She shrugs, “I think you should flirt back. Maybe get a rise out of Don. He might decide to put a label on your relationship.” I blink at her a few times. Would that work? Would me flirting with someone else get him to react? What if he just gets furious with me and it makes things worse? Erika tsks, “What is wrong with you? Adonis is going

to get pissed." Roxy raises her eyebrow, then looks over to the bartender calling him over. My eyes widened and I glared at her but she wasn't looking at me. The guy reaches us and smiles at her. His eyes flick towards me before asking, "What can I get you?" "My friend here is new to drinking and wanted to know what your specialty drinks are?" Roxy tosses her head towards me. He licks his lips, "I'm really good at whipping up screw drivers, mojitos, but my specialty is sex on the beach." I give him a tight smile and wrap my hand around the drink that was in front of me, "I'm good with this, thank you." I turn my head back to Adonis to see him looking at us over his shoulder, while still in a conversation with his friend. I look away from Adonis as the bartender says, "Come on. That's a boring drink." He leans his elbows on the counter in front of him. "I can blow your mind with my flavors." A loud slam on the counter startles me and I look down to see Adonis' tattooed hand, his credit card underneath. "She doesn't need anything from you." The bartender's eyes widened and he took the card, quickly walking away. I don't even attempt to look up at Adonis. The anger was clear in his voice. The bar man walks back, passing the credit card back to Adonis. Adonis leans forward and grabs the bartenders shirt in a fistful. He was seething, "See something you like?" The guy shakes his head in fear and I stand up facing Adonis, putting my hands on his chest. Adonis ignores me and continues, "Now turn around. And if you so much as think about her, I'll put a bullet through your head." I stood there frozen, my hands still on him, trembling. Adonis pulls away, looks down at me, his eyes blazing in rage. "Lets go." He grabs my hands and we walk towards the elevators, our friends following us without a word. Why did Roxy have to rial him up? My breathing was coming out quicker and my heart was pumping. He was so furious, I couldn't think of what to do to defuse the situation. His grip was tighter than usual around mine as we stepped into the elevator. I press my back to the wall, not removing my hand from Adonis'.

WE WALK INTO THE PENTHOUSE everyone was still silent, the air around us was suffocating. No one was able to say anything with how Adonis was acting. I was sobering up completely from all my nerves. Roxy smirks at me before walking up the stairs and I wanted to choke her. Everyone followed up and Adonis finally dropped my hand and walked towards the bar. I took that opportunity to go into our room. I take a deep breath as I enter the room. I take a seat on the bed and slip off my shoe, groaning at the soreness in my feet. I stand up and put them to the side. Walking towards the bathroom, I quickly removed my makeup. I move my hair to one side and close my eyes with a sigh as I hear Adonis walk into the room. Deciding on just facing him, I walk back to our room. He was sitting on the edge of the bed in the middle. His legs spread wide with his elbows on his knees. His palms were on his temple with his back hunched down. When he hears me walk in, he glances up at me, "Did you like it?" My eyebrows knit together in confusion, "What are you talking about?" I slowly walk towards him and he stands to his feet. "The attention of another man. Did you enjoy it?" His chest was rising and falling. His eyes looked over my body, then met mine. He was livid, I didn't know why, there was no reason for his anger. "Don, I didn't do anything." He met me halfway and he was now towering over me. I was intimidated by him at the moment, his jaw was clenched tight. "Would you rather have him touch you? Is that what you want?" He searches my eyes that widen at his words. "No, Adonis. How could you say that?" My words burn as a thick lump forms in my throat. Anger started to boil inside me but I couldn't react just yet. I needed to try to calm him down, not make it worse. "I saw the way he looked at you." His hand went up into my hair, his face centimeters from mine. His teeth were grinding together, his heavy breath was fanning over my face. "I need to know, Aphrodite. Is that what you want?"

My face heats up in anger and I put my hands on his chest to push him away but he doesn't budge. "What's wrong with you?!" His other hand grips my hip with harsh fingers. "Tell me." He says, through gritted teeth.

"No, Adonis." I match his tone of voice.

"No what?"

I close my eyes, trying to gather my thoughts. I open them, glaring right into his eyes, "I don't want anyone else but you." His eyes darken and he presses his whiskey flavored lips to mine, in a punishing kiss. His grip tightening on my hair and hip as he pulls me closer to him. I kiss him back but start to feel discomfort at his strong hold. His lips were hurting mine as he continued. I pushed on his chest until he pulled away but instead of stopping, he grabs me and pushes me against the nearest wall. I tried to ignore the slight pain and kiss him back but his kiss was bruising. I push him again, “Adonis!” He ignores me and leans back in but I shove him, “You're hurting me.” I whisper this time, tears welling in my eyes. I didn't like this side of him, I have never seen him this way. He blinks a few times, looking my face over as if realizing what he was doing. He steps away from me and I stay plastered on the wall. “Baby,” He whispers and looks down to his hands. “I’m so sorry, I don't know what got into me.” I wrap my arms around my midsection, looking down. I try to regain my breathing and slow down my heart. I looked back up at him and he was looking at me with so much remorse, my heart broke. He really didn't mean to hurt me. His anger got the best of him. I take a step forward but he shakes his head, “Don’t come any closer.” “You wont hurt me, baby.” I whisper and he frowns sadly. “I’m still so angry, let me calm down.” I take a deep breath and walk up to him, wrapping my arms around his neck. I needed to make sure he understood I wasn't going to do anything with anyone else. He needed to understand that I only saw him. “Adonis, I…” His eyes look into mine, softening, “I only want you. Everyone else around us means nothing to me. All I see is you.” He visibly gulps, “You make me feel so much.” He closes his eyes for a second, then continues, “I don't know how to handle it.” He puts his forehead to mine with a sigh. I close my eyes, “You make me feel too.”

Chapter Fifty-Two

You Know I Am

I step into the limousine and look out the window, purposely avoiding Adonis. I was so angry with him. I shut my eyes for a second and take in a deep breath. This morning, I woke up to find the right side of my neck filled with love bites. I thought he was over his anger last night but I thought wrong. I was too consumed by him last night to realize what he was doing. I felt dirty when I saw all the hickies he left on my skin. He was in the living room, about to leave to meet with Benjamin and the rest of his people. I marched right up to him and demanded he explained to me what his problem was. He claimed he didn't know what I was talking about but I know that was bullshit. All the other boys looked at me with wide eyes as they noticed all the marks on my skin, making me feel worse. He was making a statement, showing the world I was his. I was livid, I told him, even though I regretted what I said, that I was not his. I even told him that we were just friends and he had no right to mark me. Hurt flashed in his eyes but I didn’t let him answer. I walked away and left him with his mouth gaped open. I haven't seen him all day, he left to work and I hung out with the girls. We didn't do much, just went out to eat and we walked around, then came back to get ready. Tonight is Adonis’ boxing match. He texted me an hour ago telling me he was coming to pick me up. That we were leaving earlier than everyone else so he can warm up. I didn’t even reply. I could have said no but I felt bad about what I said today. So when he texted me saying he was down stairs, I came right down, throwing my hair over my right shoulder. I was wearing a long, black satin strapless dress with matching elbow length gloves. I adjusted the layered pearl necklace that was around my neck nervously. The air around us felt uneasy. I knew he wanted to say so much but didnt even know

where to start. “You look ravishing, Aphrodite.” I only let my eyes move towards him. He was sitting directly in front of me. The car was simple, it wasn't a stretch limousine. There were two rows of chairs and they were facing each other. He was wearing the same clothes from today, a white button up and grey pants. “Are you still mad at me?” I move to glare at him, “Yes, I am.” He leans forward and puts his hand on my right knee, through the opening of my dress. He rubs his thumb in soothing circles and I look down at his hand. I breath in through my nose trying to calm my nerves. His one touch made every nerve flare. He looked at his hand, then back up at me through his lashes. “Baby girl, don't be mad at me.” He frowns at me, “I felt on edge knowing that you were upset. What can I do to make it better?” His hand moved a little higher on my leg as his eyes searched mine. My stomach clenches in anticipation but I try to ignore the feeling. “Adonis, you fucked up.” I sigh and bite down on the inside of my lip. He cocks his head to the side, “I know.” I gulp as his hand rises higher on my leg, I grind my teeth. “Adonis.” My glare becomes a scowl, “What are you doing?” He blinks, “Making it up to you.” I lick my lips as my mouth dries. I bring my hand to his and try to move it away. “You know you want me to touch you.” His hand moves higher up my leg, ignoring my hand on his.
“No, I don’t.” I looked away but that right there was my tell. I was lying, of course I was. I wanted him to touch me. He laughs, the noise making me feel a pulse where I shouldn't be feeling right now. I should be shoving him away and telling him not to get near me. My body was a live wire right now. I don't know how one little carres and a few words can make me panting with need. “So you're telling me, you're not wet for me right now?” As soon as he says those

words, his hand meets my core and he hisses as he touches me immediately with no barrier to keep him from feeling me. His finger slides between my folds and his notched eyebrow arches, “What was that?” I bite down on my lip to keep any noise from coming out of my mouth and also, so I won’t fuel his large ego. He puts his other hand on my opposite knee and opens my legs a little and I can't find it in me to protest. His torturous finger continues his slow assault. He leans in closer, his legs opening wide. His scent invades my senses. I was trying so hard to act cool and collective but as soon as a finger slips into me, my head goes back and I moan softly. I grab onto the edge of the chair with both of my hands, then meet his heated stare. “You’re so fucking pretty, princess.” I lean forward, our faces centimeters apart, “Don’t call me princess.” My teeth are gritted together. He grabs my face in his large hand, “I can call you whatever I want. You are *mine*.” I open my mouth to speak but he swallows my words with his lips, owning me with them. I loved how he wanted me so badly, how he wanted to have me all to himself. It made me have hope that we will be more than this one day. He pulls back, my face still in his hold. He grins wickedly, pulling his hand away, letting them linger on my inner thigh. I whimper at the loss of his touch, my eyebrows knitting together. “Say it, and I'll make you cum.” His voice is thick with lust. My chest rises and falls rapidly, “What?” His grip on my face tightens a little and he gets closer, “Tell me your mine.” Deciding on not answering him, I press my lips back to his. His hand moves to my hair, kissing me harder. As I am about to deepen the kiss, he pulls my head back, making me gasp. His lips touch my chest and he kisses upwards, his finger going back from where it left. This time I feel more stretched as he added a second digit. "Say it." He says along the base of my throat. He continues peppering kisses along my neck. "Or I'll-leave you- like-this. Greedy- desperate and-a-wet-mess." His words are said between kisses and when he reaches my collar bone, he licks up to my ear, making me pull in a sharp breath. His teeth latch onto my earlobe and he slowly pulls down, a moan coming out from his lips with it. I can't help but match it. He knows I'm his, he shouldn't doubt it. I always was his but maybe he needed reassurance. Maybe he felt insecure and this was his way of proving that I was his. The anger inside me dissipates as I admit, "I'm yours, Adonis. You know I am." He brings my face back to his and kisses me hungrily. His fingers working on me just how I needed them to. He knows exactly when I get close to the edge. His lips left mine, my eyes were still shut as he continued to pleasure me. His hand still in my hair, "Look at me." I open my eyes and the first thing I notice is that his breathing matched mine. "I want to see your blue eyes as you cum on my fingers." He starts a faster pace and my lips form an "O" as I get closer and closer. "Now." I gasp loudly as I reach my orgasm, just when he wants me to. His forehead presses to mine and he slows down his pace, prolonging the pleasure. My heart stammered in my chest at the way he looked into my eyes. There was so much emotion in his pastel eyes. I didn't know what it was but all I know is that I wanted more of it. As my breathing slows, he releases his hold on me and pulls back his fingers. He leans back in his chair, putting the two fingers that he used on me into his mouth. I feel myself tighten and I close my legs shut. How can I already be so needy? He cockily smirks and he puts both his hands on his stretched out thighs. "Don't worry, baby. I'll fuck you good tonight." He looked so perfect, as if nothing just happened. His hair was in place, his clothes didn't even look wrinkled. And it's good that I wore stainless red lipstick. If not, his face would have been covered with it. I don't even dare speak. I just look him over, my eyes landing on his tight pants. His hand brushes up towards the middle of his legs. My eyes quickly meet his, his smirk falling. "I'm all yours." I lean back in my chair and cross my leg over the other, my hands doing the same on my lap. I try to seem nonchalant, "Good." He looks at me with a very meaningful look, the same look he gave me a few minutes ago. I tilt my head to the side, "I wonder what you're thinking when you look at me like that." His eyes bore into mine, "I think of how easily I can get lost into your eyes. I think of how beautiful you are. I try to understand how I lived so long without you but I realized I wasn't living. I am only alive when you are around me." He takes a deep breath. "There is no one like you in this world." My heart fills and I feel my eyes glaze over at the emotion in his voice. My hands trembled so I interlaced them. He looked down for a second and when his eyes met mine, I almost gasped at their intensity. "I am a very bad person. But you, you are the only good in my life. You make me want to be better for you." Wanting to console him, I move so I can sit next to him. I lean into him, wrapping my arm around his waist. He brings his over my shoulder, pulling me closer. "Adonis." He looks down at me, "You are perfect. You mean everything to me."

Chapter Fifty-Three
The Great Gatsby

Music was blasting and Adonis was sliding into the boxing ring. Tonight was different than last time I saw him fight. Everyone was booing as he stepped in. Adonis didn't seem bothered by it though. He was still his cocky self, rolling his shoulders as he looked upon the crowded arena. This place was different from The Undergrounds. The chairs were elevated. With each row, it got higher, steps leading up towards the back. We were in Adonis' corner. Cain, Hudson, James, Liam, Roxy, Erika, and I. We all crowded around anxiously. My shoulders were stiff and my heart was hammering in my chest as I waited for the fight to begin. The music changed and all the jeering turned into cheering. Adonis' opponent stepped into the ring and was pumping his fist up towards the sky and grinning at his fans. He was intimidating, that's for sure. His name was Alexandro, he had dark hair, thick eyebrows, and dark eyes. He wasn't as built as Adonis but he definitely had muscle under his golden tan skin. He was a part of Benjamin's allied mafia and apparently, Adonis' good friend. But when they step into the ring, they are now rivals. They shake hands and start walking around each other, both of them itching for the other to throw the first punch. Adonis' face comes into view and I see him smirking at his friend, saying something to him. Alexandro's head tilts back as he laughs, then says something back. Adonis makes the first move, taking a step forward and jabbing him in the chest. Alexandro just shakes his head with a smile, then punches Adonis in the nose, making his head fly back. I bite down on my lip so hard, I can feel the metallic taste of blood on my tongue. Adonis laughs. *He laughs!* This is fun for them, they were enjoying this. While I stand here with my stomach churning. “What the hell is their problem?” Roxy asked me and I closed my eyes for a second breathing in. “They’re apparently, really good friends.” I looked at her but her eyes were on the fight ahead. “That’s just...” She shakes her head and I couldn't agree more. This wasn't a time to be joking around. They needed to take this seriously. There were a few other hits and ducks but nothing too bad. I hiss loudly, turning my head away from the hit. Alexandro hit Adonis right in the gut, making him hunch over in pain. My eyes caught Benjamin leaning on a black pole a few feet away, watching the fight. Our eyes meet and I quickly look away. Adonis was on his opponent. Alexandro’s back was pressed to the ropes and Adonis was punching him rapidly. The crowd was completely silent and you can hear each hit and grunt from the fighters. Now it was getting serious. Alexandro was trying to shield his face from the blows. “Don’t worry too much about him.” I turn my head to Benjamin as I hear his raspy voice speaking beside me. He was wearing a navy blue, three piece suit. Before I can reply, he continues, “He is very smart. He knows what he is doing. He doesn't go into things blindly.” I turn my face back to the fight, watching them again. Alexandro and Adonis are circling each other. I look back up at Ben, his eyes fixed on me as I say, “You're very fond of him.” He chuckled, putting his hands in his pockets, “I see him as the son I always wanted.” His words warmed my heart and his gaze was on Adonis. Benjamin's eyes were filled with pride. “I know I haven't known him for long. From the moment I met him, I knew he was going to be someone important. I didn't know he was going to be important to me. But as time passed, I noticed how much he reminded me of myself.” I wince as Adonis gets an elbow jab to the shoulder. Adonis quickly recovers and gives an uppercut to the other guy's chin. Benjamin begins talking again, “He loves you.” I turn my face to look at him wide eyed. “I have seen that look in his eyes before. I know that look. My wife, she was my life, she was all I had…and all I could have.” I frown sadly at him and he matches it with a tilt of his head and a small shrug. I could tell this man went through so much in his life. In his eyes, you can see that he has moved on from it. Or at least has been trying to. We both turn our heads to a loud groan with a matching grunt.

Alexandro punched Adonis so hard in the face. Adonis’ face flew to the side, his body going down with it. My eyes were saucers as I ran to the edge of the stage. Adonis was on the floor, his head to the side and his eyes closed. My ears were ringing, my heart stopped as all the noise in the building did. The boys started yelling at him to wake up but there wasn't any response. My voice was lost, I couldn't even fathom what I was seeing. Fire starts building up in my throat and the only thing that can relieve it, is me screaming his name, ”Adonis!” I repeated his names several times, in a desperate manner. “Wake up! Right now! You have a fight to win!” The more I scream, the hotter the sensation in my chest gets. He needs to get up right now or I'll never forgive him for putting me through this. The referee was sitting over him, looking at his watch on his wrist, checking for the time. If he goes over a certain time, he will be officially knocked out. I opened my mouth again, screaming like I never had before, “Adonis!” His eyes flash open, and he stammers to his feet. The crowd goes wild and I take a deep breath of relief but I was definitely still worried. Adonis straightens his back and brings his fist up. He punches Alexandro but doesn't get a

chance as he ducks out of the way. As they start prancing around again, the bell rings. I watch as James slides in a little chair in Adonis' corner. Liam, Hudson, and Cain quickly slide in the ring, all of them holding something different in their hands. Hudson holds Adonis' face as soon as he sits down, making sure Adonis can focus on him. Cain was holding a bottle of water with the straw in Adonis' mouth, squeezing water into it. James was cleaning up his face with a wet cloth. Hudson starts reprimanding Adonis, "What the fuck was that out there?" Adonis shakes his head, trying to get out of his hold, looking for something in the crowd. I move into his view and our eyes lock, my stomach tightens. He pushes Hudson off of him and slides off the chair to his knees, holding onto the ropes right in front of me so we are at eye level. He puts a hand to my cheek and I lean into his wrapped palm. He looked at me in concern, his eyes searching mine. I narrow my eyes at him, "What happened to getting in and getting out?" His whole face was swollen and blotchy, his eyes and lips the worst. He chuckled, "You have a whole mafia behind you now." I frown at him angrily, "That doesn't mean you can take your time in there."
"That's enough Adonis! The match is about to start!" Adonis gives me a meaningful look before standing up and getting back to his little wooden stool. Hudson starts speaking as Cain and Liam start working on him again. Hudson tells Adonis what to do and what to stay away from. Adonis just nods, taking in his words. The bell rang and Adonis stood up and attacked Alexandro, giving him no mercy. After Adonis won the fight, Alexandro had a huge grin on his face as they shook hands. I was amazed at how they went back to friends so easily. We all waited for Adonis to get ready and then we got out of there. We

got in a stretch limousine together, everyone raving about the fight and talking about all the details. I just stared at Adonis' bruised face, as our hands were intertwined, I wanted to take all the pain away from him. If there was a way I can have those marks on my face instead of him, I would. We were now walking into a huge mansion. We were invited to a party by Benjamin's allies. It wasn't what I was expecting. It was a raging party, flashing lights and people everywhere but somehow, it still managed to be posh and elegant. There were waiters serving snacks and drinks on platters. The men were wearing tuxedos and the women were wearing dresses. We walked through the house, passing rooms filled with people doing different things. Adonis was leading the way with his arm wrapped around my shoulders. As he passed men, they all greeted him in different ways and he smiled and shook their hands when needed. We ended up at the backyard of the house, passing large french doors. We step down the rounded steps and I look around at the extravagant view in front of me. In the middle of everything was a large fountain. To the right was a bar surrounded by people and lots of round tables scattered around it with chairs. To the left was a white dance floor crowded with dancers but they didn't only dance there. People were dancing wherever they wanted. There were twinkling lights overhead, running straight down for miles ending at a pool. Benjamin was waiting for us at the bottom of the stairs with a huge grin on his face. Before anyone can say something, Roxy says, “So, um...where's Gatsby?” I couldn't help the laugh that came out of my mouth at her question towards Benjamin. I guess she's right, this party did seem like it came out of The Great Gatsby. Benjamin smiled at her, his eyes crinkling on the sides.

We walk with Benjamin as he ushers us to a group of people. I turn my face up to look at Adonis, “Is this the kind of parties we’re going to start going to now?” He laughs, meeting my eyes, “Maybe. Do you like it?” My lips curl up at the corners, “I love it. It's amazing.”
“Everyone!” Benjamin shouts over to the group of about fifteen people in front of us. Men and women turned towards us, some smiling and some frowning in confusion. “Our winner, Adonis Clark!” They started cheering, raising their glasses in the air. “Someone! Get our guests some drinks!” A man with an Italian accent, who I don't know, says as he steps forward and extends his hand out to Adonis. Adonis unwraps his arm from me and grabs the man's hand, shaking it. Adonis smiled at the man respectfully. “How are you Lorenzo? long time no see.”
“Adonis!” The man releases his hand and then quickly throws a little greeting gesture to the boys. Turning back to Adonis and I, he says, “Who's this? I thought you were going to wait for my Valentina?” I narrowed my brows together at the tall man, who had black hair and green eyes. He looked a little like Hugh Jackman. Adonis tilted his head back in genuine laughter. When he looked back at the man he said, “This is Aphrodite, my girlfriend.” My heart stopped but he paid no attention to how stiff I got as he continued. “Mr. Guzman, we still have eleven years till she's eighteen. We have time.” He flicks his hand in a casual manner. Lorenzo holds up a finger, “Ten years. She just turned eight a few days ago.” The man was clearly joking, his eyes were shining in contagious amusement. I couldn't help it as my lips curled in happiness. Adonis shook his head with small laughter and a waiter came by with a tray in his hand, holding drinks towards us. They were flutes filled with champagne, my mouth watered at the sight of them. Adonis grabbed one and

passed it to me, then grabbed one for himself. Our friends grabbed some, then wandered off to find something better to do, I guess, leaving me and Adonis with all these people. We talked for, what felt like hours, Adonis introduced me to what I came to realize was the Italian mafia and Lorenzo Guzman was the leader. I even met Alexandro, the man that fought against Adonis tonight. He was a really down to earth and funny guy. I was really enjoying myself. I didn't think I was going to. After some time, Adonis and I slipped away to look for our friends and have some fun. I couldn't get my mind off of what he said; *My girlfriend*. My stomach erupted in butterflies just thinking about it. I look up at him and it's as if he feels my eyes on him, he meets my gaze. My heart fills with so much joy at the way he looked at me. His eyes matched his grin as they shined so bright. He pulled on my gloved hand and met my lips to his. I close my eyes at the feel of his lips on mine, his taste tingling in my mouth. I smile against him, my eyes softly closed. We were in the mix of a crowded house, people surrounded us. Music was blasting, lights were flashing but all I could focus on was *him*.
He pulls back but stays close enough that I feel his lips move as he speaks. “Why are you smiling?” I stick my tongue out to touch his lips and chuckle, “I'm happy.” He wraps an arm around my waist, pulling me into him. Feeling his warmth pressed to my body made my toes curl. He put his forehead to mine, taking in a deep breath, his strong spicy smell was filling my lungs deliciously. He pulls away and we continue walking, Adonis' fingers swirled in mine as he pulls me through the groups of people. When we finally found our friends, they were in a huge room in the house that had high ceilings and marble floors that were being used as a dance floor. I was shocked

at what I was seeing. Roxy dancing with Liam. I decided on ignoring it and just shook my head with a smile. Those two didn't even notice us. Erika and James greeted us and continued to dance. Hudson was a few feet away dancing with a red head. Cain was on the opposite side, dancing with two girls, one behind him and one in front of him. I look up with wide eyes at Adonis and he shrugs with a toothy smile. The song changes to, “Take You Dancing” by Jason Derulo. Adonis pulls on my hand and gives me a twirl, pulling me into him. I giggle and we start dancing to the beat of the music. My back was to him and his hands were on my hips as we swung to the song. I twisted my hips, going down and he bends his knees following me. My stomach clenched at how he was moving. I turn around on my way up and wrap my arms around his neck, his going around my waist. His eyes bore into mine and we continue to dance in sync. “Wanna go get a drink?” Adonis asked me as the song finished and I nod breathlessly. As we went to another room in the house, it was set up as a lounge, the music was quieter in here and there were a few rounded couches scattered around for more private seating. In here, you can see smoke swirling around in the air as men smoked on cigars. Adonis led me to take a seat, saying he was gonna get us drinks. I cross my legs, adjusting myself on the large red couch that was empty. I watch Adonis as he tells the bar keeper his order, my eyes moving over his strong body. He was looking sexy in his black, double breasted pinstripe suit that was tailored to him perfectly. I choke on my spit and sit up straighter as a woman walks up to him, putting her hand on his shoulder. It was Adriana. My eyes open in shock. I had no idea she even came on the trip with us. My blood starts boiling as I see Adonis talk to her with no intentions of throwing her off. I clench my hands together, trying to see through my envy. Trying to push it down, knowing Adonis wouldn't do anything to hurt me intentionally. Her hand starts going lower down his chest and Adonis grabs her wrist and flicks it off of him. Saying something angrily to her, her response is a sultry laugh, tilting her head up a little. Now she presses her body to his, her perfect breast aligned to his chest. The jealousy was getting harder to contain. I felt myself tremble in rage, I wanted to rip her hair out and pull her away from what was *mine*. Adonis peels her off of him, as if she was gum on the bottom of his shoe. He says something that pisses her off because she crosses her arms over her chest. The bartender comes by with the drinks. Adonis grabs them and walks back to me, shaking his head in disgust. I smile, my bitterness slowly turns into amusement. He sets the drinks on the little table in front of me and takes a seat beside me. My eyes lock on Adriana's as she looks at us with an ugly scowl on her face. I turn towards Adonis, throwing my leg over one of his. He puts a hand on my thigh, holding it in place as he bends down to meet my kiss halfway. My eyes stay on the woman that tried to seduce *my* Adonis tonight. My possessiveness gets the best of me. I push my body into his, showing her who he belongs to. Telling her with my actions, who is going to have him in their bed tonight. I felt him bite down on my lower lip and he pulled back squinting his eyes pointedly, a smirk playing on his rosey lips. "What was that about?" I tilt my head to a fleeting Adriana, "What was that about?" I lean back, putting my hands on the chair. His smirk deepens and he gets closer to me, his lips pressing to mine again.

Chapter <u>Fifty-Four</u>

Jinxed

I look at Roxy bewilderedly, “What?” She throws her head in her hands, groaning loudly. We were at a cafe having lunch. Just us girls, the boys were out working. Today was our last day in New York, we were leaving tomorrow morning so us girls decided to see as much as we could today. But as we sat here, Roxy mumbled something that sounded a lot like a confession, “Don't make me say it again.” She whines. She looks back up as Erika says, “You're gonna have to, we didn't understand anything that came out of your mouth.” She closes her eyes for a second before saying, “I slept with Liam last night…three times.” I pursed my lips to keep myself from laughing, she gave me a flat look. I roll my eyes, “It's not a big deal. You guys were drunk.” I wave my hand in the air, brushing it off. “We weren't drunk this morning.” This time, Erika and I couldn't help it. We both let out a little laugh. I gave her a reassuring smile, “What are you so worried about?” She puts her fingers to her temples and rubs a little to try and relieve the tension. “I have too many feelings when it comes to Liam. I don't like feelings, they make you weak.” Erika puts a hand on her arm, “Just talk to him about it. Maybe he feels the same way.” She gives me a look, waiting for my input. I nod, agreeing with what Erika said. We had so much fun the rest of the day. Sightseeing and walking around. We tried to finish as much as we could in so little time. Everything was better than I imagined. We were now back at the penthouse in the living room area, watching a movie in our pajamas. I was exhausted over our day today, my feet were sore. The shower I took helped a little but not quite how I wanted it too. It’s way past midnight and the boys haven't gotten back yet. I was getting antsy, I couldn't even pay attention to the movie playing in front of me. “Stop fidgeting. The boys are fine." Erika throws her hand over my shoulder, pulling me into her. She was always so calm, I loved that about her. She rubbed my arm with her hand and I nodded, "Yeah, you're right. What's the worst that can happen?" Roxy sighs loudly and turns off the TV with the remote, "You bitches just jinxed everything!" She stands to her feet and starts pacing. I stand up and walk towards the bar, grabbing a bottle of water to calm my nerves. Erika joins me while saying to Roxy, "Why do you have to be so dramatic?" Roxy turns towards us, putting her hands on her hips. She opens her mouth to say something when the elevator doors chimed open.

We all turn our heads to the noise and I gasp at what I see. The boys in the elevator, all of them full of blood and all their clothes disordered but the weirdest thing was that there was someone else in the elevator with them. Hudson and Adonis were holding a thrashing man, keeping him from escaping. And James was holding Liam up while Liam was hopping on one leg, the other clearly hurt. We all ran towards them and Roxy couldn't help herself as she said, "I told you guys!" "What is going on?!" I say, exasperated. Adonis and Hudson walk past me, soaking in blood that clearly wasn't theirs. I turn to see them lunge the man on a chair next to the window. Roxy and Erika follow Liam and James to the couch. Cain runs towards the bathroom. I follow Cain to ask him for answers and I see him bending down, searching under the sink. "What is going on, Cain?" I repeat my question hoping he would answer. Cain stands up pulling a first aid kit out of the drawer, "That man followed us back here, he shot Liam and tried killing us but failed." He walked past me. I take a deep breath telling myself I will freak out later. I form my hands into fists to keep them from shaking and walk

out. Adonis was on the man, speaking menacingly into his face, anger clear in his stance. Hudson was holding the man from moving, holding down his shoulders. The man wasn't speaking. He had a smirk on his face and a crazy glint in his eye. I ran my eyes over Adonis to check if he had any injuries but couldn't find any at the moment. Adonis stands straight and catches my eyes, "Take care of Liam's wound." His demand came out as he pointed towards a groaning Liam. He turned back before I could reply. Cain peeled off Liam's pants, leaving him in his boxers. I hissed when I got close enough to see the bullet piercing. I grab his ankle and lift it up, trying to see if it went through or if it's still inside him. Thankfully there was an exit wound. "Okay guys, luckily the bullet is no longer in his leg but we need to clean it right before I stitch it up." Cain passes me the first aid kit so I can look for what I need. There wasn't the right stuff to clean up an injury this deep. The little alcohol pads were not good enough. I look up, "Erika, go get me a vodka from the bar!" Without a question, she runs to the bar. "I could use a shot too, good thinking." I hit Cain in the back of his head, "It's for the wound." He nods with wide eyes.
Roxy was leaning next to Liam, who looked like he was in a lot of pain, "Roxy, go get a few towels and pain medicine." She looks towards me and stands to her feet looking a little lost. "Roxy, don't worry. Go! And wet one of the rags to put on his forehead." She walks away in search for what I asked her. Erika passes me the vodka and I look up at Liam, "This is going to sting." He Looks at me with his eyes as wide as saucers and shakes his head. I lift up his legs again and pour the vodka over his wounds, causing Liam to scream out in pain. Roxy runs back holding the towels and she passes me one that I use to dry off

the gashes. After I'm done cleaning it up, I pass the bottle to Liam, "Drink." Roxy gives him the pills and he swallows them down with the liquor. I hear a loud yell coming from Adonis and I flinch turning my head to see Adonis punch the man in the face. The man had no reaction, his face came back as if nothing happened. I turn back to Liam's leg with a large intake of breath. I get the needle and set it up so I can stitch up the two large tears. I will myself to keep my hands steady. Adonis' yelling was not helping me concentrate but I needed to drown him out for now. I look back to Liam, "Bite down on something." He grabs the towel the Roxy was using to clean his forehead and stuffs it into his mouth. He nods once, telling me that he was ready. I pierce into his skin and he groans into the rag, I drown him out too. I pretend that it's just me practicing my sutures on an orange like I have thousands of times before. As I do, I work quickly on both wounds. When I am done, I add some antibiotic ointment on the closures and stand to my feet. Liam was laying his head back with his eyes closed. I wiped my hands on a towel and sat down on a step that led to the living area, my knees shaking too much for me to stand.
I turn my body towards Adonis and Hudson as they interrogate the man. My face screwed up as I saw Adonis choking the man. I finally allowed myself to hear what he was saying. "You fucking piece of shit! Tell me!" The man doesn't even attempt to open his mouth, his eyes hold nothing but amusement. "Who sent you? You are not part of the Irish mafia. You would have been dead, like the rest of them." My breath stills at his words. I knew they did crazy things when they did jobs for Benjamin but killing a whole mafia? A whole family? Adonis rubs a hand over his face as he takes a step back, his back was stiff

meaning he was full of rage. He is passed the line of control. At this moment, all Adonis sees is this man and all he knows is that he needs to hurt him. My gut was churning. This wasn't going to go well. My breathing was heightened and my legs were jittering even more. I put both my hands on my knees to keep them steady. Adonis continues, "I'll give you a choice." Adonis gets into his face again, "You tell me what I want to know and I'll let you go. Probably with a broken bone or two, to remember me by." Adonis stood again. He looked so calm and collective on the outside but inside, he was an inferno of fury. He was scary in a way that made your skin crawl. "If you don't cooperate, I will have no choice but to send a message to your boss and you know what that is." Adonis looks towards Hudson and shakes his head, answering Adonis' silent question. The man finally speaks, "I am not going to tell you anything." Adonis shakes his head with a dark chuckle, "If that's your choice." Adonis reaches behind his back and pulls out a Glock. He presses it to the man's forehead. My head spins, my heart stammers and my breath stilled. This wasn't going to happen. This couldn't happen. It's probably a show to scare the man off. He wouldn't kill him. He can't. The man smirked even though Adonis had the tip of the silencer to his head, "He is coming for all of you." The man's cold eyes meet mine and his smirk turns into a grin. "Especially her." Adonis doesn't even turn to see where he is looking, he pulls the trigger. My heart leaps and my stomach bottoms out. The man's head flies back and the glass behind him gets splattered in blood. The noise was minimal due to the silencer but I can still hear it repeat over and over in my ears. I couldn't hear myself screaming but I know I was. My face was numb but I know tears were running down my face. I tried reaching out to stop Adonis but he already did it. I feel arms wrap around me but I continue to thrash around, trying to somehow stop him. That's all that was running through my mind, even though it was too late. “Calm down,” I hear James' voice and I throw myself to the floor in full force and my sobs take over my whole body. I look up as Adonis crouches down in front of me. I felt bile rise up in my throat. He puts a hand to my shoulder and I flick it off. “Don't touch me!” I scream loudly and his eyes fill with dread. He puts his palms up facing me, “Baby girl. Please relax. I am not going to hurt you.” His words came out softly but I didn't want to hear them. “Get away from me! You're a murderer!” I don't want anything to do with him. He looked disgusting to me. That man could have had a family that needed him. He took his life away. He didn't have that power. Who does he think he is? He isn't god. He was no one. Adonis stands to his feet and steps away from me, his hands still up in surrender. His expression was filled with fear and regret. “Baby, please. Don't do this. It had to be done. I shouldn't have done it in front of you.” I stand to my feet and glare at him, my whole body trembling. “You shouldn't have done it at all!” His face fell, “I told you, I'm not him anymore. This is what I do now. This is who I am.”

“I thought I could handle all this, Adonis but I can't do this. It's too much for me to even fathom.” I shake my head and give him a disgusted look, “I can't even look at you.” I turn around and leave him there. Erika was sitting down, tears falling down her face and Roxy gave me a worried look as she was kneeling next to Liam. She went to stand up to come to me but I raised my hand halting her movements. I walked down the hall into my room and closed the door.

My back hits the door and I slide down it. Tears start falling down my face in large droplets. I'm tired. So tired. I put my face into the palms of my hands and try to calm my breathing. What I just witnessed was flashing through my eyes on repeat. That wasn't the first time he killed someone, it was too easy for him. He didn't even flinch. Adonis had regret in his eyes but the regret wasn't that he killed him. The regret was that he killed him in front of me. Benjamin was wrong about me. I can't just stand by him and allow him to kill people. What he did tonight does change everything. When I said nothing he does can come between us, I was wrong. Murder didn't even cross my mind at the time. This is something that will keep me from being in his life. My heart breaks at the thought. I love him so much but I can't be part of something like this. The tears come down faster as I think about not being with him anymore. I wish there was a way I could turn back time until just an hour ago. I wish I can live in that bliss of not knowing him as a murder forever but all that peace of mind was over now. The moment he pulled that trigger, everything changed. He did not only murder that man, he killed our relationship and he killed me. He murdered any future we had together. He was the only one that could keep me from him and he managed to do it. He tore me apart. Knocks come from behind me and I don't react. The knocks turn to slaps on the door but then the slaps holt and the hand slides down the door and I hear something fall to the floor and I know it's his knees. "Aphrodite?" I don't answer Adonis so he continues, "I'm sorry. Let me in so we can talk about this." For Adonis to say sorry, was a big deal. He was taught by his father a long time ago, not to apologize for anything. But tonight, he was sorry that I was here, not for what he did. "He would have had the same fate, either way. If I would have let him go, his boss would have killed him. I gave him an easier death. They would have tortured him for days." I couldn't help but laugh humorlessly. Oh it's not a big deal, Aphrodite. He would have died anyway...wow, he said it so easily. Minutes passed by without a noise coming from either of us. Then a small thud on the door sounds and I imagined it was his forehead leaning on it. "I need you. I can't lose you." I feel a burning ache in my chest at his words. I shut my eyes tight and lean my head back tilting my chin towards the ceiling. "It breaks my heart to know I already did." A sob is released from my lips and he takes a deep shaky breath. "I thought I had you forever." A new round of salty tears stream down my face and I shake my head no. He didn't have me anymore. I wasn't his forever. How is this happening right now?

Chapter <u>Fifty-Five</u>

Don't Turn Back

I pack our bags and take a deep breath. I haven't slept at all. I hope to get at least a few hours of sleep on the plane. Every time I closed my eyes, all I saw was the man's head as it swung back and the blood spattering on the window. The sound of the gun being fired was still so real to me. I couldn't forget any of it. I look at the alarm clock next to the bed. It was seven in the morning. Our flight was leaving soon so we need to leave in the next hour or so. I finished packing all of mine and Adonis' things. I know I shouldn't have fixed his stuff but I needed to distract myself. When I start cleaning and organizing, that's when I can calm my nerves a little. I grab my purse, leaving all the other luggage on the bed, knowing someone else will take it downstairs. I walk towards the door and pull it open. My eyebrows knit together and I frown at what I'm seeing. Adonis was sleeping on the floor, a pillow under his head and a blanket thrown over him. He slept here next to the door. I had no words. I step over him and walk down the hall, trying my hardest to not look back at him because if I do, I know that I will crawl next to him and forgive him, telling him I didn't care. But I did care. I walk up the stairs and towards Roxy's room.

THE DAYS PASSED BY with so much pain and tears. I haven't moved from my room, only to get something from the kitchen to keep from dying. There were times that I cried so hard, I couldn't breath. I would hyperventilate. After the thoughts of Adonis being a murderer, new thoughts pop up. I lost him. A new round of sobs came from my chest until I finally cried myself to sleep, only to be jolted awake by nightmares. There's two that keep replaying every night. The first is that I'm the one in the chair instead of the man. Hudson is holding me down while Adonis holds the gun to my head and when I wake up, all I can think about is how he killed us when he murdered that man. The second dream, Adonis would walk towards me with that swagger he has, his eyes filled with desire, me sitting on a bed surrounded with perfect white sheets and pillows. Waiting for him to come towards me. Then, he would ask me, in his menacing voice, "What are you most afraid of?" His clothes would suddenly be all bloody. His face turns sinister instead of lustful. The sheets around me would be shredded with red stains and before I can answer, I look down to my hands and scream, finding them full of blood. My screams jolt me awake and all I can think of is his question. And the answer was, him. I was scared of him. I never thought I could be afraid of my best friend. But I was. He would text me in the mornings and my phone would ring every night with his caller ID but I didn't have enough strength to answer. Roxy came over a few times but we didn't even talk, we both would just stay there in silence until she had to leave. My mother was worried about me but she just thought Adonis and I were fighting. No one understands the pain I'm going through and they wouldn't be able to if they tried. I lost a large chunk of my heart and soul. This isn't nearly close to the emptiness I felt in London. After being with him, having him in so many more ways than just a friend, it's different. It's different because this time he has my whole heart with him instead of just a piece. I am in love with him now and the emptiness I felt, it was like my heart was literally missing. Sometimes, I lay down pressing my hand to my chest, silencing my breathing. Trying to make sure there was still a pulse to see if he didn't really have my heart. I know he wasn't mine anymore and never will be again. It has

been around five or six days since we flew back from New York, I'm not really sure. All the days were meshing together lately. I had to pull myself together because my classes started in just a few weeks. I needed to get up and get out of the house but every time I tried, my knees would collapse and I couldn't walk out the house. I was laying on my bed. It was starting to get late already when my mother walked into the room looking tense. I sit up on the bed and give her a questioning look. "What is it?"
"Johnathon Clark got arrested." My eyes go wide at her sudden statement. She sits down at the feet of my bed, then continues. "Apparently, he was running a sex trafficking organization. He has been doing it for years. Adonis found out, he's the one who got him locked up."
"When was this?" I was so confused. I didn't know anything about this. Adonis did say something about his father doing something bad but he said he would tell me that story another day. We never got around to it, I guess. My mother sighs, putting her hand on my leg. "I barely heard from Mary today. She was devastated but it was yesterday when it all happened." I shook my head, I had no words for this. My phone rings. I look at the caller ID. It was Mary, Adonis' mother. I answer without a second thought and put it to my ear. "Hello?" She breathes out in relief, "Aphrodite, I am so glad you answered. I'm sorry to bother you but I need your help." I answered her right away, "Yes, anything." I hear movement and then she asks, "Is there any way you can come over?" My breath stills but she continues. "I heard about you and Adonis. Not from him because he hasn't been home all week but he came home today. He went straight to his room and wont let me in. I keep hearing things crashing in there but he won't even answer me

when I ask if he is okay." I hear a long sigh come from her as she says, "Please, if you can come over. Maybe you can get through to him." I bite down on my lip in thought. This is not something I can do. She is asking for too much. "Can't you ask one of his friends?" I looked up to my mom and she was frowning in confusion. "Sweetie, he is not okay. You're the only one that can get through to him." My mind goes on overload. I try to convince myself not to go but there is another part of me that wants to make sure he is okay. Okay, Aphrodite. Just go. Ask him what his problem is, make sure he isn't harming himself and leave. That's it. Just get in and get out. "Okay, I'll be there soon." I hung up the phone and my mother stood up with me, "Where are you going?" I close my eyes for a second, "I'm going to go see him." I walk into my closet and quickly throw on jeans and a t-shirt. I grab my tennies and walk out, taking a seat on my couch to put them on. "What happened between you two?" I shake my head at my mother's words, "I don't want to talk about it." She sighs, "Okay sweetie, just know I'm here for you." I nod and she walks out. I don't even want to go into the bathroom to look at myself. I know my face was blotchy and my eyes were swollen. My hair probably looked like a birds nest. I grab my keys and helmet and walk out of my room, dreading every step I take down the stairs. Mary's worry is the only thing keeping me from turning back around and going back into my little shell. I step out of the door and lock it behind me, my legs shaking as bad as my hands. I look at my red Ducati that was in the driveway and frown sadly as memories from the day he gave it to me run through my head. I think about how far we came from that moment and today, so much has changed. I take a deep breath and walk towards the motorcycle, throwing my helmet on. I straddle the bike and roar it to life in one go. I turn out of the driveway and speed down the street towards the Clark's house, hoping everything goes as I planned.

Chapter Fifty-Six

Vulnerable

I stand in front of Adonis' bedroom door. I try to keep my knees from falling to the floor. I keep myself steady, clutching my legs hard enough to bruise. A sound comes from the other side of the door and I flinch. It sounded like he was throwing things around. I close my eyes. I try my best to convince myself to knock on the door and ask him to let me in but all I see is what he did. Him killing that man. So I open my eyes and wish I could keep them that way forever, so I wouldn't relive that scene. I didn't know what I would see when he opened that door and to be honest, I was terrified. I ran my hand through my disheveled hair and took a deep breath before tapping my knuckles on the white door. He doesn't answer so I knock again. A loud groan comes from Adonis, then he says, "Leave me alone!"
I sigh before saying, "Adonis...It's me."
Silence...nothing, no noise comes from the room. His name releasing from my lips after so many days, made my heart stop for a second. The knob twists and the door slowly opens. My stomach bottoms out at the sight of it opening and when my eyes land on him, I feel like my breath was stolen. His hair was in different directions, probably from pulling it so much. He has dark circles under his eyes and thick stubble on his face. He wasn't wearing a shirt, all he had on was grey joggers that were rolled up on his hips. His muscles looked more defined and a lot larger since last week. His pale green eyes look dazed and confused. He was rooted in his place, his body tense. His eyes roamed all over my body, searching for answers. "What are you doing here? Is something wrong?" I look around his room, not able to keep my eyes on him. The room was a wreck, there was stuff everywhere. I answered him, "Your mom wanted me to make sure you were okay." I hear him take in a

deep breath, “What do you think?” I try my best to keep a straight face, even though I was dying on the inside. “I think you need to get your shit together. Your mother is worried about you.” He runs a hand through his crazy hair, “As if it's that’s easy.”
“Okay, so I guess I’ll be leaving.” I turn to walk away from him. I need to leave before I break down right here in front of him. I can't stand another second of being around him. His expression of hurt and loss was killing me even more.
“Why are you really here?” He asked and I stopped in my tracks. Not turning towards him, I say honestly, “I don’t know.” It was the truth, I didn't know why I came. I didn't have to. I could have said no to Mary. I just used her as an excuse to come see him. My heart needed to know if he was okay. Also, I needed to see him at least one more time before I pulled myself together and got ready for my classes at UCLA. “I know why.” He whispers. I turn on my heel and narrow my eyes at him, “Why?”
“Because you feel empty. Because you feel lost. You feel like your heart is missing.” His chest starts moving faster as his breathing quickens. “You can’t breath. You can't sleep. You eat because you have to but most of the time, you want to throw it all up.” His lip trembles, “You feel as if everything and everyone around you is just a blur.” I swallow the lump in my throat. How can he say these things to me? Why is he treating me this way? Just because I'm vulnerable without him, he doesn't have to rub it in my face. My hands form into fist as annoyance builds inside me, “What's your problem?” His eyes look sad as he speaks, “Because that's how I feel.” My heart hurts and I can’t help it, I raise my hand to rub my chest to try to relieve the pain. “So no, Aphrodite. I am not okay.” I feel my eyes glaze over and I try to blink

away the unwanted tears, trying my best to keep them from falling. I can't give in to his words. I just can't. "I still see it, Adonis. Every time I close my eyes. All I see is you pulling that trigger." He steps closer to me and raises his hand. I take a step back, not letting him touch me so his hand deflates. "I hate that you had to see that." Anger boils inside me and I grit my teeth, "You still don't understand, that's not the point." He grabs my arm this time and I try to shake him off but he just pulls me into his room and closes the door behind us. He puts a finger to his lips, shushing me, "My mom is listening in."

"It's fine. I am leaving anyway." I pull my hand out of his grasp that was making my skin heat up. I hate the way he made me feel. I hate that he still had an affect on me. I didn't want to feel anything towards him. His eyes go unfocused and his breathing quickens, "Aphrodite, I'm helpless without you. Don't leave me like this." My lips turn down, "Adonis." His name comes out of my lips almost pleadingly. "I can't pretend everything's okay when it's not."

He shakes his head no, in desperation, "I don't want to feel like this anymore." My only thought was, *me neither.* "What do you want me to do, Adonis?" I look down for a second, trying to gather my thoughts. "I want you to tell me that you're still mine. I want you to tell me that you don't care about what happened in New York." I bite down on my lip to keep it from trembling, "I can't do that. I wasn't really ever yours anyway." Maybe hurtful words will help my departure. "We weren't anything." The lies burned my tongue but I still continue to say them, even though the hurt was evident on his face. "It didn't mean much. It was just sex. You can find someone else to give you what you want." I hold in any look of hurt. I hold in any tear that threatens to fall and when I go home, I will allow myself to break down but right now, I will keep my chin up and tell him all these lies to make it easier on both of us. For a man so adapted to killing, his eyes were filled with tears as he says, “You don't mean that.” I square my shoulders, getting ready to walk away, “Adonis-” My words get stuck in my throat as he falls to his knees in front of me. I couldn't believe what I was seeing. I felt my heart squeeze in pain. “Please wait. Don’t leave yet. Just give me a few minutes.” Tears fell down his cheeks, “If this is it. If this is our last time together, let me try to make this right -” He chokes on a sob, then he grabs onto his hair. “I can't have you leaving this room. To leave me for good, without you knowing.” The tears that I have been holding in, start to run down my face. They were burning my skin. I nod, not able to speak, as my heart was broken from seeing him this way. He blinks, then quickly stands to his feet. He grabs my hand and pulls me towards the bed to sit down. His hand was lightly coated with sweat and I wondered if it was because he was nervous. I reach up to wipe my itchy cheeks as he walks towards his night stand. He pulls out a little wrapped rectangular box. He walks back towards me and hands it to me. I grab it and look at him confused. He pulls his lips into his mouth before speaking, “April twelfth. I went to go see you.” I give him a perplexed look but he continues. ”I was so excited when I landed. I called your mother right away to ask her where to find you. I asked her not to tell you so I could surprise you. I was finally going to see my best friend. I haven't spoken to you in so long and at the time, I also wanted to escape. I just wanted to feel whole again and I knew only you could do that. Only you can put me back together.” He takes a seat beside me on the bed. “But as I saw you laying there in that beautiful blooming garden, the one that you said I wouldn't like. I couldn't make myself walk up to you." I couldn't breath. My chest was rising and falling rapidly. He was there in London, on my birthday. His eyes met mine and he continued. "I sat down on a bench and just watched you from a distance," He chuckled, "If you would have taken your nose out of the book you were reading, you probably would have seen me. You wouldn't have recognized me though. That's one of the reasons I didn't go up to you. I was scared of your reaction to my new look. You looked so happy, laying there. I didn't want to take that away and then my mind came back to reality and I remembered who I am now. And I didn't want to bring you into it. I couldn't just pretend for a few days that we were back to normal, then leave. I would've had to ignore you again and that would have left you even more devastated. I couldn't do that to you. I couldn't be selfish. I called your mother and told her. She went off on me but I already made my decision." Anger was masking my shock, "You are selfish. You are the most selfish person I know." I don't know where this burning sensation in my chest was coming from but I needed it gone. He shakes his head, not letting me continue, "You know that's not true." He takes a deep breath, then stands to his feet. He walks into his closet and walks out with a box that I recognized. It was a present I sent him for his birthday. It was still perfectly wrapped. He sits back down, saying, "You sent me this just a couple weeks later on my birthday and I couldn't bring myself to open it. I felt like such a coward for not giving you yours. I didn't deserve to open it." He sets it aside and closes his eyes for a second before looking into mine, "I should have realized then." I knit my eyebrows together and he continues, "I should have realized I was in love with you then." His words made my body spasm in a way it never has. I search his eyes but all I see is sincerity. "I love you so much. I always have. It took me too long to understand that. There were a lot of times that my actions screamed it but I wouldn't listen. I was too scared to lose you. But since I already did, I'm telling you now. I am madly in love with you." He slumps his shoulders in defeat, "It kills me that I lost the only reason for my existence." Silent tears were streaming down my face as he spoke. I look down to my lap. For weeks, I have been wanting him to say these words to me. I wanted him to tell me he loved me so I can run into his arms and tell him how I felt. I always thought that he didn't feel the same way or that he couldn't but now as he admitted to me how he felt, I am at a loss for words. I couldn't just drop everything. Drop all my fears and doubts because I love him. He was still a murderer. That will never change and I don't think I can ever move past that. He rubs his hands over his legs as he continues to speak, filling the silence. "I know you will never feel the same way and I know I am a monster in your eyes and it's okay. I understand. I love you enough to let you go. I crossed too many lines and I know you will never see me the same." Minutes passed in silence and I decided to tell him the truth. "I am in love with you." I couldn't look at his face as I heard his breath hitch. I continued to talk, "But I can't make myself push all my fears away. I am so scared, Adonis. What I saw the other day, has been imprinted into my mind and it will be there forever. Every time I look at you, all I see is blood on your hands. I won't be able to be in a relationship with you." He stays silent at my words and I look up at him to see his eyes already on me and they were widened with unshed tears. "You love me?" He whispers. My eyebrows narrow down. Is that all he heard? "Adonis. Yes. Of course, I do but you need to understand, we are at a point where the love we feel for each other, doesn't make a difference." He grabs my face in his large hands, "Listen to me. I will never hurt you. I will always protect you but I also need you to understand that I am working for a very powerful man and there are a lot of people that want to hurt me and the people I love and I can not allow that to happen. So if a man comes and threatens you or anyone else I care for, I will put a bullet in their head without a fucking hesitation and if that's too much for you, then I understand. But if there is anyway, at all, that you can push past all that and be mine, I promise I will forever be yours." I stand to my feet, put the box on the bed and start towards the door but instead of walking out, I pace the room. Everything he said was running through my head on repeat and I was trying to piece together my thoughts and feelings. He just sat there watching me walk in circles like an idiot. I close my eyes and the dream where Adonis asks me what I am most scared of, pops into my head. I realized I wasn't scared of him. No, he would never hurt me. My biggest fear was and always has been, was losing him. Maybe right now, I am still a little shaken up by what I saw him do but he's right. If someone threatened Adonis or tried to hurt him, I feel like I would want to hurt that person and maybe even kill them if I had to. The man's sinister eyes pop up into my mind as I remember how he looked at me. A shiver runs down my spine. I try to picture myself in Adonis' shoes and as I think of the man looking at *him* that way, as if he was excited for *him* to die. All I want to do is shoot the man in the head. All I want to see is the blood splatter on that window. I know those thoughts were wrong and that is the opposite of what I have been thinking all week but I wouldn't let anyone hurt *my* Adonis...I turn to him, putting a hand to my mouth and shake my head with wide eyes. He was looking at me with slight fear in his eyes. He's scared I am going to leave and never come back. He doesn't know how wrong he is. "Baby," I whisper and lower my hand. His eyes open in shock but I continue. "I understand. I would do anything for you without a second thought."

"What are you saying?" He was so vulnerable. I've never seen him this way before and I never wanted to see him like this again. I take a step forward, my eyes not leaving his, "I would hurt," I take another step forward, "I would kill." I was standing right in front of him now. I put my trembling hand to his cheek. "For the ones I love...and I love you, Adonis. *I am willing.*"

Chapter Fifty-Seven

The Undergrounds

It's been two weeks since Adonis and I got back together…well, started officially being together. We were in his new car. It was a shiny red Ferrari. He said he wanted to match my motorcycle. He got a new car because he destroyed his Porsche. Like literally, destroyed his Porsche, with a sledgehammer. I was shocked, to say the least. We were on our way to The Undergrounds, Adonis had a big fight tonight. He squeezes my bare thigh, then puts his hand back on the gear shifter and I look at him through my lashes and the curtain of my hair. I was wearing a red dress that had a slip going up my left side. The dress was off the shoulders and framed my body well. "You look," He bites down on his bottom lip before continuing, "So beautiful."
"Thanks, baby." I feel my cheeks heat up and I smile up at him. He winks at me as I put my hand on top of his. I grab it and put it on my lap, intertwining our fingers. He slows down as we turn on the road and brings my hand to the gear shifter as he switches gears. Then, he brings it back to my lap. I felt butterflies in my stomach and rubbed my thumb soothingly on his hand. As he speeds up the car, he uses the hand he was holding the steering wheel to switch gears again, while holding the wheel steady with his knee. He was too sexy for his own good. He continued to do that until we arrived at the beaten down shopping center. He parked in the back of The Undergrounds, I reached over to open my door when he said, "Let me." I sit back and wait for him to walk around the car and open my door. He reaches out his hand and I grab it. He helps me out and closes the door behind me. As I go to walk, he presses my body into the side of the car. My stomach flips as I look up into his light green eyes. He caresses my face with the back of one finger, his face centimeters from me.

His eyes were gazing into mine with so much love, I was melting. He brings his finger down to the bottom of my chin and tilts my face up so my lips could meet his. I bring my hands up his arms and to the back of his head. I pull him in closer as he deepens the kiss that had my knees wobbling. He pulls his lips away, his forehead leaning on mine, “I love you, baby girl.” I felt as if a hand was squeezing my heart at his full hearted words. I bite down on the corner of my lip before saying, “I love you too, Don...so much.” He leans down and gives me a lingering kiss before pulling me towards the entrance of the locker room. Adonis quickly changes into his fighting outfit, which was just a pair of loose shorts and shoes.
We stepped into the gym and all the boys and Benjamin were there waiting for us. Roxy wasn't here because she was on vacation with her family. They wanted to spend some time away before school started and Erika was busy with her mother tonight. Adonis takes a seat on the chair that they had ready for him by the mirrored wall of free weights. As Adonis starts talking strategy with Ben, Liam and Cain start wrapping Adonis' hands. I couldn't get my eyes off of him tonight. His muscles flexed in his tattooed arms. His chest was pressed against the spine of the chair while his legs straddled it. He caught my lingering eyes and smirked at me with a little lick of his lips. My eyes go straight there, zeroing in on his glossed lips. My insides clench and my eyes meet his again. His eyes darken and he stands to his feet. The guys finish up wrapping his hands and Benjamin wishes him good luck before walking away. Without taking his eyes off of me, he says, “Meet you guys out there. Okay?” I look down to the floor, feeling the blood pumping through my veins. “Alright Don, we'll be waiting for you in your corner.” James says. I hear

footsteps walking away. I look up through my eyelashes and see Adonis stalking towards me. I gulp as he steps into me, his wrapped hands grabbing my waist, "Hmm...baby. Last time you looked at me like that while we were in here, I had to have you on my lap." My insides melted at his words and I felt my core clench. "Is that what you want, Aphrodite?" His eyes search mine, "Do you want me to take you right here?" My lips part and my breathing speeds up. He smirks and pulls me towards the dumbbells by the waist. He turns me around and faces my body towards the mirrors while he stands behind me. I bite down on my lip and put my hands on the weights while pressing my lower half on him. My eyes don't leave his as I arch my back down. He raises an eyebrow and grabs onto my hips, pulling them back so my back flattens. "You are such a naughty girl." I blink innocently, my eyes never leaving him. "We don't have long." He growls and lifts my dress up, bunching it around my back, "I only need five minutes." My ass was in full view of him now and he clicked his tongue, shaking his head as he noticed I wasn't wearing anything underneath. "Were you ready for this, princess?" His eyes meet mine again and I nod. He takes a deep breath and I see him tug on the elastic of his shorts, pulling them down, taking his boxers with him. He puts the tip of himself to my entrance and his eyes burn mine as he thrust in, in one quick move of his hips. I moan loudly and he reaches his wrapped hand over to my mouth and covers it, "Shh...baby girl. I don't want anyone hearing the sounds that are meant for my ears only." I don't know why but the fact that he was wearing his fighting wraps, makes me even more consumed in lust.

Adonis Throws a hard uppercut to his opponent's chin and the man's head flies back, taking his whole body with him. The man lays there, the referee over him counting down the time. This whole fight was brutal. The fighter was as good as Adonis. They went three rounds of hard hits. We were cheering him on. He loved the attention. As soon as the referee calls out knockout, the crowd goes wild and Adonis starts prancing around the ring, throwing his fist up in the air in victory. I grin like an idiot as I watch him dance around. Then, suddenly a loud gunshot was heard and I ducked down, covering my head out of instinct. People started screaming and shouting. I look up to see people running around and men with full on swat style outfits holding huge guns and aiming at people. My ears were ringing, everything was going in slow motion. I look up to see two men on Adonis. I stay there frozen, unable to move. He manages to fight them back, taking the gun away from one of the men and shooting them both. My heart was hammering in my chest and I didn't know what to do and how to do it. Everything the boys taught me was lost in my mind. Adonis turns to me. He starts towards me when I see another one of those guys jump into the ring, I scream for Adonis to turn around but it was too late. The person already jumped him. I turned to find help but the boys were already in their own fights. There was so much going on everywhere. When I look back to Adonis, a hand goes to my mouth and I start thrashing as the person behind me wraps their arm around me. I am guessing it was a man because the build I felt behind me was huge. I scream into his hand and start squirming. I looked around and tried to find someone to help me but no one even noticed, everyone was fighting their own battles. The guy lugs me away from the scene. I tried to calm myself down and I elbowed the guy in the ribs with all my strength. I rewind all the classes the boys gave me in my head.

The guy grunts in pain and he lets me go. I whirl around and knee him right where it should hurt the most. He crunches over with a groan. I'm about to turn and run when I get another arm wrapped around me. My eyes bulged as I felt a cold metal to my temple. "Try something and I'll blow your brains out." My breath hitched and he pulled me towards the exit. I couldn't move, I couldn't scream. I was stuck. My eyes roam around searching for Adonis as I am being pulled away and I see people fight, people shooting other people. I was so far from him. He was too busy fighting men to notice I was getting taken. This can't be happening. This isn't real. God knows what they're going to do to me. Before I can disappear through the door, I scream, "Adonis!" Adonis' head whips and his eyes meet mine and they go wide. The man that was holding me puts his hand to my mouth and says with a Russian accent, "You stupid suka!" He drags me up the stairs quickly and my stomach churns, my blood pumping in my veins. We reach the top and he lifts me higher, then throws me over his broad shoulder. He starts jogging and yelling at someone in Russian and the fear inside me becomes worse and tears start falling down my face. "Let me go!" I started yelling through my sobs and hit his back. I heard a door being slid open and he threw me, my back hit a metal, causing me to hiss in pain. I looked up to see I was in a van with no chairs in the back, there were only chairs in the front of the car. The man looks at me and smiles wickedly. My eyes open in terror as he grabs the door and I scream, "No!" But it was for no use, he slid the door closed.

Chapter Fifty-Eight

-ADONIS-

“**A**donis!” My head whips towards Aphrodite’s scream. My eyes widened as they met hers. Someone was grabbing her and pulling her towards the exit. I quickly grab the AK-47 from the guy in front of me, who was trying to take me down. I shot him in the head in one quick movement and run out of the ring, sliding under the ropes. I ran towards the hallway, shooting anyone that was trying to get in my way. I run into the locker room, grab my keys from my locker and sprint up the stairs. My blood was running cold through my veins. They took her. They took my girl. I am going to murder them with my bare hands. Then, I am going to find the mother fucker who started this and I am going to destroy him, slowly. I get into my car throwing the gun on the passenger seat. I start it, slam the door, and drive towards the front of the shopping center. I see the guy that was holding Aphrodite, climb into a black van and he starts driving out of the parking lot. I am not going to let him get away with her. I follow him as fast as possible. I was on his tail as we hit the street. He speeds up, climbing out of his window with a Glock in his hand. He shoots towards me but misses completely. It was very late at night so there weren't people or cars on the streets. This man had no chance at all, I have an 812 while he has a shit van. I was gonna fuck him up. I grab the gun from the side and open the window, aiming straight for the man’s tires. The car skits to a stop and I switch lanes, driving so I am beside the car and quickly drift the car around so I was facing the van. I took a deep breath calming myself down, I needed to get Aphrodite out of this and to safety. I climb out of the car, leaving it on. I aimed the AK-47 up towards the driver, the back of it pressed to my shoulder. The man looked at me, still in his seat, with his palms up in the air. I was focused, nothing and no one was gonna keep me from taking my girl back. I open his door and press the guns mouth to his temple, “Who fucking sent you?!” I scream loudly, wanting to shoot his brains out right now. “Adonis!” Aphrodite yells from the back. My stomach drops. She was so scared. “I’m right here, baby! Don’t worry!” I grab the man’s shirt and pull him onto the floor. His eyes were wide and he looked scared shitless but he wasn't planning on telling me shit. His lips were sealed. That's the thing about omerta. When you belong to a mafia, you are bound to a code of silence. Getting information from other mafia men was sometimes impossible. “Tell me! Who sent you?”

I felt my face red hot in anger and my breathing was out of control. He doesn't say anything, and that was getting me more pissed. I aim the gun to his chest directly over his heart. “Talk!” The guy closes his eyes and puts his palms together. He wasn't begging me, he was praying. He does the sign of the cross and kisses his fingers. I shoot his leg and he yells in pain. “You're testing my patience,” I grind my teeth together. “You can’t stop him.” The man shakes his head. His voice was thick, it sounded like he was trying to mask an accent. “Trust me, I will.” I aim the gun back to his chest and fire multiple shots into his heart. I throw the gun down and walk over him, sliding the door open. Aphrodite’s eyes meet mine and she jumps into my arms. Air finally fills my lungs as I wrap my arms around her. She sobs as I lift her and she wraps herself around me. “Shh...it's okay. I have you, baby.” She hugs me tighter, choking on her sobs. I grab my phone as I walk towards my car, her legs wrapped around my waist . I dial Cain's number and put the phone to my ear, he answers on the first ring. “Hey, Don. So glad you're alive.” I hear him sigh. “Cain, I need you on Third street, near The

Undergrounds. Is everyone okay?" I walked around to the passenger side and opened the door, Aphrodite was trying to calm herself down. "Um...yeah, everyone's fine. The Undergrounds is empty now but there were a lot of casualties." I lean down and help Aphrodite sit. Our eyes met and she had a sad look on her face. I put my hand on her cheek and pressed my lips to her forehead for a second before standing up. "What do you need me to do on Third?" Cain asked. I move Aphrodite's dress into the car before closing the door, "I killed the man that tried taking my girl." I walk around the car and I hear the sound of Cain's motorcycle start through the phone as he said, "I'll be right there." I hung up the phone as I stepped into the driver's seat. I turned my face to look at her and her cheeks were stained with tears. Her makeup was running down her face. "Who were those people, Adonis?" Her voice was shaky and full of fear. I start the engine, "I don't know but I plan to find out." I grab her trembling hand and look her in the eyes, "No one will ever lay a hand on you again. I promise." She tightens her hold on me and I search her whole body with my eyes, looking for injuries. "Are you okay? Did they hurt you?" She shakes her head, "No, they didn't." As soon as I see Cain, I drive off. Leaving him to do what he has to with the body and car. I took a quick glance at Aphrodite, "I need to go back to The Undergrounds so I can see what they need. Then I'll take you home. Okay?" I was not going to take her out of my sight. Not today and not ever. "Okay," She whispers. We park in and I unwrap my gloves. This is the last time I will have them wrapped. I will never fight in a boxing match ever again. I don't need this in my life. I am done with it and after I find the man that wanted Aphrodite and after I torture him for days, I am done with the mafia too. I needed to protect what mattered most to me. I don't want her to be a target forever. I open the car door and step out, throwing the wraps on the floor. I go around to open the door for Aphrodite and grab her hand, pulling her out. I wrap my arm around her shoulders and pull her towards the back entrance. She wraps her arms around me and buries her head in my chest. Having her by my side, after everything that just happened, it made me feel like I finally had control after losing it. We pass the locker room and walk down the tunnel, towards the arena. The whole room was silent. All of our people are cleaning, trying to put everything back together. There were bodies everywhere. Aphrodite pushes her face into me after looking around. I see a few people surrounding something next to the boxing ring and I feel the blood drain from my face. Something was wrong. James sees me from far and jogs over to me, his hands and shirt full of blood. His face was stained with tears. "Adonis," James warned as I pushed him out of my way, letting go of Aphrodite, leaving her with him. I step up to the guys and what I see has me pushing them away. My heart dropped at what I saw before my eyes. Benjamin's lifeless body. My breathing accelerates and I fall to my knees next to his head, grabbing him in my arms. "No," I mumble. I look down at him, raking my eyes down his body. His shirt was soaked in blood. I couldn't accept what I was seeing. "No," I say a little louder now, I could feel tears running down my face. I look back to his face, his eyes closed and his hair matted down. "No!" I scream loud now. This wasn't supposed to happen. He wasn't supposed to die. He had too much to live for. I still need him in my life. "Benjamin!" I shook him, I don't know why but I just needed him to wake up. I needed him to be okay. "Please wake up." I whisper, "I need you." My face burns as the tears fall down my face and I wipe them so they won't fall on him but they were coming down too quickly. The sobs were taking over my whole body and I pinch my eyes closed. My body was shaking as I held on to him, hoping this wasn't real. I stay there holding him for, I don't even know how long, before I feel a hand on my shoulder and I look up to see James with tears running down his face. "We need to move him." I nod in agreement and turn back to Benjamin. I tightened my hold on him, "They're going to pay for what they did." I promise him. I set him down, setting his head down gently and I shakily stand to my feet. I see all my boys standing there. Aphrodite in the middle of them, tears running down her cheeks. I put a straight face on and square my shoulders, "I want this place cleaned up. And I want Benjamin in his house. So the police can find his body there." I turn to Cain, "You know what you need to do to make sure it looks real." Then, I turn to Liam. "I need you to clear the cameras on third street." James was waiting for his order already, "You stay here and make sure this place looks perfect. It's what Ben would have wanted." I looked at Hudson. His eyes were dark and swollen, Benjamin raised Hudson. When He had no one. "Help me move him."

Epilogue

-Adonis-

I watch as they lower the casket down into the ground, my teeth grinding together. I need to keep myself from breaking down right here in front of hundreds of people. It wasn't only Benjamin's followers. People from all over America came to his funeral. Dons from other mafias came to pay their condolences.
Benjamin was very well respected by everyone.
Benjamin wasn't all smiles, people were terrified of him. Ben didn't mess around. He was always in a good mood but you definitely didn't want to get on his bad side. I squeeze Aphrodite's hand as people take turns shoveling dirt into his grave as a symbol.
Benjamin was in my life when I needed him most but he left too soon, there was still so much that needed to be done. I still needed him in my life. I don't know how to continue without him. Who will I go to for advice? Who will be there to tell me what to do?
Benjamin was more of a father to me than mine ever was. He always had the right words and never put me down. Hudson passes me the shovel and I grab it, walking towards the pile of dirt. I take a deep breath as I press it in. I shovel up the dirt and carry it. I stand over his grave, the shovel hovering. I wanted to be tough, I thought I could hold it in. A tear falls down my face as I whisper, frowning. "I can't do this on my own, Ben." I shake my head and shut my eyes for a second before saying, "You were the father I always wanted and I should have told you sooner." I throw the dirt in and I pierce the shovel into the dirt in front of me. I turn around and Aphrodite looks at me worriedly but I shake my head and put my hand on her arm and walk past everybody, needing to be alone for a minute.
My steps get faster as I see a tree a few hundred feet away. As I finally reach it. I crouch down, putting my face in my hands, sobbing into my hands

uncontrollably. I felt my heart crushing in my chest. My lungs couldn't fill with air, they were squeezed tight. I was hyperventilating. Brining my hands up to my hair, I tug on it in desperation. I look up and try to catch my breath. This was way too hard. It's funny how I wanted to kill my father but here I am at Benjamin's funeral and I couldn't even breathe. A man that I haven't known for long. Benjamin managed to be in my life and in such little time, do more than my father ever has. I try to calm myself down, taking large breaths. I hear the grass crunching as footsteps come towards me. I turn my head to see Carter. I stand up and clear my throat, running my hands over my face trying to look presentable. Carter was Benjamin's right hand man and he is now the Don of the American mafia here, in California. Carter was tall and of a lean build. He was around Benjamin's age, maybe a little older. His rich chocolate complexion and sharp features made him look sophisticated and smart. His hazel eyes were sad as he approached me, holding a manilla envelope. "Carter." I greet and clear my throat as my voice comes out croaked. "Adonis." He tilts his head in greeting, then continues speaking. "Benjamin really cared for you. I know this isn't the right time but Ben left an order and I need to live by it." He passes me the envelope. "He gave this to me. He said if something ever happened to him, to give this to you as soon as possible. He didn't want me to wait." I frown in confusion and grab it. I opened it quickly, wanting to know what he left. I pull out a bunch of papers. I glance at Carter questioningly, clutching the papers in my hand. "He left you everything, Adonis." I looked down with narrowed eyes, not understanding what he was saying. I take the paperwork out and put them over the envelope and start going through all the sheets with a heavy heart. I swallow as my mouth goes dry. He's right. Everything is under *my name*. Benjamin's house, his business. His vehicles. His money. And his *Mafia*. This is something I didn't want. It was already too late. When a mob boss officially passes you his title, only death can take you out. I was Without Choice. My heart clenches as I realize I was now a mafia boss. A Don Of The American Mafia.

Wait! Don't stop there! There's more!! Keep reading for Bonus Chapters in Adonis' POV Hope you like them - E

Bonus Chapter 27.2

-ADONIS-

I look up at her house as I harshly close the door shut of my car. I felt like shit for leaving her alone right now but I needed to go find Nick Walker and show him what happens when you mess with me. As I pull out of the driveway, I click on the screen of my car and search for James' name on my recent calls. I rev my engine as soon as I reach the street and I speed down it as fast I can. After a few rings, James answers, "Don?" Running my free hand over my hair, I asked, "Did you find him?" He replied bitterly, "Yes. We have him. We are waiting for you at The Undergrounds." I hang up and take a deep breath. Flashes of her face when I was in the ring run through my mind and my knuckles turn white on the steering wheel. Her sweet pink lips were busted and her jaw was swollen and red. That mother fucker punched my baby girl on her perfect face. After I'm done with him, he won't be able to recognize himself. She looked so scared, she was shaking in my arms. It broke my heart when she thought I was going to get mad at her. I would never blame her, she didn't know better...but I did. I should've fought harder. I shouldn't have let her go out with that guy in the first place. I have to admit to myself, it was killing me that she was out with him. The thought of someone else having their hands on her, killed me but right now, I am in a worse predicament because he didn't touch her sexually. He hurt her. I grit my teeth and hit the middle console angrily. How I could I let this fucking happen?! I park behind the building that leads to the back door of The Undergrounds. I look at my unwrapped hand and watch as I open and close my fist. Normally, my hands are always wrapped. No matter if I'm in the ring or not . If I am hitting someone's face for Benjamin or for The Undergrounds, I always make sure my hands are protected. At this moment, my hands are not wrapped and that's just the way I want them. I want to feel Walker's skin under my closed fist. Slamming the car door shut, I walk towards The Undergrounds back door and open the door that was already unlocked for me. I walk in and down the stairs. I hear muffled yelling coming from the arena and I grind my teeth together. My breathing gets heavier as I get closer with every step. That fucking piece of shit hurt an innocent girl, an innocent girl that belongs to me. He is going to pay. My fist was trembling in anticipation. Walking through the tunnel that leads to the arena, Nick's pleads get louder and it's like music to my ears. I wanna hear him beg for his life. He fucking knows what's coming for him. I grin as I see the boxing ring. Nick was sitting tied up to a chair and gagged. All my boys were surrounding him. Nick spots me walking towards them and his eyes widened and he starts thrashing out of his chair. My steps weren't rushed, they were long strides. He knew what was expected to happen. Liam pulls out the rag that was in Nick's mouth and Nick starts pleading while trying to break free. I grab onto the ropes and pull myself up on the platform. I pick up the ropes and go under them. As I stand tall and walk towards him, words that I can hardly register come out of Nick's mouth in a rushed tone. “Adonis, look I'm sorry.” My ears were ringing in anger. I needed to shut his fucking mouth right now. My fist came flying into his face. His face flew to the side with a loud groan. He looks back to me, “Please, Adonis It was a mis-“ I shut him up again, pulling my fist back and punching him right in the nose. I felt the crunch under my knuckles. His face flies backwards from the hard impact, making the chair fly with him

with a loud thud. “You fucking hurt her!” I jump on top of him, grabbing onto his shirt and pulling him upwards. He looks at me dazed, blood dripping down his nose and face. Seeing that crimson color made me want to see more of it.
Aphrodite’s face flashes through my eyes. I pull back my fist and connect it with his jaw multiple times, right where he hurt *her.* I grab his shirt with both hands now and scream in his face, “You're dead! You’re fucking dead!” I say through my clenched jaw. Lifting his head a little higher by his shirt, I slam him into the floor with a loud growl, “Was she begging the way you're begging now? “ I ask him, then slam his head into the floor again, grunting out loud. I shake his head so his eyes meet mine, I don’t get a response from his so I lift up my hand and slap him a few times, “Look at me!“ I yelled in his face till his disoriented eyes widened again a little and met mine. “Did you even give her the chance to beg you, mother fucker?” Not letting him even think of an answer, I punch him in the face again. “Adonis.” I hear James warning me. I turn towards him with a glare, “Leave me the fuck alone.” I turn back to an unconscious Nick and raise my fist to punch him again but I stop as I hear her name. “Aphrodite is waiting for you. Get your shit together.” James again warns me. If he wasn’t right, I would have killed him for stopping me. I throw Nick roughly back to the floor and rise to my feet, climbing over him. I don’t give the boys a second glance as I climb out of the ring. “Cain, clean this up.” I hear James’ command as I walk into the tunnel.

DRIVING BACK TO Aphrodite’s house, I speed down the highway in anticipation, not being able to get to her fast enough. The thought of her seeing me fight, didn't even pass my mind till right now. I didn't care about that earlier, all that mattered was I needed to protect her and the asshole needed to pay but now that it registers in my head that she knows, I feel my stomach twist in anxiety. What is she thinking about it? I hope she doesn't hate me for it, or judge me. Her opinion matters to me so much. I need her approval over anyone's. That is one of the reasons why I didn't want her to know anytime soon. The other is that I needed to keep her safe from that side of my world. I tried for so long to keep her out of my life, to keep her safe. Also, to keep the people from this half of my world from knowing she even existed. She means too much to me and that is dangerous for a person like me. My mind going back to Nick, anger ripples through me again. He should have known better. I kicked his ass in the ring multiple times. He knows exactly who I am and what I can do and he knew what Aphrodite means to me. I explained that to him in little words before they went out on they're first date. I really should have stopped it there. I should have told him to turn around and leave but instead, like the idiot that I am, I let her go out with him. I remember the night I found out about their second date. Cain got a call from Roxy. Roxy wanted me to know, she knew we were all together. She spoke loudly on purpose. Roxy always likes to see me react to Aphrodite, she always has. She knew what I would do, that girl loves drama and conflict but I appreciate her telling me. When I saw what Aphrodite was wearing that night, I was livid. Crazy things ran through my mind, I can only imagine what Nick thought. My jaw clenches again as I think of that night again.

I finally park in front of her house. I open my car door and step out and shut it behind me. Walking around to the front of my Porsche, I look up at her house and lean on the hood of my car. I was now freshly showered. I couldn't come back to her looking and smelling like shit after beating up two guys in one night. Before I walked in there, she needed to know everything. She needed the option to get out of this friendship. I won't force her to be in my dangerous life. I won't make her go through that. She needs to decide if she wanted to be in my life or if she wanted to forget about me all together. Running through everything that she needed to know in my mind, made me nervous but this is something that needed to happen sooner or later. I couldn't keep her in the dark of my crime-filled life anymore. On top of everything, I couldn't get her out of my mind lately. She was all I thought about. Her sexy body, oh, how I wanted to run my hands over her body. Her lips, the things I can do to that mouth of hers. Her scent, she smelled of jasmine and gardenias. It was the sweetest smell I had ever encountered. I just wanted to put my face in her neck and breathe her in all day. Thinking back to her in my arms earlier as I drove, makes me frown sadly. She felt so good in my arms, I didn't want to let her go. I wanted to keep her safe there forever. I keep thinking these things about my best friend because that's what she was. She was the person who has been there for me my whole life and I wouldn't want her out of my life but lately, all I want to do is kiss her beautiful silky skin and all I thought about was getting her naked and tasting her. I had to shake those sinful thoughts away though. Those actions can change everything. if I act on them, they can destroy our relationship forever so I need to forget about it. I grab my phone and dial Cain's number. She answers right away, not even letting it ring. Meaning, she was waiting for my call. My heart breaks a little because I left her alone while she was scared. "Hello?" Comes her soft answer. “Hey baby girl, I’m outside.” I look up to her balcony as I hear shuffling on the other side of the phone. She looks through her curtains. “Come down here.” I whisper. “Why aren’t you coming inside?” She asked with confusion lacing her words. “I want to talk to you first. Let's go for a drive.” I see her nodding at my words but then she realizes she needs to answer and she says, “Okay, let me get dressed real quick. I’ll be right down.” The thought of what she is wearing now, makes me want to walk in there. I take a deep breath and wait patiently for her to come outside. As she does, I look down to see her wearing white Calvin Klein pants and a matching crop top hoodie, showing off her perfect slim waist and flat stomach. After she closes the door and locks it, she turns towards me. Her eyes raked over my body worriedly. When she realized I wasn’t hurt, she breathed out in relief. When my eyes reach her face, anger ripples through me again, my fist clenching at my sides. I try to mask it the best I can and give her a small smile that I know doesn’t reach my eyes. She walks up to me and wraps her arms around my midsection. I instantly hugged her back, my arms engulfing her little body.

Bonus Chapter 47.2 -ADONIS-

After showering and getting dressed, I go in search of painkillers and water. With a heavy heart, I walk over to where Aphrodite was sleeping and sit down on the bed beside her. “Baby,” I whisper, while running the back of my fingers along her cheek. I felt like shit for what I was doing. I had to leave. I didn't even have time to hold her in my arms this morning. The boys were waiting for me and I had to go. I didn't want to wake her up either but I had to make sure she was okay after last night and I also had to let her know I was leaving. I watch her beautiful face, her lips purse a little in her sleep, her eyebrows furrowing. That little look made me want to forget about everything and get under the covers with her. “Aphrodite. Wake up.” She was so tired, she barely even stirred. My lips curled up into a smile, she hated the morning on a regular day, I can only imagine after last night. She was curled up on her side, the blanket wrapped around her body. I leaned forward and peppered kisses along her cheek, whispering her name a few times. She stirs and as I reach her lips, she sighs against me, pecking me back. I pull back and she opens her slightly swollen eyes. “Hey,” her voice comes out hoarse and full of sleep. She notices that I am fully dressed. Blinking a little, she sits up, running a hand through her hair. “You're leaving already.” It wasn't a question and it breaks my heart to leave her after what we did last night. “Yes. The guys are waiting for me.” I lean forward and grab the pills and water from her nightstand. “How are you feeling?” I pass them to her and she pops the pills into her mouth and takes a sip from the water to help her swallow them. “I'm okay, just a little sore.” She shrugs her shoulder as she tries to sound nonchalant. I couldn't help but smile at that, she was just too understanding sometimes. I didn't want to take that for granted. I grab the cup from her and set it down, pressing my lips to hers for a second. I put my hand on her leg, looking into her eyes, "I don't want to leave you like this." It was the truth I meant every word. I frown but she meets it with a smile. She leans forward and puts a hand to my cheek, the warmth of her palm feels so good on my skin, I lean in to her touch. "Adonis. It's okay. You have to leave. I get it." *She always does.* She kisses me softly and pulls away, "Go." I looked over her face, making sure she was okay and she wasn't hiding pain behind her smile but all I saw was sincerity. I stand on my feet and she grabs my hand, "Don't forget about me while you're in Vegas." I laugh under my breath. I put a hand to my heart, pretending to be shocked, "I would never." Her giggle fills my ears and the sound is like music to them. "Bye, baby." She says, releasing my hand. For some reason, I blink at her a little taken aback by the endearment. It made a little twinge in my stomach appear. All she did was smirk at me and I bit down on my lip. "So I'm your baby now?" She nods, her eyes shining in amusement. *God, I didn't want to leave.* I lean down, putting my hand into her hair, taking her lips into mine, I kiss her passionately. I wanted to stay a little longer in this moment, so before I pulled away, I let my lips linger for a second. I stand to my feet and walk towards the door. Turning my face back to look at her, I say, "Bye, baby." She grinned and I walked out of the room, my smile falling as soon as I knew she couldn't see my face.

DRIVING TOWARDS HUDSON'S HOUSE, I run a hand through my hair. I was trying to stop myself from turning the car around and saying "fuck you" to everything else. I wanted to hold her and kiss her for hours. I wanted to make sure she was comfortable and felt no pain. My heart was beating in my chest loudly at just the thought of not seeing her for the next few days. My breathing was coming out heavily and my hands were shaking. I'm driving away from her as if I'm leaving a part of myself with her. I always felt off when we were apart but now it was stronger. I tried to convince myself it was because we had sex last night for the first time or because I took her virginity but the truth was, I didn't feel like she was just my best friend anymore. She was so much more. Every time I closed my eyes, I saw her bright blue eyes and beautiful smile. I couldn't get her off my mind. She was a constant thought, just there, hovering. She was always a part of me but now, I didn't want to let go. I thought this wasn't going to happen. I didn't want this to happen but it has. I am in love with her. My eyes widened at the realization and I took a deep breath. I was blindly driving now, my mind was on autopilot as I was thinking so many things at once. I love her. I love her so much. I always have. I hit the steering wheel, “Fuck!” How didn't I know this?! I put my free hand over the lower half of my face bringing it down, releasing a breath. I can't be in love with her. She is my best friend, I am going to fuck everything up. This is exactly what I didn't want. We agreed we weren't going to fall in love with each other because if we did, it would ruin our friendship. But who the fuck was I kidding? I didn't recently fall in love with her, this happened years ago. I was pissed. If I would have known sooner, I wouldn't have started this with her. I think back to all my actions over the years. Everything wasn't because I was a protective best friend...it was because I didn't want any boy around what was mine.

I park in front of Hudson's house and turn the engine off. I put my face into my hands, I can't tell her. She can't know. She doesn't feel the same way. Right now, all she is doing with me is having fun. If I tell her...I don't even want to think of how she would react. Bile rises up my throat and I quickly swallow it down. I honk the car horn a few times and wait for the boys to walk out. The passenger door flies open and James steps into my SUV, the other doors open and the guys get in the car, in a full blown conversation about who knows what. James' eyes run over my face and I know he notices how pale I am. "You want me to drive?" I shake my head no and start the car again, pulling out of the parking space. Memories of last night flash through my head and I bite on the inside of my cheek. My fingers tingled as I remembered the feeling of her silky skin under my touch. I'm not going to lie, I have been with a lot of women but being with Aphrodite…she is everything a man needs and desires, and everything a boy will never understand. The way her body reacted to me without even touching her was enough to drive me crazy. "What's up Don?" I look through the rearview mirror at Liam as he gives me a concerned look. "Yeah? What's up with you?" Cain asks and I look towards the road not knowing what to say. I try to avoid looking back at Hudson but I feel him analyzing me like he does to his victims. "Didn't get much sleep last night." My answer wasn't a lie. I spend most of the night not being able to sleep and my eyes wouldn't leave her gorgeous face. "Oh, were you saying *goodbye* to your girl all night?" Cain says the word *goodbye* suggestively and I give him a glare through the mirror. *My girl.* She is my girl. She always was and I'm going to make sure she always will be. And that is where my brain starts working on a plan to make her fall in love with me. I won't be able to keep my feelings from her for long so I need to make sure she loves me before I tell her. I tried to fill the void of her presence the whole time she was gone. I should have known that feeling of despair was because she wasn't around me anymore. I tried filling it with *sex*, I went through women without a care in the world. Not knowing their names or caring to see them again. *Drugs*. Don't get me started on drugs. I tried to numb myself with all sorts of narcotics but they just made the feeling of emptiness worse. The liquor made me miss her even more but I loved the burn. The tattoos felt as if I was writing my story on my skin, showing the world I am, who I want to be, and no one can stop me. But not even that pain filled that hole in my chest. All the anger I felt was released in my fist but that only helped for a short time and as soon as the adrenaline subsided, the ache would start again. I didn't feel whole again until she was right in front of me. Even though she hated me and we were fighting the first few weeks, I didn't care. She was close by. *That*. That should have been enough to tell me I was utterly in love with her.

Bonus Chapter

55.2

-ADONIS-

Hudson puts a plate in front of me, I look down to see a sandwich, "Eat." He says as I am sitting at his kitchen counter. I have been staying at his house for the past few days. I couldn't be around my father while I was busy piecing all the evidence against him. I take a sip of my coffee instead, not able to put food in my system. Every time I tried, I felt nauseous. I lost her. I lost the love of my life because I wasn't thinking. I acted on an impulse. "You need to eat, man. We have a lot of shit we need to take care of and we need you." Hudson says as he sits next to me on a barstool, taking a bite of his sandwich. He's right, I need to be strong for what we're going to do today. I grab the sandwich in my hands and take a bite. I close my eyes as all I taste is cardboard. I put it back on the plate and swallow it down with my coffee. I push my chair out and stand up. I leave everything there and walk straight to the front door, walking out. I slam the door shut behind me. I pull out my pack of cigarettes from my pocket and take one out, putting it to my lips. I lit it quickly, needing something to calm my shaking fingers. I take a drag from it, filling my lungs with toxic smoke. I walk down the path leading to the gate and open it. I take a seat on the hood of my car and run both my hands through my hair. I put the filter to my lips, needing that temporary fix. It was too early for anything stronger but I needed the poison in my system in order to go on. It was the only way to numb the pain. I'm broken and I don't think I can be put back together. *Don't touch me! Get away from me! You're a murderer!* Those words killed me. That night, I died with that piece of shit I killed. I shouldn't have killed him in front of her. I wasn't going to kill him just yet. I was just trying to scare him into telling me the truth. Hudson told me he wasn't going to lead up but I tried anyway. I was so lost in rage.

When he said they were after her, all I saw was red. I didn't realize I killed him till I heard her screaming. She wanted to stop me, all she kept screaming was no. But it was too late. I did it already...and I killed us in the process too. The disgust she had in her eyes as she looked at me was too much to handle. That was the last time she looked at me. On our way to the airport and on the plane, she ignored me completely. I wanted to give her space, even though it was hard. I leave the cigarette in my lips as I pull out my phone, sending another text to her.

I know I messed up but I can't do this without you.

The message is delivered but again, she doesn't answer so I send another one.

Come back to me.

Is this how she felt when she would message me while she was in London? Because I feel hopeless. I look at the message thread and I just need her response. I need something to tell me she is still here. That she is still in my life. I am waiting for something that isn't going to happen. Cain's Harley parks right in front of me and I look up at him as he walks towards me after climbing off the bike. “Still nothing from-" He stops in his tracks and raises his palms up as I glare at him. “Fine, I won't say her name.” I turn around as I hear a car rumble. Liam and James arrived and they both climbed out of the challenger at the same time. Liam grimaces at me but doesn't say anything. James doesn't give me that courtesy. “You look like shit, Don.” I feel like shit too. It wasn't like I looked like a slob. I was dressed. It's just that I have really dark circles under my eyes and the stubble on my face is darker than normal. I lean my head towards the house and they follow me back inside. We go to the dining room table and sit down, Hudson joining us. Today, we are going to finally take my father and his whole organization down. I have been waiting for this for so long. We finally got the information we were waiting for a couple of days ago and we can now take him down. We have enough evidence and intel. We just need to find a way to get all the girls out of the building before someone gets tipped off and they flee. Tonight, my father was going to get arrested for helping a mafia sell women for sex. That was something Benjamin's mafia did not agree with. When I found out about what my father was doing, I went straight to Benjamin. He told me I needed to wait and gather as much information as I needed to bring him down. That's what I have been doing. Benjamin offered me everything I needed to do what I had to. He offered me as much manpower as I wanted and also, weapons and essentials. He told me he was behind me for whatever I decided to do and for that, I was grateful. Liam laid his tablet in the middle of the table, the building's blueprints on the screen. He started telling us where everything was and we just sat there listening. The wheels started turning in everyone's heads, then we all started spinning ideas. And in that moment, I realize there isn't anything these boys wouldn't do for me. They truly are great friends. I always wanted brothers and with these guys, I got more than what I wished for and if anything ever happens, I'd be there for them.

WE WERE NOW in front of an abandoned building. On the outside, it looked like a rusted old factory but on the inside, it was the complete opposite. There

was a detective I had been in contact with today, he was a friend of Benjamins. He was waiting for my call to come in and do what he had to do with back up but first, we needed to make sure no one escaped. We all split up and bounded every exit available, even the secret ones. We met at the back of the building and Liam was on his tablet, searching for my father's location. "He is in route. He should be here soon."
I nod and grab my phone, dialing the number to detective Seeley. He answers on the first ring and I hit the speaker button. "Ready?"
"Yes. Jonathan Clark will be here soon. We boarded all the exits." I look up at the buildings as I continue. "What should we do?"
"Right now, nothing. You wanted him to be arrested so leave everything to us." Silence passes for a second before he speaks again, "Don't worry, we'll get him." I hang up and wait. Watching my father being cuffed by a police officer and having his head being pushed into the patrol car, wasn't nearly as satisfying as I'd hoped. I should have just raided that abandoned building myself and took out all his men with my bare hands. I should have taken all those women to the hospital myself. There were a lot of them but with Benjamin's manpower, we could have done it. I regret not killing my father but it was too late now. Before my father can get into the car, he turns harshly in the man's hold and his eyes meet mine. His eyes shine with a dark glint, "You don't know what you did, son." He smirks, "I am no one. You didn't just mess with me. You messed with someone so much more powerful and he has been itching to destroy your boss. This just gave him that push he needed. Keep your eyes open, boy." The officer curses at him, pushing him into the car harshly, shutting the door in his face. I get in the passenger seat of Hudson's car. I

just wanted to get out of there. That's bullshit. I wanted to go see my girl. I needed to feel her again, see her again. She would have made everything all better. I put my hand to my forehead, leaning my elbow on the middle console. She wasn't my girl anymore. I fucking lost her. I run my hand up through my hair as Hudson climbs into the car. He drives off and I relax into the seat. I took in a big sigh as thoughts came through my head. I finally put my father where he belonged but I don't feel any joy. I don't feel content. I don't think I could ever feel happiness again. There was a time in my life where I looked up to my father. There was a time where I wanted to be just like him but that all stopped a long time ago. Now I have my mother to take care of and I will do whatever I have to, to not lose her too. We park in front of Hudson's house and I step out of his car. I walk down the sidewalk and my eyes land on my Porsche. The car Johnathon gave me. Anger ripples inside me and I stomp up the walkway and behind Hudson's house to a shed where he keeps all his tools. I find a sledgehammer and wrap my hand around it. I drag it on the floor as I walk back to the car I was about to destroy. Hudson looks at me as if I had two heads. I lift the hammer and put it on my shoulder. I walk over to the windshield and swing straight in the middle. The glass shatters completely. I move and start hammering into the hood of the car, loving the harsh dents it was making. The anger was building with every blow. I pictured my father's face and smashed into the car. Then, a flash of Aphrodite walking away from me goes through my eyes and my movements get stronger. My arms flex as I lift the sledgehammer above my head. I see Hudson from my sideview and I look up to see him with a baseball bat in his hands and he starts breaking the passenger side windows. Our eyes meet and He smiles, ear to ear, at me. I shake my head, then continue walking around to the back of the Porsche and give it the same treatment. The thing that had me hitting the car the hardest was the look that son of a bitch that followed us in New York, gave Aphrodite. He said, *especially her*. And looked at her like the psycho he was and I shot him. And I'd do it again, without any hesitation. Even though it caused me to lose her, if I could turn back time, I'd kill him again...

Author's note- I hoped you liked it! Please Leave me a review. Tell me about your experience reading this book. And what you thought about it and its characters. -Elizabeth

Acknowledgments

First I would like to thank my Husband Kevin. Thank you for pushing me to do this. Thank you for believing in me, when I didn't believe in myself.

Having you in my life, means everything to me. I asked God to send me someone, and he sent me you, the perfect husband and father, to our daughter.

He blessed me abundantly with you, because frankly, no one else could handle me.

It was love at first sight. It was love at the hundredth sight and the thousandth sight too. True love is falling in love with the same person over and over again. You are my true love.

I'm gonna love you 'til
My lungs give out.
You understand me, like no one else can.
You are the inspiration for this book.
And you are my inspiration.

My princess, my daughter. Faith. I dedicate this book, and every book I ever write, to you. You are my life. You are the reason for my existence. I love you so much. “When I
look into your eyes
I know that it's true
God must have spent
A little more time
On you.”

Nicole, my Angel. My best friend. You have been in my life for as long as I can remember. It’s always been you. Even when we were apart we were still together. God put you in my life, he made you an angel just for me. I imagine your wings to be the purest of white and gigantic. I know God has your crown ready for you, full of diamonds and rubies. You make me a better person. You make me happier. I can breathe better since you have been in my life again.. I don't know if that makes sense but it's true. You're my soulmate. You're my person. You and I are like yin and yang, completely different but fit perfectly together. Like two puzzle pieces you didn't know fit together till the very end.

Mom. Thank you for everything. Whenever I needed you, you were there in a heartbeat. And I am so grateful for you. I thank god I have you in my life. When I told you about my writing I was expecting you to freak out and tell me to stop. But instead you encouraged me. The way you encouraged me in everything. I am who I am today because of you. "You were my strength when I was weak
You were my voice when I couldn't speak
You were my eyes when I couldn't see
You saw the best there was in me
Lifted me up when I couldn't reach
You gave me faith cause you believed
I'm everything I am
Because you loved me"

Dad. My super man. I love you so much. Thank you for always believing in me. Thank you for pushing me. Thank you for making me stronger. "When I look at you, I see forgiveness
I see the truth
You love me for who I am
Like the stars hold the moon
Right there where they belong
And I know I'm not alone"

To my mother in law. My confidant, the person I tell everything to. You have always been my Mom, even before I married your son. Thank you. Thank you for teaching me. Thank you for caring for me. Thank you for supporting me. I love you. You taught me so much, but the thing that always sticks is. Everything has its time. That one, was always hard for me. But you taught me patience. Also you taught me to love god on top of everything. 'We can make our plans, but the Lord determines our steps. Proverbs 16:9'

To my father in law. My Dad. Thank you. Because of you, I think before I react. I Listen, more than I speak... Well, I try. You've shown me so much. Who to trust. Who to love. Who to respect. Thank you for all your great advice. Thank you for being in our lives. Thank you for taking care of us. You never let us fall. You always make us stronger. 'Trust in the Lord with all your heart; do not depend on your own understanding.
Proverbs 3:5' -You taught me that. You taught me to ask god, before anything I do, and that I am most thankful for.

Brian and Bridget.

You guys are my role models, always were. I love both of you so much. Thank you for being in my life and cheering me on in the process. I have no idea why. But I always need both of your guys approval before I do something. When I told you guys about my writing I was shaking. Thanks for teaching me to be smarter, kinder and for teaching me life isn't that hard. Just take it one step at a time. "You can count on me like one, two, three
I'll be there
And I know when I need it, I can count on you like four, three, two
And you'll be there"

Adam and Kathy

Kat. You managed to crawl into my heart, and I didn't even notice when you did it. One moment you came into my life and the next, you wrapped me around your finger and in so little time. Adam. I laugh harder because of you and cry less. Thank you for that. For some reason I need you guys in my everyday life. I know I'm super annoying. And you

guys probably want to choke me most of the time. But I
love you guys. "I'll be there for you
(When the rain starts to pour)
I'll be there for you
(Like I've been there before)
I'll be there for you
(Cause you're there for me too)"

Momio.

I miss you so much. I know you're up there with Jesus,
screaming at me because this. Or your rooting for me, I
don't know. Probably both. You were always like that.
Thank you for being the best grandma anyone can ask for.
I
get little flashbacks every once in a while, when I am
about to do something that you taught me how to do, I can
hear your voice perfectly too. I love you. You're gone, but I
know you're up there telling God to take care of us. "I miss
you, I miss your smile
And I still shed a tear every once in a while
And even though it's different now
You're still here somehow

TIFFANY, GRACE, BELLA, NATHAN, ETHAN AND JADAN

I love you guys so much!! I want you guys to follow your
dreams! I want you guys to always be strong! And always
push yourself to be better!! Don't let anyone put you down!!
Always work hard, even when things are good. I will ***always***
be there for you guys!!

Nicole

Brandy, I could not have asked for a better friend, partner and Soulmate. You are that person who makes me feel whole and who understands me the most when the world does not understand at all. This is going to sound very cheesy, but you made me believe in my dreams that I have kept to myself. I could have never done this without you. You are the purest most real friend I ever had and I will never take you for granted. I never really paid much attention when we faded from each other but now that I looked back I was lost and blind. And now that you're back into my life I feel my spirit lift and I know it's because of you. You taught me so much and somehow you also taught how to be the person I am today.
I will never forget our journey together in this book and I can't wait for the adventures and stories we will make come true. You mean so much to me and you don't even know it. I would never find what we have in anyone else and I thank god he gave me someone like you. Thank you for giving me a chance. I'll *always* love you.

Paul, I would like to thank you for helping and believing me throughout this journey. You were always by my side. Crazy thing is I never thought you would have gotten to know this side of me. I was scared that you would have told me I was dumb and weird and that I was losing my mind but you didn't ... you looked at me like there was something in me worth looking at. You encourage me. You let me be me and that meant so much to me. You are more than anyone could ever ask for in a husband. I don't show it much but I do appreciate you and never forget that *every atom of me loves you.*

Issac, my son. My world. My everything
You are *precious* in every way. My *sunshine* in my day and the *joy* in my *soul.* But also a hurricane when u wanna be. Always know you are loved for the boy you are and the man you will become and the precious son you will always be. This ones for you.

Mom, you're the one who brought me to the world of stories. Books, romance and life itself. There are no words to compare the love I have for you. I was also afraid of you knowing this part of me. But all my doubts went away when I saw the glint in your eyes.
Thank you for supporting and
Encouraging me through this, well through everything in life too. You mean the world to me and I hope you know that. I am everything I am because you loved me. You always see the best in me when I couldn't. I can't thank you enough for *everything* you've done for me.

About the author.

I dropped out of school at a very young age, due to culture. I didn't even go to middle school. I am a self taught writer. I have learned how to write from my love of reading. I started reading books at the age of ten, I loved the words. I loved the stories playing in my head. I would always get so intrigued by each story. My eyes would just dance along the pages. I started writing when I was twelve. Nothing too big. I would just make up little stories. Every time I didn't know how to spell something, I would write it down all day, till I memorized it. But not with a pen and paper. I would

write with my finger over any surface. I was obsessed with words. I always did my reading and writing in secret. In my culture people hardly do things like this. A few years back I wrote a book on Wattpad, and got a lot of good feedback on my work. When I showed my husband, who didn't know at the time. He was ecstatic. I was shocked at everyone else's reactions. They were all good. So I started writing and editing my work with the help of a very good friend. And that is how I became a self published author.

-Follow on Instagram-
@Author_ElizabethAndrews

-Follow on tiktok-
@Author_ElizabethAndrews

-Follow on twitter-
@Author_EAndrews

The Divinity series

<u>**Book One**</u>

Without choice

<u>**Book Two**</u>

My Choice

Coming soon

<u>**Book Three**</u>

No Choice

Coming soon

<u>**Book Four**</u>

Your Choice

Coming soon

Follow me to get info on release days and more -
Follow on Instagram- @Author_ElizabethAndrews -
Follow on tiktok- @Author_ElizabethAndrews -Follow
on twitter- @Author_EAndrews
Email to contact the author and her team
Autherelizabethandrews@Gmail.com
Book edited by Elizabeth Reza reza.elizabeth4@gmail.com

Made in the USA
Las Vegas, NV
27 April 2021

22091230R10252